Imagine
a City

Imagine
a City

Glasgow in fiction

MOIRA BURGESS

First Published 1998
Argyll Publishing
Glendaruel
Argyll PA22 3AE
Scotland

The author has asserted her moral rights.

Subsidised by the Scottish Arts Council

British Library Cataloguing-in-Publication Data.
A catalogue record for this book is available from
the British Library.

ISBN 1 874640 78 5

Typeset & Origination
Cordfall Ltd, Glasgow

Printing
ColourBooks Ltd, Dublin

a few words about Glasgow
sure
but which few words

gangs
hardmen
neds
screams in the night
clichés

warmhearted
gallus
neighbourly
smiles better
likewise

east end west end
north side south side
black white brown yellow
blue green
yes

a few words about Glasgow
sure
but which Glasgow

CONTENTS

Acknowledgments

This book has been on the way for some years and I am grateful for the Scottish Arts Council Travel and Research Grant which allowed me the necessary time and space to work on it. I acknowledge also with thanks the help and interest of very many individuals and organisations whom I have approached along the way. These include James Barclay; David Branch; James Kelman; Allan MacRitchie; Andrew Miller; Nancie Miller; Edwin Morgan; Hamish Whyte; Pat Woods; Christian Wright; Constable Publishers; Curtis Brown; *The East End Independent*; Falkirk District Libraries; *The Glaswegian*; *The Herald* library; the National Library of Scotland; North East Fife District Libraries; *The Scotsman* library; and above all The Mitchell Library, Glasgow, in whose History & Glasgow and Arts departments I would probably still be burrowing if it had not seemed expedient to stop and actually write the book.

My poem "a few words" first appeared, in a longer version, in *Zwei Sprachen – zwei Städte/Two Tongues – Two Towns*, edited by Reinhard Knodt and Jack Withers (Frankfurt, 1988). The epigraph to Part III is from Edwin Morgan's *Essays* (Carcanet, 1974), and the epigraph to Part IV from Robert Crawford, *A Scottish Assembly* (Chatto & Windus, 1990). I am grateful to them, and to Tom Leonard and Stephen Mulrine, for allowing me to quote from their work.   Moira Burgess

Glasgow, January 1998

Foreword

Moira Burgess is the acknowledged historian of the Glasgow novel. Since her original research in the 1970s, and her two definitive bibliographies of the subject in 1972 and 1986, she has built up her knowledge of Glasgow fiction through her editions (with Hamish Whyte) of Glasgow short stories in *Streets of Stone* (1985) and *Streets of Gold* (1989) to the point where, with this loving and carefully researched study, she presents us at the millennium with the most complete and informed discussion available on the subject.

She is no dry scholar. To her research Moira Burgess brings additional qualifications which enrich her understanding and supply her with rich contexts – namely the fact that she is an accomplished novelist herself. With *The day Before Tomorrow* (1971) and *A Rumour of Strangers* (1987) she showed her range of abilities, from the first novel's anticipation of William McIlvanney's use of crime as a way of exploring Glasgow with its volatile mixture of warm humanity and dark violence, and the second's similar recognition of ambivalent human qualities, this time revealed in a West Highland setting. Add to this creative ability her insistence on finding real achievement, however hidden by neglect and prejudice, as in her *The Other Voice; Scottish Women's Writing Since 1808* (1987). Here she pioneered study of the relatively unexplored territory of women's concerns and perspectives, discerning a recurrent and detached irony in their attitudes towards their experience and their country very different from those of the more celebrated male writers.

And it is just this combination of enthusiasm for her subject with a clear critical detachment which makes her judgements in this volume so valuable and fair. Carefully shaped into four main parts that are in themselves the main movements of developing Glasgow, *Imagine a City* is historically balanced. Small City, Hard City, Kaleidoscope City and Deep City as internal titles capture well the movement from the restless pre-industrial university-and-cathedral town of Bailie Nicol Jarvie in Scott's *Rob Roy* in 1817 to the city of mean streets and razor gangs which became stereotypes for Glasgow for too long. But Glasgow became also a multifaceted city, kaleidoscopic in its conjunctions of sentiment and violence, with Wee Macgreegor sharing trips down the Clyde with Para Handy, with rough diamonds like Private Spud Tamson showing the other side of the razor kings by gaining the Victoria Cross; while other writers like MacDougall Hay or Patrick MacGill saw only the appalling degradation of slum conditions.

After a long unwillingness through the nineteenth century to look squarely at itself, Glasgow was at last, between the wars, imagining itself in a host of different ways; sometimes evasively, or urbanely, or condescendingly, as Burgess reveals. And moving on to a realisation of the present, with the work of writers like Gray, Kelman, Galloway and Kennedy, Glasgow's layers are indeed deep and rich, and to be treated in a myriad of post-modern and magical ways if its contradictions and subtleties are to be conveyed.

Paradoxically, while Burgess recognises the dominating influence of Gray's *Lanark* (1981) on Scottish writers of the last two decades, one of her principal achievements with this book is to challenge successfully the now famous contention of Duncan Thaw in that novel that Glasgow wasn't a place that its inhabitants imagined living in, and that it had produced but a few bad novels. Her rediscoveries, from Sarah Tytler's *St Mungo's City* in 1885, through the virtually unknown *Jean* (1906) by John Blair, with its astonishing clear-eyed frankness about social conditions, to her discussion of neglected masterpieces such as Catherine Carswell's *Open the Door!* (1920) or Frederick Niven's *Justice of the Peace* (1923), consistently suggest that the problem about Glasgow fiction – and perhaps culture generally – isn't so much that it hasn't existed until recently, but that it just hasn't been recorded and transmitted. So novelists like Edward Gaitens in *Dance of the Apprentices* in 1948 or Archie Hind in *The Dear Green Place* in 1966 – and Gray himself in *Lanark* – suggest the fundamental loneliness of the creative spirit in a wasteland west of Scotland. Their feeling of isolation may be true for them, but from Burgess's account it would seem that, if their society had only enabled them to know, they aren't alone in their dystopian imaginings.

That is not to say that Glasgow fiction does not suffer from problems of identity and confidence, and perhaps Burgess's most important contribution here is to show how debates of significance and conviction, too readily forgotten, raged through the twentieth century. Arguments such as those recently concerning the significance and artistic acceptability of writers like James Kelman and Irvine Welsh are not new. In the 1930s there were ongoing confrontations between urban and rurally based writers, and between those who wanted to banish the national consideration in favour of an international and socialist perspective.

Once again this volume breaks new ground by revealing these vital and historically important battles, and looking at them coolly and sympathetically, so that their contestants emerge as sophisticated, intelligent and decent people with the courage of their convictions. As in the case of George Blake, who came so close in *The Shipbuilders* (1935) to creating a truly great Glasgow and Scottish novel in its epic treatment of the loss of tradition in the decline of the Clyde shipbuilding industry, but finally admitting that he just couldn't get under the skin of ordinary workers, they could also admit limitations of class and vision.

There's so much more in this immensely readable book, with its relaxed, friendly and genial involvement of the reader, who is treated as someone who shares Burgess's enthusiasm and desire to explore. And for this reader, the treatment succeeds entirely in its principal aim, to see the Glasgow tradition of fiction whole, with its melodramas and sentimentalisations, but with its remarkable range, for too long patronised or neglected, so that its truly great writers, from Carswell and Gaitens, to Friel and Kelman are marginalised as eccentrics of a north Britain which mystifies the south, as well as too many of our own educationists. Moira Burgess in *Imagine a City* is an important part of the movement which is changing this.

Douglas Gifford
December 1997

Preface

> The city goes soft; it awaits the imprint of an identity. For
> better or worse, it invites you to remake it, to consolidate it
> into a shape you can live in . . . The city as we imagine it, the
> soft city of illusion, myth, aspiration, nightmare, is as real,
> maybe more real, than the hard city one can locate on maps, in
> statistics, in monographs on urban society and demography and
> architecture.

Jonathan Raban in his 1974 book *Soft City* presents an arresting
image of the fictional city – any fictional city. He considers how,
and why, that city differs from the physical, factual one. Others
before and since have noticed the phenomenon of the fictional
city – we speak quite readily of Dickens's London or Balzac's Paris.

In this book I have focussed on one city, Glasgow, and on
the fictional city built up in novels which take Glasgow as their
setting. Of course these "Glasgow novels", to use a shorthand
term, are not "about" Glasgow, but about Glasgow people. The
interaction between place and people, though, is, as I shall hope
to show, a dynamic force throughout.

But what is the fictional Glasgow that we find? On the analogy
of Dickens's London, whose Glasgow do we recognise? A
perceptive reviewer has remarked that "there are so many
Glasgows", in fiction as in fact. There's a grim, violent slum

Glasgow, adopted with remarkable unanimity over sixty years ago on the publication of *No Mean City*: Alexander McArthur's Glasgow, we may say. But generations have rejoiced in JJ Bell's couthy Glasgow, the setting of *Wee Macgreegor*. Some recognise their grandparents' or great-grandparents' Glasgow in Guy McCrone's *Wax Fruit*. Many Glaswegians today reject all these images, but find themselves, whether they like it or not, at home in James Kelman's Glasgow with its bleak realism and underlying humanity. In recent years we have discovered a fantastic future city in Alasdair Gray's *Lanark*, and a recognisable present-day city which is yet touched with magic realism in AL Kennedy's *So I Am Glad*. So many Glasgows, indeed.

This book, then, is a history of Glasgow fiction, looking at the novels and the writers who have addressed the problem of constructing a fictional Glasgow. Yet perhaps it's also something more. I have elsewhere toyed with the idea of drawing a map of fictional Glasgow to be laid over the real map, so that we can see where the two cities match and where they diverge. I hope this book may encourage its readers to look at the real Glasgow through the fictional one, and thus to find even more than at first meets the eye in this many-sided, inexhaustible, terrible and marvellous city.

I

SMALL CITY

"It's a great city, Ironburgh, or thinks so at least."
"It can hardly help thinking so."
"Quite true; it can't help it. It is a well-pleased city."
Mrs Elizabeth Taylor, Blindpits (1868)

1

An Urbane Silence?

The principal street was broad and important, decorated with
public buildings, of an architecture rather striking than correct
in point of taste, and running between rows of tall houses, built
of stone, the fronts of which were occasionally richly
ornamented with mason-work; a circumstance which gave the
street an imposing air of dignity and grandeur, of which most
English towns are in some measure deprived, by the slight,
insubstantial, and perishable quality and appearance of the
bricks with which they are constructed.

Frank Osbaldistone, a central character in Walter Scott's novel
Rob Roy, has already spotted, a long time before the public
relations slogan of the 1980s, that Glasgow's miles better. *Rob
Roy* was published at the end of 1817 and depicts Glasgow about
a hundred years earlier, at the time of the first Jacobite rising.
These were fairly early days for the Scottish novel, and also for
Glasgow as a place of importance, since by the middle of the
eighteenth century the city's population was still under 25,000.
As it developed in size and significance however, Glasgow attracted
the attentions of writers. Scott's impressions, through his character
Frank, form our first sustained view of Glasgow in fiction.

Rob Roy is not quite the first novel to be (at least partly) set in Glasgow. In 1735 Tobias Smollett had come to the city to study medicine and work for a few years as an apothecary's apprentice. The young hero of his first novel, *The Adventures of Roderick Random* (1748), follows a similar career path.

There is a slight problem about claiming *Roderick Random* as the very first Glasgow novel, since it never actually mentions Glasgow; but such details seldom deter Glasgow historians for long, and we are told that:

> Two curious little shops in Gibson's Land, at the north corner of Saltmarket and Prince's Street, used to be pointed out as the apothecary stores in Smollett's *Adventures of Roderick Random*. One belonged to Dr John Gordon, with whom Smollett served his medical apprenticeship; the other (at the corner) to Dr Crawford, a rival apothecary.

The rivals, with other Glasgow characters, are thought to be caricatured in *Roderick Random* – Dr Gordon as Mr Potion and Dr Crawford as Mr Launcelot Crab – and, while we should probably not consider the novel completely autobiographical, there is a nice air of oral tradition about the identification of Gibson's Land.

Smollett did include Glasgow on the itinerary of his motley party in *The Expedition of Humphry Clinker* (1771). Matthew Bramble approves, on the whole:

> I am so far happy as to have seen Glasgow, which, to the best of my recollection and judgment, is one of the prettiest towns in Europe; and, without all doubt, it is one of the most flourishing in Great Britain. . . Marks of opulence and independency appear in every quarter of this commercial city, which, however, is not without its inconveniences and defects. . .

It could do with a reservoir of good water, and the river is – as it was then – too shallow for large ships. Win Jenkins, however, dismisses it briskly:

> We afterwards churned to Starling and Grascow, which are a
> kiple of handsome towns; and then we went to a gentleman's
> house at Loff-Loming . . .

where she finds more in the way of interest and adventure.

We are on much firmer ground with *Rob Roy*. Scott visited
Glasgow in the summer of 1817, while he was writing the novel,
and saw the sights in the company of his bookseller friend John
Smith. He told his publisher Constable that he was going to "make
a hit in a Glasgow weaver whom he would ravel up with Rob."
His writer's instinct was sure. From the moment Bailie Nicol Jarvie
arrives at the Tolbooth he is alive:

> . . . in form stout, short, and somewhat corpulent; and by
> dignity, as it soon appeared, a magistrate, bobwigged, bustling,
> and breathless with peevish impatience. My conductor . . .
> could not elude the penetrating twinkle with which this
> dignitary reconnoitered the whole apartment.

The setting date of *Rob Roy* is 1715–16. Glasgow is, as we have
already seen, an attractive place. It is a small city, but, most
importantly, it is a merchant city.

> Not only the fertile plains in its immediate neighbourhood, but
> the districts of Ayr and Dumfries, regarded Glasgow as their
> capital, to which they transmitted their produce, and received
> in return such necessaries and luxuries as their consumption
> required.

And Bailie Nicol Jarvie is a Glasgow merchant. He knows how
many beans make five. He takes pains to explain that in agreeing
to stand bail for Mr Owen he is making no wild quixotic gesture,
because:

> "I am a carefu' man, as is weel kend, and industrious, as the
> hale town can testify: and I can win my crowns, and keep my

crowns, and count my crowns, wi' ony body in the Saut-Market, or it may be in the Gallowgate."

Neither could he ever be described as a reckless adventurer:

"I wadna gie the finest sight we hae seen in the Hielands, for the first keek o' the Gorbals o' Glasgow; and if I were ance there, it suldna be every fule's errand, begging your pardon, Mr Francis, that suld take me out o' sight o' Saint Mungo's steeple again!"

Predictably he approves of the Union of 1707:

"I say, Let Glasgow flourish! whilk is judiciously and elegantly putten round the town's arms, by way of by-word. – Now, since St Mungo catched herrings in the Clyde, what was ever like to gar us flourish like the sugar and tobacco-trade? Will ony body tell me that, and grumble at the treaty that opened us a road west-awa' yonder?"

But Frank, or Scott, is clear about the Bailie's essential human qualities:

Although . . . he considered commercial transactions the most important objects of human life . . . [his] conversation showed tokens of a shrewd, observing, liberal, and, to the extent of its opportunities, a well-improved mind.

And by the time we have seen him gamely brave the world beyond the Gorbals; veto the publicising of his adventures to people in Glasgow, especially his maidservant Mattie and his rival Bailie Graham; and marry Mattie, caring nothing for the gossip of the town, we have become rather fond of the Bailie.

He walks off the page as a living person and it seems that for a time in real life the boundary between fact and fiction became, in his case, quite blurred. Not just for Glasgow readers. Queen Victoria, on her first visit to Glasgow in 1849, asked to see Nicol Jarvie's house (and was duly shown an old building in the Saltmarket, behind the Original Bailie Nicol Jarvie Tavern).

The lively pamphleteer John Gilkison in 1873 causes his character Jean Byde (that is, Jane Boyd, but she's proud of her rich Ayrshire accent) to venture from her South Side tenement into the city centre, and there ask passers-by where Bailie Nicol Jarvie's house used to be. "Lod, the wife's daft," they impolitely comment, but her delusion is surely understandable. She might even have seen a copy of the weekly periodical *The Bailie*, first published in 1872, specifically named for Bailie Nicol Jarvie and with a cover illustration depicting him in all his portly glory.

The fiction of Bailie Nicol Jarvie's editing *The Bailie* was scrupulously maintained for most of the paper's long life. Correspondents (real or equally fictitious) addressed him as "Dear Bylie," or, in more stately mode, "my Magistrate." The Jubilee issue of 15 December 1922 ran an elaborate "biographical appreciation" of Bailie Nicol Jarvie, based, so we are told, on a manuscript *Sketch of the Municipal History of Glasgow* which had consisted of "500,000 closely written pages, containing an average of 2000 words each" but had most unfortunately been burned some years before. It is here revealed that:

> the famous Nicol Jarvie was born on the 4th March, 1670, in a house in the Saltmarket, which has been long since demolished. He was the only child of Nicol Jarvie, Deacon of the Weavers' Incorporation, and his wife, Elspeth Macfarlane . . .

It is in this connection we learn to our surprise that Captain Peter Macfarlane, better known as Para Handy, whom we shall meet later, is a collateral descendant of the Bailie's mother. (Incidentally, we are also told that the maidservant Mattie before her marriage was Martha Spreull, another name which will prove to have certain resonances for the student of Glasgow fiction.) Briefly removing tongue from cheek, the same issue of *The*

Bailie considers the question of "the real Bailie Nicol Jarvie," for some prototype, it is thought, there must have been. *The Bailie*'s candidate is Dr James MacNayr, editor of the *Glasgow Herald* for a few months in the early nineteenth century. A more usual suggestion is David Dale, "the benevolent magistrate," the self-made man who set up the New Lanark Mills.

But the Bailie's interest to us lies not so much in his ancestors as in his literary descendants. Glasgow merchants, very often in the textile trade, appear again and again in Glasgow fiction. Claud Walkinshaw in Galt's *The Entail*; Tam Drysdale in Sarah Tytler's *St Mungo's City*; Ebenezer Moir in Frederick Niven's *Justice of the Peace*; Dickson McCunn in Buchan's *Huntingtower*; the eponymous hero of George Woden's *Mungo*; Arthur Moorhouse in Guy McCrone's *Wax Fruit* – these sturdy citizens carry the likeness of Bailie Nicol Jarvie down over more than a hundred years.

Apart from the Bailie, perhaps the best-remembered Glasgow reference in *Rob Roy* is Andrew Fairservice's cadenza on the Cathedral.

> "Ah! it's a brave kirk – nane o' yere whigmaleeries and curliewurlies and open-steek hems about it – a' solid, weel-jointed mason-wark, that will stand as lang as the warld, keep hands and gunpowther aff it . . ."

Just before this loving description, however, Frank Osbaldistone observes the building in its setting, and his first impression is "awful and solemn in the extreme."

> Situated in a populous and considerable town, this ancient and massive pile has the appearance of the most sequestered solitude. High walls divide it from the buildings of the city on one side; on the other, it is bounded by a ravine, at the bottom of which, and invisible to the eye, murmurs a wandering rivulet, adding, by its gentle noise, to the imposing solemnity of the scene. On the opposite side of the ravine rises a steep

bank, covered with fir-trees closely planted, whose dusky shade
extends itself over the cemetery with an appropriate and
gloomy effect.

Almost as persistent as the merchant motif in Glasgow fiction is
the recurrence of this numinous scene: the Cathedral, the ravine
of the Molendinar, and the rocky hill above, now the Glasgow
Necropolis burying-ground. A recent commentator has noted:

> This area, the Necropolis and the cathedral precinct, is
> symbolic, emblematic, part of the common lot of every
> Glaswegian. No one comes here unaware of its history and its
> part in a legacy of Glaswegian lore and tradition.

He is writing with reference to Alasdair Gray's *Lanark* (1981), a
present-day Glasgow classic, where the Cathedral and the
Necropolis are still figuring in a dystopian future Glasgow. But
this gothic cityscape was clearly irresistible to Scott, and it is found
again, a few years later, appealing to John Galt, whose *The Entail*
was published at the end of 1822. Charles Walkinshaw, on hearing
that he has been disinherited, rushes from the lawyer's office along
the Gallowgate and . . .

> never halted till he had gained the dark firs which overhang the
> cathedral and skirt the Molendinar Burn . . . The sky was darkly
> overcast. The clouds were rolling in black and lowering masses,
> through which an occasional gleam of sunshine flickered for a
> moment on the towers and pinnacles of the cathedral, and
> glimmered in its rapid transit on the monuments and graves in
> the churchyard . . . The gusty wind howled like a death dog
> among the firs . . .

The Necropolis was not yet a graveyard when *The Entail* was
published, but we begin to see why, some ten years later, the fir-
covered hillside above the Molendinar may have seemed a good
place for a City of the Dead.

Trying to pinpoint the first real Glasgow novel, we have probably found it in *The Entail*. Galt himself told his publisher, while writing the novel, that "the chief business lies in Glasgow," and its last line reads unequivocally, LET GLASGOW FLOURISH! Certainly the lands of Kittlestonheugh lie outside Glasgow as it then was. The Grippy can be located on the north-facing slopes of the Cathkin Braes, about Carmunnock, and Camrachle, where Mrs Charles later lives, is identifiable as Pollokshaws, then a rural village. But Glasgow is in its proper place as the business and commercial centre of its area. Claud Walkinshaw, father of Charles, begins as a cloth-merchant in the Trongate and the reader learns that "Glasgow's on the thrive."

The Entail has some interest as a source of social history. The period of the novel is roughly 1700–1815, and the action is punctuated with topical events like the opening, about 1740, of "the new kirk . . . [with] the papistical name of St Andrew". Because of Galt's insistence on "real" chronology it can perhaps be presumed that 1822, the publication date, is seven years after the end of the story. Even the earliest fictional events are therefore, notionally, not beyond the reach of "family history" recollections, and the description of Mrs Gorbals' colourful costume as an example of "the gorgeous paraphernalia of the Glasgow ladies of that time" can be taken on trust. Provost Gorbals and his wife, it is pointed out, are *nouveaux riches,* and we have a beautiful picture from two generations farther back:

> " . . . had ye but seen the last Leddy Kittlestonheugh . . . and
> her twa sisters, in their hench-hoops, with their fans in their
> han's – the three in a row would hae soopit the whole breadth
> o' the Trongate – ye would hae seen something. They were
> nane o' your new-made leddies, but come o' a pedigree. Foul
> would hae been the gait, and drooking the shower, that would
> hae gart them jook their heads intil the door o' ony sic thing as
> a Glasgow bailie . . ."

More interesting still, from our point of view, is the moment of intertextuality – a testament that *Rob Roy*, five years after its publication, was a household word – when the reader sideslips into a quite obviously fictional Glasgow, as Isabella, apprenticed to a dressmaker, takes a new dress:

> . . . to Mrs Jarvie, the wife of the far-famed Bailie Nicol, the same Matty who lighted the worthy magistrate to the Tolbooth, on that memorable night when he, the son of the deacon, found his kinsman Rob Roy there.

But these are surface details. The importance of *The Entail* to the student of the Glasgow novel is its introduction, for the first time, of the literary theme of Glasgow as a commercial city. While "commercial transactions [are] the most important objects of human life" to Bailie Nicol Jarvie, this and similar attitudes are perhaps there in *Rob Roy* largely for the purpose of being played off against the old romantic way of life found beyond Aberfoyle.

In contrast, commercial transactions – money and land – are the mainspring of *The Entail* and of its Glasgow. Money, in the shape of commerce, has its good effects, and it has made Glasgow a thriving little city. But money – or the love of money – has its bad effects too, and here they are worked out in Claud Walkinshaw's remorse and despair and the tribulations of his family. In either aspect, money, or commerce, is clearly seen as a moving force; a character, we may say, in *The Entail*, and a theme in Glasgow fiction.

By the mid-point of the nineteenth century, then, Glasgow was established as a suitable case for treatment in Scottish literature. Its growth and position as a commercial centre had been noted. Its lively life and manners were under review by several novelists. But much more was about to happen to Glasgow, thanks to the event, or series of events, which now with the benefit of hindsight are called the Industrial Revolution.

In what can justly be called a population explosion, Glasgow, within some fifty years, more than quadrupled in size and more than doubled again in the next half-century. The population figures for the city of Glasgow are well enough known:

1801	77,385
1851	329,096
1901	761,712

More to the point, for the novelist as observer of city life and character, was the nature of the explosion. Where Glasgow, broadly speaking, had been a commercial city, with merchants and lawyers and shrewd old ladies to write about, suddenly it was an industrial city, with mill-owners and mill-hands, shipbuilders and shipyard workers. The factories and yards needed workers, an infrastructure of shops and subsidiary trades sprang up, and in came immigrants from the Highlands, from Ireland, from Eastern Europe, from Italy, crowding the small city with colour and noise and squalor and strangeness. What a gift, what material, for novelists of Glasgow!

Critics over the years have taken some pains to explain how this gift was disregarded or actively shunned. The theme appeared as early as 1888:

> What tolerable Scotch fiction we have tends to deal only fragmentarily with rural lives and never with the collective life of our larger towns.

The journalist and man of letters William Power repeated it in 1935, writing of turn-of-the-century novels:

> Though Scotland had been severely industrialised . . . and though Glasgow was one of the largest of British cities, it was still assumed, for literary purposes, that the majority of Scots people lived in rustic villages.

Most influentially, George Blake pronounced in 1956:

> In the meantime, Scotland had been most miserably

industrialised . . . The time came when fully two-thirds of the
population of Scotland was immured within the narrow Clyde-
Forth belt. In other words, the essential life of the Scottish
people was thus narrowly and sordidly confined.
So we ask what the contemporary Scottish writers had to say
about this almost melodramatic state of affairs . . . Was there
nobody in Scotland to tell the truth about what was
happening? And to our question we get a dusty answer. The
representative Scottish writers of the period went on – and on –
representing their coevals as either bucolic philosophers or
eagle-plumed gallants in the heather . . .

The "bucolic philosophers" represent the popular Kailyard School
of Scottish fiction, which will be examined more closely in a later
chapter. A few years earlier, writing more specifically on the Kailyard
School, Blake had adduced three possible reasons for the lack of
fiction set in industrial Scotland, which may be summarised as
follows:

> – the generally "sad state" of literary culture in Scotland,
> blamed by Blake on "two centuries of the influence of a
> fundamentalist Kirk";
> – the overwhelming impact of an industrial revolution which
> had arrived "too swiftly, and too brutally";
> – the influence of Scott and Stevenson, slanting the national
> taste towards novels of history and romance (represented
> by the "eagle-plumed gallants" above).

This was one man's view, but a recension too, as has been seen, of
the views of earlier critics. It may be worth mentioning that the
poet Sydney Goodsir Smith was inclined to apportion some blame
to Burns:

> His work, however universal its significance, was centred willy-
> nilly in the parish pump . . . Soon, with the coming of the
> Industrial Revolution, Scottish life was to become more highly
> urbanised, but our literature, both poetry and prose,
> continued, because of the enormous effect and lasting prestige

of Burns's work, to deal with subjects taken from the village or
the country town . . .

Others suggest interestingly that the city, though not overtly dealt
with until much later, *caused* the Kailyard, in a fairly direct way:

> The big, ever-expanding industrial cities with their social and
> economic unrest and injustice loom threateningly out of a
> smoke-misted horizon . . . This is the background against
> which the modern novelists write. Their reactions vary . . . The
> Kailyarders are inspired to registration. Like officials from some
> museum they "excavate" their villages, explore the quaint
> material they find there and supply the world with picturesque
> stories from a dying community.

The lack of Scottish, and particularly Glasgow, industrial fiction
has been continually and thoroughly deplored, with some excur-
sions into the realm of "if only":

> Carlyle had the genius to do it – and the passionate
> transcendental Gothic fire. If his ambition had taken him to the
> pullulating slums of nineteenth-century Glasgow we might
> have had an opus to set beside Balzac's *Comédie Humaine*.

So the received opinion ran until as recently as 1986. Then a seminal
work on Scottish fiction turned things upside-down.

> This curious notion [that Scottish Victorian fiction
> "concerned itself exclusively with an idealised rural past"] can
> be found in one form or another in most accounts of the
> subject . . .
> But this view cannot be sustained. It is based solely on an
> interpretation of bourgeois book-culture which assumes the
> Kailyard to be typical and considers further enquiry
> unnecessary, while even middle-class fiction during the period
> is largely unexplored and the real popular literature of
> Victorian Scotland is practically *terra incognita*.

In these remarks, the literary historian William Donaldson refers to the treasure-trove of Victorian fiction, mostly in serial form, contained in Scottish newspapers and periodicals from about the 1850s onwards.

> Genuine novel-length – that is 80–120,000 word – fiction now became normal in newspapers, and the very nature of the form began to change . . . The plot had to be managed with unprecedented resourcefulness and ingenuity [in order to keep the reader interested throughout a serial novel] and grew in importance relative to character and setting.

In ignorance of this source, Donaldson quite temperately observes, "a number of conclusions have been drawn" and this has led to "serious subsequent misjudgements."

In all fairness, it probably does remain true that no "great novelists" – certainly no canonically acknowledged novelists – tackled the subject of industrial Glasgow in the late nineteenth and early twentieth centuries. The topic was, too, for the most part ignored by those writers who were currently and locally popular, like the "Clydeside Litterateurs" celebrated in a book of that title published in 1898. A recent critic has observed their "strong nostalgia for the Scottish countryside, Highland and Lowland", while a contemporary reviewer also had their number:

> Some readers will perchance be astonished to learn that we have so many men of letters among us, and more perchance will think that [the editor's] enthusiasm is often greater than his powers of critical perception.

But the industrial city was making an impression on other writers. This is very evident, for instance, in the poems of Alexander Smith, and in his prose work *A Summer in Skye* (1865):

> There was Glasgow herself – black river flowing between two

29

> glooms of masts . . . And ever, as the darkness came, the district
> north-east and south of the city was filled with shifting glare
> and gloom of furnace fires; instead of night and its privacy, the
> splendour of towering flame brought to the inhabitants of the
> eastern and southern streets a fluctuating scarlet day . . .

Sometimes city life was matter-of-factly taken on board and treated with humour, as in the various series of sketches that will be looked at in Chapter Three. The Glasgow slums – the inevitable result, as it then appeared, of the population explosion – were described by novelists, though often from a middle-class viewpoint, another phenomenon which will be considered later on. Occasionally a genuinely realistic treatment of city life is found, as at times in the work of David Pae, one of Donaldson's discoveries. One way and another there were plenty of writers in Victorian Glasgow. We shall see in the next two chapters how they viewed their city.

2

The Goosedubbs of Glasgow

Was ye ever in the Guse-dubs o' Glasgow? Safe us a', what clarty closses, narrowin' awa' and darkening down, some stracht, and some serpentine, into green middens o' baith liquid and solid matter, soomin' wi' dead cats and auld shoon. . . Dive down anither close, and you hear a man murderin' his wife, up stairs in a garret . . .

Thus, as early as 1826, Christopher North in *Noctes Ambrosianae*, from the safety of an Edinburgh tavern, characterises one of the notorious slums of Glasgow. (The Gusedubs, or Goosedubbs, was a lane running between Stockwell Street and the Briggait. A short stretch of it is still there, at least in name.) While this description hovers on the border between fact and fiction, there is no lack of eyewitness accounts of nineteenth-century Glasgow to back it up.

A particular strand of Glasgow fiction, not yet fully explored, indeed concerns itself specifically with the slums, and with what was perceived to be the cause of the misery there.

"Dis yer faither drink, Jim?"
"Yes, sir."

"Yer mither, she drinks tae dootless, or ye wudna be in sic a
state as ye are. There's too mony o' her kind gaun aboot in
Glesca toon. That's the way there's sae mony like you on the
streets."   (W Naismith *City Echoes* 1884)

Elsewhere Jet Ford, rescued from the slums by a philanthropist,
returns, before leaving for the mission field, to see if things have
changed, and is edified to find that:

"Band of Hope" meetings to educate in the noble principles
"Touch not", "Taste not", "Handle not" . . . had sprung up in
all directions.   (CM Gordon *Jet Ford* 1880)

It isn't quite as easy as that, however:

"I thought if a' the spirit merchants and public-houses were
shut up and ruined, that maybe father would be himself again.
Oh, mother, think of that!"

"Oh, lassie dear, lassie dear! it's no that," said the elder woman,
sadly. " . . . It's just some folks, ministers, teetotallers, and the
like wantin' us to say if we would like tae hae the pow'r tae
shut up the public-houses roun' about us. If we would like!"
she interjected bitterly, "but what's the guid o' speaking,
they're no like to be shut up; there's owre much money tae be
made out o' the ruin o' bodies and souls for the like o' that tae
happen."   (Anon *Almost Persuaded* 1887)

These are tracts rather than novels, and it took some time for
genuine fiction to grow from inescapable fact. While the perception
of an industrial Scotland ignored by writers was not entirely
accurate, the literary scene in nineteenth-century Glasgow does
have, by all accounts, a distinctly couthy air.

Of the many literary howffs which have flourished in Glasgow,
one of the most famous was the back shop of the publisher and
bookseller David Robertson in Trongate. Here gathered such
contemporary if ill-assorted literary lights as William Miller, author

of "Wee Willie Winkie"; William Motherwell, extreme Tory editor of the *Glasgow Courier*; and Alexander Rodger, the 'Radical Poet' (possibly the first but far from the last Glasgow writer to earn that reputation). From their association emerged the *Whistle-Binkie* series of poetry anthologies (1832–43), highly popular in their time, though more recently regarded, in their sentimental simplicity, as everything that Scottish poetry ought not to be.

But the Whistle-Binkie group are poets, or poetasters. Forty or fifty years later we are able for the first time to recognise a group of Glasgow novelists. Glasgow writing had taken a swing towards prose fiction. Perhaps a key figure in this process was Dr James Hedderwick, editor, man of letters, and, in today's phrase, facilitator *extraordinaire*. Printer's ink clearly ran in his veins. His father was founder of a printing firm in Glasgow, and Hedderwick was briefly apprenticed there before his university education.

His long life gave him a unique perspective on the Glasgow literary scene. He clearly remembered the meetings of the Whistle-Binkie poets. (On less cultural matters his memory, in fact, went back to the time when sheep still grazed in St Enoch Square.) He once met a Mrs Hunter who knew Burns – "a black-a-viced man, marked with smallpox." In 1844 he attended a Burns celebration at which three of the poet's sons were fellow-guests, though they modestly disclaimed any share in their father's genius; and nearly fifty years later, still writing, he produced an autobiography, or collection of autobiographical essays, covering all these topics and many more. He was a minor poet himself, but his importance here lies in his work as an editor and his close involvement with literary Glasgow.

After five years in Edinburgh as sub-editor of the *Scotsman* he returned to Glasgow in 1842, still in his twenties, and started the *Glasgow Citizen*, a weekly newspaper with a strong literary content. His later *Hedderwick's Miscellany* was a literary periodical, and when he launched the daily *Evening Citizen* in 1864, the renamed *Weekly Citizen* took on a purely literary role. As a successful and influential editor, he was able to give a start to younger Glasgow writers as contributors or staffers. Poets, essayists, and, most relevantly for our purposes, such novelists as William Freeland and William Black were all encouraged and published by Hedderwick.

Perhaps it was a secret of his success that he recognised the calibre of his readership. He attended a Glasgow lecture on Wordsworth which the speaker had interlarded heavily with the more popular poems. These, Hedderwick observed, fell flat.

> His object was, I suppose, to come down to the supposed level of his audience, and not always to shoot over their heads. But this proved to be a mistake. Their heads were higher than was guessed. They had perhaps, like Alexander Smith, found that in the far-stretching city – "The stars were nearer to them than the fields."

However, it's possible that not everybody in Victorian Glasgow would despise the popular poems of Wordsworth. This perception, or something like it, would at first glance seem to lie behind the success of George Roy:

> Introduction – My Great Ambition – The Bath – The Bunker – The New House – The Sideboard – John's Waistcoat and my Gown – Our Daughter Mary Ann – Lessons in Music – Bailie Monro's Invitation – John's Terror and Surprise – Our New Piano.

This is from the contents page of George Roy's novel *Generalship, or, How I Managed my Husband* (1858). Part First, detailed above, expands on the writer's Great Ambition, which is to have a house with a dining-room. John's Terror arises when his daughter sits down at the piano, as far as he knows unable to play it, and shows every sign of affronting him before Bailie Monro's guests, while the Surprise is that Mary Ann, with her mother's connivance, has been taking piano lessons for six months. The episode, and the

George Roy, the author of the highly successful *Generalship, or How I Managed my Husband*, was a partner in the wholesale grocery firm of J&G Roy and a kenspeckle figure in Victorian Glasgow. Roy's humour disguised unsparing satire, and middle-class Glasgow, his own milieu, was the object of his wrath. The above caricature appeared in the popular periodical *The Bailie* in 1874

book as a whole, assumes the viewpoint that domestic tragedies and triumphs, social gaffes and successes are the only important things in life, and thus appears to mark *Generalship* as a forerunner of what we shall be calling the "urban kailyard" school and discussing at some length in Chapter Four.

The author of *Generalship* was evidently a kenspeckle figure in Victorian Glasgow.

> Most people have heard something of George Roy . . . A dozen years ago George was, as he would say himself, "a genteel lad". He was well-built, he wore his hair in long snaky locks, and he cultivated an interesting and literary look. . . But the George of today is a very different personage from the George of '62. To use his own somewhat technical expression, he has become "fat and foosey". The good things of this life are beginning to tell upon him.

These good things had come, at least partly, from authorship.

> Your *Superfine Reviewer* . . . would certainly shrug his shoulders at the claim to authorship put forward by George, but our friend could afford the *Reviewer* his shrug. When one sells twenty thousand of his book, as Mr Roy sold of *Generalship*, a shrug from a literary snob doesn't matter much . . .

Actually the shrug didn't matter at all, because George was a partner in the wholesale grocery firm of J&G Roy, "well known to every grocer and provision dealer in the West country" and, in addition, "city landlords possessing a rent-roll of over £5000 per annum." As the profile writer drily observes, "This success has enabled George to 'cultivate literature upon a good pickle o' oatmeal'."

To him that hath, however, shall be given, and *Generalship* attained large sales and lasting popularity. It was still available in a sixpenny paperback edition in 1907, at what was the height of the urban kailyard vogue.

At that time it would seem very much a contemporary kailyard

product. Its presentation, indeed, had been doctored slightly to
conform to the rather heavy-handed kailyard sense of humour.
Whereas the original 1858 frontispiece to *Generalship* shows a
handsome woman in bonnet and crinoline meditating on her book,
the cover illustration of the 1907 edition depicts a plump, smugly
smiling Mrs Young leading her dejected husband in a halter. On
the book's first appearance Mrs Young might have reminded some
readers of the Leddy o' Grippy: "I'm sure, if it were weel looked
into, the dochters o' Eve wad prove at least as great gen'rals as
ever the sons o' Adam were. . ." But she is a caricature of the type,
as her opening remarks go on to illustrate:

> . . . for I'm sure there's no woman that's married to ony
> man . . . wha manages to lead a quiet, peaceable life, and get a'
> things her ain way (which I lay down as a fundamental principle
> that it's every woman's right to get) . . . that hasna during her
> lifetime just as muckle gen'ralship to display as ever was
> required o' the Duke o' Wellington.

She is a staunch supporter of her John, her aim being to see him a
town councillor at least, with "Bailie Young" the eventual goal.
And she sees the undeviating path which he must tread towards it:

> Mr Patrick then asked me if I knew what John thought of
> the Sunday steamboat; to which I could truthfully reply, that
> one Monday, last summer, John remained in Rothesay all
> night rather than come up in the Sunday boat even on a
> week day. John said she had the mark o' Cain upon her . . .
> Mr Patrick said that the story about not coming up in the
> Sunday boat would get hundreds of signatures in any ward
> in Glasgow . . .

Her efforts to effect the reburial of her dead child in a more fittingly
marked grave tend towards the heavy sentimentality which is one
mark of the kailyard, but from which Galt, for instance, is very
largely free. Her closing remarks seem perfect kailyard:

> I was just as happy in my first humble abode as I am with my
> town and country houses . . . I, therefore, in bidding my
> readers adieu, counsel all to seek, in their respective
> circumstances, contentment – the only certain source of
> happiness.

She chooses to forget that she has displayed, throughout her memoirs, extreme discontent with any circumstances less comfortable than those of a bailie's wife with a villa at the coast. Irony, it would appear, is not her forte.

But is it George Roy's forte? *Generalship* has been discussed so far as if it were an early but genuine example of the couthy, undemanding kailyard school of Scottish fiction. The profile already quoted, in *The Bailie*, regards George Roy as an entertainer, a showman.

> Perhaps George is even better known as a platform speaker
> than as a writer of books . . . Nothing seems to come easier to
> him than to make people laugh . . . He has done much good to
> others [the takings from his platform appearances always went
> to charity] and no harm to anybody.

So popular were his appearances that many of his talks attained book publication. *Lectures and Stories* (1863) contains "rather a peculiar mixture," the foreword admits, but an explanation is given: "The arrangement of the Volume was suggested by the fact, that almost every night when I have lectured I have been called on to tell a story."

So each of the lectures, on suitably grave subjects – The Dignity of Labour, Money, The Way of Life – is followed by a story illustrating the theme. Thus, after thirty pages on Heart's Ease, we relax with the five-page story "The Stair-Head Battle". It may be surmised which part of the programme the audience preferred, because this is a richly humorous story. Battle is joined when Johnnie Carmichael and Johnnie Meiklejohn start up a boyish scuffle on the landing. Mrs Carmichael comes out and slaps Johnnie Meiklejohn around the head, to which Mrs Meiklejohn ripostes by knocking Johnnie Carmichael's head off the wall. There are words between the mothers, and then there's the unfortunate affair of the pot and the firescreens. One thing leads to another until the husbands come home:

> Mrs Carmichael commanded their attention, saying in a calm distinctness, "Yes, Mr Carmichael, come into your tea, and let John Meiklejohn into his porridge – porridge, porridge, everlasting porridge; no wonder the poor man is deaf; his naturally thick head cannot but be stuffed with porridge." Mrs Meiklejohn's reply was (and she, too, now took plenty of time to make every word tell), "Yes, John Meiklejohn, come into your porridge, and let Mr Carmichael into his tea; the poor man is new-fangled about his tea; he is the first one of the seed, breed, or generation that ever tasted tea: his old father, Daniel, that carried home the poor-house coffins, did not get much tea."

We may be sure (and contemporary allusions, for instance in *The Bailie*, confirm it) that "The Stair-Head Battle" was one of George's most popular turns.

But how popular, and how well understood, was "Mrs Gallacher" which illustrates the lecture on The Dignity of Labour? It's also very funny. The narrator, merely enquiring Mrs Gallacher's opinion of *Uncle Tom's Cabin*, is assailed by a torrential account of the ills the book has brought her. These range (for reasons too complicated to summarise) from the burning of a pigeon pie to the raising of her rent. But in the course of this diatribe Mrs Gallacher is revealed as an insensitive, humourless, racist bully, condemned out of her own mouth. George Roy comes across as an unsparing satirist, and middle-class Glasgow, his own milieu, is the object of his wrath. After "Mrs Gallacher", the reader must turn back to *Generalship* – described on the cover of its 1887 edition as A Scottish Story, Humorous and Pathetic – and question whether it is, and was always meant to be, something more than that. At the very least we may enjoy the reflection that the genial grocer was perhaps observing his Glasgow somewhat more closely than it knew.

Rather different is the work of George Mills (1808-81), whose two-volume novel, *The Beggar's Benison, or, A hero, without a name; but, with an aim*, was published in 1866. He too is writing about Glasgow, but not entirely his own Glasgow, as the narrator's tone makes clear.

> If you have half-an-hour to spare from the drawing-room of an evening, after your luxurious dinner . . . call a cab; proceed at once to such localities as the Briggate or the Goosedubbs of Glasgow; penetrate some of their closes and dark passages, and opening a door or two, peep in; there you will witness at once the realisation of what I aver. You had better, however, be attended by a policeman! [author's exclamation mark]

This is the middle-class Glaswegian displaying the slums for his reader's amazement and horror. The protagonist is a slum boy who rises to become a successful businessman: ". . . I found I could congratulate myself on being a man worth – I like to be correct and particular – no less a sum, in the aggregate, than £115,795 7s 2½d."

But George Mills never was a slum boy. He was the eldest son of a merchant who became a town councillor and Lord Provost of Glasgow, a position beyond even the dreams of Mrs Young. The family home was a villa in its own gardens on what was then the country thoroughfare of Sauchiehall Road. George, *The Bailie*'s profile-writer remarks, had "ability, education, and social position, so superior to the great majority even of prosperous business men . . . But somehow [he] never seemed to get upon the right rails."

> Had he chosen the law, with his shrewd common sense, caustic tongue, and ready pen, he would doubtless have reached, long ago, the head of his profession . . . Had he gone to study for the

pulpit – no, that wouldn't have suited George; but he might
have been drilled as an engineer . . . ; or had he persevered
pertinaciously in any of the ordinary walks of industry . . .

Apparently he didn't. James Hedderwick puts it kindly: "Young
George's career was through nearly all his life absorbing and varied.
He was in turn a steamboat-agent, a shipbuilder, a newspaper
proprietor, and a chemist." Between times he was writing, "as if,"
ventures Hedderwick, "with a wish to leave something behind
him which might live." It was not exactly with a view to making a
name as a novelist, because *The Beggar's Benison* was published
anonymously. (An earlier novel, *Craigclutha*, appeared under the
pseudonym of Mesrat Merligogels, Gent. The alert reader will
notice that *Merligogels* is an anagram of *George Mills*.)

But he did have a purpose in his writing, more perhaps than
the profile-writer gives him credit for, and more than early reviewers
of *The Beggar's Benison* discerned. In a letter to his friend George
Cruickshank the caricaturist, Mills complains:

> Nobody that has criticised the B.B. [sic] yet (and the number
> extends now to 19) has seen the real drift of it, which is to
> show that there are thousands of *good, amiable, religious* people
> going about, who are rascals, but who possess the secrets
> connected therewith, *themselves alone.* [author's italics]
> And when reading the B.B. consequently the reader should ask
> himself "am I not to some extent, the hero myself?" . . . When
> some people read the B.B., their thoughts may get a useful stir-
> up . . .

Thus we should not take quite at face value the rising young
businessman who returns to Glasgow:

> In the fall of the evening, I stole out to visit the old haunts of
> my childhood in the precincts of the Goosedubbs and the
> Briggate . . . There seemed to be the same amount of
> drunkenness, of riotousness, and of squalor. The very
> inhabitants seemed to be the same . . . with the same rude and

coarse manners to each other; the same habits of cursing and swearing; . . . and the same style of attiring themselves in rags. The locality presented no pleasing reminiscences for me. *I had only visited it impelled by curiosity to know if it still existed* . . . [my italics]

He attributes his rise, incidentally, to the eponymous benison, bestowed on him by the vagrant Girzie Galbraith but refused to his stepfather, who is shortly thereafter hanged. Girzie sees success and riches in store for our hero, and they come to pass. "Who then will despise a beggar's benison?" he muses, and we can see that this expression of simple gratitude to unseen powers also needs to be scrutinised with some care. George Mills was not entirely the well-off dilettante sketched in *The Bailie.*

But *The Beggar's Benison* never set the Clyde on fire, let alone the Thames as was his hope. In the letter quoted above he dreams of "a favourable critique in the *Times* . . . it will be the salvation of the B.B. – But I fear – I fear!"

A month later he is planning to send a review copy to Ruskin with an artfully worded covering note, pointing out how imperceptive critics have so far missed his meaning: "This will perhaps set *Ruskin* thinking, and we'll see what comes out of that."

He reports rather dolefully in the same letter that *The Beggar's Benison* "is making *way* here – at least it is much talked of . . . If a few more good critics come out it will perhaps take a start that will astonish us . . ." But three years later the publishers are proposing to remainder the work. George Mills isn't at all keen on the idea of "hawking" his book, but he has lost heart and agrees that it must be done ". . . in the hope that we will soon get this d----d first edition on the shelves, or down the WCs of the community." Strong words for a Victorian gent, to which he adds in a later letter by appending a pen and ink sketch of 'Mr Hawk' peddling books in the street with the cry, "Will you buy the 'Beggar's Benison', ye Beggars – "

Perhaps his dilettante reputation worked against a serious

reception of the book by Glasgow readers (from *The Bailie* it is evident that his authorship was a fairly open secret). Perhaps the message about whited sepulchres was a little too strong for the time; perhaps it was a little too well-hidden. *The Beggar's Benison* is full of vivid local colour, such as the matter-of-fact and detailed description of the Rookery, a slum tenement in the Goosedubbs. (Its garretful of children live by stealing silk handkerchiefs from passers-by; how much of this is down to personal knowledge and how much to *Oliver Twist* might bear further consideration.) George Mills could write "a story", which, he complained, was all that reviewers saw in his book. Perhaps he couldn't balance this easy readability with his serious purpose in such a way that his readers would have no choice but to see "the real drift".

There is one startlingly macabre sequence describing a hanging which does have the ring of truth:

> My stepfather held the kerchief in his hand . . . At last he dropped it, while a kind of shudder, or "sough", as the Scottish idiom expresses it, went through the crowd, seemingly as if its very blood was curdling.

One criminal is successfully turned off, but a second is only half-choked and has to be revived and hanged again. Whether or not George Mills had in fact witnessed a hanging in Jail Square – the last execution on that site was in 1865 – he comes out, in the Notes which follow the text of *The Beggar's Benison*, as an opponent of capital punishment, and justifies the passage by quoting at length from contemporary newspaper reports of bungled hangings. He takes pains to point out that he includes this sequence not to dwell on the process of execution, but to convey its horror. This sudden declaration of purpose alone, without the evidence of his letters, might give us a hint that there is more to George Mills than just a story-teller.

On the superficial level, however, *The Beggar's Benison* does stand as an early representation of the slums and underworld of

Glasgow. It is to some extent an outsider's view; yet not so much so as parts of David Pae's *The Factory Girl, or, The Dark Places of Glasgow* (1868).

David Pae was, in William Donaldson's opinion, "little known in his own lifetime, and utterly forgotten today, [but] still probably the most widely read author of fiction in Victorian Scotland." He was a prolific writer whose work appeared in serial form in newspapers and magazines – notably the *People's Friend* (which he edited for fourteen years) and the *People's Journal* – and was widely syndicated. Comparatively few of his stories were published in book form.

The Factory Girl is a long, melodramatic, romantic novel, "showing evil over-ruled for good, iniquity punished, and virtue rewarded" (to quote its sub-title). The authenticity of its depiction of Glasgow life is perhaps somewhat diluted by the fact that nearly all the characters speak an impeccable, even stately, Victorian English. The exceptions are Hugh the honest knife-grinder – the only Scots speaker – and the criminals, who, as Donaldson points out, converse in London thieves' slang:

> "Now, old covey, you must be quiet. I say, Bob, shall I take the mitten from his cheese-trap?"

There is particular interest for us, however, in one fairly minor character, a novelist (from Edinburgh) who wants "to write a tale, sir – a novel – a story descriptive of Glasgow life." To acquire local colour, he is anxious to visit a well-known city-centre haunt of thieves, but reckons that he needs police protection for this enterprise. (Perhaps he's read *The Beggar's Benison.*) He goes to the police station and makes his case:

> "I write tales, dramas, and things of that kind; and I have come to Glasgow to study the various phases of life in the city, in order to write a true and faithful story of Glasgow life. I have heard that one of its phases is to be seen most vividly in a notorious place called the Tontine Close, where thieves and

murderers reside, and I want to explore that close, and have a peep at the dwellings and their inmates."

But the police superintendent isn't at all cooperative.

"Well, Mr Hay, I think Glasgow has been very much abused by people of your sort, who have professed to describe life in the closes. There is a book just now which is very much circulated, and which, while it contains a small amount of truth, is full of absurdity and exaggeration."

Mr Hay goes anyway, in company with a missionary, and falls into the hands of a gang of thieves, thus (he must have felt) proving his point. But what we should note is the superintendent's staunch defence of Glasgow and rebuttal of any derogatory image, an attitude which, as will be seen, is repeated much later on in the tale of Glasgow fiction.

Twelve years pass and we move on to "the second epoch of our story." We have rather romped through "the secrets of the Tontine Close," but David Pae indicates that he now has a more serious purpose.

That reign of undisguised rascality and guilt we shall not revisit, neither shall we revert to a similarly low class of criminals. The richer and more spacious villains we have still on hand . . .

He is looking at industrial Glasgow and evaluating its good and bad aspects; exactly what, in the canonical view accepted until Donaldson, Victorian novelists had failed to do.

The slanting beams of the descending sun fell brightly on the Clyde as it skirted the southern boundary of Glasgow Green . . . Across, on the south side of the river, and far down by its eastern bank, and away verging to the north, were tall chimneys and long blocks of high square buildings, with many rows of windows, which flashed back the beams of the sinking

orb of day. From these many buildings came puffing jets of
smoke – and the rush, rush of the engine, like great heart beats,
and the clanking noise of the machinery, which uttered its voice
in its iron-labour-song, harsh and uncouth as its own hard
self . . . These were the cotton factories and other large works
which give such character and importance to Glasgow.

It is a striking and thoughtful cityscape, and we look forward to a
consideration of the human element in this industrial scene,
especially when the narrator adds:

> . . . all this while we are on the outside of the large iron gate,
> listening to the rushing sound of machinery within, quite
> bearable from where we stand, but strong enough to show us
> that it must be terrible inside, where we mean to go.

But David Pae has his readers to consider and the strands of a
romantic story to tie up. He does observe and comment on the
factory system – and Donaldson adduces evidence that this was a
large part of his purpose – but the reader is irresistibly pointed
towards our heroine Lucy and the handsome overseer.

> Very beautiful she was, with her light auburn hair, braided
> smoothly towards her ears, and her blue eyes, so heavenly in
> their expression . . .
>
> . . . a young man of frank address and winning manners, whose
> appearance came something near our human ideal of manhood.

As a background to these beautiful people, we see the factory girls
at work.

> The monster apartment contains some five hundred power-
> looms all going, each tended by a young girl just at, or
> approaching the age when lovers are in their thoughts, when
> their eyes reveal the feelings of their hearts, and send out soft
> killing glances from beneath silken eyelashes . . . They look quite

brisk and happy, though day after day they had to keep watch by
their looms in the midst of the deafening roar of machinery,
while the sun shone without, and the flowers bloomed in the
woods . . . [here follow six lines of nature description, involving
birds, streams, flowers, bees and butterflies] . . . All this these
busy factory girls knew little of, yet did they not seem sad or
languid. *Some of them were, indeed, pale and sickly* [my italics];
but others wore the rosy hue of health on their cheeks, and had
laughing lips and sparkling eyes.

The picture is as rosy as the cheeks, and we must suspect once
again that this is an outsider's view. The suspicion is confirmed by
the writing of an 'insider', a real-life Glasgow factory girl: Ellen
Johnston, who published her autobiography in 1867. She went to
work at the age of eleven, had a daughter (probably to her abusive
stepfather) when she was sixteen, and died destitute in the Barony
Poorhouse, aged only thirty-eight.

By the later decades of the nineteenth century, then, it is safe
to speak of "the Glasgow novel." The city's potential as background
and source of material was being recognised. The poet John
Davidson, who lived and worked in Glasgow before moving to
London, plays on this recognition in his first novel *The North Wall*
(1885).

"I am going to create a novel. . . [declares the unsuccessful
novelist Maxwell Lee] We shall cause a novel to take place in the
world . . . You will aid me to begin the art of novel-creation."

"Do you propose to make a living by it?" inquired Briscoe [his
brother-in-law].

"Certainly."

Briscoe rose and without comment left the house . . .

Briscoe proceeds to kidnap a millionaire in the middle of Glasgow,
from which action, sure enough, arises the novel *The North Wall*.
If this is not sufficiently post-modern, Davidson supplies a very
funny coda. Lee offers to write descriptions of his romantic leads

for the use of any readers who may need the help, indicating meanwhile that such readers are beneath his contempt:

> "Do you see him, O unimaginative lady reader? Do you understand that he is wholly unlike your own male friends . . .?"
>
> "O unimaginative male reader, I loathe the thought of your having any knowledge of the person of Murielle . . ."

William Black was one of the young Glasgow writers encouraged by James Hedderwick, contributing to the *Weekly Citizen* for some years and working as a sub-editor for a short time. While on the *Citizen* he wrote his first novel, *James Merle* (1864), set in eighteenth-century Glasgow. It did not meet with great success and Black never had it reissued. This was not, his biographer believes, entirely a case of the famous writer disclaiming a piece of juvenilia.

> It seems probable that he disliked it and would fain have removed it from the knowledge of the world because, although it was the autobiography of a fictitious character, it reflected much of the writer's own life. One is allowed to see in its pages the conflict between the artistic temperament of a young man of talent and enthusiasm and the dreary creed [i.e. Calvinism] with which Black was made familiar in his youth . . . The heaven that lies about us in our infancy was . . . too deeply tinctured with a sombre creed to furnish congenial or sympathetic memories to a man who, in the process of mental evolution, had advanced to another and a more liberal plane of thought . . .

In fact he had advanced to writing immensely popular romantic novels, certainly some distance from the discourses of Calvinism.

In 1864, the year of *James Merle*'s publication, Black moved to London, following other West of Scotland emigrants like his friend Robert Buchanan and the poet David Gray. He had to work as a clerk for some time while writing in the evenings, but gradually gained a foothold in journalism and began to publish novels. The success of *A Daughter of Heth* (1871) enabled him to give up his day job and write novels in his own then-acclaimed style for the next twenty-five years.

While not all his settings are Scottish, he was regarded, and is remembered, as a novelist of the Highlands, specifically of the romanticised Hebrides beloved by the Victorians. He specialised in scenery, particularly Hebridean sunsets. However, a contemporary remarks that he "contrives to get his native city into every novel he writes", and by 1877 this peculiarity had come to the notice of *The Bailie*, which granted him a chapter in a spoof serial parodying various novelists of the day.

> The two stood on the wild, weird range known to the daring yachtsman and the solitary artist as the Glaisghu Briochoomie-lauch. Far to the north there cleft the sky the lonely peak of Tieannhant's Lhum, its awful head ever enveloped by dark and mysterious mists. . . It was indeed a weird spot. Weird especially by night, when the wind howled, and the pass of Jammhackih Brieag was dangerous to cross, and the belated wayfarer caught sight of the mysterious glow in the southern sky which the superstitious people shudderingly called Dhuiksohn's Bleaishes.

(These Glasgow totems, Tennant's Lum and Dixon's Bleezes, like the Broomielaw and Jamaica Bridge, will appear again in Glasgow fiction.)

The Bailie, in fact, was not a great fan of William Black's.

> [His] new novel, *White Wings, a Yachting Romance*, which has begun in the July *Cornhill*, will hardly add to his reputation. Its hero is a middle-aged Commissioner of Police at Govan, who walks and talks and conducts himself generally in a manner that no Govan Commissioner, or indeed any other man of common sense, could possibly think of doing . . .

A few weeks later, as the serial publication of *White Wings* continued, *The Bailie* gloated "This has accomplished the bursting of the William Black bubble." But the bubble floated on as Black produced his more or less annual novels. It was his custom to spend his spring holidays fishing in Scotland and his autumn breaks in different locations – often in the West Highlands – which he proceeded to write up in the current novel. His biographer admits that his work was becoming slightly old-fashioned to British eyes, though it remained popular in the United States. All his life, however, he retained some British admirers, and he is, in the view of one at least, fully qualified to be called a Glasgow novelist.

> In transporting his two principal characters [in *White Heather*] to Glasgow he casts a spell over their movements in the big city which creates a love interest far stronger than that which attached to their idyllic life at Inver-Mudal . . . Many of the local [i.e. Glasgow] scenes pictured in *White Heather* are also to be found in *A Daughter of Heth*, the best novel Black has ever written . . . William Black has entered into the romance of Glasgow life, and many a time has he seen it with the love-lit eyes of his hero when "for him Glasgow was no longer a somewhat commonplace and matter-of-fact mass of houses, but a realm of mystery and dreams which love had lit up with the coloured lime-light of wonder and hope."

It is an image of Glasgow which we have not seen before, and may not see very often again.

A considerably drier view is taken by Martha Spreull, eponymous heroine of a novel published in 1884. The author appears as "Zachary Fleming, writer", but this is a pseudonym adopted for the occasion by Henry Johnston, one of the few "Clydeside Litterateurs" who did take a look at his own city, though much of his other fiction is set in rural Ayrshire. (He was in fact born in Northern Ireland, but his contemporaries counted him as a Glasgow writer, since he had moved to the city with his family at the age of three.)

Martha Spreull: being chapters in the life of a single wumman, which first appeared as a series of sketches in the Glasgow periodical *Quiz*, shows its origin in its episodic form, and (like other sketches which will be considered in Chapter Three) tends to a fairly light-hearted view of social problems. Martha, for instance, casts a disapproving eye on an early city improvement scheme.

> Eh me! sic a changed place. The auld Bell-o'-the-Brae [the top of High Street] is clean cut awa. Hale streets hae been dung doon, and fine new anes wi' bonnie big lands o' hooses planted i' their place . . . I mind when I lived in George Street, whenever I became discontented wi' myself or my hoose, I just took a walk doon the High Street and back by Bell's Wynd. It was a grand cure, for I aye saw sae muckle dirt and misery there that I generally cam hame thankfu' and happy . . .

The elaborate pretence is made that the sketches are written by Martha herself and edited by her old friend Zachary Fleming. A tremendous coyness pervades Martha's dealings with Mr Fleming, whom eventually she marries in a happy ending redolent of the Kailyard which was just coming into flower. Comic mis-spellings are a great source of humour throughout the book, and minor characters tend to be named after the fashion of Peter Spale the cooper and Beeny Fortune the spaewife. (This trick has an honourable enough ancestry; we remember, among many others, Mally Trimmings the mantua-maker in *The Entail*.)

In spite of this heavy humour there is a certain freshness about *Martha Spreull*. The sketches are in a well-sustained Scots, and Martha's view of Victorian Glasgow, as in the passage quoted above, holds some interest for us. The setting may be precisely dated as 1870, since in the course of the book we find Glasgow University moving from High Street to Gilmorehill, causing a distressing upheaval in Martha's career as a students' landlady. And there are rather appealing glimpses of a still earlier Glasgow. If we allow Martha to be a lady in her fifties, it would be about 1830 that she took the "chincough" (whooping-cough) and had to be taken "doon to the waterside at Govan for a change of air . . . I used to sit on a plaid on the gress . . . makin' up babs o' buttercups and listenin' to the whir o' the shuttles, and the daud daudin' o' the lays i' the loomshops."

Finally we come to a very considerable Glasgow novel, which even George Blake acknowledged as an exception to the perceived lack of fiction about the commercial and industrial city.

> . . . a completely forgotten but remarkably solid novel called *St Mungo's City*, by Sarah Tytler, with some excellent detail about Glasgow's textile industry in the early nineteenth century . . .

"Sarah Tytler" was the pseudonym of Henrietta Keddie, who was born in Cupar, Fife, second youngest of a large, close-knit family. Her autobiography *Three Generations* (1911), while not telling us as much as we would like to know about her literary career, is a warm and lively picture of rural and small-town life (though Keddie does not fudge facts: we hear in her measured tones how the "white scourge" of tuberculosis carried off seven of the ten children in her mother's family, one by one).

Like so many writers, Henrietta Keddie, educated at home by an older sister, read incessantly.

> As a necessary, almost inevitable, result . . . I took to scribbling the stuff and doggerel children perpetrate . . . I took to laying nefarious hands on my father's quill pens, employing them on my own behalf, when, of course, as my handwriting was even viler than might have been expected, I rendered them useless. . . His naturally hot temper was satisfied with the indignant explosion: "That child has been at my pens again!" So far as my conscience was concerned, I was in such a fine frenzy of composition that I felt as if I could not help myself . . .

Money was short, and so Henrietta and her sisters opened a girls' school in Cupar. She could write only in her spare time, but gradually stories in *Fraser's Magazine* and the *Cornhill* set her on the way to a writing career. Under both her own name and the pseudonym Sarah Tytler she became a prolific author, nearly as prolific as her contemporary Margaret Oliphant. Like Oliphant, she was obliged by economics to produce a good deal of hackwork:

> . . . it may be summed up as a good many novels, historical and present day stories for girls, historical sketches, a people's *Life of Queen Victoria*, and a *Life of Selina, Countess of Huntingdon*.

But, again like Oliphant, she was well able to rise above that level. She proves it in at least two of her novels: *Logie Town* (1887), a sharp and affectionate portrait of her home-town Cupar, and *St Mungo's City* (1884).

St Mungo's City is a long, leisurely, but far from uneventful family story, set in Glasgow in the earlier part of the nineteenth century. A critic has described it as "an evangelical sentimentalising" of *The Entail*, but he adds that this is not meant in any pejorative sense. Certainly the three Miss Mackinnons are in the clear line of descent from Galt's ladies whose hoops "soopit the whole breadth of the Trongate." In fact they are great-granddaughters of a tobacco lord: "' . . . a' Glesgy,' as Miss Janet was wont to say, 'trim'led at the wag o' his finger.'"

They have come down in the world, but still refer *passim* to the *nouveaux riches* as "the cotton and iron dirt." They are reduced indeed to utter poverty, hanging on from day to day in expectation of a long-delayed legacy; but they are indomitable old ladies, and when the will, eventually made public, does not please them, they take a short way with it.

> "It's twa shirra-officers, I think," [reports Miss Bethia] "come in a cab, sayin' they have a warrant for us."
>
> "A warrant!" cried Eneas [their grand-nephew] horrified . . . "There must be some huge blunder . . . These are my aunts – the Miss Mackinnons – who have lived here for more than half a century . . . You may as well accuse them of setting fire to his house as of burning his will. What do you say, Aunt Janet?" asked Eneas almost cheerfully, his

53

confidence re-established by the incredibility of the charge.
"That we brunt it, sure enough, and what for no?" demanded
the undaunted woman . . .

Beside these splendid ladies, their kinsfolk, the young Drysdales,
cannot help appearing a little conventional. Yet in the story of
their romances, and in the general picture of life at Drysdale Hall,
we have a genuinely appealing example of the novel of manners.
Sarah Tytler pokes fun most affectionately at the senior Drysdales'
small talk:

> "I believe the takes of salmon are not promising well, Sir
> Hugie; every fish costs five pounds to this day. Let mother help
> you to another slice, Leddy Semple. The lamb ought to be
> first-rate, Sir Jeames, from what it fetches . . . "

And if the Drysdale daughters, proud Claribel and unsophistic-
ated Eppie, are rather typical Victorian novel heroines, there is a
distinct spark of originality about the son, young Tam. When we
first meet him he is a somewhat dour, awkward young man, college-
educated but unwilling to take his place in society or at business,
or to do anything definite with his life. At the root of his greensick-
ness, we find, is nothing else but the first stirring of a social
conscience. Says his mother:

> " . . . It's just that our Tam, poor chiel, has ower kind a heart
> and tender a conscience. He's no easy about the rich and the
> poor, though I'm clear the Bible owns them baith. He cannot
> bide that the one should be so well aff and the other perishing
> for lack of the necessaries of life . . . "

But his father, "auld Tam", has little patience with this nonsense:
"We're not here to mend the whole economy of things . . . We can
but make the best of what we find, and well for us if we do as
much."

And in fact, before the story is half over, young Tam has recovered from his attack of uneasy egalitarianism. His fellow-feeling for the working classes is sadly shaken when he joins them on a Clyde steamer trip "doon the watter" to Rothesay at the Glasgow Fair. The chapter is a fine piece of observation, from the sunny freshness of the morning, through the refreshments, the broadening jests, the quarrels, to the jaded, wearisome return journey. Tam is eager to take part in the people's holiday; he has taken care to dress like the rest of the company (in a frock-coat and a chimney-pot hat), but it doesn't work: "Young Tam lingered on the least popular side of the funnel, and could not tell for his life how he was to fraternize with any of the groups around him."

No one wants him there; no one talks to him; he is even regarded as some kind of spy. If the steamer trip does not deal the final death-blow to his dreams of brotherhood, at least we soon hear of him buckling down to his father's business and taking part in the mild social whirl of city and county. Tam is himself again.

Meanwhile a young English visitor has come to the district:

> Sir Hugo was delighted with Glasgow life. Its powerful vitality, innumerable lights and shades, and the magnitude of its achievements, took hold of his large stock of sympathy . . .

And it is for this picture of a bustling, enthusiastic, attractively naive nineteenth-century Glasgow that we chiefly value *St Mungo's City*. This is the commercial and industrial Glasgow which has been sketched in *Rob Roy* and *The Entail*, only here given extended treatment.

> Never had the hammers of the boiler-makers and the ship-builders rung with more inspiring din, sending sonorous music down the misty river. Never had such strings of casks rumbled heavily in and out of the sugar warehouses and the spirit vaults. Never had St Rollax [sic] and its sister chimneys vomited forth heavier volumes of tainted smoke. Never had the Exchange been so thronged and so busy, or Buchanan Street so crowded

with promenaders and purchasers, or the Broomielaw so
besieged with the shipping of all nations.

A full chapter is devoted to "auld Tam" Drysdale, head of the
dyeing and calico-printing firm which appears on his brass plate as
"Messrs Drysdale" (in the hope that "& Son" can be added when
young Tam gets over his radical turn). Auld Tam is most carefully
and sensitively described, both in his character and in his physical
appearance.

> Tam Drysdale had the scorn for prodigality and the
> disgust at intemperance which might be expected from a
> man whose rise in the world had been, in some degree,
> the result of his prudence and sobriety from youth to
> middle age. But he had mercy on a feather-headed lad
> who had got into debt for a gold watch and chain before
> he had earned them . . . He was below the ordinary
> standard of his native district with regard to size . . . He
> was little above the middle height, and he was so finely
> built that he looked less than he was. But it was a wiry
> slightness, and a delicacy that was tempered like the
> keenness of steel . . .

We are persuaded that Tam Drysdale is a real person, whether
invented or – as does seem possible from these loving details –
drawn from life. References to Henrietta Keddie's father in the
pages of *Three Generations* are worth comparing with the descriptions above.

This raises an interesting question. Why and how did
Henrietta Keddie, born and bred in small-town Fife which she left
to live in London and later Oxford, come to write the thoroughly
Glasgow novel *St Mungo's City*? Her autobiography gives no indication that she knew Glasgow well, though her brother, a civil
engineer, worked for a time in Glasgow and his sisters spent some
holidays "by the Clyde". A contemporary reviewer does not fail to
point out, kindly enough, that the author is "a foreigner."

The impression given by the whole book is that the author has pretty thoroughly explored modern Glasgow, always keeping a watchful eye on its antiquities, and that she has carefully studied the section of its past social life in which she has embedded her clever and ingenious romance . . . Of the life of Glasgow, either in its depth or in its breadth, she has clearly no conception; but with the single phase of it which has been the object of her study she is tolerably familiar.

And this seems to have been the way she worked:

When Miss Keddie wrote *Citoyenne Jacqueline*, a tale of the Great Revolution, she had never been in France, but founded her book upon a close and sympathetic study of the best literature of the period, deriving her knowledge of French character from the various French teachers who had come under her observation.

This information, together with a few lines in *Three Generations*, opens up one intriguing possibility. While living in London Sarah Tytler, by now an acknowledged and popular author, encountered many of the literary lions and lionesses of the day. Her view of their work is not without interest, and her personal observations, frequently delivered in the bracing tones of Cupar, are a joy:

[Mrs Oliphant] was not tall, and she had a tendency to the stoutness which she was apt to describe in her mature women characters under the style of "matronly bountifulness." Mrs Craik was a good business woman . . . It is within my knowledge that she received two thousand pounds for the copyright of one of her stories.

Among many others of varying status, she mentions that

There was Charles Gibbon, who came up to London with William Black, a pair of bold adventurers from old "St Mungo's City". . . Black was certainly the more gifted of the two men,

with the keener and more delicate insight, but Gibbon had his
own special faculty, his broadly humorous perceptions . . .

It is tempting to imagine that Sarah Tytler obtained some
inspiration – even some local colour? – from the home thoughts
of these Glasgow exiles, and proceeded to write a better novel
than they ever achieved about nineteenth-century Glasgow.

3

Stra'bungo Must Be Free

Victorian and Edwardian Glasgow, writes the historian SG Checkland, was:

> . . . a city of more than Mediterranean crowding, with a large part of its labour force packed into its heart . . . One of the consequences of this concentration was to make Glaswegians urbanites of a special kind, unique among the provincial cities of Britain, identifying with their city to a remarkable degree.

Reading today through nineteenth-century volumes of the previously-quoted Glasgow weekly periodical *The Bailie,* we get a strong sense of this small city; by no means small now in population, but growing only gradually in area. Such events as the City of Glasgow bank crash in 1878, or the *Daphne* disaster in 1883 when a steamship capsized at her launching with the loss of 146 shipyard workers, reverberate through the pages of *The Bailie,* and, we are persuaded, through the whole of Glasgow.

Did *small* equate with small-minded? We have to ask this after even a short exposure to *The Bailie*'s rather relentless style of humour. Highlanders, Irishmen and Americans – or stereotypes of these – are continually presented for our amusement, their idiom travestied, their pretensions or their misapprehensions of Glasgow life mercilessly mocked. So are people from Paisley, the neighbouring large burgh, very evidently seen, from a Glasgow perspective, as too big for its boots. So are the residents of the smaller burghs – Hillhead, Crosshill, Partick, Govan and others – which, when *The Bailie* began publishing and for some years thereafter, were not yet part of Glasgow. *The Bailie* grew quite apoplectic at the thought of Partick people, for instance, strolling in the West End Park (wearing out the grass, it is more or less implied) while contributing not a penny towards its upkeep.

All this would seem to indicate a domestically-minded, parochial readership, receptive to the couthy tales of the urban kailyard, and equally well-matched to the humorous sketches which proliferated in Glasgow (and elsewhere) from the middle of the nineteenth century onwards. It would be as well, however, to look closely at these Victorian sketches before consigning them to the kailyard. While the Victorian novelists were more visibly and perhaps more respectably at work, the sketch-writers had their view of Glasgow too.

One reason for according them attention is their easy and natural use of the vernacular. As William Donaldson has pointed out:

> Many papers circulated within homogeneous speech-communities where Scots was a fundamental social bond. As "The Voice of the People" it was inevitable that the popular press should use it freely, the more so as journalists often came from a similar social and linguistic background to their readers . . . And so it was that a new phonographically-inspired prose, often of great orthographic inventiveness and freedom, sprang up in all the major dialect areas displacing "book Scots" – that is, standard literary Scots.

Glasgow periodicals were not behind in this movement. A few months into its long career (1872–1926) *The Bailie* was publishing a humorous vernacular sketch in the form of a letter from "A

Causeyside Cork," that is, a Paisley master weaver. Its purpose (perhaps predictably) was to make fun of Paisley idiom; one "homogeneous speech-community" differentiating itself from another, for *The Bailie* accepted Glasgow idiom, by and large, as the norm.

Further vernacular sketches and letters from (fictitious) correspondents followed thick and fast, signed by "Wanderin' Wull", by "Ane wha's no abune speerin," by "Saundy MacFaurlan," by "Bauldy," by "Tummas Tamson." *Quiz* (1881–98) is an almost equally rewarding field for study; publishing its first vernacular sketch, "The Gathering of the Clan McFush" in 1882, it soon acquired such correspondents as "Archie Macnab" and "Dauvit" in the 1880s, and the rather splendidly named "Scobie Garnkirk" in the 1890s.

The second reason to value these sketches is their breadth of reference, revealing, as Donaldson says, a mental world "utterly removed from the douce and kirk-gaun, meek, mim-mou'd, brainless yokelry of Barrie, Maclaren and similar middle-class book novelists."

"Dauvit" of *Quiz* may stand as a good example. He does indulge in the occasional kailyard episode, like the almost obligatory auction scene where he and his wife unwittingly bid against each other for "a superior inlaid walnut commode with large mirror back" (a description which he keeps getting wrong purely to annoy her). But he has a wider view than this would imply; in his first few letters he is already covering politics and the then-current topic of mesmerism. His letters are addressed to "the Professor", who, we learn, is a proponent of Darwin's theory of evolution. Dauvit is worried about this. Humorous as his fundamentalist objections are, we get a clear impression of sincerity too:

> I wid raither gang doon tae Auld Sanny wi' some o' my aul'
> cronies, than up in a balloon to sing psaulms wi' some
> hypocrites I ken. But, man, that's my very reason for tryin' tae
> knock this nonsense oot o' ye'r heed; for it's certain you an'
> me'll no' gang the same gate if I don't get ye brocht back tae

the richt wey o' thinkin', an' I want tae be aside ye, nae maitter whaur ye gang.

We return, however, to *The Bailie* for the apotheosis – anyway in Glasgow – of the Victorian vernacular sketch. The correspondent is "Jeems Kaye," whose letters appeared at intervals in *The Bailie* for over ten years, from 1876 until the late 1880s. Evidently Jeems was soon a household word, at least among *Bailie* readers.

> Wee Mary: "Papa, what paper's that you're reading?"
> Papa: "*The Bailie.*"
> Wee Mary: "Is there a letter in't frae Jeems Kaye?"
> Papa: "No."
> Wee Mary: "Tuts, it's no' worth the readin'."

Better evidence, perhaps, than this all too typical *Bailie* joke are the large advertisements for a Glasgow drapery firm, carefully crafted in Jeems Kaye style and idiom, which ran for some eight weeks in late 1876 and early 1877, just a year after the first sketch had appeared.

It is clear how his fame had spread by 1883, when a selection of the sketches was published in book form as *Jeems Kaye: His Adventures and Opinions.* The first issue sold out on publication day and the second within another week. Two further selections followed, in 1886 and 1888, and a sturdy collected edition in 1903 consolidated Jeems's place in Glasgow fiction.

The sketches were published anonymously in both periodical and book form, and the author's possible identity was much discussed in Glasgow. He was Archibald Macmillan, a commission agent with his business in Glasgow and his home on the Ayrshire coast, who wrote for several periodicals of the day, under various names, we are told, so that much of his output has yet to be tracked down.

His character, Jeems Kaye, is consistent, well-drawn and bringing along a supporting cast of friends and relations, like his long-suffering wife Betty and Mr Pinkerton with the wooden leg. His letters emanate from The Coal-Ree, Strathbungo (which is a real district on the south side of Glasgow).

> Our friend cannot say why he fixed on a coal-ree as the base of operations. His choice of Strathbungo is accounted for in this way. The first day he was in Glasgow . . . he met a lad who was going a message to "Stra'bungo", as he called it. Archibald thought it a very odd name, and it stuck to his memory . . .

But to describe Jeems Kaye as a coalman is seriously to undervalue him, for he is a man of many roles. A good citizen, he serves as a juryman and a school board member and helps with the census of 1881:

> In my next close wis an auld woman I knew, and she put down her age as 65. On looking ower the sheet I says –
>
> "Hoot toot, Mrs Paterson, this is no richt; ye're surely mair than 65 – in fac' I ken ye are."

As a corporal in the volunteers he attends the Royal Volunteer Review of 1881, where Queen Victoria asks specially for an audience:

> "Really, Mr Kaye, I'm prood tae see you. I've taen in *The Bailie* since the beginning and hae them a' bound noo, and I often thocht o' orderin' a hunnerwecht or twa o' coals frae you when I'm doon at Balmoral. It's a prood day for me, Mr Kaye, and if it wisna that a' the seats roon aboot me are full o' my grandchildren, I wid ask ye up."

This event has gone down in history as the Wet Review, because of the incessant rain on the day. You wouldn't have guessed that, however, from the original sketch in *The Bailie* on 24 August 1881, since it was published the day before the review took place and understandably omitted to mention the rain. Readers were delighted and there is much jocularity in the columns of *The Bailie* (though by the time the sketch appeared in book form, rain had been added).

Jeems is much involved in the politics of the day. He is fully aware of his importance in the democratic system, spending indeed so long in the box pondering how to vote that the polling clerk has to intervene:

> "Sir," I says, looking at him sternly, "are ye aware ye are only a paid servant o' the county, sworn tae keep the pencils sharpened and alloo nae boys in? Go awa' back tae yer post, sir, and leave me, a free-born Briton, and a taxpayer, forbye an elder, tae record my vote according tae my conscience. Hoo daur you, and thae three faces behin' ye, presume tae prejudice my vote, eh?"
> "But these gentlemen want in to vote too," he says.
> "Weel, put up mair boxes," I says, "am I tae be discommoded because o' your defective arrangements?"

Later he appears as a canvasser, and later still as a parliamentary candidate, promising not only free education but:

> . . . free books, an' slates, an' free pinafores, an' free bonnets – aye, an' free peevers an' free bools – in fac', everything'll be free.
> *Mr Sampson* [the dominie] – An' whaur's a' the money tae come frae?
> *Mr Kaye* – Oh! we'll just fin' that oot as we go alang . . .

He has better luck in local politics, and is finally seen as Lieut-Col Sir Jeems Kaye, Provost of Stra'bungo, in which capacity he appears at a meeting of the Boundary Commission.

This is a very topical reference, as in many of his adventures. At the time (in 1888) the city of Glasgow was proposing to annex many of the adjacent burghs to gain more space for its greatly increased population, and of course more contributions to St

Mungo's purse. The small independent burghs resisted with much spirit, proud of their identity and of their public services, which they maintained were better than Glasgow's. (A number of them were annexed in 1891, but Govan and Partick, for instance, held out until 1912.) Strathbungo, fictionally, also fights its corner.

> "What are you noted for?"
> "The finest park in Scotland, the Crossmyloof bakery, the only place in the three kingdoms whaur ye will see a baronet selling coals by the hunnerwecht . . . "
>
> "You don't wish to be annexed to Glasgow?"
> "Annexed tae Glesca? I should think no. The Glesca folk come rinnin' oot tae us looking for hooses. Ye never hear o' Stra'bungonians wanting tae flit intae Glesca."

Eventually:

> The Chairman said, "Whatever we do with Crosshill and Govanhill, and all these mushroom burghs . . . Stra'bungo must be free."
>
> "An' unfettered," says I.
> "An' unfettered," says he.
> "Free as the ostriches or the eagles that soar in the heavens," says I.
> "As free as them," says the Chairman.
> . . . So we adjourned, an' that's the way Stra'bungo wis saved.

It is satire of the most good-natured kind. Many of Jeems Kaye's letters, it is true, are on purely domestic affairs. He is given to holding disastrous New Year parties and his visits to Millport and Paisley Races are little more successful. But his observation of Glasgow life is full of interest for us. He makes a memorable journey, for instance, on the newly-opened "underground railway" (now the low-level line from Queen Street), an adventure the more harrowing since the tunnels are lighted only at long intervals.

"A' the folk that writes tae the papers come oot here [at Charing Cross], so there's nae need's gien' lichts tae the Finnieston folk; it wid jist be throwing awa' money gien' them lichts."

His very first letter, "The Caars" ("The Caurs" in book form) retains, a hundred and twenty years later, a topical, not to say timeless, quality for travellers on Glasgow public transport. Though he doesn't like the (horse-drawn) tramcars, comparing them unfavourably with "oor auld tartan 'busses o' Menzies and McGregor," he and Betty are forced by circumstances, one cold night, to wait for a car.

The first siven that came up were gaun tae the Goosedubs, and that, I need hardly say, was no' oor road . . . Up the eighth caur comes. "Whaur's that ane gaun tae?" says Betty. "Nine and sixpenny troosers," I reads . . .

"Hut tut, abin that!"
"One an' echtpenny tea. No, that's no it."
Weel, after a facht, I read in dirty yellow letters – "Goosedubs and Dobie's Loan."

"Awa' oot o' my sicht," says Betty. "Goosedubs! dae they think a'body stops in the Goosedubs? Goosedubs atweel!" . . .

The correspondence had long ceased by the time of *The Bailie*'s golden jubilee in 1922, but Jeems Kaye (evidently still well remembered) sent a message of goodwill on the occasion. When Archibald Macmillan died three years later, *The Bailie* obituary was perceptive as well as warm. Jeems Kaye is likened to such other fictional characters as Mansie Wauch, of *Blackwood's Magazine*, and Tammas Bodkin, of the *People's Journal*.

The "Jeems Kaye" sketches will be treasured as valuable contributions to the vernacular literature of Scotland. The field in which Mr Macmillan worked is worthy of further exploitation.

And, it may be added, of further exploration, because its richness was largely unrecognised until Donaldson's two books on the subject, and there is more to be found yet.

4

The Urban Kailyard Syndrome

The Kailyard School of Scottish fiction is well-known and has been frequently examined. A recent critic has summed it up, not unsympathetically, as "a dozen books or so written by three Scotsmen in a single distant decade". The three Scotsmen are JM Barrie, SR Crockett, and 'Ian Maclaren' (John Watson), and the decade is 1888–98, which saw the publication of the most typically kailyard works of these writers.

What is a kailyard work? Again, the term has been thoroughly discussed. Recent studies have begun to rehabilitate the kailyard, but 'kailyard' as a shorthand term still tends to imply a body of work characterised by sentimentality, narrowness of vision, and the acceptance of a code of unshakeable assumptions regarding conventional conduct and belief. Kailyard practitioners are not in general regarded as considerable writers, though again there has been some recent re-evaluation, particularly of Barrie. The difference has been expressed by comparing a kailyard writer to an emphatically non-kailyard one:

> For Hardy [in *Tess of the D'Urbervilles*] there is the threat of social change which may corrode the lives of his characters, and the dark perversity of a hostile or uncaring universe which may destroy them. For Crockett [in *The Lilac Sunbonnet*] it is

enough to create a world in which real-seeming people act out
a drama with a happy ending.

There is, however, one further defining characteristic of classical
kailyard: its rural setting. 'Ian Maclaren' indeed published some
short stories with urban backgrounds (of which one, "The Minister
of St Bede's", is set in Glasgow). In a different vein, the Glasgow
periodical *Quiz* was sharp enough to have the kailyard in its sights.
Crockett is the target in "A Strayed Kailyarder".

> It so chanced that I reached a city on the West Coast hard by a
> running stream that the folk there call Clyde . . . I came up the
> Stockwell . . . In the dark I was beset by an ill-favoured loon
> wha dang me doon . . . but being a buirdly chiel and licht o'
> the feet as a wild cat, and although the blow had moidered my
> head somewhat, I got up and gave him a mighty clour on the
> head. So I have had to bide here many days . . .

But these are exceptions which prove the rule that kailyard is set in
rural countryside, in villages, or in small towns.

Yet sentimentality, narrow-mindedness and convention can
be found in the urban milieu too, and in fiction set in that milieu,
as the most cursory survey of Glasgow novels will reveal. It was in
an attempt to isolate this strand of Glasgow fiction that the present
writer, some thirty years ago, coined the not very inspirational
term "urban kailyard". Though it was only meant to serve until a
better phrase came along, it seems to have passed into the common
usage of Scottish literary criticism, and may as well continue to be
used here.

Urban kailyard is fiction with an urban setting which
otherwise shares the attributes of the kailyard proper. Though, as
has been seen, there are hints of kailyard in Victorian Glasgow
fiction, urban kailyard came into full flower a little later than the
rural version, in the first decade or two of the twentieth century,
leading up to, and just surviving, World War I. In Chapter Five
several of its practitioners will be considered. First, however, we

should probably offer proof of its existence by spotting those telltale characteristics in one or two Glasgow classics of the time.

JJ Bell's *Wee Macgreegor* comes readily to mind, though some critics see more than kailyard in these amiable tales. When Macgreegor commits yet another *faux pas* before his Aunt Purdie (by reciting a poem about fleas), her reaction is purest kailyard, but she's a figure of fun. It is his mother Lizzie's reaction which is of particular note.

> With a face of disgust, [Aunt Purdie], holding up her hands, exclaimed, "Sich vulgarity!"
>
> Lizzie appeared to swallow something before she quietly said: "Micht I be as bold as to speir, Mrs Purdie, if ye refer to ma son, Macgreegor, or to the words of the pome he recitet the noo?"

Clearly we are within an ace of umbrage being taken; a phrase which itself belongs to the constricted, uneasily genteel world of the urban kailyard.

The "Erchie" sketches by "Hugh Foulis" (Neil Munro) are definitely more than kailyard, but sentimentality does creep in:

> . . . True daughter of the city, [Jinnet] loves at times the evening throng of the streets. That of itself, perhaps, would not send her out with her door-key in her hand and a peering, eager look like that of one expecting something long of coming: the truth is she cherishes a hope that some Saturday to Erchie and her will come what comes often to her in her dreams, sometimes with terror and tears, sometimes with delight.

(This being the return of her sailor son, which does in fact occur some time later, giving rise to a perfect welter of pawkiness on Erchie's part.) And Spud Tamson, hero of several books by Captain RW Campbell, is treated throughout in kailyard style: viewed, that is, from a patronising height. In the first volume of the series,

Private Spud Tamson (1915), he tells his "fond and proud parents" that he has enlisted in the Glasgow Mileeshy:

> "I'm prood o' ye, son," said Mrs Tamson. "Here, take yer faither's shirt and Sunday breeks and pawn them. You'll get twa shillin's on them. And bring back a gill o' the best, twa bottles o' table beer, an' a pun' o' ham. We'll hae a feast . . ."

Urban kailyard can probably also be detected in the work of Annie S Swan, as well, of course, as the rural variety, for her fictional world is wider than it is deep. The case for her books, as seen by her legion of faithful readers, has been put by James Drawbell with (perhaps unconsciously) appropriate fervour:

> To be taken out of themselves . . . to turn aside from the daily anxieties and be able to identify themselves with a background where living was pleasant and people were kind and considerate and loving. Was there anything so dreadful about that? Was it so much to ask for?

The novels of "O Douglas" (Anna Buchan) might seem to qualify as kailyard, but at its best her writing has a humorous sharpness which suggests that she is observing, rather than subscribing to, the ethos of the urban kailyard. The Thomsons, minor characters in *The Setons* (1917), are planning an ambitious party and the anxious daughter is supervising her less sophisticated mother's arrangements.

> "I do hope Annie'll manage the showing in all right," went on Jessie. "The Simpsons had one letting you in and another waiting in the bedroom to help you off with your things."
> Mrs Thomson drew herself up.
> "My friends are all capable of taking off their own things, Jessie, I'm thankful to say. They don't need a lady's maid; nor does Mrs Simpson, let me tell you, for when I first knew her she did her own washing."
> "Uch, Mamma," said Jessie.

We should not however be too quick to describe urban kailyard as a phenomenon of the early twentieth century. It outlasted that era, and (like rural kailyard) can still be found today. A staunch upholder of kailyard values is the Dundee firm of DC Thomson, which publishes, among other periodicals, the classically kailyard *People's Friend* and *Sunday Post*. In the early 1990s, a century after the recognised kailyard decade, Thomson's guidelines for aspiring contributors made this clear.

> The *Sunday Post* offers a market for its own special brand of short story which appeals to a wide *family* readership . . . A simple story, well told, but with strong human interest, reflecting the drama of everyday life and the emotions of people we know and understand, the familiar folk around us . . . We do *not* want the depressing, fantastic or sordid.
>
> [DC Thomson's italics]

The very easiest way to explain urban kailyard to a group of Scots is to cite the *Sunday Post* cartoon family The Broons. (This approach works with such a wide range of age, intellect and social class that the Thomson claim to reach every home in Scotland begins to seem no idle boast.) For some years during and just after World War II, similar success would have attended a mention of The McFlannels, who featured in a long-running radio series on the Scottish Home Service scripted by Helen W Pryde. Five books based on the series were published between 1947 and 1951, and George Blake had no doubt as to their kailyard credentials.

> Helen W Pryde has conceived a Glasgow family on the social level that might once upon a time have been safely described as somewhere between the superior artisan and the lower middle-class strata. During the war years its means and status have advanced, and much of the fun rests on the first encounters of simple folk with social pretensions more spacious than those to which they have been accustomed.

(The shrewd reader will note the inevitable Kailyard trick
of playing on the acute Scottish awareness of distinctions
of class, wealth and manners.)

The McFlannels was immensely popular in its day. A generation of
Scots over the age of fifty could probably still, if asked, give the
names of the McFlannel parents Wullie and Sarah; of, at least,
their two youngest children, Maisie and Peter; and of their would-
be upper-middle-class neighbour with her appropriately Kelvinside
accent, Mrs McCotton. As readily recalled are the two chief catch-
phrases, Wullie's comforting "We never dee'd a winter yet", and
Sarah's affronted "Wullie, don't be vulgar!" (which alone places
her in the kailyard, even if all other indications fail).

Such widespread popularity may be partially explained by
reference to special conditions favouring *The McFlannels*: its
production on radio, for instance, before the arrival of television
provided a larger selection of entertainment options; or its
appearance in wartime, when, it might be argued, the uncertainty
of real life drew the audience back to the security of the kailyard.
While this may be so, we should not overlook the more recent
popularity of television series like *Dr Finlay's Casebook* and *[Take
the] High Road*. (Scottish viewers do seem to be happy in the
kailyard, and greatly enjoy *Hamish Macbeth*, without always,
perhaps, recognising a send-up of the genre in its shortbread-tin
titles and its hero's frequent recourse to a soothing spliff.)

Also in recent years, it may noted that the term "urban
kailyard" seems to have acquired an additional and slightly different
meaning. Opening the Glasgow Garden Festival in 1988, the Prince
of Wales alarmed the lieges by essaying a passage of Glasgow verse.

Oh where is the Glasgow where I used tae stey,
The white wally closes done up wi' pipe cley;
Where ye knew every neighbour frae first floor tae third,
And tae keep your door locked was considered absurd.
Do you know the folk staying next door to you?

These are the opening lines of Adam McNaughtan's poem "The Glasgow I Used to Know", which has attracted both praise and censure. Its nostalgic view of a largely vanished Glasgow is sharply challenged by another songwriter:

Where is the Glasgow I used to know?
The tenement buildings that let in the snow,
Through the cracks in the plaster the cold wind did blow,
And the water we washed in was fifty below . . .

This argument will be explored in detail later on. But many of McNaughtan's phrases and images –

And where is the wean that once played in the street
Wi' a jorrie, a peerie, a gird wi' a cleek?

– recur, in spirit at least, throughout Glasgow fiction.

When editing a collection of Glasgow short stories representative of the half-century from the 1930s to the 1980s, the present writer and her colleague had to impose a strict quota, or tales of weans playing keepie-uppie in back courts would have monopolised the book. This is what the columnist Jack McLean has identified as Wee Black Sannyism, a specially Glasgow *nostalgie de la boue*. It is encapsulated in Stephen Mulrine's poem "Glasgow Number Seven":

When we were wee
it was aw berr feet
an who likes candy
an nane o yir cheek
an see us a lenny
an dreepin aff dykes
an kick-the-can
an shots oan bikes
wis rerr . . .

And it is demolished in Tom Leonard's poem "Dripping with Nostalgia", which reads in full:

> while the judges
> in the Snottery Weans Competition
> were still licking clean
> the candidates' upper lips
>
> the "Dear Aul' Glesca" Poetry Prize
> for the most heartwarming evocation
> of communal poverty
> was presented to the author of
>
> "The Day the Dug ate ma Ration Book"

The painter Joan Eardley produced, during the 1950s and early 1960s, a series of fine Glasgow pictures in which neighbour children are seen in and around her studio in Townhead. In 1988 a critic wrote less than enthusiastically about some of her later works:

> The figures . . . are flattened out against graffiti covered walls
> in a pastiche of child-like drawing. Any physical defects . . . are
> exploited for pathetic effect. These scenes of urban kailyard
> must have had special appeal to the bourgeois buyers who were
> now beginning to acquire her work.

"Urban kailyard" is here being used, it will be seen, in a new way. The Eardley children (in this critic's opinion, not shared by all) and the wee boys in their black sannies may indeed be viewed through the prism of sentimentality which is one characteristic of kailyard; but the question of narrow-mindedness does not arise, nor is there any sign of the attempted gentility which Blake and others have identified in the kailyard. Explains Mrs Young in *Generalship*: "Ye see the Bailie's folk move in a circle, or maybe half a circle, aboon us." That (even if ironically observed) is urban kailyard. Another name is needed for the perfectly valid sub-genre identified by McLean and Leonard. The snottery wean school, perhaps?

The sentimental strand of Glasgow fiction has survived in various guises and co-exists with the powerful strand of urban realism which will soon be considered. At the time of writing, a couthy view of tenement solidarity in the blitz shares the shelves with James Kelman's Booker prizewinner and the fantastic postmodernism of Alasdair Gray. Glasgow fiction is as varied as that, and has been for many years; because the early twentieth century, the golden age of urban kailyard, also saw the publication of some startlingly honest and clear-eyed views of Glasgow.

5

The Kailyard and the Rat-Pit

Returning to Scotland in 1910 after a five years' residence in
London, I was thus enabled to get a new impression of her
general position in letters . . . The atmosphere was intensely
villatic and narrow, yet people were beginning to suspect that
Kailyaird and *The Bonnie Brier Bush* scarcely represented the
last word in Scots fiction . . .

Thus, looking back in 1935, writes Lewis Spence, a poet and
man of letters (as that *villatic* may have led us to suspect).
Though he was apt to deny with some spirit that any such
movement had ever existed, Spence was well-regarded at the time
of the Scottish Literary Renaissance. Having cited half-a-dozen
Scottish writers of the early twentieth century, he continues: "Other
than the output of these . . . I cannot recall any effort worth noting
between the year 1910 and the beginning of the War in 1914 . . ."
and, like many other commentators since, he rightly sees a change,
if not a renaissance, in Scottish literature after World War I.

Interestingly to us, the handful of writers he does mention
includes the names of JJ Bell and Neil Munro, who are part of the
picture of Glasgow fiction. If, unlike Spence, we draw a line at the
end, not the beginning, of World War I, we see further intriguing

things happening in Glasgow. These two decades, 1900–1920, are not to be dismissed out of hand.

We must begin with JJ Bell, perhaps the central figure of the urban kailyard, even though, of his many books, only some half-dozen are definitely set in Glasgow, and of these only one can be said to have attained lasting fame. That one book, however, is *Wee Macgreegor*, the unpretentious collection of sketches about the small son of the working-class Glasgow family Robinson which became, and remained, immensely popular from its first appearance in book form in 1902. The sketches first appeared in the Glasgow *Evening Times*, and had an eager readership there, but the book was rejected by several publishers on the grounds that its appeal was purely local. Bell brought it out at his own expense. He wrote later:

> The book was published on 23rd November, and we wondered anxiously what was happening to it. A week passed; then came a telegram from Mr Oliver. The first printing was exhausted; a second was on the machine. By the end of the year the sales were 20,000.

> The Press notices were extraordinarily generous . . . There was much pleasant correspondence from all parts of the world . . . Presently appeared Wee Macgreegor lemonade, matches, china, "taiblet", picture postcards, sardines, and so forth. Sober-minded persons called it a "craze", and I should be the last to contradict them . . .

Bell would also have been the last to deny that not absolutely everybody liked *Wee Macgreegor*. Among all the kind and congratulatory letters ". . . there was one, I recall, bitterly abusive, which, I confess, hurt me very much, though, no doubt, it was good for me." (He is recalling it over thirty years later; a glimpse for us of the vulnerable man whom his friends knew.)

He does not record what his abusive correspondent had against Macgreegor, but the author of the spoof *Mair Macjigger*

Perhaps the central figure of the urban kailyard, JJ Bell's *Wee Macgreegor*, the unpretentious collection of sketches about the small son of the working-class Glasgow family Robinson, achieved immense popularity from its first appearance in book form in 1902

(1903) evidently felt, rather like some writers in our day, that one could have enough of appealing wee boys. The following is not, of course, usual procedure in the Robinson household, but there are times when its possibilities can be recognised.

> "He's – phew – he's been tae ane o' thae fush an' tattie shoaps," said his father . . .
>
> Macjigger bowed his head and commenced to mop his eyes with the corner of his bonnet . . .
>
> "Haven't I tell't ye dizzens o' times yer no' tae gaun tae thae nesty shoaps?"
>
> "I furgot, maw." . . .
>
> "He's been smoakin' tae," interposed his father . . .
>
> "Aw," said Mrs Dobinson, "smoakin' has he . . . varra weel." . . . She seized her son by the nape of the neck, struck him a terrific blow on the side of the head, and roared out – "Tak' that, ye imp o' Satan ye . . . Tak' that an' awa' tae yer bed."

Less extreme, but typical of some sections of the Glasgow reading public through the years, was the reaction when Anna Buchan (O Douglas) included Macgreegor in her programme of readings.

> I enjoyed letting myself go in the speech of the Gorbals. My enjoyment was, however, not shared by two genteel ladies at a concert, who were overheard saying: "What can her mother be thinking about to let her speak that vulgar broad Scotch; and quite a refined-looking girl too."

Wee Macgreegor is not specifically set in the Gorbals, but the Buchan family, as genteel south-side residents, may have considered *working-class* and *Gorbals* to be interchangeable terms (see John Buchan's 1922 novel *Huntingtower*). These ambiguities raise the question of how, in fact, we are to regard *Wee Macgreegor*. Is it a true flower of the kailyard, as George Blake implies?

> Bell enjoyed for a space an immense commercial popularity in
> Britain and the United States – perhaps the last wild wave of
> enthusiasm for a product of the Kailyard . . . It is all as simple
> as you please, inevitably sentimental . . .

Yet it can hardly be called sentimental at all beside some of Bell's
rural kailyard pieces like *Jess and Co.* (1904), or, even more
strikingly, one of his later collections of sketches about impossibly
winsome children, like *Kiddies* (1916). In comparison with these,
Wee Macgreegor verges on the realistic.

Is it, then, a classic of Scottish humour? CM Grieve considers
it from this angle.

> I realise its inability to stand against the great comic creations
> of other literatures: and yet although it is merely superficial
> comedy and fails to realise the tremendous *vis comica* resident
> in Scottish life . . . I am of opinion that it, far more than merely
> proportionately to the literary stature of modern Scotland
> compared with other European countries, provides a Scottish
> equivalent to the best humorous literature that has been
> produced anywhere in the twentieth century.

Is it, on the other hand, a social document? An article published
in 1927 to celebrate *Wee Macgreegor*'s silver jubilee quotes William
Archer as saying:

> We are as far from the lymphatic sentiment of the Kailyard
> School as from Little Lord Fauntleroy, but we are closely in
> touch with some of the best elements in Scottish working-class
> character.

The writer of the article himself disagrees:

> The Robinson group . . . are sentimental types that were
> unrepresentative of the Scottish working-class community even
> in the easy-going far-off years before the city became the
> headquarters of the Wild Men.

But thirty years later a sociologist asserts:

> There is only one broad division between social classes in
> Glasgow and Scotland . . . On the one side there is the great
> majority of families [consisting of] man and wife devoting
> themselves to the task of bringing up their children to be
> reasonably honest and kindly and well-behaved men and
> women . . .

and considers *Wee Macgreegor* one of "the two outstanding
expressions in this century of Glasgow family folklore" (the other
being *The McFlannels*). He sees little evidence in *Wee Macgreegor*
of ambition to "move up" to a better house or a white-collar job.

> In this JJ Bell may have been describing a more easy-going and
> satisfied society which is now no more. But in most other
> respects *Wee Macgreegor* is perennially fresh. It is sentimental
> and even mawkish in parts. But it is strikingly true to present-
> day family life in its main outlines . . . The supreme importance
> – rediscovered by contemporary psychologists – of warm
> mutual affection . . . was no secret to John Joy Bell . . . And it
> is as clear about the importance of moral guidance and
> discipline as it is about the child's need for love.

So what are we, nearly a hundred years after its publication, to
make of *Wee Macgreegor*? In its modest pages we can find
sentimentality galore.

> "I've broke Maw's teapot." And then he gave way to grief.
> "Ye've broke yer Maw's teapot!" echoed Mrs McOstrich [who,
> having broken it herself, has cravenly wrapped it up and sent it
> back via Macgreegor].
>
> Her moment of relief had come, and yet – and yet. . .
> It was but a feeble flame of gas on the stairhead, and the boy's
> eyes were half blinded with tears, so that he did not see the
> changes on Mrs McOstrich's plain, hard countenance. He only
> knew that, after a long period of suspense, the parcel was gently

removed from his hands, and he himself was drawn close to a bosom, which, if not quite so soft as his mother's, was yet a refuge whereon he found comfort.

"Ye're that kind, ye're that kind!" he whispered, whereupon the childless woman shivered for an instant, and then held him closer.

We can find, on the other hand, a clear and rather tender depiction of the working-class matriarchate – Lizzie's word is law – which will be a recurrent motif in later Glasgow fiction, as well as a splendid send-up of the social climber, in the person of Aunt Purdie.

"Robert is keeping well, thank you; but he's sorry he cannot leave the shope this evening. His young man was unfortunately rin over by an electric caur yesterday . . . Robert's young man got conclusion of the brain," said Aunt Purdie with great solemnity. "He was carrying a dizzen of eggs an' a pun' of the best ham when the melancholy accident occurred."

"Dae ye tell me that?" exclaimed Lizzie. "An' wis the eggs a' broke?"

"With two exceptions."

Generations have found humour in the sayings and doings of Macgreegor himself, so surely it's there. But humour is in the eye of the beholder; we can at least say that *Wee Macgreegor* tickled the Glasgow funny-bone of its day.

Though he is now known almost exclusively for *Wee Macgreegor*, JJ Bell was no one-book wonder, publishing, indeed, two or three books a year for over thirty years. The original *Wee Macgreegor* of 1902 was quickly followed by a sequel, *Wee Macgreegor Again* (1904), and sketches from both collections appear impartially in today's collected editions. Macgreegor found love in *Courtin' Christina* (1913), the *enfant terrible* Christina having made her appearance in *Oh! Christina!* (1909) which is not set in Glasgow. By this time Macgreegor is a clean-cut and honourable adolescent, and some of his charm seems to have departed with his small-boy rascality. But Bell's bibliography continues with a kind of relentless winsomeness: *The Nickums, The Braw Bailie, Meet Mr Craw, Hoots!*, and more.

This sounds very much like over-production, and so, in a way, it was. JJ Bell, says an enthusiastic profile written towards the end of his life, "is a frequent contributor to many of the leading and popular magazines and his short stories are always greatly appreciated."

Bell's friend George Blake had a more informed and sadder tale to tell.

> We might see him once in a month when he had business in town and would slip across the street to join us in a coffee. Only time for a coffee, he had to get back to the desk and the daily thousands of words he must turn out in the form of serial stories, comic sketches, and the like. In fact, Joe Bell, a sweet innocent if ever there was one, had suffered grievously one of the hazards of our trade. The affluence promised by the first success of *Wee Macgreegor* in book form escaped him, thanks to a quirk in publishing practice. It is difficult to recapture the techniques of a popular success, and for too many years it was for Joe an unending battle to keep the serial stories moving and catch the last possible post for Dundee . . .

This is the gentle, honest, vulnerable man who wrote *Wee Macgreegor* and never, perhaps, quite managed to find that chord again.

Neil Munro did not know Bell when *Wee Macgreegor* was published, but his generous reaction to it was remembered warmly by Bell.

> My earliest memory of Neil Munro is the memory of a kindness. Long ago, shortly after the publishing of my first little book, he sent me a letter, in which he declared that if the little book's circulation did not promptly stop, he would come across the water with the family dirk and stop the author's.

Wasn't I the proud and happy young writer?

They became friends, and in the 1920s George Blake, then a journalist on Munro's *Evening News*, knew them both. He too had pleasant recollections of Munro:

> . . . kenspeckle for his height and shock of greying fair hair, for the faint dandyism that expressed itself in good suits of blue or brown and handmade tan shoes highly polished – no arty scruffiness for this Highland gentleman.

Like other critics before and since, Blake saw Munro as "a quite singular case of artistic schizophrenia."

> He was the gifted prose stylist, the successful author of Highland romances . . . and he was also the "Looker On" who on Mondays chronicled in the *News* the doings of Para Handy or the observations of Erchie, My Droll Friend . . . In both capacities he was accepted by Glasgow, and one sometimes thinks that he was Glasgow's prisoner, playing in maturity, though with agonies neither of his publics could envisage, his part as public entertainer in two fields.

Bell, apparently, saw no evidence of these agonies:

> Only once . . . do I remember his saying, in passing, that he wished the day's darg would leave him time and energy for another novel or two, but he did not say it complainingly or impatiently.

But perhaps Munro felt able to express himself more frankly to Blake than to the gentle Bell.

> . . . he could be bitter about journalism. [writes Blake] "The jawbox," he called it, meaning a receptacle into which you poured everything and got nothing back save a faintly bad smell.

Munro's novels, from *John Splendid* (1898) to *The New Road* (1914), were not only popular but critically admired in their day. They have fallen out of favour in recent years, but a re-evaluation is under way. Most are historical romances with Highland settings. A contemporary believed that Munro could and should address the question of Glasgow on an epic scale; another example of the "if only" tendency peculiar to those in search of the great Glasgow novel.

> It has been asserted with truth, I believe, that no really great novel of Glasgow life and character – a novel on something like the scale of *Vanity Fair* – has yet been written. Munro, in collaboration with Foulis [see below], is the man to write it. Will he? Possibly not. A busy working journalist, even if only middle-aged, is always a sad and weary man by evening.

Munro never did, though he was inspired to a tongue-in-cheek effort by the news that Zola was to visit the slums of Glasgow.

> It was almost closing-time, and Alphonse went out into the Rue de Sauchiehall and turned down the gas above the abat-jour . . . Waggons from the Department for Cleansing lumbered noisily; the dust being blown from their open lids across his face. It seemed as if the garbage of the world had been concentrated into a bouillon, then dried and shaken out of a pepper castor. And this odour, though he did not think of it, was the pungent expression, the symbol, the sad and awful evidence of the foul humanity around him in the teeming and slumbering city . . .

But Alphonse's overtures to a "young woman, French Polisher" (the very type of artisan he's looking for), in the Rue de Lyon, Garscube Road quartier, are doomed to failure. "'Whit dae ye want at this time o' nicht? . . . Are ye the Prudential?'" and Munro, or Foulis, pursues the matter no further.

"Hugh Foulis" was the pseudonym used by Neil Munro for

his *Glasgow Evening News* sketches featuring Para Handy, Erchie, and Jimmy Swan. All three characters have Glasgow connections, but only the Erchie sketches are set exclusively in the city. They look at Glasgow with humour and perception, as the Victorian sketches did before them, continuing (recent research has brought to light) for several decades, from the first years of the Edwardian era until the mid-1920s.

"On Sundays he is the beadle of our church; at other times he Waits." Thus, in the *Evening News* of 1902, Munro introduces us to Erchie, with more than a hint of the kailyard narrator who observes his simple characters from a sophisticated height. The patronising air survives, however, for only a couple of sketches, and the narrator disappears, perhaps because he can't get a word in edgeways.

> "I saw him and her [King Edward VII and Queen Alexandra] on Thursday," said Erchie, "as nate's ye like, and it didna cost me mair nor havin' my hair cut. They gaed past oor kirk, and the session put up a stand, and chairges ten shillin's a sate.

> "'Not for Joe,' says I, 'I'd sooner buy mysel' a new pair o' boots'; and I went to Duffy [the coalman] and says I, 'Duffy, are ye no' gaun to hae oot yer bonny wee lorry at the heid o' Gairbraid Street and ask the wife and Jinnet and me to stand on't?'

> . . . "I thocht first Jinnet maybe wadna gang, her bein' in the Co-operative Store and no' awfu' ta'en up wi' Royalty, but, dod! she jumped at the chance.

> "'The Queen's a rale nice buddy,' she says; 'no' that I'm personally acquainted wi' her, but I hear them sayin'. And she used to mak' a' her ain claes afore she mairried the King.'"

Erchie, My Droll Friend appeared in book form in 1904. We learn that he and Jinnet have been married "four-and-forty year", so that his early married days are roughly contemporary with Martha Spreull's spinsterhood. Like her, he lives in a tenement, decidedly not the same thing as a slum. Tenement life for Erchie is cosy and lively and neighbourly.

> "[Duffy] and me was mairried aboot the same time. We lived in the same close up in the Coocaddens – him on the top flet, and Jinnet and me in the flet below. Oor wifes had turn aboot o' the same credle – and it was kept gey throng, I'm tellin' ye . . . Duffy's first wean was Wullie John. Ye wad think, to hear Duffy brag aboot him, that it was a new patent kind o' wean, and there wasna anither in Coocaddens, whaur, I'm tellin' ye, weans is that rife ye hae to walk to yer work skliffin' yer feet in case ye tramp on them."

At times Erchie is not wholly free of kailyard sentimentality – "If God Almichty has the same kind o' memory as a mither, Jinnet, there'll be a chance at the hinderend for the warst o' us." – but generally he steers clear of this pitfall in his sharp observation of city life. Among his more particular remarks on the contemporary scene we may quote from "Erchie in an art tea-room".

> "Ye'll no guess where I had Duffy. Him an' me was in thon new tea-room wi' the comic windows . . . We began sclimmin' the stairs. Between every rail there was a piece o' gless like the bottom o' a soda-watter bottle, hangin' on a wire . . . I lands him into whit they ca' the Room de Looks . . . There's what Jinnet ca's insertion on the table-cloths, and wee beeds stitched a' ower the wa's the same as if somebody had done it themsel's. The chairs is no' like ony ither chairs ever I clapped eyes on, but ye could easy guess they were chairs; and a' roond the place there's a lump o' lookin'-gless wi' purple leeks pented on it every noo and then . . ."

And contemporary photographs of the Room de Luxe in the Willow Tearoom, designed in 1903 for Miss Kate Cranston by the great Charles Rennie Mackintosh, bear Erchie out in every detail, insertion, chairs, leeks and all.

Munro was, of course, a skilful journalist, whose posthumously published selections of pieces, *The Brave Days* (1931) and *The Looker-On* (1933), include many vivid glimpses of Glasgow in the 1880s and 1890s. At times in *Erchie* he captures the very tone of the urban kailyard, couthy and contented, with an eye for the customs and curiosities of its own small world.

> "It's a wonnerfu' place, Gleska . . . There's such diversion in't if ye're in the key for't. If ye hae yer health and yer wark, and the weans is weel, ye can be as happy as a lord, and far happier. It's the folk that live in the terraces where the nae stairs is . . . that gets tired o' everything. The like o' us, that stay up closes and hae nae servants, and can come oot for a daunder efter turnin' the key in the door, hae the best o't. Lord! there's sae muckle to see – the cheeny-shops and the drapers, and the neighbours gaun for paraffin oil wi' a bottle . . . It's aye in the common streets that things is happenin' that's worth lookin' at, if ye're game for fun."

But (as his neighbours possibly knew) Erchie's is a sharp eye, no less so because his observations are softened with humour. At the 1911 International Exhibition in Glasgow he visits An Clachan, a recreated Highland village; a theme park, in today's phrase.

> "Whit I like aboot An Clachan," said Erchie, "is that it's fine and self-contained. The inns is handy to the smiddy, and the kirk's next door to the Inns; everything's contrived for comfort and conveniency. I don't see mony people croodin' to the kirk, either, they're a' at the picture post-caird coonter; faith, naething seems to have been overlooked."

During the 1990 City of Culture extravaganza, where hype and mud-slinging were so strangely intermingled, Glasgow was in need of a commentator with Erchie's calm and ironic eye.

Into the urban kailyard, as into British life as a whole, World War I broke with an impact we can now only imagine, or appreciate through books. Writers responded in their individual ways. Anna

Buchan, whose youngest brother was killed at Arras, wrote (as O Douglas) her Glasgow novel *The Setons* (1917) with the specific aim of recalling a happier pre-war world.

> It was really written for my mother, an attempt to reconstruct for her our home-life in Glasgow . . . It was supposed to begin in 1913, so the War came into it: the last chapters were written after Alastair had gone, and into them went some of my own grief.

Neil Munro's son Hugh was also killed in action, but Erchie continued his musings – perhaps it helped a bit – on Zeppelins, Crown Prince Wilhelm, allotments, rationing, and wartime marriages.

> "He's a kind o' Sergeant in the Fusiliers . . . Ten minutes after they were married he went awa' back to the Front wi' a bit o' the bridescake in his pack . . . Such a carry-on! Him awa' to the trenches, and them wi' a waddin' party that's shakin' the very land! And they're only engaged since Seturday!"

Wee Macgreegor Enlists (1915) appeared as a predictable sequel to the earlier books: nothing less could be expected from the upstanding young man Macgreegor had become.

> "I've enlisted . . . The 9th HLI . . . Glesca Hielanders – Kilts."
> "Ye're under age, Macgreegor. Ye're but eichteen!"
> "Nineteen, Uncle Purdie."
> "Eh? An' when was ye nineteen?"
> "This mornin'."

But surely there has never been a stranger war novel than *Private Spud Tamson*, published in 1915.

The author, Captain RW Campbell (who rose to become a lieutenant-colonel before his death in 1939), served in the Royal Scots during both the South African War and World War I. He commanded a battalion at Loos, where he was mentioned in despatches and awarded the DSO. He knows whereof he speaks, therefore, but – as becomes painfully obvious – from one viewpoint only.

> [The Colonel] was a gentleman, but he knew that these men were victims of environment. In their dreary crime- and drink-sodden homes they had learned to emulate the law-breaker, to idolise the criminal, and applaud the football god . . . While he cursed them in his stern way, that was simply because these men knew no other tongue . . . Often had Colonel Corkleg amazed his guests at his country seat by hauling a dirty old blackguard off the highway and introducing him as "one of his boys".

These are the men of the Glesca Mileeshy:

> . . . a noble force, recruited from the Weary Willies and Never-works of the famous town of Glasgow . . . Just as our aristocrats enlisted in the Guards, so did the sons of tramps, burglars, wife-beaters, and casuals enlist in the Mileeshy . . .

As the reader may have gathered by now, they are a source of great merriment. Spud Tamson enlists in this force, not without some difficulties in the recruiting office.

> "When did you have a bath last?"
> "Last Glesca Fair" . . .
> "What! Ten months ago?"
> "Ach! that's naething; ma faither hisna had a waash since he got mairret." . . .
> When Spud emerged from the water he was a different lad . . . He looked fit indeed with the exception of his spurtle legs and somewhat comical face.

He goes to the front, after a send-off by his neighbours of Murder

Close, Gallowgate, and ends up as Sergeant Spud Tamson, VC, having been "bayoneted in the chest while gallantly rescuing his colonel from a band of lusty Bavarians." He survives, however, and the penultimate sentence in the book – the last being the report of his wedding, at the Colonel's own residence, to his Gallowgate sweetheart Mary Ann – runs: "The whole Empire cried 'Well done', and all the world wondered at this hero from the slums."

The Glasgow historian CA Oakley tells us that Spud Tamson "became a national figure for a time." Certainly his popularity lasted long enough to allow an equally heroic sequel, *Sergt. Spud Tamson, VC* (1918). After the war, in *Spud Tamson Out West* (1924), he emigrates to Canada and joins the Mounties, convincing a dubious Major that he is Mountie material by the simple expedient of slapping his VC down on the desk. Returning to Scotland, he's just the man to sort out the disaffected miners in *Spud Tamson's Pit* (1926). Oakley very reasonably remarks: "Perhaps, if he had been conceived twenty years later, his creator . . . would have been criticised in some quarters rather than praised for having created him."

No such doubts seem to have troubled RW Campbell, who wrote half-a-dozen further novels, including *Snooker Tam of the Cathcart Railway* (1919):

> All smiling, [Tam and Maggie] boarded the tram and splashed fourpence on the ride to the historic and sentimental Rouken Glen. No expense was spared on arriving. A ham tea (two eggs each), cookies and "terts", as well as a big bag of caramels to chew for dessert . . . [They] were secretly pleased to hear a sooty-nosed gamin say "Aw jings! Look at the wee toffs!" Tam somehow felt he was "a heid yin" at last . . .

Even dearer to his author's heart is Jimmy McCallum, eponymous hero of a novel published in 1921, who escapes from "Water Loan, off the Garscube Road . . . not remarkable for its salubrity or its sanitation" by dint of joining the Boys' Brigade. "You have the making of a fine man, Jimmy, so we must have you in The Boys' Brigade," writes none other than its founder Sir William A Smith and, sure enough, in due course Jimmy wins the VC too.

But these flowers of the urban kailyard were by now years out of their time. As is well known, the kailyard had been effectively ploughed under by the realism of such novels as George Douglas Brown's *The House with the Green Shutters* (1901) and John MacDougall Hay's *Gillespie* (1914). Brown actually planned a Glasgow novel, *The Incompatibles*, which, as an exposé of middle-class mores, might have been something to see.

> "Chapter V – a dinner of Glasgow bodies," he wrote. "Make it as bitter a satire as you know how. Get in (1) their scandalous talk of other folk and (2) their lowness of ideal – material estimates of things and people." . . . What Brown wanted to do was to show the hidden tensions of domestic life, the unceasing conflict of emotions between man and woman.

Brown died, however, not long after the publication of *The House with the Green Shutters*, and *The Incompatibles* was never written.

Though Hay's urban novel *Barnacles* (1916), set in the slums of Paisley, is in every way a lesser work than *Gillespie*, among its passages of melodrama and unashamed sentimentality can be found some vivid and even humorous moments.

> Barnacles . . . was directed to the middle stair. At the top of it there was a sink smelling badly, and a passage floored with wood. This floor had many holes, in one of which Barnacles tripped. He brought himself up betwixt two doors near the end of the passage. He knocked on the one on the right. It was opened by a little stunted boy of some seven or perhaps nine years, it was difficult to tell, so pitiably thin he was, with a white face and big eyes. There were sores on his face.
> Barnacles smiled sweetly on the boy and said: "May I come in?"
> A voice which he recognised shouted "Ay! if ye're no' the factor."

But Hay too died before he was forty, and we can only speculate on whether the realism in *Barnacles* might have led in time to an urban novel with the power and passion of *Gillespie*.

Before turning to the darker shades of realism, however, we should consider Frederick Niven, a Glasgow novelist who belongs to neither the kailyard nor the realistic school. Niven sees, and conveys, the beauty of the industrial city, as in *Justice of the Peace* (1914).

> Martin . . . had been much haunted by a memory of those iron works situated near Gushetfaulds – at the top of Crown Street. "Dixon's Blazes" they are called . . . There had been a fog hanging over the South Side when Martin last saw these iron columns with the monstrous torches atop of them . . .What had been a haze at Mount Florida (a pallid haze, with sun struggling through and lighting it elusively) was a thick vapour in Govanhill, and a little farther on was sheer, undoubted fog. It was like pea-soup at Gushetfaulds. And high up in it was a radiance, a fanning and wavering of ruddy gold in the murky sky.

Niven was born in Valparaiso and spent over twenty years in Canada, but all his life he retained the clearest visual memory of the late nineteenth century mercantile Glasgow which he knew as a boy and young man. Though he wanted to be a painter, he yielded to parental misgivings and became instead an apprentice in a soft-goods warehouse.

> The intention was for me to pass through the various departments and *learn the business*. I began with winceys and it was Charlie Maclean, head of the wincey department, who informed me, gazing at me solemnly one day, "Freddy, the plain fact is that ye dinna gie a spittle for your work."

In his memoirs, forty years later, Niven remembered another colleague:

> Watson, the cashier in the office, was . . . a painter in water-
> colours on summer evenings and on his annual vacation. . . .
> When he saw anything he liked in the way of tones of the day
> on Ingram Street walls he would huskily whisper, "Did ye see
> yon licht on the chimney-tops the day?"

Watson must have seemed a kindred spirit to Niven, who was
attending evening classes at Glasgow School of Art. He was also
reading voraciously; he spent hours in bookshops and libraries,
sent out on errands by the understanding Charlie with the hint
that he needn't hurry back. Eventually the great Fra Newbery,
head of the Art School, observed, as Niven recalls, "The sooner
you decide whether you are going to draw or write, the better."
Writing got the upper hand, but the Art School years were far
from wasted. Newbery, Niven acknowledges, "taught me to see."

What he saw we can see too in *Justice of the Peace*, considered
by many to be Niven's best work. George Blake recognised that
Niven in his quiet way was an innovator, even if "the very first", as
we have suggested earlier, slightly overstates the case.

> For the very first time a writer of talent had taken the
> commercial world of a Scottish city for granted and made a
> good story out of the career of a man of business . . .

Justice of the Peace, set in the soft-goods warehouse of Ebenezer
Moir, patently draws to some extent on Niven's apprentice days.
Not the least of its virtues is its accurate and humorous rendering
of warehouse conversation, still perfectly fresh to our ears.

> "Is Johns still here?" asked Martin.
> "Johns? The packer? No, man! Oh, he made an awful mess of
> himsel' – drink and hoors, ye ken – an awful man! . . . What are
> ye hemming and clearing your throat for, Jimmy?" said Archie,
> looking round . . . "Aye man, Johns got full value for his
> money I assure you. He died in the Infirmary imagining he was
> being gnawed by ferrets."
> "Rats," said Jimmy.

It draws too on another strand of Niven's experience. There is evidence of an exceptionally good eye for the beauty of the city:

> A high window, fronting the west, showed a reflection of the ultimate glow of sunset that might have been taken for interior illumination at a cursory glance, only that it had a surface sheen, a smoky blending of purple and gold.

Such observations, in the novel, are in fact made by Martin Moir, Ebenezer's younger son, who wants to be an artist. The mood of the time is with him, as even his father the warehouseman can see: "Glasgow is getting an arty touch about it – New Art they call it . . ." though of course, in Ebenezer's terms, art is useless. If Martin must take up art, he suggests, couldn't it be Applied Art, which is all the rage just now? "Yes, I know. Making things, making chairs for tea-rooms," replies Martin, not impressed by the illustrious contemporary whose chairs had earlier been evaluated by Erchie and Duffy.

So *Justice of the Peace* is a loving recreation of a Glasgow where – in real life as in the novel – both warehousemen and Glasgow Boys are at home. It is more than that, however. George Blake was right to focus on the character of the "man of business". The casual reader may incline to take Martin's side; who wouldn't sympathise with a young would-be artist whose father wants him to go into trade? But the novel's title gives us a contrary direction, and Niven surely intended to be even-handed at least.

It is notoriously difficult to convey the quality of good-heartedness without making a character sentimental or boring, but Niven succeeds here. Ebenezer Moir comes over clearly, vulnerable for all his bluff earnestness. He loves both his wife and his son; he is torn between them, because Mrs Moir isn't an easy person to live with. Like any reasonable man, he considers that Martin will never make a living as an artist, but supports him loyally and eagerly in his own way, ordering a copy of Martin's etching of a timber-yard for his brother: "He'll like it – for the thing itself, and for the subject. He has an interest in timber."

Niven has a complex set of family relationships to handle. Husband and wife, mother and son are well enough done, given the situation of a pathologically jealous woman hostile to her son (because of her quite unfounded suspicion of her husband's infidelity, shortly before the birth of the boy). The father-son relationship, however, is treated with the greatest sensitivity and originality. Ebenezer makes every allowance for his neurotic wife and shows patience with her cranky friends, but at every overture of friendship from the reserved and highly-strung Martin he shows touching delight. *Justice of the Peace* has at its centre this immensely appealing man, Ebenezer Moir.

In the dedication to the novel Niven wrote, "I do not know but what, if I had not to exist as well as live, I would unravel all this book yet once again, and again begin on it." (Though as he reasonably remarks, "there would be no end to that kind of thing.") Certainly *Justice of the Peace* is not perfect. The Mrs Moir sequences tend to melodrama, and Martin comes to life principally when he is drawing. His love-story does not entirely grip us: "'Well, anyhow,' said he, 'you are an awfully decent sort.'" Though popular in its day, the novel has been long out of print.

Towards the end of Niven's life, as his widow recalled, there was a possibility of a new edition.

> His agent suggested he should cut it and try Penguin. He did so and at the time I thought he cut too much. However, Penguin rejected it . . . About six months ago I transferred some of the cuts (they tied the pattern together better) but left in those parts that were for readers not "skippers" . . . Penguin have had the doubtful honour of rejecting it twice.

For its picture of the real merchant city, not the currently hyped version, and for the character of Ebenezer Moir, *Justice of the Peace* – preferably uncut – deserves to be looked at again.

But the merchant city did not constitute the whole of Glasgow then, any more than it does now. *Children of the Dead*

End: the autobiography of a navvy, published, like *Justice of the Peace*, in 1914, reminds us of that.

> I got a job on the railway and obtained lodgings in a dismal
> and crooked street, which was a den of disfigured children and
> a hothouse of precocious passion, in the south side of Glasgow.
> The landlady was an Irishwoman, bearded like a man and the
> mother of several children . . . We slept in the one room,
> mother, children and myself, and all through the night the
> children yelled like cats in the moonshine.

The author is Patrick MacGill, who was born in Donegal, and as a boy of fourteen came to Scotland to find work. He was by turns a farm-hand, poacher, tramp, navvy, and platelayer on the railway. During this odyssey he discovered literature and himself began to write, at first verse and then the largely autobiographical, though fictionalised, *Children of the Dead End*.

A recent commentator praises the opening sequences in rural Ireland, and the powerful Moleskin Joe (later the leading character in a novel of the same name) whom the narrator meets in the Highlands, but considers that:

> The further MacGill moves away from his Irish roots and the
> nearer he gets to the modern industrial city of Glasgow the less
> able he is to cope with his life-material artistically. He was
> equipped neither by sensibility nor by ideology to penetrate
> beneath the scum surface of degradation and alienation which
> lay over the much more fluid and complex urban proletarian
> community of modern Scotland.

Alternatively it might be suggested that the grim slums of Glasgow all but overwhelmed the young MacGill, still only in his early twenties when he wrote *Children of the Dead End* and its companion *The Rat-Pit* (1915). These are parallel novels telling the story of Dermod Flynn, the navvy, and his sweetheart Norah Ryan, in their separate journeys from Ireland to Scotland in search of work. The first book employs Dermod's viewpoint and the second Norah's, to the extent that many of the early Irish sequences, and the whole of the last chapter in each novel, comprise exactly the same events seen from different angles: a device used by much more consciously stylistic novelists than MacGill.

The Glasgow slum sequences form a comparatively minor part of *Children of the Dead End*, but in *The Rat-Pit* they are of major importance. Norah, seduced by the young master on the farm where she is a casual labourer, has come to Glasgow to give birth and bring up her child. The "rat-pit" is a female lodging-house where she stays briefly, but MacGill says in his introduction:

> The underworld . . . has always appeared to me as a Greater Rat-pit, where human beings, pinched and poverty-stricken and ground down with a weight of oppression, are hemmed up like the plague-stricken in a pest-house. It is in this larger sense that I have chosen the name for the title of Norah Ryan's story.

His intention is made clear in the lines which follow:

> There were some who refused to believe that scenes such as I strove to depict in *Children of the Dead End* could exist in a country like ours. To them I venture the assurance that *The Rat-Pit* is a transcript from life . . . Some may think that such things should not be written about; but public opinion, like the light of day, is a great purifier, and to hide a sore from the surgeon's eye out of miscalled delicacy is surely a supreme folly.

Though there are sentimental passages in *The Rat-Pit*, the description is realistic to a degree startling at this early date.

> A four-square block of buildings with outhouses, slaty grey and ugly, scabbed on to the walls, enclosed a paved courtyard, at one corner of which stood a pump, at another a stable with a heap of manure piled high outside the door. Two grey long-bodied rats could be seen running across from the pump to the stable, a ragged tramp who had slept all night on the warm dunghill shuffled up to his feet, rubbed the sleep and dirt from

his eyes, then slunk away from the place as if conscious of
having done something very wrong.

There have certainly been descriptions of the slums in, for instance,
the Victorian tracts, but MacGill's treatment has the air of
something experienced by the vagrant – "the warm dunghill" –
not observed by the social reformer. Moreover, the tracts, as we
have seen, praise the reformers' attempts to alleviate the lot of the
slum-dwellers, while apparently taking the slums themselves as a
given fact. MacGill sees things with a different eye.

> "That's the Municipal Buildin's; that's where the rich people
> meet and talk about the best thing to be done with houses like
> these. It's easy to talk over yonder; that house cost five hunner
> and fifty thousand pounds to build."

And again:

> "Full of money she [the caretaker] is and so is the woman that
> owns the buildin'. Mrs Crawford they cry her, and she lives oot
> in Hillhead, the rich people's place, and goes to church ev'ry
> Sunday with prayer books under her arm . . . Has a motor car
> too, and is always writin' to the papers about sanitary
> arrangements. 'It isn't healthy to have too many people in the
> one room,' she says. But I ken what she's up to . . . If few
> people stay in ev'ry room she can let more of them."

If MacGill, at this stage of his writing career, found artistic
detachment hard to attain, still he got his observations and opinions
down on paper in novel form, and these two fine angry books are
early in the field of what became known as proletarian fiction.

From now on proletarian or working-class novels begin to
appear in the corpus of Glasgow fiction, accompanied by fierce
debate. This may be a genuine proletarian novel (a critic will
pronounce), but isn't that one pseudo-proletarian? This writer is a
true son of the working class, but that one's surely a middle-class
writer slumming it? Can there be such a thing, in fact, as a working-

class writer, since the act of writing itself displaces him into the middle class? Before getting into these deep waters, we should look at the little-known novel *Jean*, published in 1906, which would seem to meet most of the proletarian criteria, and that at a very early date in terms of Glasgow working-class fiction.

Its author, John Blair, was "an employee in a Glasgow factory." The brief newspaper item which reveals this also indicates that 'John Blair' is a pseudonym, and to date no more is known about the author of *Jean*. His other literary work is equally elusive. During 1908, with one stray contribution in 1909, he published a handful of short articles or prose pieces in the *Glasgow Herald*, some being depictions of Glasgow and some of a mining village. Before this, in 1907, "a volume of East-End sketches entitled *Jake*" was announced, but no copy of this book has so far been traced. Effectively, therefore, all we have is *Jean*.

It is a short book with a plot which, baldly retold, appears hackneyed in its simplicity. Jean, a factory girl, falls in love with and is seduced by the handsome stranger Jock. Pregnant, she enters upon the inevitable downward progress, goes on the streets, is rescued by her faithful lover Hughie, and dies of consumption. "Slightly crude in workmanship" is the fair verdict of the newspaper paragraph already quoted. Such a summary, however, does no justice to the book's unsentimental yet unsensational realism and its view of working-class life, generally quite unpatronising, though now and then it seems to occur to the author that all good books have a literate and detached narrator.

> Jean was tired. Her face was white and her eyes heavy; the thick shawl over her shoulders did not improve her appearance, nor did the innumerable small pieces of iron round which her dark hair was twisted.

But she is a girl of spirit and deals competently with her drunken father's threats:

> "Wull ye? Wull ye? Try it! Noo, I'm jist tellin' ye, if ye don't

stop it I'll bring the polis. An' ye ken whit the Bylie telt ye the
last time ye were up afore him. Nae mair fines. Ye'll gang tae
Barlinnie withoot the option."

Jean is an extraordinary essay in realism in the heart of the urban
kailyard era. If the writing is at times didactic and a touch clumsy,
it can break through into directness and strength. Jean and Jock
come across two women fighting in the street; one contestant tears
the clothes off the other so that she stands "absolutely nude amid
the jeering crowd." When the police have arrived, Jock remarks
"That was a great ter, Jean." Jean doesn't answer. She has enjoyed
the fight but has been embarrassed to watch it with Jock beside
her. "Somehow the naked woman on the street, she thought, was
a reflection on herself."

And here we see the most interesting element of the novel:
John Blair's treatment of women. He may affect a distance from
the factory girls, as in the description of Jean above, but there's no
doubt that he knows and is involved with their lives. Even more
startling is his clear indictment of a kind of life which has inhibited
and warped Jean's natural gifts.

> Her home life, the meagre education, the factory, had all
> tended to develop the emotional side of her character at the
> expense of will and intelligence. The reaction against these led
> to the desire for sensation, for anything which appealed to the
> emotions.

And so she can't resist the sexy Jock. This is Blair clumsily "telling"
us, in didactic mode, but he can "show" us too. When Jean is out
with Jock and slightly drunk: "She caressed and fondled him . . .
she felt in the mood for anything."

If this is pretty outspoken for 1906, what about Jean's
mother's advice when the pregnancy is revealed?

> "Weel, Jean, I'll tell ye whit I think; I can dae nae mair. I was
> like you, an' I merriet the man, but if I had it tae dae ower

again I wadna leeve the life I've led for a' the jewels in Windsor
Castle. Jean, if ye want my advice, hae yer wean, an' if need be,
work for it. If a man can dae that before ye're merriet, God
help ye efter. Ye ken whit a life I've had. Weel, I wad raither see
ye deid, an' laid oot for yer coffin, than ken that you wad hae
the same . . . Never mind whit folk'll say. It'll blaw ower in a
week. The ither wey, tak my word for it, 'll be for life."

The calm, humane sense of this remarkable passage is hardly
matched in Glasgow fiction until we reach the work of Catherine
Carswell in the 1920s, and later authors much more sophisticated
than John Blair are less successful, as we shall see, in empathising
with Glasgow women.

II

HARD CITY

Eh, ma citie o raucle sang,
ma braid stane citie wi dwaums o steel.
Eh, ma Glesca, ma mither o revolt,
daurin the wunds o time in a raggit shawl.

John Kincaid, "A Glesca Rhapsodie"
Fowrsom Reel (1949)

6

Proletarian Concerns

The great literary need of the age is a novel, or a series of
novels, dealing with the life of the common people of Scotland
after the manner of Zola . . .

So the *Glasgow Herald*'s literary columnist in 1908 reminds us
what was perceived to be wrong in Scottish literature of the
day. He is commenting on a pamphlet by James Leatham, a reviewer
for the left-wing *Clarion*, and quotes Leatham's opinion that
Scottish writers "with an artistic equipment much superior to
Zola's" – such as Douglas Brown, Barrie and Munro – "take no
note of life in our squalid Scottish towns and cities."

This has been said before and will be said again, but Leatham
has more specific ideas than some.

Are there no Scottish workmen, none of the devoted workmen
in the Labour movement, who give their evenings to reading
and community work, their weekends and holidays to unpaid
public speaking, their scanty means for election expenses and
political publications, their working time to occasional
canvassing and to service on public boards – are there none of
these whose adventures, comic and tragic and useful, could be
made similarly attractive in a fictional narrative?

Leatham has practically got it written, but the columnist has a caveat to offer, together with a succinct and sensible blueprint for an urban/industrial novel of literary worth.

> There is no dearth of men able to meet Mr Leatham's wishes from a purely artistic point of view, but novels of the class he desiderates are works of the heart quite as much as of the head, and until some Scotsman is touched with the pathos of the human suffering that abounds in our towns and cities, and touched because he has seen it with sympathetic eyes, we shall have no Scottish version of *Les Misérables*.

Neither the columnist nor James Leatham seems to be suggesting that the workman should write the book himself, though we have noted the novels of John Blair just before this date and Patrick MacGill not long after. However, as a much later commentator (in 1975) observes,

> . . . from time to time radicalism in Scotland has spoken out in a distinctive and wholehearted voice that has a claim to be heard by the world at large for the validity of the message it utters.

Radicalism is certainly on the menu by the time Glasgow fiction reaches the 1930s, even though criticism in the 1920s had tended to continue the "where's the urban fiction?" theme.

> The crowding of our Highland and Lowland populations into busy commercial centres, with the introduction of an Irish element, has created conditions which should lend themselves to dramatic treatment. Still, we have no work of fiction resembling Dostoievsky's *Crime and Punishment* . . .

And, with another selection of models:

> Here are douce citizens long settled, there immigrants fresh

from western island or Irish croft, elsewhere dark-skinned folk
very far from home. Of all this tumultuously spilled wealth of
material might be made a Glasgow as wonderful as Dickens's
London or Balzac's Paris. It has not yet been done.

As these critics acknowledge, attempts had been made, with varying
success, by authors such as George Blake, Catherine Carswell, Dot
Allan and John Cockburn, who will be considered in the next
chapter. In 1933 an article by the same John Cockburn made it
clear that in his opinion there was a long way yet to go.

> Where in our collection of Scottish novels is the saga of the
> Clydeside "tradesman"; where the story of the business-
> man? . . . or of the Clydeside shopkeeper? or of the Scottish
> working class girl who does not "get into trouble" or succeed
> in marrying herself to a "hero" who is a cross between a film
> star and a millionaire? Where, I ask, is the unembellished story
> of the folk who, year in year out, from birth to death, live "up a
> close" and to whom the incidents that occur in practically all
> our industrial novels are more or less travesties of fact?

The Scottish Renaissance, currently in full swing, "has still to prove
itself as such," continues Cockburn, "because, as yet, the vast
majority of the Scottish people . . . find no real and adequate
expression in it."

> This glaring weakness in the modern Scottish novel is a vital
> thing, undermining the "literature" which we thought we had
> been building up . . . The Scottish novelist, it seems, has
> reached the crossroads. Will he . . . turn aside into the path of
> reality? . . . The way of reality, or of truth, is a much harder
> road . . . He may reach no goal in the end: on the other hand,
> he may produce the novel that Scotland must have before the
> renaissance is a real thing.

The temper of the time was with Cockburn, so that cause and
effect might be difficult to prove, but his article was in fact followed

by a perfect spate of "realistic" Glasgow novels, such as Dot Allan's *Hunger March* (1934), George Blake's *The Shipbuilders* (1935), and James Barke's *Major Operation* (1936).

The breakthrough of working-class fiction, or proletarian fiction, had not, however, occurred in the Glasgow novel alone, or in the Scottish novel alone, as several literary histories make clear. Yet Cockburn had identified it as "the thing that matters" in the Scottish Renaissance. Under which flag, then – Scottish literature or proletarian literature – did these 1930s novels sail?

The question was live enough to be debated at some length in the periodical *Outlook* during the summer of 1936. In a three-part series, "Literature: Class or National?", Lennox Kerr, author of *Glenshiels* (set in Paisley), discussed fiction with reference to the industrial working class; Neil Gunn put the case for the rural working class, though his article is not relevant here; and the author and critic Edward Scouller summed up.

Kerr took issue with the assumption (as he saw it) of the writers' organisation PEN:

> . . . that literature is national, and that a nation [is composed of] men and women with a common heritage, a common culture and a common ideology which comes to them all by their common nationality. Therefore, the Duke of Buccleuch and Willie Gallacher, the Communist MP, are brothers under the skin . . . This, of course, is nonsense.

Maintaining that the true unity is between "two men of different nations, but of the same social and economic class," he defines the basis of class division: "The worker is controlled by economic urgency and the non-working-class man or woman is free of that conscious urgency." From this he proceeds to argue that, though art is classless, the artist is controlled, through economic pressures, by the ruling and possessing class.

We know anyone can write a book, but to do this there is

required certain training for the artist and some sort of bodily
and mental freedom to achieve the task, and someone to buy
the work of art. And there is a strong and active pressure
exerted against anyone who would bring to the art forms a
shape not agreed on by the possessing powers . . . So you have
a position where [working-class] authors are forced to falsify to
be published.

Kerr does see the approach of "the simple but horrible drama of
the working classs . . . a drama only economic, whose very beauty
is tied to a penny." Edward Scouller, in the third article of the
series, while broadly agreeing with Kerr, doesn't think that the
economic struggle should monopolise the working-class writer's
attention, and enters another reservation:

> I would seriously question whether the Scoto-Irish navvy in
> Glasgow has more in common with the Polish stockyard
> labourer in Chicago than with his parish priest or even with the
> Duke of Montrose. Perhaps he ought to have, but a realist
> artist is more concerned with "is" than with "ought" . . . At
> any rate I am convinced that . . . even if the one world-wide
> classless state should be achieved . . . the Scotsman will still be
> recognisably different in outlook from the Ukrainian, and those
> differences will be valid material for the artist.

Meanwhile the journalist and man of letters William Power, an
enthusiast for Scotland and Scottish literature, put his head over
the parapet with an honest statement of his own position, and was
promptly shot down.

> I am rootedly middle-class. I never was a labourer, a miner, a
> stoker, a deck hand, a mill operative . . . I never lived in a
> "model", or in an overcrowded house in a working-class or
> slummy district; I never stood in the queue at the Labour
> Exchange; and I confess that the thought of these things makes
> me shudder . . . Yet three-fourths of the Scottish people are
> working-class, and the majority of them in towns and industrial
> areas live as I have never lived, and would hate to live. When I

notice the *camaraderie* among them . . . I feel awkwardly "out
of it", lacking the right to speak for the majority of the Scottish
people.

This was meat and drink to the periodical *Voice of Scotland* in its
first issue.

> [This] great disability is shared . . . by the great majority of
> contemporary Scots writers of any little reputation, and it
> completely invalidates their work . . . [Power adds] that the
> younger Scots writers of the "Left" "make too much of the
> class struggle". Names, please? We have failed to detect any
> such. The fact of the matter is that scarcely anything has been
> made of the class struggle yet in Scottish literature.

But *Voice of Scotland*, we are to understand, will change all that.
     Power was another who nearly wrote a Glasgow novel.

> I once wrote a romantic-realistic novel of Glasgow, but I could
> not finish it because the elements in it were hopelessly
> disparate, and I could not weave them into a central strand . . .
> and so I consigned the bulky manuscript to the flames.

Just as well, probably, for, if not savaged by *Voice of Scotland*, it
would have been slaughtered by such critics as Jack Mitchell in
later years.
     Mitchell's important article "The Struggle for the Working
Class Novel in Scotland 1900–1939" was published in an East
German periodical, but reprinted in Britain more accessibly, though
in shortened form, in 1974.

> One of the "achievements" of decadent bourgeois literature in
> the 20th century has been the pseudo-working-class novel,
> usually the work of middle-class or declassed authors. Scotland
> has had more than its fair share of them. This type of book has
> the full support of the Establishment's commercial machine. As
> a result they . . . have been widely identified with the "Scottish

working-class novel" as such. This has conveniently obscured
the fact that there is another more genuine tradition of
working-class novel writing in Scotland . . .

In our field of the Glasgow novel, Mitchell's list of "genuine"
working-class novelists includes Patrick MacGill and James Barke,
and "pseudo-proletarian writers" are such as Alexander McArthur
(of *No Mean City* fame) and George Blake. Some "genuine" writers
are considered by him (as by Lennox Kerr) to have sold out. It
would be unfair to summarise Mitchell's arguments, and we cannot
here treat them at length, but their existence should be borne in
mind as we proceed to examine Glasgow novelists of the 1920s
and 1930s who chose the "path of reality" praised by John
Cockburn. Or, anyway, thought they did.

7

The Glasgow School

As it stands, [Neil Gunn's] *The Grey Coast* is a more significant
achievement than all the novels of the so-called young Glasgow
school put together . . .

So declared the iconoclastic poet and thinker Christopher Murray
Grieve (Hugh MacDiarmid) in one of the influential series of
articles collected in 1926 as *Contemporary Scottish Studies*. Gunn
himself echoed Grieve, no doubt unintentionally, in a letter to the
Aberdeen novelist Nan Shepherd a few years later.

In a broadcast talk from Glasgow on modern Scottish letters
. . . I gave it as my opinion that your work is more significant
than all the novels of "the Glasgow School" put together . . .

These judgments alert us not only to the existence of a group of
writers in the 1920s known as "the Glasgow School", but to the
opinion of two notable contemporary critics that they weren't much
good. In a history of Glasgow fiction it must certainly be asked
who those writers were, what made them appear to be a "school",
and what was wrong with their work?

Grieve was in no doubt as to their identity. He briskly lists half-a-dozen names – John Cockburn, John Carruthers, Dot Allan, Catherine Carswell, George Woden, George Blake, John Macnair Reid – all of whom had published their first novels between 1920 and 1925. True enough, these works – with the exception of those by Carswell and possibly Reid – have not stood the test of time. Blake, Allan and Woden went on to produce later novels considerably more interesting than their first efforts, but in the early 1920s we see an explosion in the quantity, not the quality, of Glasgow novels.

Where did they all come from, and why? In the letter already quoted Neil Gunn gives us the clue.

> . . . For we have got to that stage where we need something more than a realism which is often little more than a species of reporting designed to attract at all costs – and none the less when it is "daring" reporting!

The "Glasgow school" of fiction in the 1920s, then, was all about realism, that quality so assiduously sought by critics before World War I. Grieve might dismiss these new writers with "None of our young fictionists have anything to say", but it is very clear from even their early novels that they thought they had, and also thought they were well equipped to say it.

Gunn's letter indicates why they were of that opinion, and, as a bonus, suggests why their first novels were not of great literary worth. They were observant, and rightly critical, of conditions in their city; they burned to expose these wrongs; but they took the direct, journalistic approach to novel-writing (several, like George Blake, were in fact journalists) to the detriment of literary quality.

Though perhaps they had little choice. A recent critic refers to the contemporary perception of Glasgow as "a post-industrial city of crisis" ("crisis" being defined as "a state of languishing and lingering limbo") with consequent problems for the author. To express this "spiritual emptiness . . . [and] experience of hopelessness and despair" was not easy for anyone but a literary genius, which none of these writers ever claimed to be.

The artistic answer which the vast majority of authors who chose to write about Glasgow gave was to "stick to the facts", and thus to write a kind of realistic or documentary novel.

More worryingly, a trend had unwittingly been set. Long after this "documentary" approach had given way, in the great world outside, to other techniques, Glasgow novelists kept "looking inward":

. . . returning to the same themes over and over again and following the well-trodden literary paths of the Glasgow novel.

It is the more refreshing to find, at the very beginning of the decade, a writer who follows a different drum.

Catherine Carswell was born in Glasgow, and we have it on her son's authority that the early chapters of her first novel *Open the Door!* (1920) are based on her own family and childhood surroundings. This is turn-of-the-century, middle-class, west-end Glasgow, and we have some good description of that pleasant time and place, with a glimpse, now and then, of the essential Glasgow scene.

Perhaps after all it was only in cities of the North that one got such a voluptuous contrast and harmony as now presented itself to his gaze? Above the stony, clear austerity of the town curved the sky. It curved, holding its fill of light, ebullient, like a bubble of serenest blue; and forming that bubble's tumultuous outer rim were the piled-up, yellow, flamboyant clouds . . .

The life of the central character, Joanna Bannerman, diverges to some extent from Carswell's, but Carswell's own life was eventful enough to supply material for several novels. Her first husband was mentally unstable to a dangerous degree, and she fought and won a groundbreaking test case for the annulment of the marriage. Meanwhile she had embarked on a long affair with a married lover.

Catherine Carswell, whose own life was eventful enough to supply material for several novels, was a contemporary of the "Glasgow school" of the 1920s. Her work has outlasted most of the Glasgow fiction of the time. She was dismissed by the *Glasgow Herald* for reviewing DH Lawrence's controversial *The Rainbow* and she later wrote biographies of Burns, Lawrence and Boccaccio

She moved to London to be near him; her small daughter died; the relationship broke up; she married, had a son, and largely supported the family by her writing from then on. Even from these brief details, and all the more from her fragmentary autobiography *Lying Awake* (published posthumously in 1950), she comes across as a person of considerable character and courage, while both friends and photographs testify to her beauty and charm. William Power, a colleague for some years on the *Glasgow Herald*, was quite bowled over:

> There, on Monday nights, would sit the lady whom the world knows as Catherine Carswell, most gifted of Glasgow's daughters. She was like a blend of Mary Stuart and a Botticelli Madonna. I was afraid of her, but I have since realised that she is as kind as she is brave and brilliant . . .

A reviewer of *Lying Awake* said simply, "I never met her, but I wish I had."

Only after these major life events were over did Carswell's career as a novelist and biographer begin, at least to the public eye, though *Open the Door!* had been in progress for some years. She had by now met DH Lawrence, whose novels she greatly admired. As is well known, she lost her job as book reviewer on the *Glasgow Herald* because of her piece on his novel *The Rainbow*, though it is not exactly a rave review.

> This is a book so very rich both in emotional beauty and in the distilled essence of profoundly passionate and individual thinking about human life that one longs to lavish on it one's whole-hearted praise . . .

But she doesn't yield to the longing:

> The difficulty is to define even to one's self what Mr Lawrence's aim actually is . . . It is a pity too that the

impassioned declaration is marred by the increasingly mannered idiom which Mr Lawrence has acquired since the writing of *Sons and Lovers*. The worst manifestations of this . . . are a distressing tendency to the repetition of certain words and a curiously vicious rhythm into which he constantly falls in the most emotional passages.

Perhaps Carswell's editor didn't read beyond the first sentence, but offence lay in the very appearance of the review, since, foreseeing trouble, she had sent it straight to print without the customary pause at the boss's desk.

Before this, however, Lawrence had read an early draft of *Open the Door!* and offered an equally outspoken but encouraging critique.

You have very often a simply *beastly* style, indirect and roundabout and stiff-kneed and stupid. And your stuff is abominably muddled – you'll simply have to write it all again. But it is fascinatingly interesting. Nearly all of it is *marvellously* good . . . You must be willing to put much real work, hard work into this, and you'll have a genuine creative piece of work. It's like Jane Austen at a deeper level.

Open the Door! was eventually published in 1920, having won a First Novel competition carrying a prize of £250. Interestingly, two distinguished woman writers who reviewed it on publication were less than happy about the central character Joanna. Katherine Mansfield wondered:

How much, when all is said and done, do we really know of her? How clearly is she a living creature to our imagination? . . . We cannot help imagining how interesting this book might have been if, instead of glorifying Joanna, there had been suggested the strange emptiness, the shallowness under so great an appearance of depth, her lack of resisting power which masquerades as her love of adventure, her power of being at home anywhere because she was at home nowhere.

Rebecca West saw Joanna as, anyway, more purposeful:

> The principal motif is the development of a female more
> terrifying than anything since Marie Bashkirtseff, in search
> of a love-affair that shall be to her soul such a source of
> refreshment as the hump is to the camel. When her search
> is successful at the end of the book one feels as if the lion
> had at last found its Christian.

It's possible that in this first novel with its autobiographical elements
Carswell does not quite attain the state of detachment which she
later recommended to a fellow writer: "Nothing is any good until
you get somehow a stage *removed* from the self of the story, outside
of that self, cool, critical, perhaps even hostile."

But both reviewers recognise the novel's good points:
"eminently a serious piece of work", says Mansfield, while West
affirms that "this is a book of great importance." More recent
critics – Carswell's work was rediscovered in the 1980s after a period
of neglect – are impressed by the statement it makes, so near in
time to the couthy reticence of the kailyard, about a woman's
independence and sexuality. The influence of Lawrence is clear,
but it is with her own extreme honesty that Carswell deals with
the idyll of Joanna's first love, when "she surprised him again
(though herself still more) by pressing her body with a swift wildness
against his," and her passionate awakening in marriage, while
(unsuspected, we're sure, by poor old Mario) she retains her
intellectual curiosity:

> Wave after wave of purely physical recollections swept
> through her; but at the same time in her brain a cool
> spectator seemed to be sitting aloof and in judgment.
> This then was marriage! This droll device, this
> astonishing, grotesque experience was what the poets had
> sung since the beginning. To this all her quivering dreams
> had led, all Mario's wooing touches and his glances of
> fire!

And, even less conventionally, the reader is made aware of such emotions in Juley Bannerman, Joanna's mother.

> In the intimate chamber of their married life she was never really awakened. Sholto in the early days used to tell her laughing that she compared favourably with other women in her wifely demands, which he declared were for an almost fraternal affection. She believed this . . . But it was not the truth. She wanted utter union with him, and as he could unite with no one, she remained wrapt within herself. When she felt the stirrings of passion in herself she was dimly ashamed, and had to reason that after all this world was peopled by God's own ordinances. Only the yielding up of oneself to mere delight was sinful.

It will be gathered that the family background is one of fairly whole-hearted Calvinism, and at first glance this may appear to be why Joanna wants to open the door. The choice of a title for the novel was a subject of discussion between Carswell and Lawrence, who provided a cascade of suggestions.

> *The Wild Goose Chase* . . . Or *The Rare Bird*, or *The Love Bird* (very nice that), or just *Cuckoo!* (splendid). Do call it *Cuckoo*, or even the double *Cuckoo! Cuckoo!* I'm sure something bird-like is right . . . *The Lame Duck* – I'm sure there is a suggestion in the bird kingdom – *The Kingfisher*, which I am *sure* is appropriate . . .

Carswell herself had suggested *Bird of Paradise*, "which referred to the legend that, being bereft of its feet, that bird can never alight," perhaps an acknowledgment of the quality in Joanna – "at home nowhere" – which Katherine Mansfield saw.

But it became *Open the Door!* What door? There are several in the novel, among which critics have not hesitated to choose. The epigraph to Book I, ". . .Open the door, and flee," tempts us towards the theory of escape from Calvinist Glasgow, which Joanna, like Carswell, leaves behind. By Book II, however, we are in the New Testament and opening "a door of utterance," and Carswell's son has no doubt that:

> The clue to the title has much more to do with entering than with escape, and the "door" is "the little sunken door in the wall" which Joanna . . . sees in Italy . . .

That door leads into "the home of a woman celebrated for her loves." Joanna – like Carswell, as her autobiography makes clear – is not a refugee but an adventurer, even if, in an ending which many find unsatisfactory, she settles for the quiet man she has known all along. Catherine, of course, had by now married Donald Carswell, whom, in her son's opinion, "Lawrence Urquhart . . . reflects".

Carswell's second novel, *The Camomile* (1922), was for a time regarded as a less considerable work than *Open the Door!* It is shorter, and the epistolary form gives it a lighter effect, but, according to one recent critic, "This is a novel much darker at the heart."

The central character Ellen has, like Carswell, studied music, but now feels herself turning to writing. There are logistical difficulties, which she tries to meet (again, as Carswell did) by renting a room to write in, but the real problem lies deeper:

> Is writing – serious writing – simply a mistake for a woman? . . . The worst of it is I know so miserably well what people mean when they say it is "a pity" that a woman should write. I can *feel* why it is so different from, for instance, a woman singing or acting . . . [These arts] are in their effect womanly. But writing! . . . Is there any womanly sphere in literature?

Carswell confronts this question in her autobiography and it is the main point at issue in *The Camomile*. It can't be resolved in Glasgow; Ellen leaves for London. Like Joanna, she isn't running away. On her first night in Germany as a young music student, tucked up under a fluffy *Bettdecke* or duvet (not yet known in Britain), she has written:

> How happy I am! I am not in the least homesick. I know now that in Glasgow I must nearly always have felt homesick – sick to get away from home to some place where even the beds are different!

It is this difference she needs, because "One can never write till one stands outside."

Carswell, "outside" Glasgow not only geographically but intellectually, wrote no more novels, and her well-esteemed biographies (of Burns, Lawrence and Boccaccio) are in no way Glasgow books. She stands, therefore, apart from the rest of the Glasgow novelists of her time, a bright particular star.

In more home-grown Glasgow fiction, meanwhile, urban kailyard and realism still co-existed uneasily. RW Campbell wrote on, producing such gems as *Winnie McLeod* in 1920 and the egregious *Jimmy McCallum* in 1921. So did O Douglas, setting most of her novels in the Borders, but reprising *The Setons* to some extent with *Ann and her Mother* (1922) and *Eliza for Common* (1928).

> Mr Laidlaw [of Martyrs' Church on the south side of Glasgow] . . . had been in Dennistoun visiting two families and – "It's quite ridiculous," he said, "that they should come all that distance across the city to Martyrs'. They must pass at least a dozen churches on their way."
>
> "Well, Walter," said his wife, pausing with the teapot in her hand, "I do hope you didn't put that into their heads. If we don't get members from a distance where are we to get them? You know quite well that round the church there are nothing but Jews and Catholics." (*Eliza for Common*)

The novels of her brother John Buchan were a slight cause of concern to their mother, who "after a few pages . . . would murmur, 'Tuts, they're beginning to swear already.'" But the O Douglas books:

> . . . delighted her heart. They were as pure and almost as sweet as home-made toffee, their pages unsullied by swear-words, and they were about happy comfortable people . . . My mother . . . approved strongly of reticence, so it was as well that I had neither the will nor the ability to write a "strong" book.

So we need not look for outspoken realism from O Douglas.

Similar considerations may have affected her contemporary "Mary Cleland" (Margot Wells), another daughter of the manse brought up in Pollokshields. Mary Cleland does try to bring together middle-class suburbia and the near-slum tenement life which was often its near neighbour, and which she knew about, though, predictably, at one remove.

> Miss Wells's special interest lay with the Glasgow working girls, who had so few healthy places of recreation open to them after their day's work. She began a little kitchen in Kinning Park, purposing to keep it small and homely . . .

Her books *The Two Windows* (1922) and *The Sure Traveller* (1928) are parallel novels, the first being the story of the waif Molly and the second that of the middle-class girl Catherine who befriends her. Catherine longs to go to Girton, but her highly conventional mother thinks this unfeminine (it is the 1890s) and her peaceable father supports that view. The theme is promising, and its development, as Catherine submits to staying at home and turning her hand to works of charity in the neighbourhood, thoughtfully taken up. Unfortunately the books are so gentle in tone as to have a certain uniformity. One of the servants, who enters the narrative occasionally with a considerable gain in liveliness and realism, seems to share this feeling as she hears an old friend's tales of happenings in the East End:

"It's fine and cheery in the old place," she said wistfully, "with
Duke Street not a stone's throw off; aye something doing
through the week, and the Saturday night ongoings, and the
stir and the stour and the bustle. I've served here this eight
years and never once seen the polis get a person. It's fine and
exalted here on the South Side, but, woman, it's dull."

> (*The Sure Traveller*)

But neither Douglas nor Cleland gets to grips with the tenement,
which, as a more recent commentator has said, "is woven into the
fabric of Glasgow."

> As the *mise-en-scene* of urban life and experience it is the
> "foursquare" tenement block that tesselates the mosaic of
> Glasgow's robust culture . . . While some have turned the urban
> world . . . into a back-court Kailyard of couthy reminiscence and
> gritty but comforting folklore, others have pictured the
> tenemented streets of the city as prison walls behind which an
> exploited society exercised its grim existence . . .

In the opinion of the young journalist John Cockburn (whose
views on the Scottish novel were quoted in the last chapter) no
one, by the 1920s, had yet got it right, and he set out to remedy
this in his novel *Tenement* (1925). His intentions as a Glasgow
novelist were honourable:

> I have only one ambition – to put the "real" Glasgow, the real
> Glasgow people, into a book, but my firm belief in reality as
> opposed to the demand for "dramatic fiction" seems to be an
> obstacle to progress, a temporary one I hope.

But in *Tenement* – as, perhaps, in those other books which failed
to progress? – he is to a large extent writing to order, and it shows,
as CM Grieve acutely noted soon after the novel's publication:

> . . . a purely machine-made naturalistic study of Glasgow, of the
> kind that old-fashioned people still call, and regard as, realistic.

Tenement is an accurate enough picture of tenement life, though leaning well to the dark side of the cosy, neighbourly system which the urban kailyard loves to portray. The men are foolish, the women malicious gossips. The central family is well-to-do at first, but drink and injudicious speculation brings the father to bankruptcy and forces a move from the respectable Avenue to the slums. Cockburn's long "Apology" or preface, an essay-type description of Glasgow tenements and their inhabitants, does not raise the reader's hopes of having found a genuinely creative Glasgow novel:

> Drab buildings. Sheltering equally drab inhabitants. Honest uncomplaining folk who have fought hard against the overwhelming tyranny of their surroundings without much success . . . The real Glasgow is as dull as it is sensible . . . a mass of browns and greys . . . a monotonous uninteresting swelter . . .

It is not in this mood that a great novel is written, and *Tenement*, striving to be realistic, attains only a pedestrian gloom.

Meanwhile the poet Edwin Muir, who was born in Orkney but spent unhappy years in Glasgow, was attempting a Glasgow novel.

> I am going to call it *Saturday* and my subject is, in fact, that day, which in an industrial place like Glasgow, and to the bulk of the people in the British Isles, has an atmosphere quite different from that of every other day. I am going to try to render this atmosphere, suggesting as a background the other working days in the week . . . There will be a central figure: and in him will be worked out the gradual disintegration of the day . . .: the hope of the morning, the freshness of the afternoon after work, and the gradual loosening and demoralisation of the evening, the slipping of happiness through one's fingers.

Saturday, however, was doomed to be yet another nearly-written

Glasgow novel. It was never completed: "Though a good idea," writes Muir's biographer, "it was not within his power to realise." CM Grieve knew and approved of the *Saturday* idea.

> I believe [Muir] is also engaged upon a novel of Glasgow life – designed to serve as a dynamic counter-foil to George Blake's work and the other novels of the so-called young "Glasgow School".

Blake, thus identified as the leading light, or chief villain perhaps in Grieve's view, among Glasgow authors of the 1920s, went on to play an active, not to say combative, part in the burgeoning Scottish literary scene for over thirty years.

George Blake was a journalist in Glasgow during the early 1920s, succeeding Neil Munro as literary editor of the *Evening News*. Several of his novels are set in Glasgow, though he was probably both more comfortable and more successful when he began his long series of family sagas set in "Garvel", a fictionalisation of Greenock where he was born. In 1933, when Blake was already a well-established novelist, an editor tentatively expresses something of the ambiguity which still clings to his literary reputation.

> Most of [his novels] have reflected his realistic attitude to Lowland Scottish life . . . It may be, however, that the frank romanticism of his latest novel *Sea Tangle* marks a turning point in the development of a writer who has always puzzled his friends and admirers.

Certainly his first novel *Mince Collop Close* (1923) is enough to puzzle anybody. CM Grieve found it "simply inexplicable" (because of various crudities and impossibilities), considering that Blake was already "a notable figure in Scottish literature", while an extract from a contemporary review may suggest why it has scarcely survived except as an entry in a bibliography.

> Mr Blake never seems to have made up his mind what he
> wanted to be at . . . The preface indicates an initial conception
> of a work of grim realism, combined perhaps with passionate
> revolt, but before one has reached the tenth page one is into
> low comedy . . . and then without warning we return to the
> worst depth of Glasgow slumland where a perfectly incredible
> person called Bella Macfadyen lords it over a gang of crooks.

Even allowing for the teething troubles of a first novel, *Mince Collop Close* is indeed an extraordinary, melodramatic piece of work, no less amazing when viewed from this point in time because we know of Blake's later Garvel novels, solid evocations of middle-class life. The critic Francis Russell Hart struggles to find something in it:

> These early Blake protagonists elude the problems of adult
> consciousness, insulating us by their brutal innocence from the
> graphically real modern worlds we see them in.

But he too has to admit to some puzzlement:

> The question of how the author of *Mince Collop Close* . . .
> developed into the author of *The Westering Sun* [1946] is of
> interest for an understanding of the early modern Scottish
> novel.

Today it's quite hard to read *Mince Collop Close* with a straight face, but, in view of Blake's later importance in the story of Glasgow fiction, we should try to discern what he did want to do, and to what extent he succeeded in doing it.

The genesis of *Mince Collop Close* may be found in Blake's *Vagabond Papers* (1922), a collection of essays originally published in the *Evening News* and *Manchester Guardian*. In the first piece, "A Woman of Destiny", he muses on a thirteen-year-old street urchin called Bella, observed on a train organising a group of Glasgow slum children on their way back from the coast.

She will probably develop as the Queen of the Redskins of her day; she will be the belle of the Dalmarnock Road, with crimped hair, bright shawl, and broad bows on her high-heeled shoes; a capable, courageous, termagant Queen.

In *Mince Collop Close*, her destiny fulfilled, she appears as Bella Macfadyen, Queen of the Fan-Tans.

She is a figure of adolescent romance: a tall, handsome, slum-bred girl with flaming red-gold hair, attended by a faithful henchman and dowered with superhuman ingenuity, self-confidence and luck.

Her face – it was not pretty; it was thin, if anything, and hard; but it held the quality of disdain and fierce pride for which the men of Mince Collop Close are ready to draw razors . . . The police she feared not at all: from bloodshed she was never known to recoil . . . Her vocabulary of obscenity was rich . . . Nerves, conscience, remorse were never near her. Her capacity for immobile cruelty impressed even a cruel people.

The opening chapters describe Bella's childhood and rise to power. Thereafter the book falls away into a series of disconnected episodes, in each of which a hitherto unknown character is introduced, and his life-story sketched up to the point of his encounter with the mighty Bella. Chapter VII, "From the Lone Shieling", is a perfect kailyard story, the simple Highland girl, betrayed and deserted in the great city, bringing up her son for the ministry. Chapter IX, "The Jewelled Cross" is, in contrast, a lurid adventure involving a theft from a monastery and a renegade priest. We can see a prentice hand at work, and those who know Blake's middle-class sagas may take some interest in Chapter VIII, "A Caged Bird". This gentle depiction of a minister's daughter tied to her tyrannical old father is probably, until its melodramatic denouement, the most successful episode. (Bella, by the way, grows out of her gangland queen phase and stows away with her boyfriend for a new life in America.)

Yet *Mince Collop Close* is not entirely without merit. We can tell from the preface mentioned above that Blake has read a report – one of many such – by a Medical Officer of Health for Glasgow. Appalled by what it reveals, he has seen, as a novelist should, the human faces behind the statistics.

> Return to those men, women and children whose house is one apartment, and consider whether, since the world began, man or angel ever had such a task set before them as this – the creation of the elements of a home, or the conduct of family life within four bare walls.

He sets out – we may surmise – to work his angry emotions into a novel, with a strong central character (inspired by the young girl on the train) and an eye-catching title (the name, in fact, of an old vennel in his native Greenock), which will tempt people to read and, reading, discover the shocking facts about life in Glasgow slums. His eagerness, at this stage of his career as a novelist, outstrips his technique, however, and so the book, as a whole, misfires. In many places the reporter takes over:

> The single-apartment house shared by Bella Macfadyen and her Auntie Aggie was licensed by the sanitary authorities, and ticketed accordingly, to accommodate four and a half adults . . . It was not one of those convenient rooms with a large bed built into the wall in the Scots fashion. A dresser and a deal table occupied precious space. They slept on the floor.

But he can do better than this. We are drawn into sympathy with Bella's aunt, Mrs Cassidy:

> This fiery, strong, cruel niece of hers had . . . turned her into the drudge of their miserable household, flouted her and laughed at her . . . Mrs Cassidy was a woman, and jealousy tortured her. So she lay uneasy, hot, angry stuff swirling in her brutish old mind.

And it is her death which, among all the melodrama, supplies one uniquely macabre moment.

> Grimly they faced the ghoulish amenities of the chamber of death. Every night, until the cheap funeral took place, Bella and Bernard Macginty lifted the floppy, cold thing that had been Mrs Cassidy out of the way on to the dresser, and in the morning laid it again on the floor, where it lay through the day under their own bedclothes . . . They had only two days and nights of that ghastly communion to suffer.

Blake may have come across such a story as a journalist: it has the ring of truth rather than invention. But for once he has retold it with the simplicity of good writing, so that it brings home, far more vividly than any newspaper report, the reality of life in the slums.

His next novel, *The Wild Men* (1925), is somewhat less melodramatic, though as a story of Glasgow Bolsheviks it is not yet a depiction of the everyday city. He is still concerned and sympathetic when he writes about the slums:

> The child of the slums enters the world of work at the age of twelve or thereabouts. There is little room for foresight in a life of which to-morrow's breakfast is the chief cause of anxiety. The future must look after itself: all the present is occupied with the scraping of a penny here, a penny there. When the boy begins earning money by the delivery of milk, he has handed himself over to a servitude from which, saving an unlikely accident, there is no escape . . . A few years of it, and he is sharp and cunning and immoral . . . At eighteen he is casual labourer, corner-boy or hooligan, useless to himself or to the society to which he belongs, positively dangerous in that his are the impulses of the animal.

But he has stopped in the middle of a novel to tell us this. The poet and critic Edwin Morgan, with the benefit of an overview of all Blake's work, probably put his finger on it in 1961: "[Blake is] likely to endure rather as an acute social commentator and historian than as a novelist."

Yet there's *Young Malcolm* (1926), even though, at first glance, Blake seems here to make an alarming excursion into the kailyard. Malcolm, a bright boy from Greenock, graduates as a doctor with all possible distinction, goes on to do research, and marries his sweetheart earlier than planned to rescue her from a drunken father and uncongenial stepmother. He is throughout rather priggish – "He had the instinct of his class for respectability at all costs" – and has an unnerving tendency to weep in sympathy with his lachrymose bride. There is toughness in him, however, for he carries on his research in London, living with his wife in miserable furnished rooms, and refusing the offer of a well-paid but humdrum general practice. A baby arrives, but Blake resists the lure of a kailyard happy ending. The impossibility of family life as a research student finally beats Malcolm down, and he accepts the practice in a human and credible confusion of emotions. Blake as a novelist is finding his feet.

And Glasgow, as seen by a sensitive adolescent, comes to life in the earlier part of the book. Malcolm's over-sociable lodgings and his night at a boxing-match are observed with Blake's sharpest eye for the social scene. When Malcolm leaves the boxing:

> The whole affair was strange, unreal, alarming in a sense. It was difficult for Malcolm to bring himself back to the plain fact that all this was happening in Glasgow, the Glasgow of . . . the polite amenities of Arlington Street. It was like going through a shadowy door and finding oneself in a harsh world of primitives . . . To come out into the dark lane under a starry sky was like making a new discovery, or at least, a re-discovery of normality. The city was the same as ever; and that was surprising . . . A tramway car, sailing past full of light, was an astonishingly friendly thing.

It is an approach to recognising the many-sidedness of Glasgow – neither all slums, nor all warehouses, nor all manses in Pollokshields

– and to admitting that two people in neighbouring streets may very well be looking at two different Glasgows.

By now Blake had gone to London to work first in journalism and then in publishing, though he returned to Scotland in 1932. He left behind most of 'the young Glasgow school', whom we can now categorise, perhaps, as writers trying to get Glasgow down on paper, if with varying degrees of skill and success. Among them was one at least who deserves closer attention.

Dot Allan was born in Denny, the only child of an iron merchant, but lived for many years in the west end of Glasgow with her elderly mother: a middle-class life, like those of O Douglas and Mary Cleland, and potentially a restricted one, as the archetypal daughter at home.

Yet, as in Blake's young Malcolm, a certain toughness can be detected beneath the middle-class veneer. Like Douglas and Cleland, and Henrietta Keddie before them, Allan had the urge to write and pursued her calling with considerable vigour. She submitted a sonnet to the *Evening Citizen* at the age of ten, though it wasn't published, possibly because it had twenty-eight lines. Articles and poems did see the light of day, and in 1921 she published her first novel, *The Syrens*. Her Glasgow novels were only part of a large output. It seems that she didn't particularly see herself as a Glasgow writer, or even a Scottish one.

> I certainly have written a good deal about Glasgow . . . but I have
> written about other places too. I don't believe in the localisation
> of a writer's talent . . . There are no boundaries to art. That's why
> I am not altogether in sympathy with the Scots Renaissance
> movement and other allied movements, which, in my opinion,
> tend to cut us off from the rest of the world, instead of making us
> one with it. I think, in fact, [she is speaking in 1931] that a
> United States of Europe wouldn't be at all a bad idea, and there
> doesn't seem to me to be any reason why it shouldn't work.

That wide view contributes to the charm of *The Syrens*, in which Glasgow is seen as a gateway to the world. It is the story of a young man, son of the brief marriage of a naive girl and a romantic, roving sailor, who dutifully works his way to success in the grocery trade, but succumbs at last to his inherited wanderlust. His name is Goritholus, after his father's ship; a device perhaps meant to mark him out as innately exotic and unsuited to everyday Glasgow life, but tending rather to distract the reader. Allan didn't need to rely on such tricks by the time she echoed this situation in her second novel seven years later.

On the strength of *The Syrens* CM Grieve recognised Dot Allan as belonging to the "new Glasgow school", but added, "Some of her more recent work in the form of short sketches has reached a much higher level." A full tally of these sketches has yet to be made, because from the early 1920s onward Allan was a prolific freelance writer for a range of newspapers and periodicals. Her work appeared regularly, for instance, on the *Glasgow Herald*'s popular Saturday page, and while some of her contributions might not have appealed to Grieve – "Christmas Eve in Star-town" doesn't augur well – there's close observation and social comment to be found amid the whimsy. It seems as if journalism displaced novel-writing in Allan's career for some years, but *Makeshift* (1928) was worth waiting for.

The opening prologue is sharp and grim. Jacqueline's mother scrapes a living as a dressmaker working at home. She is embittered by her dealing with inconsiderate lady clients, but much more so by the marriage, to another of those romantic sea-captains, which has got her into this mess. Her husband's ship has been her rival, the mistress to whom he rushed off eagerly after every leave. She'd thought marriage would be wonderful, but:

> "Second best!" she raved. "That's what my life has been made up of, Jacqueline; makeshift all the time . . . I've missed it somehow; but there's more in life than that."

In a passion of grief she slashes a customer's material into shreds, realises what she's done – "This finishes it" – goes into her room, and gasses herself.

The main part of the novel follows Jacqueline's girlhood and growing up as she begins to write poetry, discovers sex, works in a Glasgow office and fends off the attentions of her boss. She falls in love but her lover is killed; she drifts into an engagement to someone she knows she doesn't love. It is an uneventful story in some ways, and the details are dated (crepe-de-chine lingerie tending to mark the scarlet woman). But there's honesty and frankness – Jacqueline's sexual feelings, and her awareness of the same urge in men, are not fudged – and a quality of detached observation of which Carswell must have approved. Even as Jacqueline is drawn into a conventional woman's life, she knows it needn't be like this.

> Funny how persistently the world of women revolved round that
> of men. Funny – she said the word aloud, misusing it in the
> familiar Scots fashion which causes folk to use it with no thought
> of jocularity. Funny! . . . Dear God, how happy she was!

She has just been with Owen, soon to be rather melodramatically stabbed to death.

Numbed by this trauma, she becomes her widowed uncle's housekeeper, and accepts the proposal of William, the bailie's son, almost entirely out of fear that she will become a "surplus woman" like her alcoholic colleague Miss Price. He isn't right for her, as she realises when writing friends drop in before the wedding. William is annoyed.

> What the blazes did the man mean jawing away about
> Jacqueline's poetry, puffing up the poor kid she could write?
> Write? Hell! Didn't he realise she was going to be married –
> married?

In pre-marital euphoria he lets slip the conspiracy between his parents and her uncle, whereby the engagement has come in handy to free him from an entanglement in London. Jacqueline has been used, and she's furious, but what can she do?

Fortunately a legacy has arrived from one of her father's ex-shipmates. It's an awkward device, but the necessity for it makes its own point: Jacqueline has no other avenue of escape. As it is, she seizes the opportunity, packs her poems and clothes (in that order), and catches the midnight train to Euston, full of joy. Her life is not going to be "makeshift". It is another clear feminist statement, unusual enough in Glasgow fiction of the time to earn Dot Allan considerable respect.

Possibly influenced by the contemporary feeling that tenements ought to be written about, Allan next produced her own tenement novel, *The Deans* (1929). It is not a complete success, perhaps because she has observed, but not experienced, tenement life. Beginning in realistic mode, the story takes on overtones of romance as the pretty daughter and ambitious son approach the problems of marrying into a higher social class; grave problems, it is accepted by both characters and author. As in *Makeshift*, we suffer an awkward spasm of melodrama when it is unexpectedly revealed that the mother, in order to afford a few little luxuries for the family, has been renting the spare room to prostitutes (in the afternoon, before the twins come home from school). Yet her arrest and its effect on the family are treated with sensitivity.

As in her other novels, too, Allan sees beauty in the city, and recognises that such beauty may exist because of, not in spite of, city life. She speaks here surely in the voice of her father the merchant:

> It was one of the city's singing nights, one of the nights when the hum of every passing car held a rhythm of its own, when the harsher sounds of the traffic mounting raucously at cross-roads and busy arteries projected through the quiet parts a long-drawn-out note like a minor chord repeated over and over again. Nell adored these singing nights . . . "Trade," [her father] would say when the racket grew well-nigh intolerable, "a' that means grist to some man's mill. Toys and sweeties for some wee lass."

We have heard the mercantile voice before, but elsewhere in her Glasgow novels Allan does something much less usual. We find not just sympathy for the working class – that too has been shown before, patronisingly or otherwise – but a sharp-eyed, unsparing observation, amounting to condemnation, of the middle class to which Allan belongs, and particularly the female members of that class. In the prologue to *Makeshift* the child Jacqueline remembers:

> . . . a very beautiful lady had called to ask [her mother] to make another dress. Mrs Thayer had clasped the back of a chair tightly and shaken her head. Not another stitch would she put in until she was paid for the last order, and the one before that as well. The beautiful lady had opened her eyes in pained surprise. "My good woman, I haven't got it. If I had, I assure you – " "I don't want assurances," Mrs Thayer had retorted. "I want a cheque to amount of account rendered. I have bills of my own to meet."
>
> The beautiful lady had sighed deeply as one who deplored the habits of the lower orders. Then from a ludicrously small gold-mesh purse she had produced two half-crowns.
>
> "Your milkman's bill," she had said with delicate insolence; "this might serve to meet it."

Like George Roy fifty years before, Dot Allan had observed her neighbours more closely than they knew. The results are seen again in her 1934 novel *Hunger March*, a major contribution to Glasgow fiction in the next decade, during which, as George Blake remarks, "angry young men were burning to shift the focus of interest . . . to the Gorbals and the slattern tenements of No Mean City."

8

Second City

While a mere head-count of Glasgow novels published in the 1930s is impressive, much more notable is a growth in purpose and realism. Even if it has never quite gone away, urban kailyard, like the Kailyard School in general, was no longer important. As Edwin Muir recognised, World War I was a watershed:

> All of those [pre-war] voices, from the most refined to the most pawky, had an inflection which would have been recognised and appreciated by constant readers of the *People's Friend*. Now that cannot be said by any stretch of fancy about the characteristically post-war Scottish novelists . . . The Scottish novel, then, has changed since the war; it has become less friendly to the people, less popular, less sentimental, less Scottish in the old sense, and less commercial.

This is an epic decade, marked by the publication in 1935 of two novels which, in their different ways, have become icons of Glasgow fiction: Alexander McArthur's *No Mean City* and George Blake's *The Shipbuilders*. They were joined in 1936 by James Barke's *Major Operation*, which may be a better novel than either.

But we should begin by taking a wider view. The Scottish

Literary Renaissance was under way, and Muir acknowledged Scottish fiction to be part of the new age:

> . . . fresh air has been let into it. In other words, it is no longer parochial, no longer contentedly accepts the second best as its ideal, or is satisfied to be judged by a standard which would be considered provincial or commercial in other countries.

A couple of years later he would court (and win) controversy by declaring that "a Scottish writer who wishes to achieve some approximation to completeness has no choice except to absorb the English tradition," but in 1934 he was happy to cite Eric Linklater, Neil Gunn, Lewis Grassic Gibbon, Willa Muir and N Brysson Morrison as "writers who in any country would be acknowledged to possess original gifts." In the same year Gibbon himself, with Hugh MacDiarmid, provided a longer list of young Scottish novelists, claiming:

> . . . that Scotland never at any previous time possessed so numerous a corps of novelists; that the general level of its novelistic ability was never higher; and that the "native content" of its novels was never greater or keener.

Muir, echoing an old complaint, adds, "Unfortunately, no equally vivid description of Scottish industrial life has yet been written." Similarly, interviewed early in 1935, the critic Edward Scouller:

> . . . asserts that there is more drama in the ordinary riveter's life than in any cinema star's or story book detective's, but that any portrait so far in fiction has been insulting, melodramatic caricature.

Less than two years later, however, Scouller thinks he's found the grail:

> . . . a serious artist's attempt to show working-class and

middle-class Glasgow in the trough of the economic
depression. It deliberately eschews melodrama, without which
it has seemed impossible for other writers to deal with the life
of slum and tenement. It unrolls the panorama of drab,
hopeless poverty and damns the causes that have produced
riverside Partick . . .

This is *Major Operation*, which will be examined more fully later
on.

By 1938 Scouller's view is positive indeed:

The majority of our Scots authors now concern themselves with
life in the towns and in the Industrial Belt. And he who writes
of the towns is almost forced into writing truthfully, because
the readers he hopes to attract dwell mostly in towns and know
very well whether he is describing life as they know it or
whether he is prettifying the picture . . . The serious Scottish
novelist of today is trying to reach a new reading public . . .
[which], being at close quarters with life, selects and judges its
books by comparison with life, not by comparison with other
books . . . The contemporary Scottish novelist . . . has a
dogged spiritual integrity that drives him on to write about the
sort of life that in his opinion matters.

Many of these novelists are in fact the writers of the 1920s, who
have attained through experience a technical skill to match their
serious purpose, and – in Scouller's opinion – have tapped into a
readership ready and waiting for them.

We have noted a critic's suggestion that writing about the
state of Glasgow at all, let alone writing well, was a task to daunt
most writers. Christopher Whyte takes a similar view:

Glasgow life is felt as a raw, untapped material, an unleavened
mass, and the urge is first and foremost to transcribe, to
denounce. Realism is traditionally associated with brutal and
seamier themes . . . The seeming transparency of realist
technique soothes a feeling of impotence, in the face of
material which could make a preoccupation with stylistic factors
appear indecent.

THE CANCER OF EMPIRE

work," Kirkwood, deportee and Member of Parliament, refused the invitation of the Prince of Wales on his visit to Glasgow last year. In virtue of the second, Glasgow must be rehoused. For the first meaning of this "sufficiency" is a home fit to live in. At the present time, out of a population of 1,081,983, 600,000 people, that is, two-thirds, "live in houses inferior to the minimum standard of the Board of Health" (Dollan), 40,591 families live in one-roomed homes, 112,424 families live in homes made up of a room and kitchen. There are more than 13,000 of these "homes officially condemned by the Medical Officer of Health for

[...]und hundred of them are

[...]y 32 one-roomed and 55

[...] Glasgow are empty as

[...]s Stewart, Clyde Member

[...]mself from these figures

[...]s home city, Glasgow,

[...], to hell."

[...] these gloomy statistics

[...]ing of black brick and

[...]ich a vast population is

[...]hing must be said of

[...]ouse shortage is spread

[...] every city suffers from

[...] a post-war phenomenon

[...]location of the delicately

[...]ur from the building

[...]impoverishment shown

The Cancer of Empire

I

THE Red Clyde, the smouldering danger of [...] Glasgow, owing to the swift [...] of political affairs in Britain, [...]cal anxiety, and become so [...]to the whole civilised world. [...] of trust in things as they are [...] world war and the Russian [...]tate, however geographically [...]ningly secure in possession of [...]nstitutional system, can any [...] immunity from violent, bloody [...] politic. The world is no more [...]olitically, socially, economically, [...]rown virulently infectious, and [...]tbreak in the very heart of the [...]Empire is as much a concern to [...] States as an outbreak of cholera [...]rt; and a thorough understanding [...]history, causes, and likelihood of [...]s is a necessity of high importance. [...]untry immediately affected, knows [...]ded the instinctive desire to blan- [...]Clyde, explain it away; and the

13

"In Glasgow there are over a hundred and fifty thousand human beings living in such conditions as the most bitterly pressed primitive in Tierra del Fuego never visioned," wrote Lewis Grassic Gibbon. William Bolitho's *Cancer of Empire* (1924) and many other official reports fixed an image of Glasgow in the public mind. Writing about Glasgow well in any realistic way was enough to daunt most writers and though some writers in the 1930s attempted realism, others preferred to depict earlier happier times

The kind of material he means is graphically laid out in the non-fiction work of two great Scottish writers (both of whom did also address the question of Glasgow in fiction). Lewis Grassic Gibbon famously reminds us that:

> In Glasgow there are over a hundred and fifty thousand human beings living in such conditions as the most bitterly pressed primitive in Tierra del Fuego never visioned. They live five or six to the single room . . . It is a room that is part of some great sloven of tenement – the tenement itself in a line or grouping with hundreds of its fellows, its windows grimed with the unceasing wash and drift of coal-dust, its stairs narrow and befouled and steep, its evening breath like that which might issue from the mouth of a lung-diseased beast.

And Edwin Muir supplies, albeit at second hand, such details as Gibbon has missed:

> I have been told of slum courts so narrow that the refuse flung into them mounted and mounted in the course of years until it blocked all the house windows up to the second-top storey; and I have been given an idea of the stench rising from this rotting, half liquid mass which I shall not reproduce here. I have been told of choked stair-head lavatories with the filth from them running down the stairs; of huge midnight migrations of rats from one block to another; and of bugs crawling down the windows of tram-cars. All these things, I have been assured, are true . . .

We can well imagine how contemporary novelists might be daunted by the task of fictionalising all this, but, in addition, how they felt they had to try.

Throughout the 1930s writers can be seen struggling with their "unleavened mass" of material. To get it all into one book is, artistically, a hopeless enterprise, because, as Scouller perceptively observes, "there are so many Glasgows." Most writers wisely decide to focus on one aspect, one theme.

Some novelists of the 1930s, as in every age, retreat to an earlier Glasgow. A few years after publishing *Justice of the Peace* Frederick Niven had emigrated to Canada, where he carried on a prolific writing career. Many of his novels have Canadian settings (though frequently with a Glasgow connection), but from time to time he returned in his fiction to the Glasgow of his youth, still very much alive in his mind. His widow recalled:

> When he was writing *The Staff at Simson's* his hands frequently would be wet as if they had been in water. On one occasion, looking very dazed, he said, "I have seen the pigeons in Ingram Street . . ." and he really had. He dictated a lot and at such times one could see him practically reporting what he saw before his eyes . . .

While we do not know whether Niven's *Mrs Barry* (1933) is drawn so directly from his own memories, it is worth considering as a rare (at this date) and sensitive study of a woman protagonist. Mrs Barry is a widow in reduced circumstances, driven to taking lodgers, struggling against illness and on behalf of her small son Neil. She lives in a poor district of Glasgow – a "shipbuilding parish" which sounds like Govan – but not in the slums:

> She passed turnings to tenement blocks where people did not live, as where she lived, one in a room and, at most, two in a bed. She passed mephitic and noisy side-streets where whole families existed in one room and unthinkably increased and multiplied in one room, conceiving and bearing there . . . Yes, she decided, she had much to be thankful for.

The undramatic story has its moving moments, and Mrs Barry, like Martin Moir, sees Glasgow with the painter's eye that is Niven's special gift: "She had come to the areas where the houses were built of stone that glittered in the rain . . ."

Niven's friend RB Cunninghame Graham was enthusastic

about the book and its heroine: "*Mrs Barry* is really splendid. How well you have drawn the brave and sympathetic woman. Even to read of such a woman makes one think better of humanity. . ." Compton Mackenzie was yet more impressed: "A noble story . . . one for which I shall be bold enough to claim the right to an enduring name in the literature of Scotland." To the hard-hearted reader of today Mrs Barry may seem a shade too good to be true, and Graham, gently criticising the ending of the book, puts his finger on what has been a danger all along.

> I do not like, in the last sentence, "She had found rest." It is not like the book, and it was obvious she had found it. May I suggest, without offence, that "Mrs Barry did not answer. She had not heard (or did not hear) the bell": would read, I will not say better, but more like yourself?

Besides homing in on the hint of sentimentality, Graham recognises that Niven had a voice which was distinctly himself, a combination of realism with faintly old-fashioned good taste, unsensational but unsentimental too.

This true voice is heard in *The Staff at Simson's* (1937), Niven's full treatment of the Glasgow warehouse life so effectively sketched twenty-three years before in *Justice of the Peace*. Individual characters are not treated in such depth as were the Moirs in the earlier novel, but are quickly and deftly delineated. The setting date, as before, is about 1890–1910, and each member of the staff is accompanied, in near-documentary style, through the major events of his life. Niven's main concern, however, is the to-and-fro of a textile warehouse, with its place in Glasgow business life, which he had known as a boy.

> He had the feeling of belonging to this city and of this city belonging to him . . . by a reason of a multitude of small things – such as the continuance of these two newsagents who had been there when, at fifteen, he entered Simson's. At the corner of Buchanan Street and that passage there was a jeweller and

optician . . . Almost all who passed that way had sometimes
stopped – and many of them made a point of stopping always
once a day – to check their watches with Greenwich time by his
clock . . . Office-boys, with their first watches, would halt there
also, flourish them, and pass on, proven young businessmen of
the city.

This is the near-total recall, some forty years after Niven's apprentice
days and several thousand miles away, which his widow described.

The mercantile Glasgow novel, then, was still alive, and this
decade saw another example of the genre in George Woden's
Mungo (1932). Woden was a prolific and popular author whose
career spanned some forty years. Generally he produced readable,
if rather pedestrian, novels with a middle-class background,
together with a good deal of light detective and romance fiction,
but *Mungo* is conceived on a rather more ambitious scale. It is a
family saga, tracing the lives of John Mungo and Mary Bell from
birth (indeed, conception) to comfortable middle age. Thus we
have glimpses of Glasgow in the late nineteenth century, when
John and Mary are happy newlyweds, though as John says:

> "You're no' supposed to be happy in a single apartment in a
> place like this. It's a slum. There's folk talking and preaching
> every week and the papers printing it, about the dreadful slums
> and the misery in Glasgow . . . And you talking about
> happiness! We're no' supposed to know what it is."

We also see near-contemporary 1920s Glasgow, though in some
ways it may not have moved on very far.

> "It's not gossip; it's true; I have the proofs. She has been
> seen with him down at the Coast. They have been seen
> together in the public parks – ay, after dark, and together in
> first class compartments o' the trains on the Cathcart Circle
> – ay, and in the Art Galleries; and we ken why folk go there
> in couples . . ."

But perhaps the main interest for us lies in the fact that John, like Bailie Nicol Jarvie and Claud Walkinshaw, is in the textile trade. He starts at the bottom as a "Scotch draper" or pedlar, but has plans for working up his business:

> "I'll be on my own by and by, and I can pay my book in five years. For all the outstanding money Grimmon – it's Grimmon I'm working for – well, he'll add five per cent on my purchases at the wholesale, in his name, you see, and there's three and three-quarters per cent for cash in a month – eight and three-quarters on all my turnover, though, mind you, I'll get the benefit o' him buying in quantity, maybe a shilling on, say, a pair o' blankets. You see?"

Even if Mary doesn't quite see and we too may be a bit bemused, we recognise John as another merchant hero of Glasgow fiction.

By this time, however, Niven and Woden are exceptions in continuing to tell a leisurely, almost timeless tale. From now on, as critics have noticed, Glasgow fiction shows a pervasive yearning – overt or otherwise – for a lost "dear green place", and this theme will be looked at more closely in Chapter Ten. Certainly most Glasgow novelists of the 1930s are writing to an agenda, which may well include politics.

Robert Craig has large ambitions in *O People!* (1932), a strange mixture of realism and highly romantic nationalism. The central character John Grant is a solitary idealist obsessed with the desire to see Scotland a full member of the League of Nations. Extended passages of rhyming prose glorify the kind of image of Scotland beloved by the heritage industry today. However, Grant's visionary eloquence is diverted, without his realising it, to help the cause of a Socialist candidate at a by-election. Here Craig reports with accuracy and humour the heckling at a political meeting addressed by a sprig of the nobility.

> "Is the candidate in favour of putting false teeth in the mooth o' the Clyde?"

"Is the candidate gaun tae gie us a look at his croun?"
"Hey, duke, duke! See's a fag!" . . .
"Gie the laddie a wee chance. He's near greetin'."
"Does the candidate go to the jiggin'?"
"How's your granny, wee fella?"

Catherine Gavin had political experience herself, having stood against James Maxton in Bridgeton in 1931 and cut his majority by more than half. We may infer from her novel *Clyde Valley* (1938) that she had known some rough times at the hustings. Her character Lenny Gordon is involved because of her association with the candidate, an unhappily married man. Lenny finds the proceedings unbearably sordid, and indeed it's a dirty campaign:

> The Major's first name, published on his nomination form, was Ninian, and it was well known that Ninian was an awful Catholic name, for there was even a Saint Ninian, which just showed you . . .
> Her appearance with Kennedy caused the ill-informed to ask audibly "if that was the woman" and those who knew Lenny by sight to shout: "Go on home, you, tell his wife it's her we want" . . .

Much of the action takes place in the grim surroundings of depression Glasgow, but this is not the whole story, since Lenny is brought up in rural Clydesdale and her mother has brought houseproud ways and uncompromising opinions south from Buchan. *Clyde Valley*, Gavin's first novel, is unevenly written with some alarming purple patches, but its abiding effect is a powerful one of frustrated passion, on the part of Lenny and also of her mother, who harbours a strange repressed jealousy of her.

Alongside Glasgow politics, or rather intertwined with them, runs, as ever, the issue of class. John Macnair Reid makes two serious attempts to compare the working-class and middle-class ways of life, and to conjecture what might happen if they met. His first novel *Homeward Journey* (1934) brings together the minister's son David, self-conscious and haunted by memories of his dead mother, and the shopgirl Jessie, attractive and frank. She cheerfully leads David into the back close for a goodnight kiss, little suspecting that it's his first. But close reading indicates that the suggestion is his: "Won't you show me the back?" and on this tiny point turns the subtlety and complexity of the book.

Reid does not make clear – and doesn't intend to – whether Jessie is out to catch David or David looking for a bit of rough, or, if either of these is true, how consciously the aim is being pursued. Certainly the love affair is insecurely based, and they part, David detecting an unacceptable materialism in Jessie, and Jessie deciding to "[keep] herself for her real lover, whenever he might arrive." Some self-knowledge has been acquired, but a credible ambiguity remains.

Judy from Crown Street, Reid's second novel on the theme of the class divide, is painted with a much broader brush. It was posthumously published in 1970 and its date of composition remains imprecise, though Reid's brother has explained the circumstances of its eventual appearance.

> It was only after his widow's death in 1966 that I obtained his manuscripts, typescripts, notes and so on. There were only two novels. These I had published at my own expense, as a tangible memorial . . . I am not quite sure, but I think "Judy" preceded "Tobias". The typescript suggests this. Neither was dated, but I think the decade 1940–1950 would possibly cover both books.

The setting date of *Judy from Crown Street* is 1933, near enough to that of *Homeward Journey*, but the lapse of ten or fifteen years has brought ease and liveliness to Reid's writing, if some loss, perhaps, of the delicate subtlety seen in the earlier book. The lovers are older; Judy in fact is thirty-eight, with a grown-up son, two small daughters, and a long-absent husband. She is a warm, down-to-earth woman, a development of Jessie without the element of calculation. Grannie, with whom she and her family live, muses on Judy's chequered career:

If ever there was a wee clown in Glasgow it was Judy. First, at
seventeen, Robert. And she makes the man marry her. That was
a daft-like thing to do. After a year, he buzzes off . . . And after
a while there is that student fellow. Anne isn't like Judy at all;
she's like him . . . And, begod, only three years later, wee Ivy.
Ivy was the mystery . . . The fact is, Grannie concluded
wistfully, and munching her gums the while, our family always
clicked too easily.

Judy works as housekeeper in George's big house in Pollokshields;
sharp observation of both milieux is a strength of the book. There's
a middle-class engagement in the pipeline for George, but he
masterfully stages a surprise for Judy and his mother:

"I have known that you both wondered if I'd marry Winifred
Watt. That was silly of you. Especially you, Mother. Haven't
you noticed anything much nearer home?"

"No-o. I can't say I have, George . . ."

"Ask Judy," he smiled . . . "I'm afraid you, Mother, are not a
very observant person. I've been in love with Judy for a long
time. Right under your eyes!"

As it stands, the book has an unashamed happy ending, anyway
from George's point of view. We do get a hint that Judy has some
reservations about all this, but that situation is not explored. The
writer of *Homeward Journey* and the strong character Judy, with
perhaps a bit of redrafting, could together have produced a notable
Glasgow novel, but for this Reid was not granted time; he was
prematurely killed in a road accident.

Many writers in the 1930s, it will be seen, still observe
Glasgow working-class life with a middle-class eye, or (in the case
of Muir, Gibbon and Gavin) from the more detached viewpoint
of a rural upbringing. Writers rooted in the urban working class
have so far been rare, but this is about to change.

One of the forerunners, though fiction forms only a part of
his output, is Edward Scouller. Born in Ardrossan, Scouller was

the son of a shipyard caulker who was a keen trade unionist. A biographical sketch informs us baldly that he was "brought up in poverty; developed a horror of the Scottish tenement system." He worked his way through university, but, due to lack of money, had to give up before graduation. He had various short-term jobs, served in World War I, and settled to seven years in a clerking post, at the same time beginning a parallel career in freelance journalism. He returned to Glasgow University in 1926 to complete his degree – a first in English language and literature – and taught for some years, but clearly his heart was in writing. He published many short stories in contemporary newspapers and periodicals, but there is equal interest in the considerable body of his book reviews and articles on contemporary Scottish literature.

We have seen that he asserted the drama in "the ordinary riveter's life," while John Cockburn asked for "the unembellished story of the folk who . . . live up a close." Both demands might seem to be met by *Gael over Glasgow* (1937), the only published novel by Edward Shiels, though it also has a particularly strong admixture of the "green place" theme.

> Brian O'Neill lay on the heather on the moors above
> Clydebank basking in the rare warmth of a March sun. Away far
> below in the depths of the Clyde valley, Glasgow lay in a pall of
> reeking black . . . Even from here Brian could distinguish the
> sustained snarl of pneumatic caulking machines from the close
> staccato of the riveting hammers . . . Wasn't it great to steal
> away from it all and lie up here in the quiet and feel the magic
> of the wind from the North, the keen, clean wind that had
> kissed the budding daffodils on the shores of a hundred lonely
> lochs up there.

Brian's yearning for a romanticised version of the Highlands (due, we are told, to his Gaelic heritage) is constant over the twelve years or so covered by the story. *Gael over Glasgow* is not a book of great literary quality, but Brian's milieu is clearly drawn: shipyard and factory work, unemployment, strike action, the young men filling their aimless days. The writing is sensitive and honest as the boy grows up and tries to make sense of his world. He watches his friend, an ex-choirboy, singing jazz:

> It was typical . . . of Clydebank and the Clyde, with its sharp jagged contrasts of disgusting slums and modern housing schemes; of hooligans living and mingling alongside intelligent workmen, probably the finest workmen and citizens in the world; of full-blooded modernism brawling alongside Calvinism; of materialism and Catholicism all weaving and intertwining in that puzzling pattern of Society known as Clydeside.

Edwin Muir gave the book a brief and balanced review, which read, in full: "A first novel, *Gael over Glasgow*, by Edward Shiels, shows considerable sensitiveness combined with considerable sentimentality. But it is a novel of promise." The promise could not be fulfilled. Shiels, a walker and country-lover in boyhood, had already been wheelchair-bound for some years with polio, and he died not long after his novel was published. The disappointing wish-fulfilment ending of *Gael over Glasgow* – in which a rich uncle returns from America, buys a Highland glen, and offers Brian work there – is still technically weak, but, written in these circumstances, humanly understandable.

Meanwhile a greater writer than Shiels or Scouller was beginning to find his voice. George Friel was one of a large family brought up in a tenement flat in Maryhill. (The Plottels who recur in his fiction – shiftless father, admirable mother, three brothers close in age – are generally considered to reflect his own family.) He graduated at Glasgow University, qualified as a teacher, and remained in that profession for the rest of his life.

Friel's first published short story, "You Can See It For Yourself", appeared in 1935, and seven more were published during 1936: an *annus mirabilis*, as a recent commentator points out, since only three further short stories were published during his lifetime. These are among the earliest Glasgow short stories, startling in their clear-eyed observation of people, places and attitudes. In "Clothes" the penniless Plottel children are issued with Education Authority outfits, the boy – Friel as a boy, we can hardly doubt – bitterly complaining, "Everybody will know we're poor."

> As he laced up the boots he saw there were small holes pierced
> in the uppers and arranged to form the initials E.A.G.
> Education Authority, Glasgow, he cried to himself,
> straightening for a moment rebelliously. Why don't they stamp
> it on the backside of the pants, too!

In "Home" Mrs Plottel works all day at spring-cleaning a south-side villa, but isn't paid because her employer doesn't have change. Like Dot Allan, but with more focused bitterness, Friel condemns the middle-class woman:

> . . . the smiling thoughtlessness of these people who lived in
> seven-roomed houses and had plenty of money, so polite that
> they could be sorry you hadn't an umbrella when it was
> raining, but never think of lending you one, never think you
> hadn't a penny for the bus home.

In spite of their excellence, Friel's stories remained uncollected and hard to locate until very recently, when a selection of both published and unpublished work appeared. Its editor calls the stories:

> . . . brave because they stick with and faithfully mirror the
> unfashionable world he grew up in and never left: because they
> offer no escape, or escapism.

He suggests that Friel was taking "enormous risks . . . by using working-class Glasgow for his fictional setting and then telling it 'like it is'." Certainly Friel had great difficulty in placing his work, and this continued when he turned to novel-writing, even though, of his five published novels, three at least are now considered to be in the very first rank of Glasgow fiction. They will be looked at more closely in later chapters.

Dot Allan's work in the 1930s, as in the previous decade, tends to defy categorisation. In *Deepening River* (1932), which follows the fortunes of one family – sailmakers, later in steam – over four generations and two hundred years, she produces a fairly predictable and slow-moving Glasgow epic. Her next novel, *Hunger March* (1934), goes off on a quite different tack.

Edwin Morgan has remarked that *Hunger March* ". . . does bear some marks of the self-consciousness of its 'mission', but has real imaginative force and good formal control."

It covers twenty-four hours in an unnamed but recognisable Glasgow on the day of a hunger march, one of many in the depression years. We focus in turn on the merchant Arthur Joyce, whose business is in trouble; on his cleaner Mrs Humphry and her unemployed son Joe; and on the charismatic revolutionary Nimrod, as observed by the middle-class radical Jimmy. These stories, still alive and valid, support the novel, though some of the other interweaving strands now have a dated air.

What comes out clearly, as in Allan's earlier novel *Makeshift*, is a "two cities" theme: the middle class don't care about the workers, and in fact, most of the time, don't even notice them (though by *Hunger March* the workers intend to make them notice). In a telling little scene the hunger marchers converge on George Square, watched idly by shoppers and lunchers. "It shouldn't be allowed," opines a lady in a tearoom, "I'm sure and I don't know what the world's coming to!" while the waitress in the corner silently agrees, but with a different implication to her thoughts. Allan's observation of her own class has never been sharper nor her condemnation more direct.

She does, at the same time, give full value to the despair of the businessman Arthur Joyce. The hopeful ending of *Hunger March* is based, perhaps a shade insecurely, on Joyce's determination that, for the sake of his workers, his business shall not fail. In fact Glasgow depends on him:

> The offices contained in the high stone buildings rose like a
> solid black shield warding off evil from the city . . . The
> Square was now disclosed as a moon-silvered place of grassy
> plots and statues . . . With the lights in the surrounding
> windows extinguished, and only the glitter of the street-
> lamps outlining them, these plots comprised a little
> sanctuary where dreams might be born, fresh hopes
> conceived, hopes high enough to scale the walls of the
> enfolding offices, hopes brave enough, if a tithe of them
> were realized, to increase to a splendid diapason the
> dwindling heart-beats of the city's trade.

If this can only be described as the apotheosis of the Glasgow
mercantile novel, *Hunger March* as a whole deserves to be
considered alongside two much better-known novels which tackle
the contemporary condition of Glasgow. These are George Blake's
The Shipbuilders (1935) and James Barke's *Major Operation* (1936).

To concentrate on these two novels is not to overlook the
other work of Blake and Barke, even in this decade. Blake was now
an established novelist, and – in his own words – was shortly ". . .
to retire decorously . . . and [find] his right subject among the
bourgeoisie" of "Garvel", his fictional Greenock. Before that, in
1936, he published a further interesting Glasgow novel, *David
and Joanna*. While his characters escape for a time to a "green
place" in a Highland glen, Blake – unlike Shiels – recognises the
romanticism of their dream and, even though it is implied they
will retry the good life, brings them back soberly to the city.

James Barke was best known towards the end of his life for
the ambitious novel sequence on the life of Burns which began
with *The Wind that Shakes the Barley* (1946), but he published
several novels during the 1930s. *The World His Pillow* (1933),
whose central character becomes disillusioned with Glasgow life
and returns to the Highlands, foreshadows, if more simplistically,
Barke's masterpiece *The Land of the Leal* (1939). This epic, based
to some extent on Barke's own family history, follows farm-workers
Jean and David Ramsay from Galloway to the Borders, Fife, and

finally industrial Glasgow. Galloway is their "green place", but David's return visit is not a success.

> He felt it would be an agony to come back and work in a land
> whose physical features had remained unaltered but whose
> spirit had withered and decayed. It was still to him a bonnie
> land . . . But there was no way back to that life: there was no
> way forward. He had come back to find that the past was dead
> or dying and that the future was more uncertain than ever it
> had been.

While *The Shipbuilders* and *Major Operation*, then, have their place in the broader pattern of Blake's and Barke's work, they fall naturally to be considered together. They were published in successive years and there are similarities in their handling of contemporary Glasgow themes. Critics have not failed to point out a double parallelism, in that each novel focuses on a pair of male characters, one working-class and one middle-class, and each builds up its story by presenting parallel scenes of working-class and middle-class life. Above all, however, their authors were both inspired – or driven – to write these particular novels by the Glasgow which was in crisis around them.

The Shipbuilders has caused much discussion since its publication in 1935, and opinions have varied remarkably between extremes of praise and censure. A recent critic, quoting some of these verdicts, has remarked a little tartly:

> Enough contradictions there to confuse the reader . . . even if
> the conclusions may not be as useless as those of the three
> blind persons who examined the elephant.

First reactions were favourable, to say the least.

> "Authentic" is the adjective I unhesitatingly apply to Mr
> George Blake's *The Shipbuilders*. Here is a magnificent picture
> of the Clydeside of modern depression and a magnificent series
> of portraits of Clydeside characters.

> *The Shipbuilders* . . . gives us the portrait of an authentic Scots
> working man which Goya himself might have envied in the
> profound certainty of its drawing.

These sentiments are not shared by the later critic who finds
evidence of:

> . . . excruciating sentimentality . . . the proletarian dialogue is
> stagey and artificial and the cloyingly unreal relationship
> between Leslie and Danny is a false model of human harmony.

Even a more balanced review has to admit that

> . . . re-reading the novel brings something disagreeable to light,
> and that is Blake's apparent insistence upon people knowing their
> place in a universe where status is something fixed and
> definite . . . even more objectionable is the book's creeping anti-
> semitism . . . the novel is ultimately a failure, reflecting as it does
> some of the ultra-reactionary philosophy of the *Sunday Post*.

Certainly the relationship between the two main characters, the
shipyard owner Leslie Pagan and the riveter Danny Shields, rings
lamentably false today, being patronising on Pagan's side and
uncritically devoted on Danny's. We are not convinced by Danny's
general attitude of deference to all "toffs" and ex-officers, nor
edified by Pagan's habit of dropping in to O'Glinchey's pub where
he will:

> . . . find some of the old hands at the bar there and, as he loved
> to do now and then, stand them a drink . . . those rough
> innocents whose destinies were so strangely in his hands.

It has been noted that "even when the narrative point of view is
with the worker, the language tends to remain that of his
counterpart," a persuasive indication that this is a view of the
working class from the outside.

Jack Mitchell dismisses Blake as a "pseudo-proletarian" writer. Blake himself, in a notably honest summation of his own work, would seem to agree. Referring to himself in the third person, he says,

> Blake . . . now thinks [*The Shipbuilders*] unworthy of its epic subject. He pleads guilty to an insufficient knowledge of working-class life and to the adoption of a middle-class attitude to the theme of industrial conflict and despair.

But he suggests

> It may be allowed him, at least . . . that he was the first to understand the sheer poetry of the Clyde's effort in shipbuilding, and that he had a respect for the architecture of a long novel.

Points which have indeed been allowed today by at least one critic:

> Taken on its own terms, *The Shipbuilders* is perhaps the most perfect Glasgow novel of its decade, a noble threnody on the collapse of the shipbuilding industry.

We have noticed the 'architecture', the deliberately contrasting scenes which take us from Leslie's luxurious but unhappy middle-class home to Danny's no happier working-class one; which follow the breakdown of their marriages; which chart the effects of the depression on the two men, shipbuilders both; which show Leslie escaping from stricken Glasgow and Danny staying in a milieu of domestic contentment but economic gloom. *The Shipbuilders* has, however, another virtue, not claimed by Blake but evident to a reader.

> Glasgow of *The Shipbuilders* . . . is not just background colour but fully drawn, a character itself in the novel . . . George Blake establishes a strong sense of the actuality of Glasgow. Through the use of real place names, his emphasis on the domination of the physical landscape by tenements and

shipyards, his descriptions of the buses and trams, their termini and stops, and his evocation of the city streets, Blake captures the "spirit of place".

With his journalist's eye for detail, in *The Shipbuilders* he selects scene after scene, building up a full and sympathetic picture both of Glasgow itself and of the plight of the unemployed. There is a classic description of an Old Firm football match. There is a sequence in the High Court as Danny's son stands trial with a gang of boys for murder:

> Where other eyes would have seen but a Glasgow keelie, a hooligan debased and hopeless, Danny saw his son and loved him. He saw the lad who had never had a chance . . . Peter and his kind . . . were at eighteen in mind exactly as they had been left by elementary education at fourteen . . . A boy like Peter used to go automatically to his trade, but now there were no trades to go to . . . That murder in Govan, that silly gesture with a knife, would never have been done or made by a boy on the rusty deck of a ship in the making. Waste was only proliferating out of waste.

Frequently we come back to Danny, walking the city in his idleness,

> . . . seeking strange places and discovering queer, quiet streets on the suburban slopes above Partick – streets he never knew before existed, streets that told him a doleful story of the city's vastness and complexity and indifference.

And Leslie Pagan makes a journey down the Clyde, past the many shipyards whose idleness both causes and reflects Danny's:

> Yard after yard passed by, the berths empty, the grass growing about the sinking keel-blocks . . . A tradition, a skill, a glory, a passion, was visibly in decay and all the acquired and inherited loveliness of artistry rotting along the banks of the stream.

For all their technical similarities, James Barke's *Major Operation* is very different from *The Shipbuilders*. Barke was different from Blake. His left-wing politics, a major force in his life, show up as a strong influence too in his fiction. An obituarist who had known him well in the 1930s perceptively linked the man and his work.

> As a writer he had great sympathy for the suffering and a rage against those who caused that suffering. He was a man full of humanity, a very individual man. His novels are like him. They are a little rough-hewn; he never managed a smooth and pleasing style and I guess he never tried. But he hewed out great blocks of experience and got a massive effect by heaping them together . . .

Major Operation, like *The Shipbuilders*, was enthusiastically received on publication. This is the novel which Edward Scouller hailed in a review headed "So This Is Glasgow!"

> [Barke] has entered with complete sympathy into the emotions and reactions of sections of the community (numerically the largest sections there are) in a manner that makes previous attempts to portray these sections seem tawdry, superficial and ludicrously untrue.

But, unlike *The Shipbuilders, Major Operation* fell out of sight for many years. In Francis Russell Hart's wide-ranging *The Scottish Novel* (1978) it is not discussed at all. Though it has been rediscovered, critics, even those who praise it, admit its many faults:

> It is too long, it is at times verbose and offensive in its propaganda, it betrays a lamentable lack of tolerance that hampers a politician and cripples an artist . . .

> We feel that the decisive debate has been "set up" by Barke so that he can quickly win the *desired victory* according to *his* rules . . . He is eternally narrating, telling us, predigesting for us.

> The book is schematic, didactic, doctrinaire.

The scheme, as has been noted, is one of contrasts and parallels. The bourgeois George Anderson and the workers' leader Jock MacKelvie are brought side by side in a hospital ward. (The "major operation" is carried out not only by the surgeon on George's duodenal ulcer, but by Jock on George's mind, and is also the Caesarian section which will allow the "monstrous hermaphrodite" of the city to escape from the pangs of protracted labour.) Thus their diverging points of view can be presented and argued over, sometimes at rather implausible length. The well-read MacKelvie, though a strong, well-realised character, taxes our belief when he speaks for five or six pages on Materialism, three on love, or six on the workers' movement. It is good, impassioned declamation, but possibly in a real hospital ward it would invite more comment than the mild remark by his neighbour Duff, "Why don't you write a bloody book?"

But the "massive effect" is there. It is brought about, at least in part, by Barke's technique of interlarding his narrative with striking, often impressionistic sections of description or evocation of Glasgow (not named as such, but called "the Second City").

Sometimes, as in the fine angry passage, "The Smells of Slumdom", the impression is conveyed through a character's eyes, or nose.

> MacKelvie and Connor walked down Moore Street towards their homes . . .The subway entrance breathed out its stale decayed air. Immediately beyond, where they turned into Walker Street, a warm, odoriferous waft of slumdom awaited them. It was not a smell that could be escaped. There were identifiable odours of cats' urine: decayed rubbish: infectious diseases: unwashed underclothing, intermingled with smells suggesting dry rot: insanitary lavatories, overtaxed sewage pipes and the excrement of a billion bed-bugs. MacKelvie met the waft with twisted nostrils.

In "Heat Wave" the city is scanned as if from space, dropping down now and then for a closer look at "a foreman carpenter . . .

an elderly slum mother . . ." Most notable is "Red Music in the Second City" which has been described as "James Joyce writing about Glasgow with a Communist Party card in his pocket." We are hearing the voice of the people, waiting in the drizzly street as a flute band draws near. We square up to the Lord Provost, the Labour Party, business, bookies, popular music, sectarianism, unemployment, sex, and the meaning of life:

> Who am I? I'm the Voice that breathed o'er Eden: I'm the Fly in the Ointment: I'm the Wet Blanket: I'm the Saftest o' the Family . . . I'm the Eternal Feminine and Mr Public . . . I'm the Negation of Negations . . .

> When the hell is it going to end? I'll be shrieking in a minute. Father's got the sack from the water works, the brick works, the rivet, bolt and nut works . . . Rebel Song played by the Springburn Unemployed Workers' flute band . . . So that's what all the noise was about? Well: see you later: also hear.

Jack Mitchell finds *Major Operation* "a heroic attempt to lay, almost single-handed, the foundations for the proletarian socialist-realist novel in Scotland." As such it could be regarded as the novel which sums up Glasgow fiction in the 1930s; and might be so, except that as yet we have hardly mentioned *No Mean City*.

9

The Shadow of the Gorbals

"Reeks with squalor and ends in triumph," proclaimed the *New York Herald Tribune*. "An astonishing, important and inspiring book." The book, published a few months before, was Alexander McArthur's *No Mean City*, a novel set in the Gorbals of Glasgow.

This review – at least the "important and inspiring" bit – did not exactly chime with *No Mean City*'s reception in Glasgow, where letters of outrage burgeoned in the press and a solemn decision was made not to stock the book in the city's libraries. (Anecdotal evidence indicates that other Glaswegians just laughed.) Its importance has not been widely recognised, either, by later critics; very few writers on Glasgow fiction mention it at all.

Yet *No Mean City* has gone through many paperback editions and still sells briskly, both in bookshops and on railway bookstalls. Its style and its gangland theme have had followers, not to say frank imitators, and its title crops up with some regularity in news items as well as on book pages, where reviewers seem to suffer from an eerie compulsion to describe any new Glasgow novel as either like, or else not like, *No Mean City*. Over sixty years after its first publication, why is this the Glasgow novel best known, at least by name, to the general public?

Squalor (as duly acknowledged by the *Herald Tribune*), sex and violence are the reasons most commonly suggested. Many of the local objections imply that the incidents in the novel have been invented for sensational effect. However, its joint authors expressly disclaim any such intent or method. Perhaps they should at least be heard.

No Mean City was published in October 1935 under the names of Alexander McArthur and H Kingsley Long. The publisher's preface to the first edition goes to some trouble to state how this came about.

> In June 1934 Mr Alexander McArthur, writing from an address in the Gorbals, Glasgow, submitted to us two short novels.
>
> Although neither of these was considered suitable for publication, we were greatly struck with their astonishing revelations concerning life in one section of the Empire's second city. Mr McArthur, we were told, had been unemployed for the past five years and had fought the inevitable demoralisation of "the idle years" (the title of one of his manuscripts) by writing novel after novel – without ever achieving publication . . . He wrote with complete candour . . . But unfortunately he could not present either his story or his characters in a manner that would secure the attention of the majority of readers.
>
> Mr H. Kingsley Long, a London journalist, whom we had asked to read Mr McArthur's manuscript, visited Glasgow . . . [and] called on Mr McArthur there . . . Subsequently we invited Mr McArthur to London, and in the course of a number of interviews we satisfied ourselves as to the essential truth of his account of slum life in one section of Glasgow. Mr Kingsley Long also had many interviews with him, after which he and Mr McArthur decided to collaborate. This novel is the outcome of this collaboration.

This, it will be seen, is a pre-emptive strike, anticipating objections and insisting that the material, however sensational, is based on fact. A similar defence is mounted in the appendix, which quotes contemporary newspaper reports of happenings parallel to events in the novel, and states:

> Though all the characters in *No Mean City* are imaginary and the book itself merely fiction, the authors maintain that they have not drawn an exaggerated picture of conditions in the Glasgow tenements or of life as it is lived among the gangster element of the slum population.

Cynics might ask why we should believe the publisher's statement either, but much of it, when examined, checks out. Nobody invented Alexander McArthur, who did live in the Gorbals, and was unemployed, and did write "novel after novel", and short stories, and at least one play. "Without ever achieving publication" is no invention either. Even after *No Mean City* had achieved such fame, only one piece of fiction by McArthur – a short story – is definitely known to have been published during his lifetime. Another novel, *No Bad Money,* was pulled together from surviving manuscripts by a different collaborator and published in 1969, long after McArthur's death. McArthur was not, then, a very skilled or successful novelist; the publisher's statement is right there.

The accompanying assertion – that he knew what he was writing about – is supported by various small touches of social description in *No Mean City* which do have the air of truthful reporting, although – or because? – they add nothing in particular to the story. Such are the definitions of the terms "paraffin" as a smart appearance and "hairy" as a hatless slum girl, or the limited scope of Peter Stark's dreams:

> Peter Stark never fooled himself that he would be able to set up in business on his own account. He was a rebel, but his environment limited even his own rebellious ambition. That he should become an employer and a capitalist was a dream simply beyond the reach of his imagination. All he wanted – all he ever sought – was a safe "collar-and-tie job" . . .

And there is some attempt at an explanation of the violence of the slums:

> Battles and sex are the only free diversions in slum life. Couple them with drink, which costs money, and you have the three principal outlets for that escape complex which is for ever working in the tenement dweller's subconscious mind. Johnnie Stark would not have realised that the "hoose" he lived in drove him to the streets or that poverty and sheer monotony drove him in their turn into the pubs and the dance halls . . . But then, the slums as a whole do not realise that they are living an abnormal life in abnormal conditions.

Speaking for himself in a newspaper article, Alexander McArthur expanded on this:

> Working-class people are now becoming "slum-conscious" . . . I want to see a real investigation of the Glasgow slums. Memories became so vivid that I just *had* to write *No Mean City* . . . The greater the "sensation" caused by *No Mean City*, the more was *No Mean City* required.

What about the "sensational" material so strongly objected to, even if based on truth?

> The boy was not quite sixteen and the girl only two years older, but they stared at each other with eyes that had been wide open to all the facts of sex since early childhood . . . Maggie Stark, undesired in her eighteenth year, was the victim of an inferiority complex peculiar to the daughters of the slums. And now, as the colour flooded her sallow cheeks, she saw release and triumph and self-assertion in her cousin's eyes. . .

> Men and women fell away from him. His eyes were glittering insanely and his bleeding lips were parted in an animal snarl . . . One furious slash laid open an enemy's face from cheekbone to jaw; another hideously gashed the second man's neck. Both collapsed, one of them with a thin, wild cry of anguish like a woman's.

Certainly this outdoes *The Rat-Pit* and *Mince Collop Close*; but it is 1935 now, and before long these matters, for better or worse, will appear almost commonplace in both literature and life. Such passages are at least guaranteed to "secure the attention of the majority of readers," and may therefore be attributable to McArthur's collaborator H Kingsley Long.

We have learned that McArthur's weaknesses as a writer embraced the rather crucial matter of "[presenting] the story [and] the characters." If that was Long's responsibility he may plausibly be said to have written most of the book. (Evidence suggests that the publisher took this view.) By the same token, Long rather than McArthur is surely behind the rather irritating in-text glossing of dialect words, which experience would tell him non-Glasgow readers could not be expected to understand; and possibly the phrasing, if not the existence, of the quasi-anthropological asides ("Johnnie Stark would not have realised . . .") which litter the text. But when we witness the sherricking of Razor King, or observe John Stark, senior, deciding to use the sink instead of padding across the wet landing to the stair-head lavatory, we must feel that, even if Long may be firing the bullets, McArthur has loaded the gun.

One would not expect a literary masterpiece from a novel written in this way, and *No Mean City* does not overturn expectations, as even its defenders admit. Contemporary reviewers outwith Glasgow (among them Edwin Muir), recognising this, also see what McArthur is saying: "It is impossible to lay down the book," concludes no less an oracle than the *Times Literary Supplement*, "with anything but a feeling of pity." A leader in the Glasgow *Evening Citizen* considers that "the book may positively be harmful," but, interestingly, this is because it "will tend to confirm the evil reputation of our city" – a reputation, in other words, which was already in place. *No Mean City* was not solely responsible for giving Glasgow a bad name.

Present-day critics, as has been said, tend to ignore *No Mean City*, and if they do notice it their views are fairly unequivocal.

> . . . it lifted a lid off its author's distorted and greedy mind
> . . . Such was the bourgeois-lumpen crap, *No Mean City* . . .

One or two critics, however, are prepared to concede more. Edwin Morgan considers that "crude and melodramatic though it was, [it] had a certain archetypal power about it," while Christopher Whyte, seeing a "realist fallacy" in proving the truth of a novel through newspaper quotations, and finding that "aimed explicitly at denunciation, it too often slips into titillation," nevertheless "cannot deny the novel's characters a sheer animal energy and excitement." What is indisputable is that something caused *No Mean City* to sell, and to keep on selling; and that something – its power? its titillation? its sales? – caused it to cast a very long shadow over Glasgow novels for years to come.

As early as 1940, for instance, it was followed by John McNeillie's *Glasgow Keelie*, an unrelievedly grim slum novel, pedestrian and predictable in spite of its many scenes of violence. That could have been dismissed as an example of the short-lived vogue which often follows a bestseller, but the bandwagon should have ground to a halt by 1962, which saw the publication of Bill McGhee's *Cut and Run*. The author, we are told, "was born and reared amid the sprawling squalor of which he writes," and this is "a story of the Glasgow slums . . . the teeming life behind the grimy walls of the great grim tenements." By the time it appeared in Corgi paperback, the publisher – the paperback publisher, also, of *No Mean City* – had *Cut and Run* classified: "a novel of the Glasgow street gangs – in the tradition of *No Mean City.*"

So Glasgow streets, slums and gangs seemed to be inseparable in the public mind – though in fact the mind was that of a London-based publishing trade – and the Glasgow novel, in a similar perception, had to serve up these ingredients. In Clifford Hanley's *The Red Haired Bitch* (1969), a lively light novel which centres on the staging of a musical about Mary Queen of Scots, there is a sub-plot concerning a young gangster, but it is out of place, pulling the whole book askew. In 1969 too, as we have seen, another

McArthur novel, *No Bad Money*, was exhumed, and the comparison
duly drawn:

> Nearly half a million copies of the Corgi edition of *No Mean
> City* have been sold. *No Bad Money* is as startling and brutal – a
> story of corruption, lust and squalor . . . in the underworld of
> Glasgow's slums.

Almost twenty years later John Burrowes's *Jamesie's People* (1984),
reaching its paperback edition, is promoted on the cover by quoting
the same antecedents – "A novel of the Glasgow slums in the
tradition of *Cut and Run* and *No Mean City*". This is in spite of
the fact that though the novel begins in full cry:

> Jamesie Nelson died the way he had lived . . . brutally, savagely,
> violently. Just as he himself had slashed, knifed, chibbed and
> booted his way to the height of fame . . . ,

it follows the careers of Jamesie's brother and daughter, who, if
no angels, certainly aren't gangsters. Even more distressing, as
several commentators have noted, is the treatment of Alan Spence's
fine short-story sequence *Its Colours They are Fine* (1977) in Corgi
paperback, with a sensational cover illustration quite alien to the
nature of the book.

Most interesting is the case of Hugh C Rae's *The Saturday
Epic* (1970). This closely observed and perceptive novel covers
twenty-four hours in the lives of a number of boys who, apart
from their regular preoccupations with sex, football and television,
run, as a normal thing, in gangs. They may or may not graduate to
serious crime in "the Mob"; for now, gang warfare is a part, but
not the whole, of their existence, and the blood and violence are
set against their quite ordinary everyday life, with a uniquely chilling
effect.

The Saturday Epic is not in fact set in Glasgow – the characters
take the train to Glasgow, when they can afford it, for high living
like tea and the cinema – but in one of the satellite towns of,

probably, industrial Lanarkshire. Such a detail does not deter the publisher from stating on the dust-jacket, "Twenty-four hours of violence by the teenagers of Glasgow make this *Saturday Epic*."

In publishers' terms, however, there is, in 1970, a problem with this. Around the time when *The Saturday Epic* was in the press, the singer Frankie Vaughan, amid considerable publicity, descended on the Glasgow housing scheme of Easterhouse with a project which, it was hoped, would improve the quality of life there and eradicate the gangs. So – a publisher is bound to worry – will this novel, depicting the contemporary scene, appear inaccurate and out of date? What if, by the time it's published, there are no gangs any more? Time for another pre-emptive strike.

The publisher (to quote the dust-jacket of *The Saturday Epic* again) "challenged [the author] as to whether recent philanthropy had not affected the temper of the young citizens of Glasgow." Hugh C Rae, who did know what (as well as where) he was writing about, replied, in a thoughtful piece much abridged here and deserving a less ephemeral siting than a dust-jacket flap:

> What went into this book was a measure of cold fear and a lot of disgust. You see, I needed no imagination to concoct the incidents, only a fistful of newspapers every morning to . . . supply the unimaginable details . . . It is no longer a game for gangsters and psychopaths played out in dark alleys and back streets . . . It's in the open now and in broad daylight and *still* we try to ignore it in the hope that it will go away . . . I have no ready answers. Like most Glasgow folk I resist facing up to the fact that nobody has really framed the true nature of the question yet.

The Saturday Epic, then – or at least its publisher – perpetuates the idea of a link between gangland fiction and real-life violent events. And it is not just that novelists refer to newspaper reports; it works the other way too. In August 1994 a death in the East End of Glasgow was reported under the headline: "Violent end of a hard man in no mean city". Though McArthur and Long declared that

"the characters [in *No Mean City*] . . . are imaginary and the book
. . . fiction", the victim in the 1994 killing was described as:

> . . . the middle-aged son of the "Billy Boys" razor gang leader
> featured in the 1930s novel *No Mean City* . . . His father . . .
> was the model for razor gang leader Johnny Stark, "King of the
> Billy Boys" in the novel.

Since no such title is claimed by Johnnie in *No Mean City*, there is
more than a touch of fiction, or journalistic wishful thinking, here.

Thus fiction and actuality jockey for position in the history
of *No Mean City* and its followers. The two can be seen to merge
in Ron McKay's not unreferentially titled *Mean City* (1995),
described on its cover as "the shocking novel of Glasgow gangland
life." The author is a journalist and his prefatory note could indicate
a non-fiction work:

> *Mean City* traces crime in Glasgow from the 1930s when the
> city was notorious for razor gangs, drunken brawling and crude
> extortions, to the present day, where the bullet has all but
> replaced the blade and the currency of crime is drugs.

But the first 1930s character we meet is none other than Peter
Stark, the quiet brother from *No Mean City*, and the central figure
whose career we follow is Peter's son John, named after his uncle
Johnnie, the Razor King.

Confused? The fictional plot of *Mean City* echoes, quite
closely in places, newspaper reports of Glasgow crime. The central
character, however, is not factually based, but derives from a
fictional creation. In his turn, that creation, Razor King, may have
been inspired by fact; or may not, for there are plenty of Glasgow
spokespersons who deny the whole thing, just like the police
superintendent in *The Factory Girl*: "I think Glasgow has been
very much abused by people of your sort . . ." Fact, fiction,
sensationalism, sober description: the whole question of *No Mean
City* and its shadow awaits further examination in terms of Glasgow
myth.

10

A Dark Satanic Place

A dark street of tall silent houses, a gloomy cavern with sickly
lamp moons receding under a long slice of night-sky . . . It
remained as an impression secret to himself, holding in a
heedless yet menacing way, in its stone walls and stark roof-
ridges, in its blind face that yet could see, a terrifying
immanence and power.   (*The Serpent*)

This is a young Highlander's view, transmuted into fiction by
Neil Gunn, of late-nineteenth-century Glasgow, the big, dirty,
poverty-ridden city which both sociologists and Victorian novelists
describe. Yet it is evidently more than Glasgow. The clue is that
young Tom has been approached by a prostitute and has spotted
her pimp in the lamplight, and he's trying to escape. Or not.

As he ran his mind told him with a fantastic humour, a wild
careless humour, an urgent beating humour, that he had a
shilling in his pocket, and that it was enough.

This is what gives the city night, "the scarlet night", its menace
and its hellish power.

City life is not infrequently seen in Scottish literature – very often through the eyes of an outsider, a countryman – as a kind of hell, in grim or ironic or sentimental opposition to the archetypal "dear green place". Lewis Grassic Gibbon stands by Loch Lomondside, thinking about Glasgow, and asks:

> Why? Why did men ever allow themselves to be enslaved to a thing so obscene and so foul when there was *this* awaiting them here – hills and the splendours of freedom and silence . . .

In historical terms, the answer is usually the simple one of economic necessity: the city is (or is perceived to be) where the work is. Alternatively, for the lad o' pairts, it's where he will find the university education which will open up the world to him and set him free from the narrow bounds of home. But young John Gourlay, in George Douglas Brown's seminal *The House with the Green Shutters* (1901), comes to grief in Edinburgh, and Eoghan, son of Gillespie Strang, ridden by an obsession, walks out of the Glasgow examination hall.

> Everything looked as simple as before . . . and yet all was changed . . . He flung back a look of hatred at the long front of the University. It was a long, grey cage . . . He shuddered . . . and gazed down on the roofs of Glasgow . . . In a little while he asked aloud, "Why am I here? I've made an ugly mess of things . . ." His brain burned with the consciousness that he was like an animal caught in the toils.
>
> (J MacDougall Hay, *Gillespie*)

Sometimes a balance can be found, in fiction as in life.

> The audience [at a *ceilidh*] is dreaming its communal dream in the middle of Glasgow . . . They're dreaming of the Isle of Skye, Tiree, Mull – the jewels in the sea, dim and sonorous, which sounds behind their lives even in the city . . . The dream is what makes the city bearable.
>
> (Iain Crichton Smith, *The Dream*)

But the city, at first, strikes the immigrant sorely:

> The greenhorn has everything to lose: . . . his innate
> convictions about the nature of human community, even the
> language in which he thinks and feels . . . The arrival of the
> immigrant propels him into abstractions and the contemplation
> of his own internal state of mind. It is a source of
> transformations and distortions of scale . . .

And this is what Eoghan Strang, like other fictional immigrants,
finds:

> The room began slowly to spin about . . . A loud buzzing sang
> in his ears. He staggered back towards the chair and felt himself
> sliding into an enormous space. The room had ceased spinning,
> and was receding from him swiftly, as if winged. He flung up
> his two arms and sank into the black void.

He has flu, but his nightmare perception of Glasgow remains with
him, and with us.

Gillespie, published in 1914, is an early manifestation of
something which becomes a noticeable feature of Glasgow fiction
from the 1930s on. This is the idea that Glasgow is not merely
dirty, crowded, unhealthy – conditions explicable, and curable, in
practical terms – but independently evil, a malevolent force.

> Glasgow itself becomes some sort of creeping malady, an
> affliction of the body or soul – its significance shifts from the
> general to the personal; Glasgow becomes part of our-
> selves. . . What we see developing in the thirties . . . is a
> sensibility that projects Glasgow as the detritus of industrialism,
> some awful cesspit of human depravity, and as a terrifying
> personal view of hell.

It may well be worth noting that this hell often has a sexual
connotation. We have seen what a state Neil Gunn's Tom, and his

Glasgow, got into over the temptation to go with a prostitute. Another Highlander, the eponymous Albannach of Fionn Mac-Colla's novel, had a decade before taken things further. Murdo's early impressions of Glasgow, though not exactly favourable, are straightforward enough, with just a hint of hidden depths.

> An occasional lamp darkened the shadows in a gaping close mouth or on the walls of the tall black houses, but the general impression was of a street in half-light, a dismal street . . . Decidedly he did not like the street, neither the look of it nor the smell of it, nor yet the sounds he began to hear coming out here and there. Least of all did he like those gaping close mouths. They were mirk black and mysterious.
>
> (*The Albannach*)

It's very different a few weeks later, when he has not only been with a prostitute but reaped the reward of sin.

> As he jerked himself loosely along the street he noticed a number of buildings standing solidly where they had not been before . . . He was suffocatingly aware of the fact that in the city of Glasgow there were at least a million people deformed, malformed, idiot-faced, loose at the mouth, with pendant ears . . . The black buildings leant steeply forward into the quadrangle where a huge crowd of people was seething about. All were shouting, chattering, laughing, grimacing into each other's faces like monkeys, their arms whirling about like flails or thrashing the air like the sails of windmills. Out of the corner of his eye he distinctly saw a man's arm fly off his shoulder, fly off, up, past the spire, over the roofs of the buildings.

Edwin Muir appreciated these surreal scenes.

> The passage that shows best the author's extraordinary power and sincerity of imagination is the one describing [Murdo's] half-mad terror in Glasgow after discovering that he was physically tainted. One may legitimately complain that here the author does not explain adequately the nature of the pollution

(he is frank enough elsewhere, as is right); but the description of Murdo's state of mind is nevertheless the work of a writer with first-rate powers.

But then in *Poor Tom*, published coincidentally in the same year as *The Albannach*, Muir had projected his own vision of Glasgow as hell.

Poor Tom has a strong element of autobiography. The family, like the Muirs, have come to Glasgow from the north; the father has died of a heart attack, as did Muir's father; Tom, brother of the central character Mansie, dies from a brain tumour after an apparently trivial accident, as did Muir's brother Johnnie. It is fiction, and the sequence of events, let alone individual incidents, cannot necessarily be expected to match up with real life, but yet there are many textual parallels between the novel and Muir's *An Autobiography* (1954):

> I walked through the slums as if they were an ordinary road leading from my home to my work . . . but if I was tired or ill I often had the feeling, passing through Eglinton Street or Crown Street, that I was dangerously close to the ground, deep down in a place from which I might never be able to climb up again, while far above my head, inaccessible, ran a fine, clean highroad . . .   (*An Autobiography*)

> All the same Eglinton Street was a queer place to take exercise in; not much health to be picked up in Eglinton Street. It had made him feel quite low-spirited at times, especially when he was tired . . . After passing through on the tramcar . . . one felt uncomfortably near the ground down here, as though walking along the bottom of a gully which was always slightly damp, while a little above the level of one's head ran a smooth and clean high road.   (*Poor Tom*)

While the relentless procession of real-life events in *An Autobiography* is sufficiently hellish, *Poor Tom* goes on to suggest that Glasgow is not just the location for all this illness and horror, but, at least partly, its cause. Mansie sees the hooligans in Eglinton Street as "plague spots . . . just plague spots," and the thoughts of his mother, Mrs Manson, are set forth more explicitly:

> In her heart she blamed Glasgow for all the misfortunes that had happened since they had come south . . . It was simply the portion of the corruption of Glasgow allotted to them, their private share of the corruption that was visible in the troubled, dirty atmosphere, the filth and confusion of the streets . . . it seemed to her that she no longer understood her family and that Glasgow had taken them and made them almost as strange as itself.

Tentatively in her mind, and specifically elsewhere in the novel, "the corruption of Glasgow" is seen as sexual. Mrs Manson is sure that "in the surroundings she knew and trusted" Mansie would never have stolen Tom's girlfriend. Though Tom himself, in happier days, compares the sexual conventions of the city unfavourably with straightforward, innocent country ways, it isn't so simple for Mansie, who finds a "shameful" childhood memory and the present-day experience of a blissful May Day procession melting into one another, leaving him helpless and apprehensive.

Clearly there is something very wrong here. Corruption is spreading, in whatever direction. Since Mansie is going out with Tom's girl, his distress at Tom's illness is inextricably mixed with guilt. Moreover, the doctor has a theory about the illness that startles Mansie: "'Can you tell me whether he ever went with – er – loose women?' then as if taking a plunge, 'with prostitutes?'" Back to back with this suggestion comes the strong image of the noseless beggar whom Mansie has seen by the suspension bridge:

> . . . the wide gaping nose cavity had actually looked as if it were being devoured by incredibly tiny indefatigable armies, and it was against them that the look in the man's face was protesting . . . And his voice! A subterranean snuffle rising to a soft hoot as of swirling wind in a chimney . . .

Even if we did not have chapter and verse in *An Autobiography*,

no one can read *Poor Tom* without realising that Glasgow to Edwin
Muir, for a time at least, was hell.

The city in Neil Gunn's *Wild Geese Overhead* is unnamed
and in some aspects archetypal: "a dark mythological city; a city of
tall dark walls, a prison-city," but can confidently be identified as
Glasgow:

> . . . the vast dark wall, burrowed with lights, of a tenement
> slum. Between him and that gaunt wall, a tramcar, tall as a ship
> and all a mass of light, went gliding swiftly and noiselessly
> by . . . Beyond the dock, the river slid past . . . Down past the
> building yards, where carpenters and riveters, dockers and
> dredgers, worked . . .

Gunn had been taken round Glasgow slums by his journalist friend
John Macnair Reid, and there is some straightforward description
in *Wild Geese Overhead*:

> They went up the close and into the narrow back court . . . The
> stone stair wound upward, like a turret stair in an ancient keep.
> At each landing the stair opened into the night, the orifice in
> the outside wall being protected by a grille of pointed rusty
> iron spikes.

But he – or at least his central character Will – is not exactly in
tune with the urban working class. Will's explanation chimes rather
with Blake's "rough innocents" view:

> "[Slum living's] not really as bad as it sounds to us or as it is
> written about. Their reactions are not our reactions . . . And
> the overwhelming mass of them are extraordinarily decent . . ."

What Gunn, like Muir, does feel and convey is the other-worldly
atmosphere of the city at night.

> They turned a corner and, all in a moment, were shut off from

the town he knew. The change was dramatic, and Will experienced a sensitive half-shrinking fear, as if he were intruding into a region, another dimension of life, where he had no right to be . . . The bright lights of the great thoroughfares were gone. Here was only a darkling light; and presently, as they passed a street entrance on their left and Will looked down it, his heart constricted. The electric globes went into the distance, one after another, balls of bluish light, suspended in impenetrable gloom.

And this underworld, like Muir's, is tainted (as Will sees it) with sex. A squabble between ten-year-old urchins involves "a challenging voice whipping out a mouthful of sexual filth." From adult arguments Will gains the same impression:

> The two favourite sexual words were used with increasing directness and with a penetrating rhythm. Overwork did not dull their variety or scatter their strength. On the contrary, all other oaths were sucked into them.

And he too has an encounter with a prostitute. It's more a meeting of minds, though, as with the working class, Will finds it pretty difficult to strike the right note:

> "Tell me this, Ivy. I want to be quite friendly with you. I do feel friendly, to tell the truth. You couldn't forget yourself and just be friendly with me? As you know quite well already, I am not in the right mood for the lusts of the flesh."

But the nightmare gathers, and Will is happy to end up in the country with Jenny, the companion to whom he has explained that slum-dwellers are different from you and me, who is "like Primavera, calm, with the sun in [her] yellow hair and birds about [her] head and daffodils in [her] hands." The contrasts drawn throughout the novel – city and country, darkness and light, filth and purity (for Will's and Jenny's courtship is full of daffodils and

Disney rabbits), place the city of *Wild Geese Overhead* firmly in the tradition of Glasgow as hell.

And the tradition continues. The Earl of Hell, the devil himself, had in fact appeared in Glasgow quite early in the history of Scottish fiction, in James Hogg's masterpiece:

> I hurried through the city, and sought again the private path through the field and wood of Finnieston . . . Near one of the stiles, I perceived a young man sitting in a devout posture, reading a Bible.
> (*The Private Memoirs and Confessions of a Justified Sinner*)

This is Gil-Martin, the "young man of a mysterious appearance" whom Robert Wringhim has actually met the day before; but Robert doesn't recognise him, because today he looks completely different, and indeed no two people can agree in describing him.

But the action of the *Justified Sinner* moves to Edinburgh, and the devil's next manifestation in Glasgow fiction has to wait until George Friel's great novel *Mr Alfred MA* (1972), which will be considered later in its chronological place. Tod is organising, among many other things, Glasgow graffiti, "the writing on the wall." Like Gil-Martin, he's perfectly friendly and nice and he explains his position in the most reasonable terms.

> "Badness is all . . . You can't fight me. I'm not invading you. I'm already inside. And I'm nobody."
>
> "Everybody," said Mr Alfred.

The full treatment of Glasgow as hell is Alasdair Gray's *Lanark* (1981), which again we must consider more fully later on. In the "realistic" world of Book One a minister says to Duncan Thaw, "I was six years a student of divinity in [Glasgow]. It made Hell very real to me." And he's not wrong, because Glasgow certainly becomes hell to Thaw, as the fantastic quasi-Glasgow of Unthank is hell to Thaw's *alter ego* Lanark.

A critic has observed that "there is a clear connection to be drawn between *Lanark* and the personalised horrors of Muir or Gibbon." It's equally clear in *Lanark*, however – as in any work of fiction it must be – that, for both Thaw and Lanark, hell is "already inside." Again to carry on a theme, we may note that part of Thaw's hell consists in his unsuccessful sexual overtures to a variety of girls, while Lanark's love-life is hardly straightforward either. Mr Alfred, a teacher, has been over-familiar with a pupil, and he too knows what hell is all about.

> "I know what you are all right [says Tod]. I know what you've been up to."
>
> Mr Alfred sagged with guilt. He waited to be accused of corrupting Rose Weipers.
>
> But Rose wasn't mentioned.

The fusion of Glasgow and its people in a novelist's vision – making hell not merely from a physical environment, not merely from a psychological state, but from both and the interaction between them – is something to bear in mind as we enter what has proved to be a golden age of Glasgow fiction.

III
KALEIDOSCOPE CITY

CHANGE RULES is the supreme graffito.

Edwin Morgan: Preface, *Essays* (1974)

11
Seedtime

The 1940s and 1950s are not generally seen as dynamic years in Scottish fiction. Historically the reason may be obvious enough; these are the years of World War II and its aftermath, when novelists, like everyone else, had other things to think about. The period is dominated by a few notable writers – most of whom had their formation, to use Muriel Spark's term, in the pre-war years of the Scottish Renaissance – and a few great novels: Gunn's *The Silver Darlings* (1941), MacColla's *And the Cock Crew* (1945), Naomi Mitchison's *The Bull Calves* (1947). It may be observed that these novels all have rural, Highland settings. *Happy for the Child* (1953), Robin Jenkins's second published novel, with its bleakly truthful picture of industrial Lanarkshire, points towards later developments.

Glasgow fiction of the period, equally, is not perceived as significant. Frequently quoted is the verdict of Duncan Thaw in Alasdair Gray's *Lanark*, pronounced, according to the novel's time-scheme, in the 1950s:

> Imaginatively Glasgow exists as a music-hall song and a few bad novels.

Mat Craig, aspiring novelist and central character of Archie Hind's

The Dear Green Place (1966), views his Glasgow (of probably the late 1950s) in similar terms.

> A city whose talents were all outward and acquisitive . . . its literature dumb or in exile, its poetry a dull struggle in obscurity.

But closer examination suggests something rather different. Half-a-dozen Glasgow novels of real note were published in the 1940s and 1950s, forerunners of the more extensive flowering to come, while a trawl through the *Glasgow Herald*'s Weekend Page during the 1950s, for instance, reveals Hind himself, among others later to become well-known names in Glasgow fiction, publishing thoughtful, well-crafted short stories, learning his trade.

The period was, indeed, a good one for Glasgow short stories. George Friel was continuing to write, though still finding it hard to achieve publication. An interesting if lesser-known short story writer, J Fullerton Miller, had more success in "little magazines" and on BBC radio until the 1960s, when a career move curtailed his writing time. His posthumous collection *Tenements as Tall as Ships* (1992) does contain the occasional couthy tale, but the majority of the stories are hard-edged small gems, set in the streets and shipyards of his native Govan. "Wheels for a Chariot" is a direct and compassionate examination of how a nice wee boy may become a criminal, hardly matched until the stories of Alan Spence twenty years later.

> After the birching Kenny got like one of my pattern chisels when the temper goes out of it. It's dull and blunt and botches everything it touches. And although jail's the place for him, I still think of that night in our house . . . and my mother saying in a whisper, "It's a funny boy who widna take wheels for a barrow."

These years, too, saw the early work of Margaret Hamilton, an under-appreciated writer whose many short stories can be found in anthologies. "Jenny Stairy's Hat", dating from 1947, covers a long period of time with great economy of style, and is equally notable because it speaks, movingly and without fuss, for a woman's experience in Glasgow, something which had scarcely ever been done in this way before.

> Jenny Stairy became a familiar figure in her own street and in the district where she worked – a skinny creature with her hair pulled back, because she had no time for frizzing, and hands and feet made ungainly by the chilblains which were a result of washing stairs and closes in all weather. She had a routine rather than a life: getting up in the morning, attending to her mother, going to work, coming back to attend to her mother, going to work, coming back.

Hamilton continued to write until the end of her life, latterly becoming known for her short poems in Glasgow dialect:

> See ma mammy
> See ma dinner ticket
> A pititnma
> Pokit an she pititny
> Washnmachine . . .

Her one published novel, *Bull's Penny* (1950), is a *tour de force*, being narrated by an "ordinary working man", Geordie McCallum, in a fluent easy Scots. Geordie is brought up on the island of Ramma (identifiable as Arran), moving, after some years at sea, to work in the industrialised towns around Glasgow. Like the central characters in Barke's *The Land of the Leal*, therefore, he is a countryman in the city, and this is another fine proletarian novel speaking for the rural, as well as the urban, working class. The Glasgow scenes are set, once more, in the politically active city between the wars. Geordie walks to Glasgow on 2 May 1926 and hears the beloved politician Jimmy Maxton speak. Maxton picks up Geordie's small son:

> "Never mind the police, it's this wee laddie you're to think on.

> Is he to grow up and face poverty and starvation the same as
> us? I'm telling you we have a duty this day – to ourselves, aye,
> but far more to our bairns . . . "

Hamilton wrote one other novel, *The Way They Want It*, set in mid-sixties Glasgow, which so far remains unpublished, while *Bull's Penny* has long been out of print and her powerful short stories have never been collected in book form.

The finest short story writer of the period is perhaps Edward Gaitens. Born in the Gorbals, Gaitens had left school at fourteen and worked at various unskilled jobs, spending two years in Wormwood Scrubs during World War I as a conscientious objector (as does his character Eddy Macdonnel in the novel *Dance of the Apprentices*). He began writing in the 1930s, encouraged by the dramatist James Bridie, to whom he later dedicated *Dance of the Apprentices*. His first short story was published in 1938.

His collection *Growing Up, and other stories* appeared in 1942 to good reviews. The *Glasgow Herald* was appreciative if a little nervous:

> [The stories] describe the life of a Glasgow working-class and
> slum tenement with an understanding and knowledge which
> have seldom been bettered . . . at no time does Mr Gaitens
> spoil the objectivity of his style by political or theological
> ideology . . . "A Wee Nip" shows an excellent appreciation of
> the physical virility and desperate gaiety of the Glasgow type.

The *Times Literary Supplement* considered the stories to have "poetic impulse and a power of visual imagination with a fine quality of objective lyricism," while Edwin Muir declared *Growing Up* "the most remarkable first book produced by any Scottish writer for several years." Meanwhile HG Wells wrote to Gaitens: "I do not exaggerate when I say that at least two of these stories are among the most beautiful in the English language."

Certainly there is beauty, and appreciation of beauty, in "The Sailing Ship":

One of many fine Glasgow short story writers, Edward Gaitens was born in the Gorbals, left school at fourteen, worked at numerous unskilled jobs and was jailed as a conscientious objector. *Growing up and other stories* was issued in 1942 and HG Wells wrote that Gaitens' stories were "among the most beautiful in the English language"

> Sunset met her like a song of praise and his heart went after her
> as she rippled past . . . She dipped slowly into the dying sun
> and the waters fanned out from her bows like flowing blood.
> Then the sun went swiftly down and her beauty was buried in
> the darkness. "Goodbye, lovely ship!" he called after her.
> "Goodbye! Goodbye, *France*!" . . . And for a long time he
> stood there bareheaded, unaware that darkness, with small rain
> and a cold wind, had enveloped his transported body.

Just as striking is the fact that this image is the closing one of a story which begins with such down-to-earth vigour: "Mrs Regan yelled at her son: 'Get up, ye lazy pig! Rise up an' look for work an' don't shame me before the neebors!'" A recent critic recognises the rarity, in Glasgow fiction, of this marriage of realism and sensitivity.

> Gaitens' finely-modelled prose recalls the Joyce of *A Portrait*
> and *Dubliners* . . . Prose of this quality is ultimately derived
> from Flaubert. Its annotations cannot be ascribed to any of
> Gaitens' characters, yet it transforms the slum ambience
> described, as if intensity of transcription could confer a special
> dignity and significance.

Gaitens served as a firewatcher in London during World War II. He returned to Glasgow after the war, and his novel *Dance of the Apprentices* was published in 1948. More readily available than *Growing Up*, this is the work most often cited in discussion of Gaitens, and thus tends to be the one on which his reputation rests. The verdict is favourable on the whole. The sociologist already quoted on the relevance of *Wee Macgreegor* writes:

> This story is much more true to the life of the mean broad
> streets of this famous quarter than are the more well-known
> play and novel of the same period [*The Gorbals Story* and *No
> Mean City*]. Its young men can see the stars even in the
> Gorbals sky.

Meantime Edwin Morgan recognises it as a forerunner:

To a reader in 1991, Eddy's encounter with the book is like a foretaste of the highly imaginative penetration of realistic material he [the reader] knows from the fiction of the 1980s.

An early Glasgow reviewer voiced reservations on technical grounds:

A compound of brilliant writing and weak construction . . . No sooner has Edward Gaitens convinced you that [the characters] are real people than he goes off into a series of unrelated short stories.

The review concludes that Gaitens "knows he is good and therefore imagines he can be careless", but this speculation is somewhat off-centre. The fact is that *Dance of the Apprentices* is largely an expansion of the short story collection *Growing Up*. Six of the stories from the earlier book appear, with minor alterations only, as chapters in the later one.

But these chapters, or stories, are among the best-written and most authentic Glasgow scenes in fiction so far. They have the air of being sketches from life, but their sharp detail is shot through with humour and understanding. The thread linking the episodes is the story of young Eddy Macdonnel and his friends, the apprentices of the title, as they grow up, go courting, discover politics, philosophy and literature, and go gladly to prison as conscientious objectors. Part Two looks forward some years to find them in the "world fit for heroes" to which they have returned, but the time-lapse causes the book to lose some of its impetus. It lives in vivid, if not always connected, episodes: the irresistible chapter which is the story "A Wee Nip" from *Growing Up*:

Every time Jimmy Macdonnel came home from sea there was a party and a few more after it till his pay of several months was burned right up. Even if Mrs Macdonnel had been six months teetotal she couldn't resist taking one wee nip to celebrate her son's return and that wee nip somehow multiplied . . .

together with the picture of Eddy horrified in his corner as his mother and father come to blows; the gambling school on the wasteground, a ragged boy keeping watch for the police from a slag-heap; and the young men, swinging between the attractions of culture and love, talking and laughing in the closemouth in the rain.

From one viewpoint, a notable addition to the tally of Glasgow novels during the 1940s was Guy McCrone's trilogy *Wax Fruit*, published (as one volume) in 1947. It calls for some special consideration, which it will be accorded in Chapter Thirteen, because of its divergence from the mainstream of Glasgow fiction, and because of its popularity. From the first it seemed to enter the public consciousness as a 'Glasgow novel', along with *No Mean City*, though no two books could be less alike.

Also in 1947 – though it had been written in 1938 – appeared *Fernie Brae*, the one published novel by JF Hendry. Hendry, a poet and translator, drew to some extent, like Gaitens, on earlier short stories, and an autobiographical element is also present, but in this case the novel attains coherence as a *Bildungsroman*. Its subtitle is "A Scottish Childhood", though David Macrae's story continues into young manhood. Detailed description well conveys the Glasgow of the 1920s and 1930s, but carries forward too the pervasive theme of restriction – by school and church, by conventional observances, by the whole Scottish (and Glasgow) philosophy of life.

> He always had to run to school . . . He rarely had time to dream or seek release from that iron obedience. He must "get on," they said, though they never told him where to go.

Leaving university without a degree, David emigrates to America – "Only the world is wide enough." The good things and the bad things of his previous life crowd about him, and at the last moment he achieves some sort of synthesis of Glasgow:

Then the vast hand of the sea reached up and wiped away the
inarticulate map of the fighting city, and, walking to the bows,
he stood in the inscrutable future.

While *Dance of the Apprentices* and *Fernie Brae* have been reissued
in recent years, there has as yet been no rediscovery of their near
contemporary, John J Lavin's *Compass of Youth* (1953). John Lavin
pursued a passion for writing in what time he could spare from
work – his jobs included those of coal-carrier, insurance agent and
library attendant – and through spells of uncertain health. He was
brought up in Shettleston, and we may again suspect some
autobiographical content in his picture of the east-end tenement
block which he called "The Square". One of the novel's strengths
is in its evocation of the sights, and especially the sounds, of the
Square:

> Night too brought its sounds. Suddenly a scream would rend
> the stillness, then more screams of terrified children. Fighter
> Smith is drunk and kicking his wife. Windows open and shut.
> Murmuring voices . . . Quietness settles again . . . A faraway
> engine whistle that conjures pictures of faraway places . . . A
> rumbling night lorry in the Main Street. Mysterious footsteps
> . . . Music . . . A ship's siren down the river . . . Wind without
> music, just blowing . . . The lamp at the close will be flickering
> fitfully . . . [ellipses in text]

The story is told in retrospect by a mature narrator:

> So long ago it seems to me now and far away . . . Recons-
> truction schemes have razed most of the buildings . . . The
> fountain too has disappeared and the buildings that formed the
> Square around it. A new generation lives there now . . .

Though his own departure from the Square has come about
through a fairytale stroke of good fortune (reminiscent of *Gael
over Glasgow)*, the device does allow for a detached view of the

generation he knew. Characters like the eccentric "Professor" and the clairvoyant Mrs Young modulate from figures of fun into human beings whose stories are told with considerable understanding and compassion.

The *Glasgow Herald* reviewer of the day appreciates this, if from a considerable height ("Character drawing is Mr Lavin's strong point . . ."), yet, as he issues his judicious approval, contrives to subtly devalue and indeed misread the book as a whole.

> Novels about life in the East End of Glasgow are generally very drab and very "tough". Sweetness and light never seem to penetrate into these parts. For that reason Mr Lavin's *Compass of Youth* is all the more welcome, for the life he depicts has many pleasant aspects, despite the fact that it is lived in Glasgow's East End . . . Good writing, humour, and understanding all go to the telling of this story of ordinary events, a story which should evoke the past for many Glasgow readers! [reviewer's exclamation mark]

But continually passing, as it were, across the narrator's vision are two figures of tragedy: Rab Young, the golden football hero blinded in a mine disaster, and Rachel McAllister, once his girl-friend and now a prostitute. The reviewer does indeed mention "Mrs Young and her tragic son Rab," but apparently he hasn't noticed Rachel. Yet as Lavin shows us the last meeting of Rachel and Rab his writing, always accurate and considered, reaches a stunning pitch of power and controlled emotion.

> "Rachel . . ." he echoed. "Is it you? . . . Hoo are ye, Ray?"
>
> "If ye really want to ken, I'm tired," she said. "An' I'm gey near drunk . . ."
>
> "Your voice," he said. "It hasna changed."
>
> "That's a' that hasna changed," she replied. . . . "How long is it since ye last spoke to me?"
>
> "They say it's only ten years."
>
> "That's a' it is," she said. "Ten years. Ye would hae been a

great fitba star by this time, Rab, an' years yet to play . . ."

"Oh my God," he said.

She sneered. "I used to think you were God. That was up to the last time ye spoke to me, ten years ago in this very close, when ye stood there – straight an' strong an' manlike – an' denied that the wean on the way was yours. That was the last time ye spoke to me, or saw me, Rab Young . . . The Whangie Pit exploded before the week was oot . . . God forgie ye . . . I canna."

"I'll take ma chance wi' Him, Ray."

"Better Him than me," she said, "for I'm still glad, even to this day, that the Whangie spared ye . . . to sprachle through the streets ye'll never see again."

Perhaps this was a bit too strong for a *Glasgow Herald* reviewer in the 1950s, or didn't chime with his perception of writing about the East End.

But these perceptions were about to be shaken, if not overturned, by the novels of Robin Jenkins. Jenkins had already published four novels when he tackled the question of Glasgow in *Guests of War* (1956). At the outbreak of World War II Glasgow schools, like those in other large cities, had been evacuated to rural areas, and Jenkins, then a teacher in the city, accompanied his primary school pupils to Moffat. This is the situation in *Guests of War*, which is on one level – but only one – a tragicomedy of confrontation, as "Gowburgh" evacuees meet their "Langrigg" hosts in a welter of preconceptions, misunderstandings and painful adjustments.

Out of the rich mixture of characters – urban children, parents and teachers, rural gentry, councillors and shopkeepers – we home in on the middle-aged Gowburgh mother Bell McShelvie, the centre round whom the book moves. A critic has written:

> To find Mrs McShelvie's equals we have to look back to Jeanie Deans and Chris Guthrie, those two Scotswomen of a like strength and moral beauty.

But it must be noted that this is in no way Bell's estimation of herself. Bell has moved from the country to Gowburgh as a child of six, and has never felt at home in the city. She is continually aware of her drab surroundings:

> The street was dirty with all kinds of litter. The buildings in which people lived were dirty too, sour-smelling, dilapidated, and chalked with amorous taunts or religious obscenities. There were various works and factories, with tall chimney-stacks filling the air with soot and smoke and stench. Even the shops were dowdy in this part of the wilderness, with dead bluebottles in the windows.

By extension she sees Gowburgh life too as drab and dirty, and eagerly offers to accompany the children to Langrigg. On this bald statement we might almost expect a Kailyard-style epiphany of rural beauty, or, more likely by this time in Scottish fiction, a discovery that not everything is rosy in the country garden.

In fact we find both and neither, because Jenkins is treading his own path and Bell is a creation of great complexity and power. From the beginning, though Bell is introduced to us "at the mouth of her close, dreaming of buttercupped meadows and green hills," we learn that:

> she could not despise those who had out of necessity turned these gloomy streets into home . . . She respected them always, and envied them often.

Further, though four of her children are going to Langrigg, she is leaving her husband and vulnerable teenage daughter behind, and recognises the truth of her neighbour's accusation: "You're right, Meg . . . That's all I'm doing, running away." And, the blackest sin in her own eyes, she knows that she welcomes the idea of war, with all its horrors, because it is affording her the chance to escape from Gowburgh. Her guilt over this never leaves her, and by the end she is looking for a way to atone.

Before it was too late, she must make amends to the folk she had betrayed. Returning to Gowburgh would do, but only if she returned cleansed and unresentful, prepared to create as much light there as she could, not only for herself and her family, but for her neighbours.

So she climbs the local hill Brack Fell to "make her vow." She doesn't reach the top, but she can look over Langrigg, which she sees as having "a faith as simple and courageous as any bird," and towards Gowburgh:

> . . . back to which she must soon go. With its huger, blacker smoke, its many emptier kirks, its thousands of tall chimneys, and its million people, it could not be in her vision as peaceful, innocent, or full of faith; but for that reason, because somehow of its vulnerability, it seemed to her even more dear . . . The very stones whose age and grime she had so often condemned would, if she were to touch them with her hand, prove to have more sustenance for her spirit than these rocks on the unblemished hill.

She goes down the hill, "smiling, with the tears running down her cheeks," somehow holding in suspension, as Jenkins does, the good and the bad of Glasgow together.

Jenkins further probes the city/country dichotomy, and the greater complexities of good and bad in the human heart, in *The Changeling* (1958). Tom Curdie is a bright slum child, a petty thief from a miserable home, who is befriended by a middle-class schoolmaster and taken on a family holiday to the Firth of Clyde. Tom's reaction to normal family life, and the none too enthusiastic reaction of the teacher's children to Tom, form the first sequence of contrasts, but a much more violent confrontation is set up when Tom's sluttish mother and her companions seek out the holiday-makers, audibly debating the nature of the teacher's interest in Tom and hinting at blackmail. The ending is one of shock and despair, and the solid ground is shifting for us, as for the characters.

Was the teacher, for instance, acting out of genuine charity? Was he following a golden vision of himself as philanthropist? He knows there's something else:

> Without doubt, at the very back of his mind from the very beginning had been the hope that his befriending of this slum delinquent child might reach the ears of authority. He had dreamed that at some future promotion interview some favourable councillor . . . would ask: "Is it the case, Mr Forbes . . . ?" His answer would be modest but effective.

We are far indeed by now from any stereotypes – the razor king, the shipbuilder, the Red Clydesider – which may have featured in previous Glasgow novels.

Just a year later appeared *The Bank of Time* (1959), the first novel by George Friel; but it is not so much a tailpiece to the promising decades of the forties and fifties as a forerunner of the highly exciting sixties, when Glasgow fiction began to find its full voice.

12

Write It from the Inside

Not long after the publication of his Glasgow novel *Wild Geese Overhead* Neil Gunn considered the question of realism in fiction; particularly urban fiction, and particularly that strand of it dealing with slum life.

> In the fiction of many rousing novelists . . . we come across [the] apparently objective treatment of observed phenomena . . . [but] it is nothing of the kind. It is no more than the description of a partial subjective reaction to unaccustomed phenomena, prompted in some measure by a distaste which is touched by fear . . . In a word, it is the point of view of the observer, not the point of view of the slum dweller observed, to which we are treated . . . The novelist . . . tends to put into the mind of the slum-dweller the feelings that he himself would experience had he to live in such a milieu.

It is, perhaps, an apologia for *Wild Geese Overhead*; at least it does seem to evince a realisation by Gunn that he had not managed to get "into the mind of the slum-dweller," or more generally the working-class character, any more than Blake had in his Glasgow novels. We have seen in Chapter Six the stern proletarian view that very few novelists had in fact accomplished this feat.

Gunn was writing in 1941. Thirty, forty, fifty years later – years distinguished by a veritable explosion in the quantity of Glasgow fiction published, and, it is generally agreed, an accompanying escalation in quality – there is still a perception that working-class characters in literature are not being treated properly. The columnist Jack McLean is savage about:

> . . . ladies with a pretence to an affection for wee Glasgow bauchles and who think the word "pawky" could be used to describe the Sistine bloody Chapel, being pawky is that good . . . This is the other side of the Glasgow Myth enjoyed by Scotland's middle classes, the other side of the No Mean City coin, with the jaunty features of the music-hall stage Glaswegian stamped upon its metal.

Tom Leonard, quoting at some length from Alexander Smith's 1865 prose work *A Summer in Skye* ("The 'Glasgow operative' is, while trade is good and wages high, the quietest and most inoffensive of creatures . . ."), observes:

> This passage could have been called "The Problem of Them". And so many urban poems, pieces of prose, and whole anthologies of either or both, have been produced for which "The Problem of Them" would have been the most honest title.

Having already noted the recurrence of this patronising tone in journals from *The Bailie* to the *Glasgow Herald* over many years, it's impossible to disagree.

But if it's so widely recognised that the working-class voice should be heard, why, an innocent enquirer might ask, doesn't a working-class writer get to work and make it heard? Time and space are lacking here to summarise the replies such an enquirer might receive.

Suffice to say meanwhile that Gunn in 1941 prescribed this very course.

> One gusty midnight, in what is called "the worst part of
> Glasgow," I stood and questioned a man about his native city
> and listened to what he had to say. He described the people in
> the dark tenement at which we were gazing . . . It was a highly
> respectable picture that he drew . . . Indeed I could feel in his
> voice his hurt contempt for those who had the insufferable
> conceit and complacency to come and inspect and report on
> [the residents] as if they were "some sort of specimen." Now if
> this man, who knew his tenements, were to write a novel
> around the lives of a few normal families who live in them, and
> write it from the inside . . .

Unfortunately, Gunn still leans to the patronising side in his vision
of the possible result:

> . . . a revelation of the higher virtues, of periods of hardship
> bravely endured . . . of happy times and grand nights, of a
> whole lot of gossip and not a little sentimentality.

But perhaps he does hit the mark by stating with simplicity that
the novel he has in mind must be written "from the inside."

Alexander McArthur, it seems, hoped he had done just that.
He had not only an agenda – to bring the state of the slums to
public attention – but a further aim:

> Time must also reveal that *No Mean City* is a book from the
> slums of which Glasgow will be proud! I am glad I wrote *No
> Mean City*. I am glad because it gives me gratification to know
> I am the natural "implement" which put the poorest of
> Glasgow's citizens on the map . . . I have been true to myself
> and also to Glasgow.

But there's a problem. William Power (who, as already mentioned,
was wont to explain that he was middle-class but couldn't help it)
put his finger on the trouble with a kind of brilliant naivety.

We had a lively debate in the Scottish PEN one evening on the

199

representation of the working class in literature . . . We did not
get anywhere in particular, probably for the reason that
literature has become so fixedly middle-class in outlook that a
working-class writer becomes middle-class by the very act of
writing successfully about the working class: he has had to
move out of the proletariat in order to see it.

One critic at least considers that Alexander McArthur came up
against the same difficulty after the success of *No Mean City*.

McArthur was still *in* the working-class of the Gorbals, but in a
curious sense, no longer *of* it. He seems to have had no
connection with the working-class movement any more than
with fellow-writers . . . [He] was effectively in a cultural no-
man's land.

And the problem is intrinsic to the theme of Archie Hind's novel
The Dear Green Place (1966).

It is hardly possible to exaggerate the importance of *The Dear
Green Place* to Glasgow fiction. On its own it stands as a fine
evocation of Glasgow – places, people, ethos – with scene after
scene where description and emotions blend.

He turned up past the gates of the Glasgow Green to the
parapet of the bridge from where he could see the old Clyde,
the colour of a back court puddle, winding in through the
Green towards the centre of the city. Up Crown Street was a
vista of dust and ashes . . . Above the buildings the sky was
harsh from a washy diffuse sunlight. He was standing on the
bridge looking over the parapet into the dirty water, at the very
spot where Boswell had stood and looked at the widest streets
in the whole of Europe. Gles Chu! Glasgow! The dear green
place!

But in the history of Glasgow fiction *The Dear Green Place* is
something more, because it examines – and personifies – the
problems of the working-class writer, specifically of the working-

class Glaswegian trying to write about his Glasgow.

These problems are many. On the most practical level Mat Craig, the central character, has very little time for writing, because he has a job to go to. He steals time from his work in order to write, though this causes "an awful feeling of self-division in him" since he has inherited the Calvinist work ethic. When, encouraged by his wife, he gives up work to concentrate on his novel, money soon runs short. His mother and brother help out, but that's not right either, in their eyes or in Mat's own.

> "Look," [his mother] said, "is it not about time you were starting work again? . . . Writing! You've nae time to think of things like that. You've got a wife and wean depending on you . . . Do you realise that *food* has been brought into this house?"

This arises from, and points up, the second problem, a major one: the perception – shared by his family, society as he encounters it, and Mat himself – that "writers are always other people." Mat's mother is again the one to articulate her feelings: "There's something in all this writing business I don't like. It's not for the likes of us." Mat passionately maintains that he doesn't write "because of any fancy notions . . . or to indulge a whim . . . or because of some daft social aspiration . . ." but at times he is driven to wonder:

> . . . how he, Mat Craig, a labourer in the slaughter-house, would have the effrontery to think of himself as capable of lifting himself by the bootlaces . . . of breaking through into major art.

Worst of all, his writing isn't even going well, partly at least, he begins to feel, because he is not writing in his own language, the language of the people he wants to write about. (This particular problem will be taken up in Chapter Eighteen through such writers as Tom Leonard and James Kelman.) He can't do so, it seems to him, because that language is:

> [a] gutter patois . . . [a] self-protective, fobbing off language
> which was not made to range, or explore, or express; a
> language cast for sneers and abuse and aggression . . . a
> reductive, cowardly, timid, snivelling language cast out of jeers
> and violence and diffidence; a language of vulgar keelie
> scepticism.

His struggles come together in a bleak climax when his own voice,
"a shrugging Glesca keelie voice," informs him that he's "nut
quoted. A gutless wonder like you . . . ," and on the cold deck of
a Clyde ferryboat he vomits up his disappointment and misery.
On the way home he sees "the coat-of-arms of his dear green
place, cast in iron" and as the jingle echoes through his mind:

> This is the tree that never grew,
> This is the bird that never flew . . .

we are to understand that "never" is the operative word. Yet *The
Dear Green Place* is a beginning, not an end.

Hind himself has since worked in theatre and has written,
but not so far published, a second novel. Alasdair Gray has described
the situation with gentle and humorous warmth:

> Master Hind . . . whose history of Glasgow intituled *The Dear
> Green Place* is sufficient for his fame, and who remaineth (until
> such time he overflow again) a profound cystern of
> unexpressed wisdom . . .

However, Mat Craig's literati friends have assured him that there
is:

> . . . a new something in the air, changes coming about, a new
> flowering of working-class literature, a new tone.

Mat doesn't agree; but not long after *The Dear Green Place* was published, writers like Leonard and Kelman were at work. In Glasgow fiction as a whole there was most definitely "a new something," as will be seen in Chapter Fourteen.

One further problem remains: that however well the working-class author writes about his or her own milieu, the result is going to be read mainly by middle-class people, who, by definition (as we have seen McLean and Leonard bear witness), won't understand. Leonard spells it out in his remarks on urban writing and anthologies:

> The works assume that those supposedly described don't read the literature that supposedly describes them . . .

William McIlvanney considers this question in some depth with regard to the writing of his 1975 novel *Docherty*, set in the mining community of "Graithnock".

> I knew I was after a book that would make no concessions on the truth I believed I saw to anybody, not to the people I was writing about, not to the people most likely to read it, not to the intellectual "supporters" of the people I was writing about – not to anybody . . . It meant that, while I was writing partly on behalf of people many of whom didn't read much, the prose would in no way make obeisance to that fact. It would express my vision to the limits of my own articulacy, not pretend to imitate theirs . . . This in turn meant the risk of alienating some readers by expressing the unspoken experience of characters to a level beyond their own achieved articulacy. But such a risk was central to the endeavour.

Yet even this sensitive approach has not provided the last word on working-class fiction. McIlvanney himself has been criticised for the vision of "working-class heroism" presented in the article quoted above. The novels and short stories of James Kelman, especially perhaps since his Booker Prize success of 1994, have seized the attention of middle-class and working-class readers alike, but, as we shall see, praise and censure for his work have not necessarily divided along class lines.

And in very recent years, during an East of Scotland burgeoning of new writing, the fiction of Irvine Welsh – *Trainspotting* (1993) and its successors – is famously being bought by people who don't buy books. Would Mat Craig recognise Welsh's blackly funny brutality as an aspect of the working-class life for which he was trying to speak? It's doubtful if Mat's mother would, but equally it's certain that thousands of contemporary young people do. The story of working-class fiction has far to go yet.

13

The Middle-Class Void

The discussion of Glasgow working-class fiction has brought to light one recurrent complaint: that middle-class writers have taken up working-class themes and made a mess of the job. Critical irritation at the misrepresentation of working-class life has perhaps served to distract us from questions which surely ought to be asked. What are middle-class writers doing in this field anyway? Why are they so irresistibly drawn to write about working-class life? Why is there such a small body of Glasgow middle-class fiction? As early as 1903 a history of Scottish literature had recognised:

> . . . the immense amount of stuff, as yet practically untouched and lying ready to the novelist's hand, in the life of the Scottish professional, commercial, and middling classes.

Yet ninety years later the novelist Allan Massie could still remark:

> What we know as the Glasgow Novel has a tone all its own. It is gritty and angry. It tells the story of men and women – though more usually men – who have been cheated by their experience of life . . . [But] there has always been another Glasgow; there still is, and few writers have dared to deal with it.

In fact rather more writers have dared in this direction than the reviewer implies. We have observed the strand of "mercantile" Glasgow fiction beginning with Bailie Nicol Jarvie and running through *The Entail, St Mungo's City, Justice of the Peace* and *Mungo*. George Blake's exploration of middle-class mores takes place mainly in Greenock, but one novel in his "Garvel" sequence, *The Westering Sun* (1946), brings Bluebell, the last of the Oliphants, to Glasgow between the wars. This is the very city we know from *The Shipbuilders, Major Operation* and *Hunger March*:

> The whole city was one occupied by the army of the workless. They roamed the fashionable shopping streets, finding a vague interest in windows still richly stocked with goods for the well-to-do. They stood in dark knots at the corners of their shabby streets, shadowed by the tall tenement houses. They stood in long, slow queues leading to the doors of what they called the Buroo. Now and again they demonstrated, especially the young ones. . .

Bell, quelling a nagging conscience with the reflection that "the action of the individual must be negligible", opens a tearoom, runs it efficiently, and develops it into a catering chain.

> At four o'clock of that winter afternoon Bluebell's was packed. There they were . . . the womenfolk of the suburban, provincial *bourgeoisie* crowding the place that had been deliberately designed to allure them: the tea-room that was the fashion of the hour; the tea-room that subtly flattered them with a scheme of decoration few among them could have safely chosen for themselves . . .

If Blake's gifts, as we have suggested, are in the area of social comment rather than literature, they are fully exercised here, and two sides of Glasgow come together with considerable effect.

In more recent years there have been purposive and creditable attempts at Glasgow middle-class novels, such as Evelyn Cowan's *Portrait of Alice* (1976) and Margaret Thomson Davis's *The*

Prisoner (1974) and *A Very Civilised Man* (1982). (The central characters of these novels, as of *The Westering Sun*, are women; it's tempting to see a polarisation, working-class Glasgow with its macho men and middle-class Glasgow with its feminine concerns.) One writer in particular, Ronald Frame, has shown what he could do with the Glasgow middle class through his short story "Paris", a little gem.

> Miss Caldwell and Miss McLeod had met in the late 'sixties, as recently retired ladies and as habituees of Miss Barclay's tea-room in Byres Road . . . Bizarrely it had taken them both a year and a half just to discover what the other's first name was. At last they'd found out an address too . . . but neither had invited the other to her home or could have contemplated it.

However, none of Frame's distinguished novels has so far taken Glasgow as a setting.

We have already mentioned, and should now consider, Guy McCrone's *Wax Fruit* (1947). The apotheosis of the Glasgow middle-class novel, it is also unusual among Glasgow novels because of its publishing history.

> *Wax Fruit* had one of those spectacular successes that from time to time take the publishing world by surprise. Published in 1947 in quite a modest imprint – restricted by still existing wartime paper-rationing – it was taken up by an American publisher, became chosen as a book of the month, and soon jumped into the best-seller class. Eventually, after a French translation had enlarged its readership, [it] sold a million copies.

With its sequels *Aunt Bel* (1949) and *The Hayburn Family* (1952), *Wax Fruit* follows the fortunes of the Moorhouses and Hayburns, prosperous merchants and engineers, from 1870 to 1901. It might therefore be classed as a historical novel, but that was not really McCrone's goal.

I decided that if I had any gifts as a novelist, they lay in a certain ability to portray family life. The tie of blood holds a great interest for me. I cannot tell you why . . . My first motive in going back to Victorian days, then, was merely to have room to start my family back a bit and follow it through more than one generation.

Conscientiously researching Victorian books, photographs and newspapers – especially the advertisement columns – he "became stimulated and intensely curious."

I found myself in a city that was my own, and yet was oddly strange to me. Where people with the same kind of mind as mine met their very different problems in a very different way. Where standards were less flexible, yet where emotional needs were much the same.

And so the details gleaned from McCrone's research, if sometimes a trifle obtrusive, are generally well enough assimilated in *Wax Fruit* to reach us through a Victorian, yet timeless, middle-class Glasgow mind:

A Victorian row, "commanding a beautiful view of the brilliant parterres of the Botanic Gardens, with the umbrageous woods of Kelvinside beyond", set back from the placid, easy-going traffic of a Great Western Road, where once in a while a green car rattled past on its way to and from Kirklee . . .

They couldn't have furniture that would make a fool of them. Everything must have the label solid or good . . . [Bel] spent a night entirely sleepless over a walnut china cabinet that had cost much . . . She had not been too sure of it at the time, and now that it stood in its place she had just discovered a thin line of gold metal inlay. Was that bad taste? What would people say?

Following his epiphanic discovery that Victorian Glaswegians are just like us, McCrone manages to bring life to everyone's sepia family photographs:

In his heart Arthur knew that Bel was as strong as a horse. But
the strength of horses is not romantic . . . Politer to assume
that any puff might blow her away, though you knew perfectly
– and were thankful for it – that her agile young body would
stand a hurricane.

His exploration of the younger couple Phoebe and Henry Hayburn
is interesting too. Their passionate youthful marriage and early
years in Vienna extend the scope of *Wax Fruit* beyond the slightly
constricted bounds of the Moorhouse world. A critic has noted:

> Clearly intended as a sketch of the New Woman, determined to
> live her own life, Phoebe too is enveloped by the family ethos,
> as powerful in its unassuming way as that of any London
> Forsytes. Her failure to strike out for herself makes a less
> exciting story, but it is all the truer to the facts of Glasgow
> middle-class life.

But McCrone knows that Glasgow middle-class life, like any life,
has its hidden depths. By *The Hayburn Family* Phoebe and Henry
are in early middle age and Henry's natural son Robin is part of
their family. Robin has his own adventures, and a visitor comes to
see him:

> And the part that she had played in Robin's sorry story?
> There was, of course, the harsh, the Moorhouse answer.
> But Phoebe's untamed heart refused this rigid judgment . . .

For all that the Moorhouses are the backbone of his fiction,
McCrone views them with detachment and a not uncritical eye.

After considering all possible candidates, however, we are
still left with a comparatively small number of Glasgow middle-
class novels, which, apart from *Wax Fruit*, have never greatly seized
the public imagination. "What we know as the Glasgow Novel" –
though its author by now may be either traditionally class-conscious
or theoretically classless – is, by and large, a story of working-class

life. It's as if middle-class writers find no interest or inspiration in the middle class. Why should this be so?

One possible reason was well expressed some twenty years ago, though it had been around for much longer.

> The densely interwoven street-life of the traditional city . . . has always been feared by the middle classes; who knows what unpleasant radical ideas might not be brewed up in those hugger-mugger enclaves of the proletariat?

Middle-class life, by this theory, is familiar and safe, therefore uninteresting. Working-class life is unfamiliar to the middle-class writer; slightly frightening, because of its strangeness, but fascinating for this very reason. What it hides might be just what he's looking for. And somehow it's more accessible. Middle-class life (as McCrone reminds us) can't really be devoid of human interest, because the middle class are human too. But perhaps it takes more digging to get to the interesting bits, because of a middle-class tendency brilliantly described by Alan Sharp. His west end is actually in Greenock, but its clone can be found in any town or city, Glasgow not least.

> All the closed doors and muslined windows. All the empty gardens and the tulips, the thick, pervading stench of order, of the governed, regulated world of priorities. And in its midst . . . the special school where the mutations milled at playtime. . . [Edna's] world was a west end, the landscape of her soul where the ugly things were discreetly hidden, trundled swiftly through the careful avenues in a special grey bus, special so that if you didn't want to look you didn't have to. . .
>
> (*A Green Tree in Gedde*)

But how did Edna come to inhabit this dreadful landscape of the soul? Edwin Muir has a suggestion.

> One of the distinguishing marks of Industrialism is the permanent contrast between the people who live amidst it, if

they are sensitive in any degree or even wish to exist in decency, and all their surroundings. As these people cease to feel the painfulness of this contrast – and they are bound to do so – they inevitably become insensitive; and I think one may assert without being unfair that the middle- and upper-classes of towns like Glasgow . . . have a sort of comfortable insensitiveness which cannot be found in any other class or in any other place. There may be many intelligent and humane men and women in these classes, but somewhere or other they are blunted or dead; they have blind-spots as big as a door: the door of their office or of their house.

Who would choose to write about these dead, insensitive and blind people when the (apparently) vivid, extrovert life of the working class lies ready to hand?

But Muir goes on to assign a specific reason for this acquired insensitivity:

It is not their fault, but the fault of a system which forces them to gather money out of the dirt. But the self-protective need to ignore this involves a deliberate blunting of one whole area of their sensitivity.

What he is naming is a pervasive, innate, yet unacknowledged sense of shame. To admit it is to strip off a layer of skin which protects, even though it numbs, the writer's soul. It takes painful effort, therefore, for a middle-class writer in urban Scotland to break through and write with truth.

We may recall Dot Allan's uneasiness about the role of the middle class in depression Glasgow, and, farther back, George Roy's observation of Victorian Glasgow matrons under the cloak of entertainment. Neither Allan nor Roy, perhaps, could quite throw off the skin of upbringing and convention. A great novel still remains to be written about middle-class Glasgow, but its writer may have to be particularly honest and brave.

What was happening to Glasgow fiction in the 1960s may be seen as not unconnected with what was happening to Glasgow. The photography of Oscar Marzaroli documents the demolition of large tracts of the city, Jeff Torrington's award-winning novel *Swing Hammer Swing!* (1992) is one set in this strange time.

14

Change Rules

What happened to Glasgow fiction in the 1960s? Perhaps it is not being too quixotic in bracketing it with what, during the same decade, was happening to Glasgow.

Most dramatic – because of the fame, or notoriety, of the area affected – was the slum clearance process which razed the old Gorbals, relocating people in high-rise blocks or dispersing them to outlying housing schemes and new towns. The brilliant photography of Oscar Marzaroli documents Gorbals before, during and after the demolition, while Jeff Torrington's novel *Swing Hammer Swing!* (1992) is set in this strange interstitial time.

> Fires fuelled by wooden beams burned in cleared sites. Rubble was being trucked from busted gable ends and demolishers worked in a fume of dust and smoke . . . On a gutted site near a fire that drizzled sparks on him, a greybeard sat in a lopsided armchair, placidly smoking his pipe.

The same few years saw the implementation of road development plans which effectively devastated inner-city areas like Cowcaddens, Anderston, Townhead and Govan. It was another drastic and painful *aggiornamento* which yet probably had to come. The local historian Joe Fisher has commented on some of Marzaroli's photographs of motorway construction:

> The destruction of entire living areas of Glasgow . . . in order to run concrete rivers through deserts of red blaes generated a great deal of adverse criticism . . . And yet it is difficult to stand, say, at Charing Cross and watch the dusk-rush of glowworm car lights down the deep trench leading to the Kingston Bridge and not to wonder how our horse-and-cart roads could ever have coped with such traffic flows.

But there can be no doubt that roads and rehousing between them entirely changed the face of Glasgow. Now the secure grid, "on which," as one observer has written, "the patterned play of character and narrative might be plotted," was replaced by an open city of high-rise blocks and flyovers with wastelands between, providing the backdrop to a host of other changes, good and bad.

The last tramcars ran; traditional industries closed down or were radically reorganised. Old theatres and music-halls closed, though an exciting new flowering came to the Citizens' Theatre, now standing almost alone in the demolished Gorbals. In this football-crazy city Celtic became the first British team to win the European Cup. The unsolved Bible John murders added another thread to Glasgow's dark mythology. And felt-tip and aerosol graffiti, including the mysterious notation YA BASS, became part of the cityscape, not unobserved by writers:

> On the walls of some of the old buildings Christabel was shown the evidence of real local power . . . the names of local gangsters, and some of the gangs are eighty or ninety strong. Written large: "Handy Barr Rule" – him and his weirdly nicknamed partners in fear; Wee Tam and Bike Cheyne and Pluto-with-a-knife.
> Mozart stopped the car by a disused Congregational church hall the other side of Gallowgate to show his guest a significant message chalked up in a childish hand. It read, very wee: This is Goblin Land.
> "There's Glasgow true," Mozart said . . .
> (James Kennaway, *The Cost of Living Like This*)

1960s Glasgow was a live and scary place, an ambience to which Glasgow writers were bound to respond. Some, equally, were bound to make their response in the key of nostalgia – preserving the tenements, rather than observing the demolition sites – and this is what Edwin Morgan saw in 1962.

> Too much of the experience of living in Scotland . . . is not being reflected by novelists and playwrights. Life in a "new town" like East Kilbride – in some of the huge suburban housing estates – on a hydro-electric construction scheme – at Dounreay or Hunterston [nuclear power stations] – in a recipient town for Glasgow "overspill": there is so much experience that seems to cry out for literary embodiment, for the eye of a sharp but sympathetic observer to be turned upon it.

All this experience was later to find its observers, and even in the early 1960s there are stirrings of change. Hugh Munro may seem reactionary in choosing a setting of tenements and shipyards between the wars for *The Clydesiders* (1961), but he manages to examine, in a notably even-handed way and without exaggeration, the vexed "religious question" of the West of Scotland. Chaim Bermant opens a window on the hitherto unexplored Glasgow Jewish community in *Jericho Sleep Alone* (1964). Clifford Hanley had found immediate success with his impeccably urban kailyard reminiscences *Dancing in the Streets* (1958). However he, like Morgan, had also seen that:

> . . . hordes of Scottish authors have worked on the tenements, but hardly anybody has even noticed the material in the council housing schemes. I took a nibble at this myself . . .

He is referring to his novel *The Taste of Too Much* (1960). Hanley's literary style is light and racy, and on the surface his work provides a constant rattle of dry Glasgow humour. The terrible neighbour Mrs Dougan has scalded herself:

"Oh, you're awful good, Mr Haddow," she moaned. "Naebody ever had a better neighbour, you've been that good to me this day, it was a bilin' kettle, I was just makin' a wee fly cup, oh it's terrible sore, no, it's a lot better. I would just have deceased all my lee lane if you hadn't of come, Mr Haddow, wi' naebody but the poor wee wean frightened out his wee wits. There, son, don't greet, your poor old Gran's aw right. Aw shut your girnin' face, you snivellin' wee get," she added, as the pain gave a jump . . .

But this (like *Jericho Sleep Alone*) is another Glasgow *Bildungsroman*, and the boy out with his girlfriend is groping after a different form of expression.

"I'm thinking about three thousand four hundred and eighty-two things at once . . . I'm thinking that the street lamps are shining over there, and what's the time? And this plastic mac feels shiny, and the colour of your hair, and the first time I took you home, and how nice it is to be here with you, and the rough nail on my pinkie, and the soft bit on your cheek, and I can't see any stars, and the dark colour of your eyebrows – how do eyebrows get that shape?"

Glasgow was also appearing on a wider stage. Alexander Trocchi famously clashed with Hugh MacDiarmid in 1962 over a question of nationalism and internationalism, contested no less fiercely for the fact that MacDiarmid had never read Trocchi's work. Trocchi on that occasion was appearing on a panel of Scottish writers, but his long residence abroad and his international connections have often tended to exclude him from surveys of Scottish literature. Yet he was born in Glasgow and his novels *Young Adam* (1961), set largely on the Forth and Clyde Canal, and *Cain's Book* (1963) contain sharply observed Glasgow scenes. (And this is not to mention his pornographic novel *Thongs* (1956), whose central character has the unimpeachably Glasgow credentials of being brought up in the Gorbals, daughter of a Razor King.)

The narrator of *Cain's Book*, Joe Necchi, is living on a scow on the Hudson River while writing a book (entitled *Cain's Book*), and his thoughts regularly return to his Glasgow childhood – to his red-haired mother who keeps a boarding-house:

> Her hands the texture of dried prunes – my mother used a green block of cosmetic called "Snowfire" to take the chapped look out of them, but they were never long enough out of water for it to make any difference. Including the lodgers, she had to launder for twelve people, and cook for them, and clean up their mess. It gave her great pleasure to read about and to see pictures of the Queen.

And he thinks of his long-unemployed father, a richly unexpected creation, comic yet touching, who spends his days cleaning the bathroom and defending it against lodgers who are unreasonable enough to want to use it.

> He would stamp and rage in the kitchen, shouting: "Always the bloody same! Got to clean the bloody place twice! Leave towels all over the bloody place!" . . . On bad days he was still cleaning the bathroom when those of us who came home for lunch returned. And then my mother would go nervous and angry to the door and knock on it: "Louis! Would you please finish up in there! Mr Rusk wants to use the bathroom before he eats lunch!"
>
> A cry of pained protest from my father. "Bloody people keeping me back! Can't get my bloody work done! . . ."

Of course we must not be tempted to forget the New York (and London and Paris) section of *Cain's Book*, background to the narrator's present life of drifting and drugs. A commentator has fairly observed:

> Most critics chose to praise the sections set in Glasgow for their vividness, suggesting that if Trocchi had sustained this tone and setting throughout he might have written an excellent novel. Well he might, though it would have been a very different book from the existing one.

But the Glasgow scenes are important, as Edwin Morgan has recognised:

> At a second reading, the dramatic function of the "embedded" scenes from his early life become clearer; there is a similar proceeding in Gray's *Lanark* and *1982, Janine,* and in some of the films of Tarkovsky.

The Glasgow of these early 1960s novels is still a settled city of habit and tradition; even the 'Whiteknowes' estate in *The Taste of Too Much* is, we are carefully informed, "one of Glasgow's older housing schemes." The new schemes are different, as Hugh C Rae makes clear in *Night Pillow* (1967).

> The flats, four stories high, enclosed a concrete courtyard in which a genteel architect had envisaged an adventure playground of revolutionary design, and a practical-minded contractor had eventually built a series of obstacles in defence of five stunted trees. In common with several hundred other families, the Farrells had been transplanted here from the heart of the dark clan country along the south bank of the Clyde . . .

Even more alien are the high flats:

> The side of the building dropped smoothly to the asphalt below. He could see the shine from a few lit windows on the wall beneath him, against the night air, but the windows themselves down the plumb wall were like thin pencil lines, or razor-cuts . . . He was like a rabbit in the side of a hill; no, even less individual than a rabbit: a bee in a box hive, a bee in its cell.

The story of the Farrell and Leishman families gains in bleakness, and claims our compassion, from our knowledge of this cold background.

The changes of the decade are recorded, and their impact

movingly acknowledged, by Robert Nicolson in his 1966 novel *A Flight of Steps*.

> "I see they've demolished quite a lot of the buildings," [Mr Conrad] said casually. "They're taking the street down at quite a rate . . . It won't be long before they reach here, Mrs Ross. Have you thought about where you would like to go when you have to leave this house?"
> She did not answer; but now she looked at him and her hands, in her lap, enfolded each other and worked round with a slight rasping sound . . .
> "Think about it, Mrs Ross, will you? Get used to the idea of leaving here quite soon. You know you've got to, don't you? You know you've got to go?"
> She spoke at last. "I know," she said.

Nicolson had earlier depicted this old woman in *Mrs Ross* (1961), (in paperback *The Whisperers*) and the two novels are best considered together, since they form in effect one unsentimental, humorous, tender story, a largely unrecognised masterpiece of Glasgow fiction.

Mrs Ross lives in a condemned tenement, sustained by her dreams of an imaginary past of great wealth and high position, and thinking herself continually spied on by watchers – "the whisperers" – somewhere in the building. The understanding Mr Conrad is a clerk in the National Assistance Board office to which Mrs Ross writes frequent and lengthy letters of explanation and complaint:

> "From," she wrote, "Margaret Ross, nee Cattanach, 47 Shawl Street, 2 up left, Hereditary Countess of Aird and All the Islands to the West, Comtesse de la Bruyere, Laird (on father's side) of Struther and the Adjoining Lands, Lady of the Manor of Great d'Arcy, with other titles and assistance book reference number 86-27946 . . ." (*Mrs Ross*)

In the first novel she is rescued, cleaned up, restored to health and reunited with her husband, but this is only an episode in her life, later dimly remembered.

> Had she been asleep? She thought she had and she thought that she had dreamed: something remained of distance and darkness and a voice crying a name. But had it really been a dream? She lay, now wide awake, and listened until . . . very far away, and very faint, she heard again the voices of the whisperers.

A Flight of Steps is a true continuation, its events taking place at most a year or so after those in *Mrs Ross*, even if she by now remembers them as being "a long time ago."

She has returned to her routine, her daily itinerary from home to public library via promising litter-baskets, but there's something different, which she sees but (as Mr Conrad realises) doesn't, or won't, take in.

> Shawl Street was coming down . . . Buildings not far from the one in which she lived had already been condemned and were in the process of being demolished to make way for Corporation properties where former slum-dwellers would be housed layer upon layer up into the sky in flats containing every mod.con. Already workmen were on the job, banging away at the old stones, reducing one time homes to dust and rubble. Mrs Ross looked about her, examining the new day, then chose a direction and began to walk.   (*A Flight of Steps*)

There can be no happy ending to the story, and none is attempted.

> She rested against a stone parapet; and beneath her were trees and night-darkened levels of grass, and beneath these the lights of the town streaming away through the darkness to the river and beyond . . . She leaned against the wall and gave a sound that was like a long, deep sigh . . .

Nicolson, who himself was an officer of the National Assistance

Board, sees, and makes us see, the independent, vulnerable old woman inside the grotesque behaviour and the dirty clothes. The impression which remains is of her odd happiness among the mice and old newspapers in her filthy little flat:

> Then she saw something through the dirty window. It was a star, and she saw it as though she had never seen a star before. She rubbed the dusty pane with her hand, polishing the star, and peered out at the sky above a black forest of chimneys. "Twinkle, twinkle, little star," she said, and was filled with mirth. She leaned her untidy head against the cold glass and watched the sky until the kettle boiled.   (*Mrs Ross*)

The importance to Glasgow fiction of the publication, in mid-decade, of Hind's *The Dear Green Place* has already been recognised. Equally ground-breaking – and, for various reasons, probably attracting more attention in its time – was Alan Sharp's *A Green Tree in Gedde* (1965). Again, its influence on West of Scotland writers is hardly in doubt. Liz Lochhead remembered it years later.

> Alan Sharp, there was a big discovery! I was 18 and there was this great big fat paperback book with a lot of sex in it, much of it happening in Kelvingrove Street. And I knew where that was! Alan Sharp had written this book nearly all set in Greenock, and that was nearly as ordinary a place as Motherwell . . .

Not everybody from Motherwell, or Greenock, or Glasgow, took this view. *A Green Tree in Gedde* has been quoted in connection with middle-class attitudes, and certainly Edna's west-end world was not ready to contemplate many of the relationships, heterosexual, homosexual and incestuous, explored by Sharp, far less to believe that they might be happening next door. But for Glasgow writing this kind of joyous frankness was long overdue. Apart from the sex, or rather contiguous with it, *A Green Tree in Gedde* displays a Joycean exuberance of language unknown in Glasgow fiction outside the novels of George Friel, who, as will be seen, was concurrently working along these lines but only slowly beginning to achieve publication.

Another element of *A Green Tree in Gedde* is particularly worth noting for our purpose. Though the characters follow their destinies far beyond the West of Scotland, the novel is in fact dedicated to Greenock:

> . . . to its buildings
> and chimneys and streets
> and the glimpses they have afforded me
> of the river and the hills

As this would suggest, the passages set in Greenock, and also in Glasgow, have a quality of heightened observation far beyond the merely descriptive. The observer here is John Moseby (Edna's husband, though the marriage is in a state of flux), and his current thoughts and emotions, as in *The Dear Green Place*, affect the meaning of what he sees. Indeed, he is aware of a symbiotic relationship between himself and the city.

> Outside, Glasgow. He had never really seen it before, he
> realised. Not really, not clearly . . . It blockaded the mind,
> fractured vision on its multiple baffle walls, repeated itself
> endlessly, the great inarticulate sprawl, saying stony, grimy
> words, sentences, whole pages of a prose reduced to drabbest
> utterance, an epic of the herd, sweltering in proximity.
> Through its streets the mind might wander for ever and not
> come upon a single image of transcendence . . . It made him
> see something . . . about Cathie and himself. That their affair
> was, in this new sense, Glaswegian, it had this incarcerated,
> airless aura to it, this unease that lay upon the city-dweller, that
> beyond what they had something unguessably better existed. . .

As place and people share centre stage, this important passage may surely lay claim to marking the beginning of the new Glasgow fiction.

Similarly the city is an integral part of both scene and action in Robin Jenkins' *A Very Scotch Affair* (1968). The setting here is the east end, specifically Bridgeton, which is regarded by more than one character as "a ghetto", permanently marking its inhabitants with its own depressed drabness as well as the stigma of social inferiority.

> These women, sour-faced and middle-aged most of them, laid waste by years of ghetto marriage, had come out of their caves this pale April afternoon not only to pay homage to their dead comrade but also to demonstrate their undying hatred of him who had been guilty of worse than wife-beating or child-cruelty: he had escaped, leaving his wife behind to struggle by herself with all those drudgeries and pettinesses that made up ghetto life, and that had left them, after thirty or more years of it, haggard with the onset of the menopause and repellent sexuality.

Mungo Niven, whom they hate so much, is pitilessly drawn. In an act of near-incredible callousness he has left his dying wife Bess and gone abroad with another woman. The affair has ended, and he has come home just in time for Bess's funeral. We see him through the eyes of the horrified neighbours – "Think shame, ye heartless brute. Whuremaister" – but we have also seen his version of events through his own eyes, and therefore we are left with questions about him. Can he be quite such a monster as the neighbours think him? But how can he possibly consider himself justified in such a betrayal? He inclines at times to think it was Bess's fault, and certainly never blames himself, but there's another possibility:

> He was not so sure now that she had contributed more to his degeneration than he had to hers. He had perhaps blamed and punished her for inadequacies neither of them could help.

The blame, in this reading, lies with the ghetto, and not the least of our questions about this complex and disturbing book must be whether the ghetto has in fact made Mungo the man he is. If it has – if it's not just another convenient scapegoat for Mungo – the city is, in a much more subtle way than the earlier slum novels could contrive, a prime mover in the action, and *A Very Scotch Affair* marks a high point in the story of the Glasgow novel.

William McIlvanney's first novel *Remedy is None*, published in 1966, signalled the appearance of a major writer. Kilmarnock-born McIlvanney brought a relatively new outsider perspective to Glasgow fiction. His Glasgow is the metropolis of a sprawling urbanised countryside and the action moves between city and small town. So do his characters, and their interaction in different novels justifies a recent critic's view that McIlvanney may have "achieved a fusion of his two locations to make one world of his fiction, the West of Scotland as city and post-industrial wasteland."

This achievement is still in the future with *Remedy is None*, in which Charlie Grant from Kilmarnock is, as McIlvanney was, a student at Glasgow University. The death of his father has a profound effect on him; the strong autobiographical element here – repeated in *The Kiln* (1996) – was to be suspected even if McIlvanney had not revealed it in interview. There is also, however, a calculated parallel with *Hamlet*, since Charlie's mother has deserted his father for another man, and this new marriage becomes the focus for the boy's grief and anger. The climax is melodramatic, but the book as a whole impresses as the exploration of a questioning mind at the point of unbalance.

A Gift from Nessus (1968), in contrast, is the more convincing for its avoidance of melodrama. McIlvanney here contrives a low-key tragedy. Eddie Cameron, unhappy in his work, chafed by his suburban marriage, drifting in his affair with a chance-met girl, tries unheroically but doggedly to find a way out. When he breaks off his affair, his mistress drowns herself, and he and his wife confront each other in a closely observed final scene. The ambiguity of the ending, tentatively hopeful, points forward to the complexities of McIlvanney's later work.

In the 1960s, at last, George Friel's brilliant novels began to achieve publication. *The Bank of Time*, as already noted, was in fact published in 1959, but this success followed years of effort – Friel had been writing and submitting novels since his return from war service – and did not assure automatic acceptance for his future work.

It is probably true to say that Friel's novels, for many years, puzzled people – prospective publishers, readers, and all but a few critics – because they met in some ways, yet not in all, the perceived criteria for Glasgow fiction. The editor of his short stories recognises this:

> A fiction of working-class Glasgow, but without any production-line gangsters and headline-grabbing razor kings; . . . here is no pander to the latter-day urban kailyard of a Jack House or Cliff Hanley; no orthodox Red Clydesider . . . no laconic, bad-mouthing giro novel. Friel is not *like* any other Scottish writer, and fits no handy compartment.

There is realism in his books, too much for some readers (it's the police superintendent again), as Friel himself wryly acknowledged:

> Some of the critics in Glasgow say that I should stop knocking the place . . . What am I going to do? Put my head in the sand and say that everything is lovely? . . . If I could see a lot of sweetness and light in Glasgow I would be happy to write about it; this is life.

But, as he knew and as critics have at last understood, there is much more.

> . . . Each novel is a carefully constructed experiment in parable, symbol and narrative style, full of wordplay and allusion. The subject matter of his works is that which has found its most common expression in the realist mode, but his style is modernist and experimental.

The Bank of Time is a *Bildungsroman*, though unusual, as one
commentator notes, because of its social background – "a very
unexotic, motherless, financially-impoverished and culturally-
deprived Glasgow tenement", and, in particular, because the
protagonist "is still there at the end of the book." It has autobiographical elements: the general family situation, father, brothers
and sensitive protagonist, may be familiar to us from Friel's earlier
Plottel stories, and the specific interaction of the three brothers
may well reflect Friel's relationship with two brothers close to him
in age in his big family.

The Bank of Time, perhaps the least experimental of Friel's
novels, affords certain pointers to the future. David Heylyn, like
the later hero Percy Phinn, is fond of poetry and trying to educate
himself; and he is continually concerned about words. "I didn't
know you were musical", someone says, and:

> . . . her remark sounded silly to his pedantic ear. It made
> him think of someone who emitted a musical note if he were
> prodded in the middle, or played a little tune if he were
> wound up like a cigarette-box.

It is a passing comment in the context of this book, but words and
their meanings, overt and unintentional, are to be very important
in Friel's later work.

Percy Phinn makes his appearance in *The Boy Who Wanted
Peace* (1964), and Friel's true voice begins to come through. Percy
is "a culture-hungry teenager who had failed his eleven-plus examination and come to life at sixteen." All he wants is peace and
quiet to get on with being a poet, and his problems seem solved
when the proceeds of a bank robbery turn up in the school cellar.
Nine publishers rejected *The Boy Who Wanted Peace* before it was
accepted by the avant-garde house of John Calder, and again it's
possible that they were puzzled by a "realistic" novel with such an
unlikely situation at its heart: £40,000 in cash hidden in a cellar,
worshipped by a gang of small boys.

Things fall into place once we recognise that Friel is not just describing Glasgow working-class life, but analysing it. In this society money is of great importance, whether for everyday necessities or as the key to a better life. When there's suddenly plenty of money, appearing from nowhere and belonging to no one, it is naturally an object of worship at first, but what happens then? Peace, as Percy finds, is the last thing it's going to bring.

In this novel Friel begins to play with words. The conversations which frame the story showcase his technical dexterity – coolly handling the intertwined topics of football and bank robberies – as well as his accurate ear for Glasgow speech rhythms. Percy dotes on words, finding impressive titles for the office-bearers in his Brotherhood, or gang: Claviger, Campanologist, Regent Supreme. The names of the characters are significant: the tearaway Savage, the honest child Frank. It has been observed that Percy Phinn's own name, flamboyantly un-Glaswegian, aligns him with Persephone, regent of the underworld, which is the cellar:

> . . . a sprawling low-roofed vault stretching below the main
> building and out under the playground, where it ended in
> an unexplored boundary of evil darkness. Not even Frank
> Garson had ever touched that far-off invisible wall . . .

There is much more going on here than meets the eye accustomed to the realistic Glasgow novel.

The Boy Who Wanted Peace was well enough received by reviewers, but this in no way smoothed the path of Friel's next novel, *Grace and Miss Partridge*. He sent it to Calder, in understandable expectation, shortly after *The Boy Who Wanted Peace* had been accepted in 1964, but took it back when after more than a year no decision had been reached. A proposal to televise the earlier novel caused Marion Boyars, of what was now Calder and Boyars, to look again at the later one, and she accepted *Grace and Miss Partridge* in 1967, though it was not published until April 1969.

It's no wonder that Friel, finally able to inscribe a copy to a friend, was moved to write a verse "in explanation of the long delay":

> I wrote a story in '63
> about a partridge in a bare tree.
> I typed it clear in '64
> and tried my publishers once more.
> Back it came in '65
> Ah well, I said, I'll still survive.
> It lay unread in '66
> till Mrs Boyars, promising nix,
> asked to see it again in '67
> accepted it – so all forgiven.
> I got no proofs till '68
> and that was November, rather late.
> Printed at last in '69
> . . . so now it's yours as well as mine.

After all this, *Grace and Miss Partridge* did not make a great impact on the reading public. Even the jacket blurb manages to undersell it, or sell it as something rather run-of-the-mill: "George Friel's new novel shows this witty and compassionate chronicler of Glasgow life in his finest story-telling form. The author is a schoolteacher." But one reviewer knew better.

> No account of recent Glasgow writing would be complete
> without the mention of George Friel, whose *Grace and Miss
> Partridge* is a formidable achievement, metaphysical,
> psychological, comic and chilling.

High praise, but not too high for an extraordinary novel, which has more recently been described as "a structure of endless trapdoors through which we fall from the security of the real into the glamour of the fancied and back again."

Grace and Miss Partridge opens in Glasgow realist mode.

In the tenement where I was born there was an old maid lived all alone in a single-end on the top storey. We always called her Miss Partridge to her face, but behind her back she was Wee Annie.

The tenement children inhabit the back court, the girls playing singing games while the boys add "bawdy variations." Vigilant mothers rest their arms and bosoms on windowsills; young lovers kiss and cuddle in the back close; we appear to be in the comfortable world of the wee black sannies. Indeed the narrator, fully in the urban kailyard tradition, is, or was then, one of the children:

She didn't like boys, and we couldn't get playing in peace in the backgreen for her shouting at us over the staircase window.

But he knows more than can be seen from the back court. Wee Annie invites her favourite little girl Grace Christie in for cake and lemonade:

"Boys aren't nice. You'll know what I mean when you get older, and you'll thank me for it. Boys always want to, I'll tell you some day. O-my-O-my! Just look at those knees . . ."

She knelt and washed the child's knees with the soapy flannel, travelled slowly down the sturdy legs that were in fact quite clean and up the stalwart thighs to the brief knickers. And when that was done she went over it all again, massaging the legs from knickers to ankles with a skimpy towel, lingering over each limb.

Who is this apparently omniscient narrator? Though one of the tenement children, he's nameless (though, once more, his family details resemble those in the Plottel stories) and never takes part in the action. His mother comments that he never did:

"You always were a devious little prig. A fly wee bugger as your father called you. Sitting in a corner with your nose in a book but aye listening to whatever was said, aye adding things up."

229

We know at an early stage that now, writing the story, he has Miss Partridge's diary and there are other references to his sources:

> Miss Partridge confided in my mother and my mother confided in me when I was older . . .

> I met Main again many years later . . . He told me a lot I had only guessed.

But we lose sight of him until in the last chapter he appears as an adult, discussing the book he has written – this book – with his mother.

Like David Heylyn and Percy Phinn, he is fond of words. *Grace and Miss Partridge* shows Friel's Joycean wordplay in its full form.

> She was womanly weak, Dross's weekly woman . . .

On the following page we learn that she's a reader of women's magazines, though *Woman's Weekly* isn't actually specified.

> Jig keys, hall keys, keys as trig as his head . . .
> . . . a bawdybill show . . .

We should also note the conversations between Miss Partridge and "the inspectres"; they may remind us of Mrs Ross and "the whisperers", and something similar will recur in Friel's masterpiece *Mr Alfred MA*. This is adventurous writing:

> Given: A girl and her river.
> Required to: Get her across.
> Construction: A bridge. Abridge her life.

But more than that, it begins to let us into Miss Partridge's secrets: what lies behind her love of little girls, her desire to keep them safe, her sense of sin.

Grace in her bare scuddie, eh? That would be something to
refumble! Like you played on your daddy's knee in your nightie-
night-Papa. Something you'd like to retumble. And what would
Mama say if she knew that Papa knew what Papa knew?

Anyway, the narrator thinks that's how it was. Friel, who is after all
behind the whole story, allows us to think that it may have been
so; but then in the coda he forces us to think again. As a critic
suggests:

> These final revelations dissolve the whole texture of the
> previous presentation, unravelling the surface of the story and
> revealing new potentialities which the novel itself will neither
> affirm nor deny.

The narrator's mother reckons he has made most of it up. He
admits he has had to "mould the material, give it a shape, make it
mean something. . ." He's shocked to discover that there is a
volume of Wee Annie's diary which he has not seen. And now we
learn, what he has never hinted in the narrative, that he is married
to Grace; he has always loved Grace; in his mother's opinion at
least, he was jealous of Miss Partridge. He's hardly the unbiased
observer we had imagined; from the very beginning his perceptions
may have been skewed. What is the truth of the tenement where
he was born? *Grace and Miss Partridge* presents a Glasgow full of
secret lives, ultimately unknowable: the hidden face of the city.

15

The Glasgow Group

In the early 1970s Philip Hobsbaum of Glasgow University chaired a writers' group which met in his west-end flat. Some of the writers who read and discussed their work had been part of an earlier group run by Hobsbaum in the late sixties; some were published local authors; some were recruited from a concurrent extra-mural class in creative writing. Hobsbaum has since said that "the Glasgow Group, retrospectively, looks like a peak of literary culture." It does indeed, since it was attended by – among others – Tom Leonard, James Kelman, Liz Lochhead and Alasdair Gray.

While the official meetings of the Group came to an end in spring 1975, the continued association, personal and professional, of these writers has proved seminal for Glasgow literature of the present day. On an individual level, they have "discovered" and encouraged other gifted writers, such as Agnes Owens and Janice Galloway. To public view, they remain a group (however that is defined) and as such have attracted media attention, bringing about – most notably perhaps in the 1980s and early 1990s – a general perception of Glasgow as a city of writers,

A soundbite like "The Glasgow Group", however useful, comes loaded with certain assumptions which it might be as well to examine here. Firstly, such a phrase tends to deny the writers any individual concerns, viewpoints or achievements. Of course, each pursues his or her own vision; no two writers could be less alike than – a random choice – Kelman and Gray.

Secondly, the concept of such a group implies isolation, either from the literary world outside Glasgow, or from the non-writing Glasgow scene. Two pieces of work by Alasdair Gray dismiss any such view. His witty calligraphic presentation – well worth close study – in the preliminary pages of *Unlikely Stories, Mostly* (1983) unambiguously sets Glasgow writing in the wider context of Scottish literature, so that "Kelman, agnamed the Cool . . . Lochhead of Motherwell . . . Master Hind, agnamed dear Archie . . ." share the spotlight with MacDiarmid, Muir and MacCaig.

Just as significant is the series of thirty paintings and drawings which Gray produced for the People's Palace museum during a placement as Artist Recorder in 1977. His brief was to show "aspects of Glasgow and Glasgow people in the 1970s." Nine of the works depict Glasgow writers – Kelman, Leonard, Lochhead and Hind are there, with Clifford Hanley and Jack House, the poets Edwin Morgan and Alexander Scott, and the dramatist Tom McGrath – but they are accompanied by portraits of other contemporary Glaswegians known and unknown, and streetscapes with buildings in survival or decay. There could be no more telling expression of the identity of Glasgow writing with its city.

Finally, in the 1970s as in any period, not all Glasgow writers can be aligned with, or belonged to, a group. Our view of the seventies, for instance, should not overlook the work of Matt McGinn, the fiercely gifted singer/songwriter whose one novel *Fry the Little Fishes* (1975) draws on his experiences in an approved school; or of Evelyn Cowan, previously mentioned in connection with novels of middle-class Glasgow. Her memoir of a Glasgow Jewish childhood, *Spring Remembered* (1974), was followed by a much under-appreciated novel, *Portrait of Alice* (1976). Alice, stranded in status-seeking suburbia and a loveless middle-aged marriage, struggling out of a nervous breakdown, is a new voice in Glasgow fiction, sensitively presented by Cowan.

And it is right to consider the career of Margaret Thomson Davis, if only because she may be said to have founded a new school of Glasgow fiction. Her first novel, *The Breadmakers* (1972), received considerable press coverage from the romantic angle that Davis was "an ordinary housewife" (though a successful writer of magazine stories) who suddenly had five novels accepted at once. The book itself was an immediate popular success. Set in 1930s Govan, its aim is to encapsulate a certain view of Glasgow:

> Life was Glasgow, tough, harsh, complex, warm with humanity, with generous helping hands, with caring in abundance.
>
> It was the caring that mattered.

In *The Making of a Novelist* (1982), an autobiography-cum-creative writing manual, Davis describes the process by which she developed her central character Catriona, a naive sixteen-year-old from an area a cut above Govan who comes to live above the bakery as bride to the frightful Melvin.

> I chose characters that were as different to one another as possible. Contrast and conflict are essential . . . Because I've made Catriona timid and lacking in self-confidence, I make Melvin the opposite – an aggressive, conceited bully.

A "well-made novel" then, with perhaps undue concentration on the waif-like qualities of the amber-eyed young heroine and the bulging eyes and muscles of her earthy husband. *The Breadmakers'* most successful character, Sarah Fowler – to outward view a cheerful brassy blonde, in fact a sick woman badgered by her husband and mother-in-law, and at last driven to fatal retaliation – does come alive. Davis herself realised this:

> I was sitting at my desk writing and suddenly, unbidden, out of a blank mind – or was it out of my subconscious? – I heard Sarah say something that was perfectly in character with her but something that was quite alien to me. And I saw her. She

shuffled across my mind's eye – as clear – as clear – I cannot tell you. My stomach flips nervously over even yet.

The Breadmakers is, however, only the first volume in a trilogy.

> I had meant *The Breadmakers* to cover about eight years or so in the lives of my characters . . . However, once I'd written what I thought was an average booklength manuscript I found only a year had passed. That's why I had to press on and write a second book . . . New characters kept popping up with new storylines . . . I had to press on and write a third book in which to work everything out to a satisfactory conclusion.

This pattern has been a recurrent one in Davis's prolific writing career (which comprises, to date, some twenty novels, many of them grouped in trilogies.) The majority of her novels are set in the past, whether recent, as in the *Breadmakers* trilogy, or farther removed, as in the trilogy which began with *The Prince and the Tobacco Lords* (1976), set in eighteenth-century Glasgow and Virginia. It may be repeated that her books are extremely popular and, as has been suggested, she can be seen as the founder of a dynasty. Glasgow and its hinterland has since the 1970s become the setting for a number of big, colourful, eventful family sagas – generally coming in threes – by such writers as Jan Webster, "Jessica Stirling" (a pseudonym of Hugh C Rae), Christine Marion Fraser and Frances Paige.

In the same year as *The Breadmakers*, but to rather less populist acclaim, appeared George Friel's fourth novel, *Mr Alfred MA*. Like all his novels, this too had a protracted journey towards publication. He submitted it in 1967, on the acceptance of *Grace and Miss Partridge*, but Calder and Boyars excelled themselves by mislaying the manuscript. It was found and accepted in 1970. Since another book had by now been published under Friel's original title *The Writing on the Wall*, that had to be changed. Because of rising costs it was then decided to produce the novel in a form of near-print, "a perfectly disastrous solution", as one commentator temperately observes. *Mr Alfred MA* appeared in January 1972 in a sort of typewriter script, with unjustified margins, blank pages and "widows", enough to make a booklover weep.

Reviews, where they did not focus on the deplorable production, were favourable, though – as seems to have been Friel's destiny – several got the book quite wrong. Auberon Waugh in the *Spectator* objects to Friel's use of "obscure and archaic" language, drawn from "Liddell and Scott . . . the British Pharmacopeia and . . . equally unfamiliar slang expressions from Clydeside." What he misses is that the novel is all about language and communication, or rather non-communication. Mr Alfred, failed writer and failing English teacher, can't communicate with his colleagues, or his pupils, or the Glasgow people around him. They can't communicate with each other; and, it has been pointed out, in their natural tongue they, and most of Scotland, can't communicate with the English establishment (certainly not with Auberon Waugh). Friel has deliberately crafted the language of the novel with this in mind.

The *Glasgow Herald* review can best be described as very *Glasgow Herald*. The complex, ambiguous, sensitive situation in which Mr Alfred offers more affection than he should to his first-year pupil Rose Weipers gets short shrift: "It is a poetic thought; but instinctively one sides with suspicious authority . . ." As ever, the *Herald* is mindful of its reading public: "His story is set in that lurid wasteland of Combies and Tongs where few other *Glasgow Herald* readers would care to venture." And the final paragraph quite spectacularly misses the point of the novel:

> If this book is to be accepted as an impressive indictment of the empty assertions and confident pretensions of many modern educational theories it is devalued by the extravagant note of melancholy farce upon which the story ends. There may also be considerable reasons to mock modern psychiatrists; but it is foolish to fight two battles in one book!

Needless to say, observant and funny as the school and psychiatrist scenes are, this isn't what *Mr Alfred MA* is trying to do.

With the rest of Friel's work – he published only one further novel, *An Empty House* (1975), and, sadly if typically, did not even receive his author's advance copies before his death – *Mr Alfred MA* fell out of view for some years. On its rediscovery and reissue in 1987, one critic at least was in no doubt as to its value, and his voice was joined by others.

> This is one of the greatest of Scottish novels . . . In its expression of bleak negativity, [it] stands comparison with Golding's *Lord of the Flies* and Conrad's *Heart of Darkness*.

Mr Alfred, MA(Ord) – he had to give up his honours course when his father died, "then his mother went and died too" – resents his lowly position in a bad school, his poor salary, the dull classes he has to teach. He's sure he deserves better. He has a collection of poems which he has never managed to get published. He is unmarried and an alcoholic. In his longing for love, or human contact at least, he's drawn into familiarity with twelve-year-old Rose. He is transferred to a worse school and mugged by an ex-pupil. He finishes up in an asylum. We have noted the theme of non-communication; at the end he can't communicate at all, and yet he can: "Turned out nice today. No sign of children," he'll say to passing fellow-patients. It is an unsparing portrait of a disappointed, unloved, inadequate man, and also a portrait of contemporary Glasgow, with its bleakness, violence, graffiti and young gangs; once more, the symbiotic relationship of man and city is there to be seen.

In Part II, which retained the title "The Writing on the Wall", Mr Alfred becomes obsessed by the graffiti of "Wasteland Glasgow". Non-communication again:

> He saw a new rash break out on the scarred face of the city. Wherever the name of a gang was scribbled the words YA BASS were added . . . It upset him . . . He brooded over the inexplicable words that turned up irregularly alongside YA

BASS. He noted FUZZ, JOEY, DOTT, PEEM, MUSHY, BUNNY, ETTIE, CLAN, BIM and forty more. Sometimes the gang name was followed by OK instead of YA BASS, sometimes it was preceded by YY, but he couldn't find out what YY meant.

There was indeed a quantum leap in Glasgow graffiti during the 1960s, thanks no doubt to the development of aerosol cans and felt-tip pens. Many a writer has put it to work as realistic scene-setting, but in Friel's hands it becomes something much more significant, leading into what has been rightly recognised as a key passage in modern Scottish literature.

Mr Alfred, having been mugged, comes round in a tenement close, hearing a gentle, sympathetic voice. Realistically the voice belongs to a kind passer-by in this famously friendly city, but Mr Alfred is in another world.

"You used to teach me. Not remember?"

"Your face I think," said Mr Alfred. "But your name I don't, no."

"Tod," said the speaker. "Not remember?"

Abruptly translated to "the house where Tod lived," a notorious condemned squat, which he has never actually seen (does it exist?), Mr Alfred gravely debates with this mysterious figure the problem of delinquency and the derivation of YA BASS. Tod claims credit for both. Like Hogg's Gil-Martin, he can't be fully accounted for. His explanation "You can't fight me . . . I'm already inside" allows him to be the projection of a fevered brain, or, alternatively, to be what he says he is.

"I was, I am, and I always will be."

"You think you're God perhaps?" said Mr Alfred.

"No, the other One," said Tod. "The Adversary . . . I'm nibbling away at the roots of your civilisation. I'll bring it down. The felt-pen is mightier than the sword."

In Friel's dark vision Glasgow (with the rest of the world) is going to the devil, and here the devil, unforgettably, takes up his place in Glasgow fiction.

Meanwhile William McIlvanney had moved to his alternative location "Graithnock" for the setting of *Docherty* (1975), the massive novel of working-class family and community which put him firmly on the map of Scottish writing. His next Glasgow novel was eagerly awaited. When it appeared, in the shape of *Laidlaw* (1977), a considerable furore ensued, because *Laidlaw* is – or appears to be – a detective story. Had McIlvanney gone down-market, sold out?

Of course he hadn't. This has become ever more clear as the character Jack Laidlaw has appeared in further novels, but it was there for all to see from the beginning of *Laidlaw*.

> Out of what burrows in you had the creatures come that used you? They came from nowhere that you knew about.
> But there *was* nowhere that you knew about, not even this place where you came and stood among people, as if you were a person. You could see who people thought was you in the mottled glass . . .
> Nowhere in all the city could there be anyone to understand what you had done, to share it with you. No one, no one.

Since these are the thoughts of the murderer, we may at least be sure that we are not embarking on a whodunnit. Naturally this was no accident, as McIlvanney has explained, clearing up at the same time a few more mistaken preconceptions about *Laidlaw*.

> People keep judging [*Laidlaw*] in terms that don't apply to it. It's like having done the long jump and finding yourself assessed on the height achieved.
> *Laidlaw* has been called a police procedural. It isn't . . . partly because such procedures have little to do with what I was after . . . *Laidlaw* has been called a mystery. It isn't. . . .
> The book begins with a crime committed and the criminal identified. That, in the usual sense of a mystery, is the story

over. It's not a whodunnit. It is a whydunnit – only in that area
does the book contain any mystery.
Laidlaw is less an example of the traditional detective story
than an attempted challenge to it . . .

But it's a Glasgow novel too. What McIlvanney has done is to fuse
a specific, accurate, and lovingly observed Glasgow background –
streets, atmosphere, conversation – with a universal hero. McIlvanney had long intended to write about Glasgow – "the strength of
my desire . . . perhaps came from the fact that I am not a native of
the place" – and in *Laidlaw* – sometimes, as here, speaking through
the character Laidlaw – he does so to some purpose.

> "At each of its four corners, this kind of housing-scheme.
> There's the Drum and Easterhouse and Pollok and Castlemilk
> . . . Just architectural dumps where they unloaded the people
> like slurry . . . Glasgow folk have to be nice people. Otherwise,
> they would have burned the place to the ground years ago."

But this isn't where a novel comes from.

> The idea remained lifeless. The electrical charge that would
> transform a possibility into a compulsion was still missing.
> Then, if it doesn't sound too much like Joan of Arc, I heard a
> voice. I noted down what it was saying . . . Slowly, from jotted
> remarks and tentative notes, the man behind the voice
> emerged. He was a detective in Glasgow and his name was
> Laidlaw, Jack Laidlaw.

The tough, vulnerable, unsettled and unsettling Detective-
Inspector Laidlaw lives in the mind long after the book has been
read. McIlvanney has returned to him in two more novels, *The
Papers of Tony Veitch* (1983) and *Strange Loyalties* (1991); he and
his world develop further in each book. McIlvanney has said: "The
central mystery of *Laidlaw* is Laidlaw."

Though – or perhaps because – McIlvanney as a writer is

held in high esteem by both critics and the reading public, various accusations have been levelled at him over the years (and he has defended himself with spirit in essays and interviews). There's the question of a perceived fascination with violence; there's the view that his treatment of women characters is less than politically correct. There's the suggestion that he overwrites, overdosing on colourful imagery and idiom, a tendency which may have peaked in *Tony Veitch*. Of most concern to us is the indictment that he takes a rose-tinted view of Glasgow.

> It was a place so kind it would batter cruelty into the ground . . . No wonder he loved it. It danced among its own debris. When Glasgow gave up, the world could call it a day.
> (*The Papers of Tony Veitch*)

However, this again is Laidlaw's view, and the reader learns in the course of the three books that Laidlaw is not a Glaswegian, any more than McIlvanney is. In *Strange Loyalties* an eighteen-year-old student comes up to Glasgow in search of digs: "'For me, travelling from Kelso to Glasgow was like taking the Golden Road to Samarkand. What would I find there?'" It's certainly not the view of a native Glaswegian, but perhaps it's necessary to give our picture of Glasgow in fiction a fully three-dimensional effect.

The picture, as can be seen, is now growing year by year, even month by month. 1977, the summer of *Laidlaw*, also saw the publication of Alan Spence's short story collection *Its Colours They are Fine*, greeted immediately in a perceptive review:

> It is necessary to point out what he has overcome and ordered: that is, the inexhaustible richness and energy of Glasgow life.

The reviewer, acknowledging that most of the stories had been previously published in magazines and anthologies, goes on to emphasise "how much they gain from being put together; one is aware of a pattern, a unifying concept." This is the first key to *Its*

Colours They are Fine: that it is not just a collection of stories, but a story sequence. That's important, because a quick glance at some of the earlier stories might suggest that we are in wee black sannie land again.

> On Friday night Shuggie and Aleck set out early for the shows. On their way down to Govan Cross for the subway, they stopped in at Louie's fish supper shop and they each bought a bag of chips for their tea. They walked on, eating greedily, the chips at first burning their fingers and their tongues.
>
> ("Gypsy")

In this story Shuggie and Aleck are wee tough guys of ten or eleven years old. But we have earlier met Aleck aged six, looking at the reflection of his Christmas kitchen in the tenement window:

> He imagined it was another room jutting out beyond the window, out into the dark. He could see the furniture, the curtain across the bed, his mother and father, the decorations and through it all, vaguely, the buildings, the night. And hung there, shimmering, in that room he could never enter, the tinsel garland that would never ever tarnish.
>
> ("Tinsel")

We are going to meet Shuggie aged thirteen:

> He was bigger and stronger than Aleck or Joe and he tended to boss them. He'd been too much for his mother, ever since his father had been killed. That was about a year ago, and it had made quite an impression on all of them.
>
> ("Silver in the Lamplight")

A few years later we meet them again, though their paths have diverged: Aleck has gone on to high school while Shuggie has found unskilled work in the shipyards. Shuggie goes to the dancing, loses the girl he fancies, picks a fight with the boy who has won, waits for him outside:

"This should be good," said Eddie. "Didye see that wee guy's face when ah says we wur the Govan Team! Jist aboot shat is sel! That wis the best laugh. Fuckin tremendous!"

Shuggie laughed and reached into his pocket, feeling the steel comb with the long pointed handle.

"Mental!" he said.

"Brilliant!" said Rab.   ("Brilliant")

This sort of thing is familiar enough in Glasgow fiction from *No Mean City* onwards, but the reviewer already quoted recognises that Spence has here done something unique.

> He has portrayed the development of the Hardman, without any secret thrill of identification, without glamour but with understanding and pity.

Spence, of course, knows exactly what he's doing, and has continued to do it in a small but distinguished output of fiction, poems and plays (a novel, *The Magic Flute*, appeared in 1990 and another short story volume, *Stone Garden*, in 1995).

> My writing often has a harsh surface realism, but something else keeps breaking through. And it's that *something else* I want to celebrate. The moment, the glimpse, the insight. A sense of astonishment and wonder. *Here we are!*

A bookshop browser in the late 1970s would have found, sharing the shelves with *Laidlaw* and *Its Colours They are Fine*, a small book published in 1976 under the modest title *Three Glasgow Writers*. Something of a collectors' item now, it is a significant volume, because the three writers were Alex Hamilton, Tom Leonard and James Kelman. Hamilton was experimenting with the transcription of Glasgow speech.

> "Heh," goes Tommy, "Ah'm gaun orr therr tae see aboot this.

> Wullie must be daft ur sumhin, shoutin at that f'lla. E'll get is
> heid done fur im."   ("Gallus, did you say?")

Leonard's work in the same field, which will be considered further
in Chapter Nineteen, was already attracting attention. *Three
Glasgow Writers* included prose as well as his better-known poetry:

> A canny even remembir thi furst thing a remembir. Whit a
> mean iz, a remembir aboot four hunner thingz, awit wance.
> Trouble iz tay, a remembir thim aw thi time.   ("Honest")

Kelman had been publishing stories in magazines and anthologies
for some years but had not so far achieved book publication in
Britain, though an enterprising American publisher had produced
a collection of thirteen stories. In *Three Glasgow Writers* he supplied
a short introduction to the stories included:

> I was born and bred in Glasgow
> I have lived most of my life in Glasgow
> It is the place I know best
> My language is English
> I write
> In my writings the accent is in Glasgow
> I am always from Glasgow and I speak English always
> Always with this Glasgow accent
>
> This is right enough

This statement will be something to remember when the flowering
of Kelman's reputation and influence is considered, such a
prominent feature of the Glasgow literary scene in the 1980s.

IV
DEEP CITY

A chapter closed
And silently in Glasgow quick hands began
Angrily making cushions.

Robert Crawford:
"The Scottish National Cushion Survey"
A Scottish Assembly (1990)

16

The Unthank Epiphany

It undoubtedly will stand as one of the greatest of Scottish
novels . . . But this – though true – denies the novel its other
singular achievement; which is, that it effortlessly manages to
find equal footing and fruitful comparison with the best of
great surrealist, dystopian fiction throughout the world.

In 1981, in such warm terms, a critic greeted *Lanark*, the first
novel by Alasdair Gray, which, suitably appearing near the start
of a new decade, marks a new beginning in Glasgow fiction.

Lanark had been a long time in the writing: thirty years or
so, nearly three-quarters of Gray's life. Its chronology is laid out
by one writer in the useful collection of critical essays *The Arts of
Alasdair Gray*:

> *Lanark*'s most remote ancestor is the improbably titled *Obbly
> Pobbly* from 1951 . . . From this point onwards Gray worked at
> a series of books which combined or juxtaposed a realist semi-
> autobiography with an epic allegorical fantasy in ways which
> culminated in the solution achieved by *Lanark* . . .

Gray himself has reasonably (if emphatically) pointed out, "*I didn't spend 25 years writing it,* I was doing lots of other things." The other things included scene-painting and mural painting (for Gray attended Glasgow School of Art and his painting and writing careers have always run side by side); teaching (soon abandoned) and lecturing; writing plays for radio and television. But as the same chronological survey explains, *Lanark* was always around:

> The big novel continued to develop throughout Gray's time at Art School, always named after its protagonist who mutated from Obbly Pobbly to Edward Southeran, Gowan Cumbernauld, then becoming Ian, Hector, Gowan and finally Duncan Thaw.

Chapters, or what later became chapters, were published in magazines here and there; the eventual Book One was submitted to a publisher as a complete work, but rejected; parts were read, and the enterprise encouraged, at meetings of Philip Hobsbaum's Glasgow Group; *Lanark*, now completed, was offered to another publisher, but rejected on grounds of length. Finally it was accepted in 1978 by the Edinburgh publisher Canongate, and published early in 1981, a 560-page "Life in Four Books", with Gray's own artwork – dustjacket, title page, and frontispieces to the four books – adding to its distinctiveness and significance.

It was well-received and perceptively reviewed. Unusually for a Scottish book, the *Times Literary Supplement* gave it a full-page. Reviewers, satisfactorily, called it an epic, which had been Gray's aim, and drew comparisons with, among others, Blake, Dante and Hieronymus Bosch. Its visual and dramatic qualities were commented on (it has since been adapted for the stage with sensitivity and some success, while plans for a film version have been drawn up though not so far carried through). Following on this first response came sustained and serious consideration of *Lanark*'s place in literature; not merely Scottish literature, as the quotation at the head of this chapter shows.

Academic criticism of *Lanark* could by now, indeed, fill a

Alasdair Gray's *Lanark,* appearing in 1981 with Gray's own distinctive artwork , marked a new beginning as writers realised that Glasgow novels need not follow traditional lines

volume on its own. Given a novel on this scale, it's not surprising that critics have come at it from many directions, asking many questions, finding many and varied answers. There's discussion, for instance, of what would appear to be a strong autobiographical element in the 'realistic' Books One and Two. As presented here, Duncan Thaw's life from childhood to young manhood, in the 1940s and 1950s, does have certain correlations with the biography of Alasdair Gray, who was born in 1934. Gray has written, "My most densely and deliberately autobiographical writing is in Books 1 and 2 of *Lanark*," though he immediately stresses that much of his life is "not copied" in the novel.

Then, critics ask, does Duncan Thaw die at the end of Book Two, when he wades into the sea? If so (or if not), what is his relationship to Lanark, the protagonist of Books Three and Four, whose experiences echo Thaw's in unsettling ways? The options have been clearly presented in one introductory essay:

> We may accept [the Thaw and Lanark stories] as substantially the one tale, however come by, simply following on from each other sequentially. [Or] we can take the Thaw story as a version of actual facts (autobiography) or possible facts (fictional biography) and the Lanark story as a fable projecting fears about an after-life or a co-existing and contemporaneous underworld. We may take it that Thaw actually drowned and that was the end of him; or we may interpret his end metaphorically, with "immersion" as a plunge into worlds of the subconscious and unconscious. Or . . . we may regard them as representing a person at two different *stages* of life, stages defined by quite different levels or kinds of consciousness . . .

And do we have here one novel, or two connected novels, or even two separate novels, as a footnote in *Lanark* itself appears to suggest?

The fact remains that the plots of the Thaw and Lanark sections

are independent of each other and cemented by typographical
contrivances rather than formal necessity. A possible
explanation is that the author thinks a heavy book will make a
bigger splash than two light ones.

But this footnote, as we might guess from its second sentence, is
(probably) not to be taken seriously. It is presented as commentary
by a pedantic academic on the Epilogue to *Lanark*. The Epilogue,
which is not at the end of the novel, features a conversation between
Lanark, the character, and a figure described as "the author", who
is currently engaged in writing *Lanark*, the book. This leads us,
and the critics, to the question of *Lanark* and postmodernism,
discussion on which is too lengthy and wide-ranging to be summarised here.

    Theories and counter-theories on the novel and its meaning
continue to proliferate. As only one example, another footnote
informs us that "Most of *Lanark* is an extended Difplag [diffuse
plagiarism] of *The Water Babies*" and if we do take this seriously, it
has been claimed, "the details of the two books are close enough
to make it possible to see *Lanark* as a re-creation of *The Water
Babies*." But this critic goes on to point out that the influence of
Kingsley's work has probably been in technique rather than
outlook, as Gray himself has said, or anyway hinted, in interview:
"I particularly liked *The Water Babies* because of the business of
mixing genres." It should be added that Gray's many helpful
interviews on his works may not provide the last word, as he has
with equal helpfulness told his bibliographer:

> Alasdair Gray points out that since several of these interviews
> were tape recorded, rather than written, the omission of a
> crucial *negative* from the printed transcript has sometimes
> entirely reversed his intended meaning.

There is one critical passage, written by a poet, which appears to
say it all.

A writer who is also an artist, with a strongly developed visual imagination and a distinct flair for portraying the grotesque and the strange, tries his hand at the novel. He sees this literary form, this great tract so ill-defined in shape and purpose, apparently welcoming a lavish and indulgent play of imagination, a story-telling rich with fantastic incident, whose sole necessity is to enthrall. This is a freedom he will find deceptive, but only partly deceptive. He discovers that the "necessity to enthrall" involves him willy-nilly with human feelings and experiences, and that the novel is oddly tenacious of its verisimilitudes, even when it is shading towards fairy-tale or allegory.

Unfortunately this isn't about *Lanark* at all. It's Edwin Morgan writing in 1960 about Mervyn Peake's *Gormenghast*; but oddly, paradoxically, and suitably so in connection with this odd and paradoxical novel, it does somehow relate to the problems of understanding – and creating – *Lanark*.

Since we are looking at the image of Glasgow in fiction, however, one particular aspect of *Lanark* has to be considered here. On the narrowest possible reading *Lanark* qualifies as a Glasgow novel. By now we recognise something familiar in the opening pages of Book One.

Thaw lived in the middle storey of a corporation tenement that was red sandstone in front and brick behind. The tenement backs enclosed a grassy area divided into greens by spiked railings, and each green had a midden. Gangs of midden-rakers from Blackhill crossed the canal to steal from the middens.

The real Glasgow presented in Books One and Two is precisely dated. "The Thaw family came home to Glasgow the year the war ended" and we can work back and forward from that. We meet Duncan Thaw at the age of five, and follow him to secondary school and art school, through asthma attacks, friendships, and (consistently unsuccessful) approaches to sex. Books One and Two of *Lanark*, in short, comprise a *Bildungsroman*, like *Fernie Brae* or *The Bank of Time*. And Thaw's world, the Glasgow of the late 1940s and early 1950s, is meticulously described.

> There was daylight in the sky but none in the streets and the lamps were lit. Boys of his own age strolled on the pavements in crowds of three and four, girls walked in couples, groups of both sexes gossiped and giggled by cafe doors.

> The factory was near the river and he descended to it by narrow streets where many small factories stood between tenements and scrapyards.

> There was a chill wind outside and a sky bright with the green and gold of a slow summer sunset. Drummond said he knew of a party and led them up Lynedoch Street, a normally shallow hill which tonight seemed perpendicular.

We don't, though, begin reading *Lanark* with Book One. We begin with Book Three, which is set in another place.

> The city did not seem a thriving place. Groups of adolescents or old men stood in occasional close mouths, but many closes were empty and unlit. . . . After a while we came to a large square with tramcars clanging around it . . . Some soot-black statues were arranged round a central pillar . . .

This place is just "the city" until, some distance into the story, we learn that it's called Unthank. But if you know Glasgow when you begin to read, or if you turn back to Book Three after reading Book One, this city sounds weirdly like Glasgow, and 1950s Glasgow at that (closes, tramcars, soot). We can probably say with some confidence, in fact, that it is Glasgow, drawing on a statement as unambiguous as anything in *Lanark*. Asking for information on the "geographical and social surroundings" of Unthank, Lanark (the character) receives the "dry academic" reply: "The river Clyde enters the Irish Sea . . . Before widening to a firth it flows through Glasgow . . ."

253

A novel, however, doesn't depend on geographical and social data. The exciting thing which Gray has done in *Lanark* – which makes it a significant text in Glasgow fiction – is to transmute Glasgow into Unthank. As Edwin Morgan explains:

> He was perhaps the first person to see that Glasgow could be, well "mythologised" is perhaps the wrong word – but something like mythologised. It had to be a real presence, it was a real place, but at the same time it had to be given a resonating, a reverberating kind of existence that you would expect a big place to have, and he was able to do that.

We have said that Gray's writing and painting careers ran concurrently. In 1964, when he had already written Book One of *Lanark*, he was working on a large oil painting called *Cowcaddens 1950*. (Apart from their chronology, the link between book and painting is hardly in doubt, for a variant of the picture appears in the top left-hand corner of the title-page of *Lanark*.) There are the tenements, the small factories, the darkening streets and lighted lamps; a courting couple; three young men on a night out, coming down a steep street. It's definitely the cityscape of Books One and Two.

But what comes into the mind of the reader of *Lanark* on first seeing *Cowcaddens 1950* is a passage from Book Three.

> The cross was a place where several broad streets met and they could see down two of them, though the dark had made it difficult to see far. And now, about a mile away, where the streets reached the crest of a wide shallow hill, each was silhouetted against a pearly paleness. Most of the sky was still black for the paleness did not reach above the tenement roofs, so it seemed that two little days were starting, one at the end of each street.

Quoting this and considering *Cowcaddens 1950*, a writer on Gray as a visual artist boldly declares, "Unthank and Cowcaddens on a murky day are one and the same."

So Unthank is Glasgow. As time, in the novel, shifts and changes, it's not always the same Glasgow, but it is all the more recognisable to the reader who (like Gray) has known the city in different phases. One such commentator makes the point, which we have touched on in Chapter Fourteen, that

> . . . so little had changed, it seems, from the Glasgow of the thirties to the forties to the fifties to the early sixties. Yet only five or so years later things would be different. In a sense . . . these were the last years of the old Glasgow, before the full impact of the Modernist revolution, and it is this Glasgow which Gray uses to inform his fantasies.

Following this, he sees – and it's there to be seen – the new Glasgow of the late 1960s and early 1970s in the altered Unthank to which Lanark returns in Book Four.

> He remembered a stone-built city of dark tenements and ornate public buildings, a city with a square street plan and electric tramcars . . . but below a starless sky this city was coldly blazing. Slim poles as tall as the spire cast white light upon the lanes and looping bridges of another vast motorway. On each side shone glass and concrete towers over twenty floors high with lights on top to warn off aeroplanes. Yet this was Unthank, though the old streets between towers and motor-lanes had a half-erased look, and blank gables stood behind spaces cleared for carparks.

There's a third Glasgow, still more distant from the old, to be found in *Lanark*, if we accept the persuasive argument of another critic about Provan, which some have considered to be a different city.

> It is true that Lanark . . . flies from Unthank to Provan, but he flies through an intercalendrical zone, and as his bird-machine gradually descends and he looks down at the landscape it is obvious that he sees such familiar places as the Firth of Clyde,

the River Kelvin and Glasgow University. The city is clean,
sunlit, attractive . . . nothing could seem further from the
image of Unthank; but it is still a metamorphosis of Glasgow,
and not necessarily to be relished because it looks appealing . . .
If Unthank is a "city of destruction", so Provan may be too, in
a different sense, with its great scientific achievements and
discussions ranged against rather than for humanity.

But let us return for the moment to Unthank as we first see it. It is
certainly the 'old' Glasgow, the city in which Duncan Thaw grows
up; yet it's not quite the same.

Beyond the rooftops were rows of cranes with metal hulls among
them. The train travelled toward these and crossed a bridge over
the river. It was a broad river with stone embankments, cracked
khaki-coloured mud on the bottom and a narrow black stream
trickling zigzag down the middle. This worried me. I felt, and
still feel, that a river should be more than this.

It worries the reader too. Gray has carefully constructed Unthank
to be like Glasgow, but a skewed, wrong Glasgow. What does he
have in mind? What is Unthank saying about Glasgow?

Nothing good, because Unthank is a threatening, dreadful
place. People in Unthank disappear. People suffer from strange
diseases: mouths, softs, twittering rigor, dragonhide. These diseases
may bring them to "the institute", a sort of hospital where patients
go salamander and explode, and, worst of all, the food is processed
from the bodies of those who die. Lanark, as he recognises, is in
hell. Logic would suggest the next stop: Gray is saying that Glasgow
is hell.

But what kind of hell? There's disagreement among critics
on whether *Lanark* is "about" society, politics, culture; or whether
it is the exploration of a personality (or, of course, two person-
alities). As Douglas Gifford suggests, there is plenty of evidence
for the "social" view:

The symbolism indicates through exaggerated form real

Glasgow problems: unemployment, apathy, "disappearance" in the sense of the weak and economically unimportant becoming non-persons. To disappear is to fall off the bottom rung of society's ladder, and the pit of the Institute is filled with those who do. Such victims supply employment for Institute members, who are in real life doctors, social workers, civil servants.

(And we have seen that a city in which these problems seem to have been solved, Provan, may be another kind of hell.)

But the same critic acknowledges that the realistic Glasgow of Books One and Two constitutes a personal hell for Duncan Thaw, the sensitive, artistic boy at odds with the world and with himself. He offers a particularly interesting reading which suggests that Books Three and Four are nightmares or hallucinations in the mind of Duncan Thaw; that Thaw's world has already begun to break up at the end of Book Two of *Lanark*, when we see and hear what isn't there:

> Suddenly words came to him out of the air, whispered by an invisible beak . . . Mrs Colquhoun's cat sat in the opposite doorway looking at him. Part of her head and throat was missing. The right side was cut away and he saw the brain in section, white and pink and pleated like the underneath of a mushroom . . . The whisperer was a black crow which flew behind his head. In the great silence its orders were very discreet.

Thus the apparent realism of Books One and Two is not necessarily so, and Thaw's city, Glasgow, is already on the way to becoming Lanark's city, Unthank. Yet the critic sees a difficulty in this reading:

> If the only viable way to read *Lanark* is to see it as happening inside the head of a disintegrating social failure, how can we trust the assessments of society that are implicit in that trapped account? Either Lanark is a flawed personality with whose hallucinations we sympathise *or* he's a trustworthy guide through a sick society.

In this maze of ambiguity we are uncertain how to read the ending of *Lanark*, when the cathedral and Necropolis – in Unthank, but recognisably the features to be found in real-life Glasgow – are nearly immolated in a tidal wave, but not quite. It is a considerable tribute to the power of *Lanark*, the novel, that our last sight of Lanark, the character, as he awaits death, is so simply satisfying and right.

> The chamberlain vanished. Lanark forgot him, propped his chin on his hands and sat for a long time watching the moving clouds. He was a slightly worried, ordinary old man but glad to see the light in the sky.

The significance of *Lanark* to Glasgow fiction should by now be clear. While it has been argued throughout that the interpretation of Glasgow in fiction has been a continuing process, and some high points along the way habe been indicated, it is hard to think of any previous Glasgow novel which could have been discussed at such length or mined for meaning to such an extent as *Lanark*. Yet *Lanark* presents in Books One and Two the kind of realism frequently found in the work of earlier Glasgow writers. Gray has started from the same place but taken a great leap forward.

And as the poet and short-story writer Brian McCabe recognised in an early review, the influence of *Lanark* extended beyond Glasgow.

> *Lanark*'s importance consists in the fact that it has opened a very large door in the windowless little room of Scottish fiction, a door we did not know to be there, and only now can we begin to realise how much scope there is.

The novelist Iain Banks has acknowledged this with a specific example:

> Certainly of all the books I've written, *The Bridge* is the one

that was most influenced by any other single work, definitely
Lanark – I don't think *The Bridge* would be the way it is at all
if it wasn't for *Lanark*.

But our minds are concentrated on Glasgow fiction by a passage
in *Lanark* so often quoted since 1981 as to be almost a cliché.
Duncan Thaw says:

> Nobody imagines living here . . . If a city hasn't been used by
> an artist not even the inhabitants live here imaginatively . . .
> Imaginatively Glasgow exists as a music-hall song and a few bad
> novels. That's all we've given to the world outside. It's all
> we've given to ourselves.

Readers of the present work may feel confident of identifying the
"few bad novels", and a critic surveying Glasgow novels has
indicated that they are not so few:

> By the time of the 1970s the Glasgow novel had not only
> become utterly predictable but it had also manoeuvred itself
> into an artistic stalemate.

Things were about to change. By recognising the tradition of
Glasgow fiction till then, and by subverting it, Gray, in *Lanark*,
worked a miracle of sorts.

Referring to what he, like many, identifies as "the failure of
the greatest density of living Scots to produce, between Galt's
Entail and Archie Hind's *Dear Green Place*, an interesting, imaginative account of themselves," Gray in interview has generously
disclaimed any credit for bringing about an improvement.

> Surely the cause of the failure is a combination of poverty and
> unimaginative education. At present good writers are appearing
> in Glasgow whose education and nurture were ensured by the
> postwar welfare state and social security system, the National
> Health Service and Education grants.

But writers themselves, as we have seen, would not put it down entirely to cod liver oil and orange juice. The critic just quoted agrees that there's something more:

> The reader of Gray's work observes the artistic re-examination of what I call, for want of a better expression, the "Glasgow tradition" . . . Gray shows a remarkably liberal attitude when it comes, in terms of Scottish urban writing, to the choice, arrangement, and artistic transformation of traditional Glaswegian motifs. To write about a recognisable Glasgow is no artistic predicament for Gray.

After the epiphany of *Lanark*, Glasgow writers realised that, equally, it need not be a problem for them.

17

Imagining Glasgow

In the 1980s Glasgow was re-invented, both on the ground and, post-*Lanark*, in fiction. Even as the two operations proceeded it could be seen that two different cities were coming to life.

In town-planning terms this, like the sixties, was for Glasgow a decade of change, inevitably accompanied by argument, objection and controversy. The sixties' redevelopment started from perceived Glasgow problems – perceived not just by planners but by Glasgow people – such as sub-standard housing, and aimed to ameliorate them. (To what extent it worked, and where it went wrong, are elements in a long-running story which cannot fairly be summarised here.) The make-over of the eighties, the Thatcher decade, was different. It had the air, as sniffed by Glasgow people, of being imposed from outside, inspired by ideals remote from Glasgow concerns. There's a chilly, alien ring to the phrase which came to stand for these changes: the New Glasgow.

> What is the New Glasgow? Well, it has been practically impossible to walk the streets of the city or open a page of the popular press for the last few years *[the writer is commenting in 1990]* without being told of the re-vitalisation of the city, a new feeling of civic pride, the rediscovery of Glasgow's true self.

It's difficult to pinpoint one event which marks the arrival of the New Glasgow. Was it the decision, early in the decade, to renovate the old Merchant City south and east of George Square? Was it the launch in 1982 of the "Glasgow's Miles Better" campaign with its ubiquitous daffodil-yellow Mr Happy logo? Was it the success, in 1983 and 1986 respectively, of the city's applications to host the British Garden Festival and to become European City of Culture, or was the New Glasgow not fully in place until the staging of these events in 1988 and 1990? Looking back, the snowball effect is clear; round these official nuclei there came to cluster shopping centres, yuppie flats, an arts revival, restaurants and cafe-bars. This was exactly what the planners hoped for: money was coming into the city. In the 1980s, Glasgow was on a roll.

Or so it seemed from outside. Significantly for the present purpose, no such feel-good factor is mirrored in Glasgow writing of the 1980s. A number of writers, indeed – their voices growing stronger in the Year of Culture 1990 – target the New Glasgow idea with furious satire and polemic. Others make fun of it:

> "It's not done these days, you know, McCann. Glasgow's miles better and much nicer; head-butting is out."
>
> "Oh, Christ, aye, European City of Culture nineteen-ninety, eh? Bloody garden festival . . ." He snorted and drank.
>
> "More hotels."
>
> "An anuther fuckin exhibition centre."
>
> (Iain Banks, *Espedair Street*)

> "First tell me about the European Cultcha Capital thing," says the dealer. "Why Glasgow? How has a notoriously filthy hole become a shining light? Is it an advatising stunt?"
>
> "Certainly, but we have something to advertise!" says Linda.
> ". . . The city centa is a mastapiece of Victorian and Edwardian architectcha. But in those days it was unda such a thick coating of soot and grime that only the eye of a masta could penetrate it. Even moa off-putting wa the people . . .
>
> (Alasdair Gray, *Something Leather*)

Others again ignore the New Glasgow altogether; and not because of nostalgia for the old Glasgow. If celebration of cafe-bars and shopping centres is absent from 1980s Glasgow fiction, so, largely, is celebration of cosy tenements. Glasgow writers in this decade are looking at a contemporary city with clear and informed eyes. After *Lanark*, they are able to acknowledge its rich and deep variety and tap into a new confidence; but they are still searching for their city, and it's the same city, with all its problems, personal and economic, multiplying rather than decreasing on the journey through the Thatcherite eighties. Promoters of the New Glasgow notion should really have wondered why the most thoughtful Glasgow writers, when they weren't decrying it, found it totally irrelevant to their concerns.

Old-style Glasgow images were, of course, still being presented. Most of them turn up in Clifford Hanley's *Another Street, Another Dance* (1983), which sweeps in time from 1926 to 1945, taking in love, politics, incest, neighbourliness, and a good helping of wee black sannies, or equally traditional footwear.

> Charlie was the boldest of the bold . . . Once he even swore to run right to the top landing, three flights up, and ring every bell in the building. . . He crept into the close and upstairs; or tried to creep. His tacketty boots rang and echoed on the stone stairs.

Margaret Thomson Davis continued to produce action-packed sagas of life and love in Glasgow.

> He smiled down at her, a wonderful smile that softened his dark eyes. It melted her gut and knocked her heart off its regular beat. They were in "the Tally's" by this time, as the Italian-owned ice-cream shop was called. Here, despite its marble counter, mirror-lined walls and marble-topped tables, neither she nor Drummond was intimidated. This was Springburn, their territory.
>
> (*Rag Woman, Rich Woman*)

And there's the curious case of Emma Blair, whose career as a novelist began in 1982. Into the pages of *Where No Man Cries* are packed class conflict, sectarian violence, a poor boy's rise to tycoon status, and his humiliation of the foundry owner who cheated his widowed mother out of compensation for his father's death in a works accident, all occurring in a broadly delineated Glasgow. Ten prolific years later the press announced with some glee:

> At Exeter Magistrates Court on Thursday, Ms Blair, the scribe to whom thousands of readers turn for escapist fantasy, and a runner-up in last year's Boots Romantic Novel award, was revealed as a beefy male six-footer from Glasgow . . . It was his publisher who suggested that his books would be easier to market if he wrote under a woman's name.

Who suggested the marketability of Glasgow clichés is not so clear, but "Emma Blair" has been a bestseller from the start.

The shadow of *No Mean City* was still apparent in the eighties. Gang warfare supplied the springboard for John Burrowes' *Jamesie's People* (1984), though Burrowes completed his Gorbals trilogy in less hackneyed style, considering Glasgow's Asian immigrants in *Incomers* (1987), and the sixties' migration to the housing schemes and overseas in *Mother Glasgow* (1991). Glasgow's reputation as a villains' playground turned to a sort of fame in 1983, when the long-running TV series *Taggart* first appeared, offering a gruff Glaswegian with a heart of gold (another cliché, warmly welcomed by viewers), who investigated intricately plotted crimes in Glasgow locations both traditional and new.

Almost as notable in terms of Glasgow fictional crime was the debut of Peter Turnbull with *Deep and Crisp and Even* in 1981. Turnbull's police procedurals feature the officers of P Division, notionally based at Charing Cross. Upper-crust Donoghue, ageing Sussock, trendy Montgomerie, conscientious Hamilton, glamorous Willems, are well enough sketched to catch the reader's attention, though their characters hardly develop throughout the long series.

At his best Turnbull can supply a striking image of Glasgow:

> The man thought this city was a bitch. A wild, red-haired Irish
> bitch. She had the long flowing hair of the Campsies, two long
> limbs which lay either side of the river and met at the intimacy
> of the grid system at her centre. This city would love you or
> hate you, but she would never be indifferent to you. Not this
> bitch. The solitary figure was a policeman. His name was
> Hamilton and he knew he'd never leave her, not this bitch.
>
> (*Deep and Crisp and Even*)

But the traditional themes of tenements and crime, however
popular, were no longer regarded as the beginning and the end of
Glasgow fiction. A shift had taken place, and not only on the writers'
front.

> [From the thirties to the sixties] the images have been there
> even if the sad thing has been that the audience of the general
> public, schools and universities has been less than enthusiastic.
> At last the audience is changing . . .

The observation comes from the programme of the Strathclyde
Writers' Festival which was staged in 1984 as part of Mayfest, the
arts festival held annually in Glasgow from 1982 until 1997. The
nine-day event covered fiction, poetry and drama, publishing,
literary magazines, writers' circles and "Glasgow's heritage and
prospects," with talks and readings from over fifty writers, well
fulfilling its aim "to celebrate the achievement of Glasgow writers
in the last twenty-five years and draw attention to the new wave of
West of Scotland writing." (That wave, in 1984, was only gathering
strength. Organisers of a similar festival today would have to
consider including a further fifty writers at least.)

In 1985 the London Weekend Television series *Book Four*
screened a programme on Glasgow writers. "Forced to choose a
manageable number," the programme featured Alasdair Gray,
James Kelman, Liz Lochhead and Agnes Owens, while its

265

accompanying notes mentioned Morgan, Leonard, Hind and McIlvanney as being "among other important Glasgow writers." Glasgow writing had been noticed south of Watford. During the eighties, and increasingly into the nineties, it was also being studied in schools and universities – at least in the West of Scotland – another level of recognition gained.

There was plenty to study. A second edition of the present writer's bibliography of the Glasgow novel appeared in 1986, considerably enlarged from its 1972 original, and was itself quite out of date within a couple of years. Nearly seventy titles in all were published in the 1980s (a total, it is true, boosted by the regular productions of Blair, Davis and Turnbull), and many of these were first novels. The quality of the "new wave" and the attention it was receiving worked together, it seems, with an empowering effect on Glasgow writers. It is difficult to detect a trend, to isolate a typical 1980s Glasgow novel, but this is a good fault. The diversity of genres and themes, of ways to look at Glasgow, is a symptom of the richness of the decade.

Grim Glasgow was still in evidence. There's not much sign of the New Glasgow, for instance, in Iain McGinness's *Inner City* (1987), one of the novels which snarls at the official view that everything's miles better.

> Glasgow is quite a big place, but it's getting smaller. It's getting smaller just like a grape shrinks when it's left in the sun to dry, and, like the raisin the grape becomes, Glasgow is turning black and wrinkled and disfigured as all of its lifejuices evaporate into the atmosphere. Also like the raisins, Glasgow is wrapped in an appealing cardboard and cellophane package which diverts the eye from what lies within.

Most of *Inner City* concentrates on "what lies within", and deep gloom envelops the three main characters, Sam the teacher, Pat the car worker, and Alec the clerk with a double life. We look with interest at the novel for another reason, however, since McGinness, like James Barke in *Major Operation*, interleaves episodes in his characters' stories with brief savage bursts of satirical description: "Selected Information for Tourists," "Linguistics," "Scottish Recipe Page: Suicide Supper." The theme of sectarianism is bitterly recurrent: colours, names, songs, and the mindset which lends them a warped significance. McGinness's Glasgow is a million miles from the City of Culture.

Equally unreconstructed is the Glasgow of Alex Cathcart's *The Comeback* (1986). We first meet Hamish Creese in the 1960s when he annoys the debt-collector Gaffney and for his trouble is nailed to the floor in the Clyde Vaults bar. When he returns sixteen years later from prudent exile in Australia, the scene is different but hardly improved:

> On the right-hand side, at the junction, held in the arms of the apex, lost and forgotten, one tenement block stood, ragged blinds flapping through square holes which once were windows in somebody's home . . . The Clyde Vaults. Still standing.

Another change is that Gaffney has emerged from a stretch in prison as a poet admired by the literati. Hamish doesn't approve, though his New Glasgow woman friend lectures him:

> "I think you're just a touch silly about it . . . you don't want to learn; you don't want to improve your ways . . . Hamish, this is the nineteen-eighties."

He sticks to his old ideas and he and Gaffney fight to the death in the rubble of the Clyde Vaults. Through melodramatic events and a deliberately repetitive style, this is another voice saying that things haven't really changed.

The young central character in Joseph Mills's *Towards the End* (1989), the first openly gay Glasgow novel, doesn't see much evidence of the New Glasgow either.

> The East End of Glasgow looked far worse than I remembered

it looking when I stayed there as a child . . . even though it was
well after nine at night, the broken, litter-covered streets ("We
should have hired a tractor not a van," I said to Pat) were
teeming with hordes of wild-looking youths . . .
"They make documentaries about this street," I mumbled to
him as we got out of the van.

Admittedly it is something else he is looking for, and in some
measure finds.

I could see what was wrong with the Christmas display: every
now and then one of the circuits of light glowed too brightly,
overpowering the other, which dimmed and flickered
precariously, threatening to blow out the whole thing. But
when both burned with equal intensity all the coloured lights
merged into one vibrant fusion which radiated all the colours of
the imagination.

The haunting Glasgow seen by the unnamed narrator of Frederic
Lindsay's *Brond* (1984), as he blunders through webs of mystery
and terrorism, is both old and new.

The light was dim like a church but the walls smelled of evil
and too much poverty. It was a bad church . . . I came out of
the front of the close into another street of desolate tenements
and walked out of it into a hallucination of green fields. They
had demolished streets of buildings and sown the vacant places
with grass. These dazzling plots glowed like jewellery in the
vivid light.

That location is unidentified, but the spell works in a geographically
exact Glasgow too.

At the corner I hesitated about walking through to Great
Western Road, but turned instead into Gibson Street . . . As I
came on to the bridge, I passed a boy who was pulling himself
up to get a view. His behind stuck out as he hung by his elbows
from the narrow parapet of iron . . . I looked back at the boy in

time to see a man put the flat of his hand under the little
wriggling behind and give one good heave in passing that lifted
him over the parapet. It looked effortless but then the boy had
been drawing his weight up so high.

By the end of the decade Glasgow fiction had matured enough to
encompass Frank Kuppner's *A Very Quiet Street* (1989), described
on its cover as "a novel, of sorts". Kuppner is a poet and thinker,
and his novel (if it is a novel), while grounded in historical fact,
acknowledges few limitations of chronology or structure, epitom-
ising the post-*Lanark* freedom of the Glasgow writer. Into its pages,
just as the whim takes him (or so it seems), he packs research into
the 1908 murder of Miss Marion Gilchrist in West Princes Street;
memories of his childhood, by coincidence spent, fifty years later,
in the house next door to Miss Gilchrist's; and musings on the
character of Glasgow in these different decades, and on the links –
causal and accidental – between people, buildings and events then
and now.

I find that I am thinking of an extremely bright sunlit
morning of what – of slightly over 20 years ago . . . I looked
down from my high window . . . and watched the postman
leisurely enter and leave in turn all the closes across the street.
No-one else was out and about so early, and the whole
episode was so obviously happening outside time that to have
to consider it dissolved into the normal fabric of some
unspecial month or other of the 1960s seems hopelessly
counter-intuitive. That this memory seems to have nothing
whatever to do with Marion Gilchrist is, I might say, exactly
its point. This was the same street in which an old lady had
been horrifically murdered by an unknown hand nearly sixty
years before. (Indeed, my view then was a sort of higher
distortion of hers.) The thought, what else might not have
happened in that street, flickers for a moment in the
consciousness . . .

This individual, absorbing book is far indeed from the 'traditional'

Glasgow novel, and the same could be said for Alasdair Gray's *1982, Janine* (1984), except that to describe *Janine* as a Glasgow novel would be ludicrously reductive. It is regarded by some as Gray's masterpiece, and its complexities are too rich and extensive for discussion here. Yet there are connections with Glasgow:

> It was a sunny summer in Glasgow, the streets quieter than usual. Perhaps it was the start of the fair fortnight. I walked along St George's Road and saw Alan strolling toward me round the curve of Charing Cross Mansions, arms folded on chest, great face surveying the white clouds. I was filled with delighted relief and laughter, I ran to him crying, "You're not dead! You're not dead!"
> He smiled and said, "Of course not, that was all just a joke."
> And suddenly I grew terribly angry with him for making such a cruel joke. And then I awoke, unluckily.

Between *Lanark* and *Janine* Gray had published a collection of short stories, *Unlikely Stories, Mostly* (1983). As the stories themselves – fantastic, satirical, experimental – testify to Gray's great and influential originality, the appearance of the collection as a whole marks the burgeoning of the short story form in Glasgow fiction.

An article published in 1982, "The Glasgow Short Story" – which opens with the words "A title to raise an eyebrow, but . . . there is such a genre" – acknowledges the achievements of Gaitens, Friel and Margaret Hamilton, but identifies "distinction in the short story" more generally as a feature of Glasgow writing in the seventies. Alan Spence, Gray, Kelman and Carl MacDougall are rightly named as outstanding in the genre. While all had been featuring for some years in literary magazines and anthologies, only Spence, when the article appeared, had published a substantial collection of stories in this country. Things were due to change; the remaining years of the decade saw the publication of five or six short story collections by Glasgow writers, including MacDougall's impressive *Elvis is Dead* (1986). Recognition of the Glasgow short story further resulted in two anthologies edited by the present writer and Hamish Whyte, *Streets of Stone* (1985) and *Streets of Gold* (1989).

Alasdair Gray had much to do with the publication of *Lean Tales* (1985), apart, that is, from his contribution (customary in his own books) of stories and prose pieces, illustrations and book design. In a "Postscript" he explains how *Lean Tales* was made:

> A director of a London publishing house asked him if he had enough stories to make another collection. Gray said no. There was a handful of stories he had intended to build into another collection, but found he could not, as he had no more ideas for prose fictions . . . Even if his few unpublished stories were stretched by the addition of some prose portraits and poems they would still not amount to a book. The director asked Gray if he could suggest two other writers who would join him in a collection . . .

One of them was Agnes Owens, whose "discovery" as a gifted writer is described in the same Postscript. Her short stories and novels, at first glance, fit well enough into one accepted image of Glasgow fiction: realistic, clear-eyed, plain-spoken. But there's a dimension of surreal black humour to some of her work. The story "Arabella" surfaced at an extra-mural writing class.

> Arabella . . . took hold of her father's hand, which was dangling down loosely. She clasped it to her sagging breast and was chilled by its icy touch, so she hurriedly flung the hand back on the bed saying, "Daddy darling, what advice can you give your little girl on how to get rid of Sanitary Inspectors?"
>
> He regarded her with a hard immovable stare then his hand slid down to dangle again. She looked at him thoughtfully and pulled the sheet over his face. "Mummy, I think Daddy is dead."
>
> Her mother took out a pipe from her pocket and lit it from the fire with a long taper. After puffing for a few seconds, she said, "Very likely."
>
> Arabella realized that the discussion was over . . .

"If you enjoyed that story," observes Gray, "you will know why Lochhead [the class tutor], Gray and Kelman were greatly excited."

The remaining writer in *Lean Tales* was James Kelman, probably the key figure, apart from Gray himself, in 1980s Glasgow fiction. As we have seen, his road to recognition had been a long one. He was a member of Philip Hobsbaum's "Glasgow Group" (see Chapter Fifteen), and his stories were being admired in magazines and anthologies throughout the seventies, appearing also in the seminal *Three Glasgow Writers* (1976) and in a small-press publication, *Short Tales from the Night Shift* (1978). He had in fact published a collection of short stories several years earlier, but not in Britain. The Postscript already quoted supplies the background:

> An author who liked Kelman's work was Mary Gray Hughes, one of North America's best short-story writers. She visited the Glasgow group . . . and through her representations Puckerbush Press of Maine published in 1973 Jim Kelman's first collection of stories, *An old pub near the Angel* . . . It proved to those who cared for such things that Jim Kelman was a professional writer. Ten years passed before his next book of tales found a publisher . . .

That next book was *Not Not While the Giro*, published in 1983. Years later again, in 1994, an interviewer recorded how Kelman

> . . . recalls with quiet amazement well-meaning academics asking him if he ever revises, if he's ever read Joyce, as if he were some miraculous aberration of nature sprung fully-fledged from Govan . . .

He is of course an exceptionally painstaking writer, a craftsman. No word or phrase in his stories and novels is there by accident, and strong beliefs power both what he writes and how he writes it. He has often spoken of this, very concisely in one talk published in 1992:

Along with Alasdair Gray, James Kelman is probably the key figure in 1980s Glasgow and Scottish fiction. This portrait by Alasdair Gray is from the 1985 collection of stories, *Lean Tales*, which featured work by Gray, Kelman and Agnes Owens

273

The stories I wanted to write would derive from my own background, my own socio-cultural experience. I wanted to write as one of my own people, I wanted to write and remain a member of my own community . . .

Nobody issues such instructions. It's all carried out by a series of nudges and winks and tacit agreement. Go and write a story about a bunch of guys who stand talking in a pub all day but if you have them talking then don't have them talking the language they talk.

The two paragraphs, a couple of pages apart in the talk as published, go far to summarise his concerns and his style.

His community, he finds, is not represented in "English Literature". He expands on this in interview:

One of the things that goes on in say English Literature is the wee dialogue going on between author and reader about character. All the wee signals and codes . . . a wee game going on between writer and reader and the wee game is "Reader and writer are the same and they speak in the same voice as the narrative, and they're unlike these fucking natives who do the dialogue in phonetics . . ."

He sets out to short-circuit the wee game by various techniques.

[interviewer]: You've stated that you are trying to obliterate the narrator, to get rid of the narrative voice.

[Kelman]: Not every narrative voice, just the standard third party one, the one that most people don't think of as a "voice" at all – except maybe the voice of God – and they take for granted that it is unbiased and objective. But it's no such thing. Getting rid of that standard third party narrative voice is getting rid of a whole value system . . . Let's just go for the factual reality here.

He goes for it through, typically, a kind of interior monologue or dialogue – again, the point is debated in interviews – where the narrator is not distinguishable from the character, and where colloquialism switches to formality and back again. A reviewer particularly interested in Kelman's style has tried to pin it down:

> Sometimes, in monologues or narratives rooted entirely in the perceptions of a single character, he puts the style at his subject's disposal, as an articulating instrument; at other times, in more fantastic or more fragmentary pieces, it is imposed upon action to produce – through the inhumanity of its elaborations – a black, humane comedy.

A year or two earlier, an interviewer was perhaps taken aback by the thoroughness of Kelman's answer to a simple and indeed sympathetic question:

> [*interviewer*] I remember thinking as I was reading *The Busconductor Hines* that this was the first time about, or one of those rare times, when there was a realistic amount of swearing in a piece of literature.
> [*Kelman*] Well, even in the way that question was said. For instance, what makes you think it's swearing? You see when you use the term "swearing" it's a value; I don't accept that it is swearing at all you see. How can you talk about it? "The use of the four-letter word"? That's not satisfactory . . . So in that sense I object to taking part, for instance, in a discussion that hinges on the use of swear words in literature, because right away you've begged the question of what those words are, you know, and you're involving me again in a value system that *isn't your own to deny*. I mean I deny this fucking thing, but suddenly you find that you've affirmed it; the very fact that you're talking about swearing means that you've affirmed it, you know . . . *[the full answer is considerably longer than this extract]*
> [*interviewer*] Anyway, I just thought I'd mention that I thought you had the eh four-letter word proportion about right, for the first time.

Chapter Twenty will look at this vexed question, since the reaction to Kelman's brilliant, Booker-prizewinning *How Late It Was, How*

Late (1994) produced the extraordinary statistic that the novel contained four thousand instances of the word "fuck". By this time, however, it should be unnecessary to say that "the use of the four-letter word" is simply one component of the flexible, rhythmical, immensely articulate voice of Kelman's stories and novels: the very voice of his own people, his own community.

During the eighties Kelman published two collections of short stories and three novels. *Not Not While the Giro* (1984) revealed him at once as a master of the short story form. The horrifying one-paragraph "Acid" is already a classic, while "Jim dandy" has been described by a critic as "quite simply the funniest sexy story I know." It established, too, the parameters of Kelman's Glasgow (which, as it were, accompanies the central character even when the story's setting is London, Manchester or a Highland construction site). The title story enters the mind of an unemployed man as he daydreams, plans, muses on his neighbours, contemplates suicide, because his giro cheque won't come until Saturday and it's only Thursday now. Kelman's grim humour has never been stronger.

> 3.30 in the afternoon this approximate Thursday. I have
> until Saturday morning to starve to death though I wont.
> I shall make it no bother. The postman comes at 8.20
> – 7.50 on Saturdays but the bastarn postoffice opens not
> until 9.00 and often 9.05 though they deny it.

Greyhound for Breakfast (1987) attracted widespread critical attention. (Perhaps not coincidentally, it was Kelman's first book with a 'big' London-based publisher.) Reviewers spoke of "a powerfully sustained description of modern urban life," detected the influence of Kafka and Beckett, called his books "sheer art and wild wit." There's understated menace in "Old Francis", surreal humour in "The Small Family", and again, in the title story, deep exploration of a man in distress, who buys a knackered greyhound, he doesn't know why. But we do, in a way: his teenage son has gone off to London without warning.

Where to keep the dog for instance. The boy's room. Could he keep it there? Would Babs accept it? Would she fuck. She would just fucking, she would laugh at him. Quite right as well.

Between these two collections Kelman had published two novels. The eponymous central character of *The Busconductor Hines* (1984) is another man in trouble, no less desperate because his troubles are such everyday affairs. He isn't a very good bus-conductor, he'll never become a driver, and bus-conductors are being phased out. He and his family live in a "no-bedroomed flat." His in-laws don't approve of him and his wife might just go home to mother. We observe him at home, at work, and walking about the Glasgow streets, often overhearing his thoughts.

> There is a crack in the pavement a few yards from the close entrance; it has a brave exterior; it is a cheery wee soul; other cracks can be shifty but not this one. Hines will refer to it as Dan in future. Hello there Dan. How's it going? Cold yin the night eh! This fucking weather wee man. Never mind but, the ice and that, helps you expand. Pity cracks don't wear balaclavas right enough eh!

The first sentence of *The Busconductor Hines* is: "Hines jumped up from the armchair, she was about to lift the huge soup-pot of boiling water" and this attracted some comment on publication, as if we had here an author who didn't know what a sentence was. As always in Kelman's work, it was no mistake.

> *[interviewer]* Let's talk about the opening sentence of *Hines* – in particular about its punctuation. You know what I'm talking about – the fact that it's two sentences separated by a comma.
>
> *[Kelman]* I know that opening sentence of *Hines* quite well and I do not accept that at all. I spent a lot of time on it. You cannot make it a semi-colon; you can't make it a colon: it's got to be a comma, there's no question . . . He jumps up because his wife is about to lift over a pot of boiling water – an inadequate pot . . . It's got to begin in a really unemphatic way;

even a semi-colon makes it emphatic, you know. It's got to be
something that's so everyday. I remember Alasdair Gray
reading that for the first time . . . and saying it was really
terrible for him to wonder . . . if this girl was actually going to
fill the bath without scalding herself.

And in that sentence Hines, an ordinary guy who cares deeply
about his wife and son, a most attractive character, in fact immediately comes alive.

The life of Tammas, protagonist of *A Chancer* (1985), is,
deliberately, even more ordinary. He is twenty years old, unemployed, vaguely looking for work, investigating sex, a regular gambler.
He lodges with his sister, who worries about him. A critic has said:

This is the closest anyone has come to presenting the real,
elusive heartland of Glasgow . . . This is the most depressingly
fair and sophisticated picture of Glasgow life, at one of its most
significant levels, that has yet been written; I respect its craft
and truth enormously.

Kelman's third novel, *A Disaffection* (1989), opens uncomprom-
isingly: "Patrick Doyle was a teacher. Gradually he had become
sickened by it." Patrick teaches in a comprehensive school and
hates himself for being in the employment of a repressive government, though his teaching method goes some way to making
amends.

Children, there is little to say and I'm not the man who can say
that little. I'm a man who is fucking sorely bemused, sorely
bemused . . . Repeat after me: We are being fenced in by the
teachers . . . at the behest of a dictatorship government . . . in
explicit simulation of our fucking parents the silly bastards . . .
Good, good, but cut out that laughing . . . Okay then that last
bit: viz the suppressed poor! . . . Cheering.

Again we hear his thoughts – sorely bemused though they are, as he fancies a married woman colleague and plays music on a pair of old cardboard pipes – and again there is no resolution. We leave him walking home in the rain, accosted by the police, or is he imagining that?

> What are they shouting. They're just shouting they hate him
> they hate ye we fucking hate ye, that's what they're shouting. It
> was dark and it was wet but not cold; if it had not been so dark
> you would have seen the sky. Ah fuck off, fuck off.

A Disaffection was shortlisted for the Booker prize, focussing further media attention on Kelman and his work, and on Glasgow writing in general. On Glasgow itself, one would say; except that Glasgow was now firmly in line anyway for media exposure, due to inherit the title of European City of Culture in 1990.

18

Entirely in Glaswegian

Discussion of the use of Glasgow language in fiction has to begin with the famous one-sentence put-down in the majestic *Scottish National Dictionary*, written in 1931.

> Owing to the influx of Irish and foreign immigrants in the industrial area near Glasgow the dialect has become hopelessly corrupt.

Given its date, this might be seen as an expression of the *zeitgeist*, the search for pure Scots which was one benchmark of the contemporary Scottish Literary Renaissance, except that it does not stand alone. It had been foreshadowed:

> "She [Effie Deans] is a Scotchwoman, and speaks with a Scotch accent . . . [but] you must suppose it is not the broad coarse Scots that is spoken in the Cowgate of Edinburgh, or in the Gorbals."   (Walter Scott, *The Heart of Midlothian*)

It is a view that has followers right up to the present day. A fairly sympathetic commentator writing in 1981 damns the native tongue with faint praise: "The Scots of here and now for millions is the thin Scots of the cities . . ." It was a distinctly unsympathetic voice contemplating the fiction of 1984 that observed: "There is even a novel written entirely in Glaswegian. Lacking a dictionary, I soon gave up." Coarse, corrupt, thin, unintelligible: Glasgow language is thus portrayed, over more than a century, as being hardly fit for everyday communication, let alone for literature.

Of course, there's a different view.

> Glasgow speech [is] that aspect of the city in which I see most hope for the survival of its identity undiluted . . . Even a cursory acquaintance with that speech will reveal that it is not merely a collection of slightly different words. It is the expression of a coherent attitude to life, a series of verbal stances as ritualised as one of the martial arts. But it is also continuingly inventive, an established style within which individual creativity can flourish.

Thus William McIlvanney, in an essay expressing his relationship with Glasgow and the city's importance to his writing, gives full credit to the language which, especially perhaps in his Laidlaw novels, he uses with power and purpose. Further, he refers readers to a standard work of reference:

> Anyone who wants a quick and painless introduction to the essential Glasgow should read Michael Munro's excellent dictionary of Glasgow speech, *The Patter*, full of superbly creative examples.

The Patter (1985) is excellent indeed. Though lighthearted, it should not be confused with what its introduction mildly describes as "various jokey books about Glasgow parlance that contrive to present it as a language for inarticulate idiots." On the contrary, writes Munro:

> I maintain that Glaswegian is a rich, vital, and above all valid regional dialect which gives a true reflection of the city and its

inhabitants with all their unattractive features, such as deprivation, bigotry, and pugnacity, but with all their virtues too, such as robust and irreverent humour, resilience, and abhorrence of pretension.

Illustrating not only Glasgow speech but Glasgow life, *The Patter* goes far to prove the point. Two adjacent entries, randomly chosen, may give the flavour of the book:

hen A term of affection for a girl or woman. It is often used when speaking in a friendly way to a stranger: "Is that your glove you've dropped, hen?"

Her, Him The Anonymous Spouse. Many married people tend to speak of their beloved without referring to her or him by name. It is almost as if the marriage partner has attained such a talismanic status that it would be bad luck to utter the name aloud: "I'll need to be away hame to give Him his tea."

The Patter sold well, not only in Glasgow. Anecdotal evidence indicates that a bulk order was placed for British consulates overseas, as an aid (it is assumed) to the repatriation of emotionally disoriented Glasgow football fans.

While *The Patter* disclaims any intention to be a scholarly work of lexicography, more academic studies of Glasgow language (or dialect) were also appearing during the 1980s. Importantly for our purposes, these began to investigate the use of the language in Glasgow literature, something which was a fairly recent phenomenon at that time. In early Glasgow novels like *Rob Roy* and *The Entail* a rich Scots is employed, but it is a traditional Scots, not distinctively Glaswegian. The same applies to Victorian sketches like *Jeems Kaye*, possibly because the features now seen as typical of Glasgow dialect were not yet in place. "Nineteenth century Glasgow", observes one specialist, "was something of a linguistic melting pot."

The same authority notes that:

Even the famous *Wee Macgreegor* stories of JJ Bell are written
in traditional dialect, and could have been set anywhere
between Ayr and Helensburgh as far as language is concerned.

Bell himself confirms that the *Wee Macgreegor* dialogue did not
necessarily come from the contemporary city around him.

> I am well aware that I have been suspected of eavesdropping on
> tramway cars and elsewhere, and of furtively lurking in close-
> mouths, and in sundry other places, in order to gain my know-
> ledge, such as it is, of the Glasgow, or Lowland, dialect; but . . . I
> had never made any effort to "learn" the speech of the people of
> the period. While I was familiar with the older men in my father's
> factory, who used the vernacular as a matter of course, I feel
> certain that I acquired little or nothing there . . . From the lips of
> my paternal grandmother . . . fell all the quaint words and phrases
> – many of them embodied in nursery rhymes – into my memory,
> there to lie quiet till the years should bring a use for them.

His reference to "the Glasgow, or Lowland, dialect" may be noted,
with no indication of any difference between the two; and also
observe that this particular grandmother in fact came from Paisley,
which, as we have learned from the columns of *The Bailie*, wasn't
quite the same thing.

By the 1930s Glasgow dialect may have been considered
"hopelessly corrupt," but it was at least different; so much so that
Alexander McArthur in *No Mean City*, or more probably his English
collaborator and publisher, deemed it necessary to put such idioms
as "eleven of a family" and "awa' oot to get a wee drink" in quotes.
Often Glasgow phrases, and slang phrases in general, are actually
glossed, even in moments of narrative excitement:

> "Nit the jorrie (Leave the girl alone)!" he yelled.

Sometimes they are considered earnestly in a kind of anthro-
pological way:

> In the language of the Gorbals, he was "well put on" and
> proud of his "paraffin". There was actually a paraffin dressing
> on his sleek black hair, and perhaps there may be some
> association of ideas between slumland's passion for smoothed
> and glistening crops and its general term for a smart
> appearance.

The phrases thus highlighted in *No Mean City* are much more commonly connected with what Munro calls the city's "unattractive features" than with its virtues. George Blake in his exactly contemporary *The Shipbuilders* (or at least his middle-class character Leslie Pagan) also equates Glasgow language and unpleasantness:

> The ugly tongue of Clydeside assailed his ears, every sixth word
> a fierce and futile obscenity.

Thus when a new wave of Glasgow writers wanted to express the life of their city in its own language, there was a lot of baggage to discard, as Tom Leonard has inimitably observed:

> right inuff
> ma language is disgraceful
>
> ma maw tellt mi
> ma teacher tellt mi
> thi doactir tellt mi
> thi priest tellt mi . . .
>
> po-faced literati grimly kerryin thi burden a thi past tellt mi
> po-faced literati grimly kerryin thi burden a thi future tellt mi. . .
> even thi introduction tay thi Scottish National Dictionary
> tellt mi . . .

Archie Hind, speaking for a working-class Glasgow writer, explored this question in *The Dear Green Place*:

Where did the failure of his work come from? . . . Was it in the
language he spoke, the gutter patois into which his tongue fell
naturally when he was moved by a strong feeling?

The breakthrough came after – and very likely because of – *The
Dear Green Place*. Edwin Morgan has noted that:

> The seventies was a decade when Glaswegian began to fight
> back, in fiction, drama and poetry. The "gutter patois" of
> Archie Hind's soured hero became both an area of experiment
> and a badge of pride.

A key text in the seventies is Alan Spence's *Its Colours They are
Fine*, with its beautifully observed dialogue:

> "Fancy gin doon tae the ferry efter tea?" [Joe] said.
> "The ferry?"
> "Aye, we could nik acroass tae Partick an play aboot therr 'nen
> come back. Disnae cost anythin."   ("The Ferry")

And once again we must turn to the slim paperback *Three Glasgow
Writers*. Here are poems by Tom Leonard "in a transcription of
Glasgow speech," sometimes directly concerned with this question:

> . . . if
> a toktaboot
> thi trooth
> lik wanna yoo
> scruff yi
> widny thingk
> it wuz troo. . .

The accompanying short story "Honest" transfers the same
technique to prose, again considering the problems involved:

> Ifyi sayti sumdy, "Whaira yi afti?" nthey say, "Whut?" nyou say,

"Where are you off to?" they don't say, "That's no whutyi said thi furst time." They'll probably say sumhm like, "Doon the road!" anif you say, "What?" they usually say, "Down the road!" the second time – though no always. Course, they never really say, "Doon thi road!" or "Down the road!" at all. Least, they never say it the way it's spelt. Cos it *isny* spelt, when they say it, is it?

Alex Hamilton also follows this line:

"Cumoan," I says, "Tam's right. Fwi jiss get oan wi it thill no boathir us. Ah mean, thid oanlie want a gemm wi thi likes a us if we wir thi oanlie wans wi thi baw, widint they?"

Hamilton's short story collection *Gallus, did you say?* (1982) declares on its cover:

This collection is a landmark in publishing history, representing as it does the first conscious decision to reproduce in extended written prose the sounds of Glasgow English, as faithfully as non-phonetic transcription will allow.

The stories by James Kelman in *Three Glasgow Writers* are in fact in English, though the near-contemporary "The Hon" uses Glasgow dialect with irresistible effect.

Auld Shug gits oot iv bed. Turns aff the alarm cloak. Gis straight ben the toilit. Sits doon in that oan the lavatri pan. Wee bit iv time gis by. Shug sittin ther, yonin. This Hon. Up it comes oot fri the waste pipe. Stretchis right up. Grabs him by the bolls. . .

But *Three Glasgow Writers* contains, as has been noted, Kelman's statement: ". . . In my writings the accent is in Glasgow/ I am always from Glasgow and I speak English always/ Always with this Glasgow accent . . ." Various components of his style have been isolated and described. The use in many of his stories, for instance, of formal Standard English in both narrative and reported thought, is examined in the article which previously looked at *Wee Macgreegor*:

> This deliberately stilted style contrasts with the indigence and desperation of the characters, and clearly implies a proposition about language and thought, to the effect that the language of inner speech is free of the social differentiae of the spoken word.

His narrative style in "Young Cecil", in *Three Glasgow Writers*, is further compared to that of John Galt in *Annals of the Parish*:

> Like Galt, Kelman uses a mixed style, in which certain categories of Scots forms, mainly lexical forms, are used alongside Scottish StE . . . Unlike Galt, however, Kelman also treats the reported speech in the same way, so that the language of the narrator and the characters, who share a social background and milieu, is homogeneous.

What all this adds up to is a totally distinctive style, sensitive and accurate, yet variable. The orthography of his 1994 novel *How Late it Was, How Late* is slightly different from that of the 1989 *A Disaffection* (*doesnay/ doesni*, for example) as Kelman hones his "Glasgow accent" to represent more exactly what his city says and thinks.

19

Glasgow Women

There is a perception that all Glasgow novels are about men, the hard inhabitants of this notoriously macho city. Like other perceptions that we have examined – for instance, that there were no city novels at all for many years, and that there are still no middle-class Glasgow novels – this one is false; yet, on a quick consideration of landmark titles, it's possible to see how it has taken hold. Razor King in *No Mean City*; the paired male characters of *The Shipbuilders* and *Major Operation*; sensitive Eddy in *Dance of the Apprentices*; struggling Matt in *The Dear Green Place*; complex Laidlaw and tortured Thaw/Lanark; the list goes on.

Of course there are female characters in all these novels, just as there have always been women in Glasgow, and strong women too. We have already observed the recurrence of the strong woman character in Glasgow fiction, from Galt's Leddy o' Grippy in *The Entail* down to McCrone's Bel Moorhouse in *Wax Fruit*, or indeed Bel's widowed mother Mrs Barrowfield. We first meet this genuine Glasgow matron as she ensures that her housemaid comes in at the stroke of eight every morning to re-lay the bedroom fire: "A body's not much worth, if she's come to the age of sixty-five and still lets her girls get the better of her".

Sometimes, indeed, the strong-minded woman is laughed at, as in *Martha Spreull* and *Generalship*. Just as often she is admired, though rather to excess and not always for the right reasons – think of George Blake's fearsome Bella Macfadyen in *Mince Collop Close*. (But then Bella, though strong, is ridiculous. Bluebell Oliphant in *The Westering Sun*, two decades later, is much more credible, attesting to Blake's greater maturity as a writer by that time.)

We have seen how the character Bella Macfadyen sprang from Blake's observation of a lively, confident young girl on a train. A nineteenth-century versifier had earlier captured another most attractive little girl.

> A deil o' a lassie to scamper an' rin;
> Bare-fitted, bare-headed, and wild as the win':
> For ever in mischief, and whiles in a haud;
> O, weel dae I mind o' ye – Shoosie, ye jaud! . . .
>
> A' lassie bit playthings aside ye wad fling;
> But gie ye a "peerie" wi' plenty o' string,
> Or a big spinnin' "tap" wi' a whippin' skrudge ca'd,
> And ye lick't a' the laddies clean – Shoosie, ye jaud! . . .

What with her unconventionality, skill and courage – "Ne'er fearin' a fa', nor a broo-duntin' daud", the poet is in no doubt that "Ye ocht to had breeks on ye – Shoosie, ye jaud!" But time brings changes. It's sad (from today's viewpoint) to see how Shoosie settles down, and how whole-heartedly the onlooker approves. He is clear about the chief end of women, and certain that Shoosie has done right to recognise it.

> And whiles it's the roughest and tooziest bairn
> That grows up the doucest; and prood I'm to learn,
> (Tho' misunderstood lang, and muckle misca'd),
> Ye're baith wife an' mither noo – Shoosie, ye jaud!

And that's one trouble about the depiction of women in most

Glasgow novels: their joys and problems are linked to those of their men. William McIlvanney has been criticised in this regard.

> There are three basic types of women in McIlvanney's novels. The first is the wee "decent wumman" epitomised by Tam's wife Jenny Docherty . . . The second type is austere and "as clean and about as yielding as stainless steel". She belongs mainly to "the lumpen middle class" . . . The third type of woman is an amalgam of the first two types – middle-class, physically attractive and emotionally open . . . Absent from this list are strong, attractive female characters and women who act independently of men.

But it is probably unfair to single out McIlvanney among many others who portray their woman characters as objects of desire, or wives, or mothers. The last, in fact, is a special case. It would be possible to compile a sizeable anthology of heroic mothers in Glasgow fiction.

> Neil should have new boots. Her shoes had holes in the soles . . . Yes, Neil required new boots. Neil required new underclothing to be warm. She skimped herself of food often so as to give him sustaining meals. He was a growing boy.
> (Frederick Niven, *Mrs Barry*)

> Her limbs heavy and aching after her long day's work, she would not think of the ten miles' walk before her, but the rain again soaked into her shoes, and she knew she would be drenched and ready to collapse before she was even right into the city. And away at the other end of it her family were waiting, expecting her to be coming back with money in her pocket and warm fish and chips, in a vinegar-smelling parcel, under her arm. (George Friel, "Home")

> Rather than squabble meaninglessly [in the wash-house], . . . she would withdraw into her kitchen to wash as many clothes as possible in the sink, until her quick, unquestioning hands were split and cracked with hacks from long immersion in water, and the gathering forks between her eyes fought against the dim light. (J. F. Hendry, *Fernie Brae*)

Is the writer quite sure about those "unquestioning hands"? (And was the earlier poet sure that Shoosie didn't harbour notions of rebellion under her dutiful apron?) It's very seldom in such tributes to saintly mothers that we get a hint of any objections to the motherly role, any ambition beyond the simple, dedicated one of keeping the family and home together.

The subtle Robin Jenkins does allow Bell McShelvie, the central character in *Guests of War*, to want something more. As she accompanies some of her children to evacuation in the countryside, however, she is seen by a chorus of neighbours to be abandoning the rest of her family, and the strictures of the other women are as nothing compared to her own guilt. At the end of the novel she resumes the yoke of returning to the city "prepared to create as much light there as she could".

A year or two before the publication of *Guests of War*, Jenkins, writing on the theme "My Scotland", had epitomised, perhaps unconsciously, another approach which has hobbled the Glasgow woman in fiction.

> Here is a theme that teases my imagination: a woman with a
> Highland name, middle-aged, with four or five children,
> married to a labourer, say, with a small wage, living in a typical
> city tenement in one of the poorer districts . . . the protectress,
> indeed the sheet anchor of her family, yet tormented by
> girlhood ambitions and still older ancestral memories of
> another kind of life . . . Such a woman would best convey my
> Scotland.

This woman sounds not unlike Bell McShelvie, though Bell, as she appears in *Guests of War*, has acquired added complexity and humanity. The original "my Scotland" woman labours, however, under one big disadvantage: she is not a person but a personification. Of course personifications of Scotland as woman are not rare in Scottish literature, from Lewis Grassic Gibbon's Chris Guthrie to Gray's Janine, but treatment of a female character in this way carries its dangers. A mother seen as the personification of Motherhood, with however much filial love and respect, may lose the chance to say how she sees herself; to say who she thinks she is.

Among all these women on pedestals, the half-mad jealous mother in *Justice of the Peace* is a rare exception, but Frederick Niven is most concerned with the effect of her neurosis on her husband and son. There is a slightly unconvincing attempt to explain it (the trouble began when she was pregnant – say no more), but little insight, from this often sensitive writer, into the anguish of Mrs Moir herself. We have seen John Blair in *Jean* and Patrick MacGill in *The Rat-Pit* attempt, if clumsily, to provide the woman's point of view. Archie Hind might have achieved more in *Für Sadie*, his long-promised second novel, "the story of a middle-aged, working-class woman from Parkhead who decides to learn the piano". We see Sadie, certainly, through the music teacher's eyes:

> When she moved it was with constraint, with a particular kind of action which McKay had often thought to himself [sic] as "the close-mooth shuffle". He had seen hundreds of these women during his life in Glasgow, scuffling up and down tenement stairs, crouching over their breasts which were held clutched in their forearms like valuable parcels . . .

But there's also an attempt at a Sadie's-eye view:

> . . . during the last chromatic run she had felt the notes like loving fingers playing delicately on the spine of her backbone. She was moved by a strange feeling, almost of power, as she sat there on the stool.

Apart from a few fragments, however, *Für Sadie* has, at the time of writing, never been published and cannot fairly be evaluated.

There is one factor, though, common to all the fictional Glasgow women mentioned so far in this chapter, from the Leddy of Grippy to Razor King's moll, from Nora in the rat-pit to Sadie at the piano. They are all depicted by male authors. Until very recently, the perception with which we began had a corollary: Glasgow novels are written by men.

An article some years ago (which unsurprisingly began "Although I have little sympathy with feminism . . .") attempted to expand on this.

> Women novelists have approached the city half-heartedly, with their eyes averted and their minds on other things; they have retreated into a shell of personal relationships, leaving to their male contemporaries not only the grimmer side of the city, but the major themes of industrial life.

Since this strange sentence appears to imply that Glasgow novels ought not to deal with personal relationships, it should probably be forgotten as we consider what these hermit crabs calling themselves women novelists have in fact written.

The answer has largely been given already in earlier chapters, where such accomplished writers as Sarah Tytler, Catherine Carswell, Dot Allan and Margaret Hamilton have been dealt with in their chronological place. To these should be added, at least, the names of Joan Ure, better known as a playwright, whose quirky, steel-hard short stories have been occasionally anthologised but not yet collected, and Evelyn Cowan with her one outstanding novel *Portrait of Alice* (1976). It was described by a contemporary reviewer as "a taut book of loneliness, despair and rejection"; hackneyed enough themes perhaps, but not (anyway in Glasgow fiction) as treated here, in the context of the mid-life crisis of a middle-class woman.

But still, traditionally, the well-known Glasgow novels have been those written by men. A parallel may be drawn with the situation of Glasgow women artists in the early twentieth century, many of whom were brilliant students at the city's School of Art at the time of the renowned "Glasgow Boys".

> They were recognised as artists and were able to earn their living through their art . . . Yet [they] vanished from most

> accounts. Even on a 1955 commemorative scroll representing
> the history of the School . . . the visible women of the early
> history of the School . . . had vanished.

Other essays in this thoughtful collection allude directly to women writers.

> Women painters, like women writers, have been more harshly
> judged and more quickly consigned to the storage rooms of
> history than their male counterparts . . . Women were isolated
> from the mainstream of artistic production and then criticised
> for the "triviality" of the work they produced in effective exile.
> As with many women in the literary arts from this era, women
> in the visual arts were consistently faced with barriers to which
> they were by force of circumstance compelled to respond or
> acquiesce.

We may think of Dot Allan, living with her elderly mother in genteel Kelvinside, and writing, in "effective exile" from influences which might have pointed out its unnecessary purple patches, the uneven, romanticised, yet sincerely feminist *Makeshift*.

We may also note that Allan's central character Jacqueline is forced to leave Glasgow (and Scotland) in the end, in order to have any hope of realising her potential as a writer and an independent woman. So does Ellen in Catherine Carswell's *The Camomile*, while Joanna in *Open the Door!*, in her pursuit of freedom, certainly doesn't contemplate finding it in the west end of Glasgow.

As the nineteen-eighties moved into the nineties, with developments in Glasgow fiction and in social conditions jointly working towards empowerment, things began to change. Glasgow women writers, among them Janice Galloway and AL Kennedy, began to attract the critical attention they had always deserved, and the woman's viewpoint became acknowledged as an element in Glasgow fiction. The work of Galloway and Kennedy will be looked at in its chronological place in the next chapter, but it's interesting to ask here whether these writers do present us with the image of strong women, confident, in control.

The answer is not entirely straightforward. On a superficial view, Galloway's Joy in *The Trick is to Keep Breathing* and Kennedy's Jennifer in *So I Am Glad* are definitely not in control: Joy is struggling out of a nervous breakdown, and Jennifer, though she thinks she is "calm", is in fact unable to experience emotion, except when she goes over the top in sado-masochistic lovemaking.

But their problems, unlike those of Mrs Moir, are – to apply our previously-used phrase in a new context – written from the inside. Where the women are viewed in relation to men, the emphasis has changed. These relationships, indeed, have been skewed and damaging, as both Joy and Jennifer come to recognise. What we begin to see, in each case, is a great underlying strength. Each story ends in a gleam of optimism, as the heroine, truly independent, prepares to get on with life.

Probably this same strength is what empowered the traditional "strong woman" of the Glasgow novel, the wife and mother running her home and supporting her family; but Joy and Jennifer, single working women, do not align with this recurrent figure. Has she disappeared from Glasgow fiction? No, she's there, though totally subverted, in Agnes Owens's *A Working Mother* (1994).

Betty, who narrates the story, is independent all right. She goes to work because "We owe money. The kids need clothes, apart from the fact that we like to eat." So far, so traditional, it would seem; but her attitude is not quite what the saintly mothers in Niven, Friel and Hendry would recognise.

> "Singing, are we?" said Adam when I arrived home clutching my plastic bag of groceries and humming "Lili Marlene".
>
> "I hope it's not a crime."
>
> "No. It's nice to see you in a good mood. But I just can't help wondering what you've been up to."
>
> "Lamb chops, that's what I've been up to. Lamb chops for supper and a bottle for afterwards."
>
> Adam and the kids regarded me with blank stares.
>
> "There's no pleasing you lot is there?"

She's singing because she has conned thirty pounds out of the dirty old man who is her boss, and "Lili Marlene" is specially chosen to annoy Adam, who attributes his neuroses to his war service. Betty doesn't entirely believe his harrowing tales, but she herself lies as readily as she breathes, telling everyone what best serves the purpose of the moment. She briskly manipulates her boss, her colleagues, her husband Adam and his oddball friend Brendan, while sleeping from time to time with both Adam and Brendan and drinking with them non-stop. It all rattles on at a great pace, heartless and extremely funny.

But is it so funny? Towards the end of the short novel we find that Betty has been telling all this to her room-mate in a mental hospital where she has been brought "shouting and screaming", out of her mind with drink. None of the story, she says, is true. Or maybe some of it, she corrects herself. The room-mate complains "It seems to me you don't know what the truth is," and Betty replies, "When you're in here everything gets so jumbled up it's hard to know the truth".

So it's possible that she has in fact burst out of a humdrum and rather miserable marriage with a neurotic husband to carry on this hilariously amoral life; it's equally possible, though, that the bleakness of the marriage has driven her to fantasise it all. Drink is the constant factor, and what's certain by the end is that she is detached from a reality which (whatever it was) has proved too much to bear. *A Working Mother* at last, and with disturbing effect, brings a Glasgow woman into the full light of the Glasgow novel.

20
Culture and After

"Culture" is the motif-word of the conversation: ancient
Scots culture, future Scots culture, culture ad lib. and ad
nauseam. . . The patter is as intimate on my tongue as on
theirs. And relevant to the fate and being of those hundred
and fifty thousand [Glasgow slum-dwellers] it is no more
than the chatter and scratch of a band of apes, seated in a pit
on a midden of corpses.

Lewis Grassic Gibbon wrote that in the 1930s, but something
very like it was being expressed at the tag-end of the 1980s,
in the run-up to the *annus mirabilis* of 1990 and Glasgow's
coronation as European City of Culture for the year. There were
differences, of course: as we have seen, the notorious Glasgow
slums cramming the inner city had gone. Instead, on the cold
outskirts, thousands of Glasgow people lived in the "schemes"
where, as Liz Lochhead caused a character to observe, "the only
culture's whit's growing on my walls." A journalist observed:

The Festival city, the city of smiles: for more than one in
five, and one in three in Royston Road [in the north of
Glasgow], it remains as miserable as it was before the first
tenement block got its sand-blasting job so long ago.

He noted, however, that "Even the media is sucked into this conspiracy. Any criticism is shouted down in the name of consensus." Sustained criticism meanwhile was coming from within Glasgow, notably, though not exclusively, from the members of an organisation called Workers City. Their anthology of the same title, edited by the writer Farquhar McLay and published as a warning shot well ahead of Culture Year, contains writing by working-class people from the eighteenth century to the twentieth, giving voice with dignity and anger to a long tradition. Their point was clearly made:

> There is widespread acceptance that [Culture City] has nothing whatever to do with the working- or the workless-class poor of Glasgow but everything to do with big business and money: to pull in investment for inner-city developments which, in the obsessive drive to make the centre of the city attractive to tourists, can only work to the further disadvantage of the people in the poverty ghettoes on the outskirts.

1990 was ushered in with fireworks in the city parks and with a fanfare in the *Glasgow Herald*, which earnestly assured its readers that Culture Year would not be an exclusively middle-class affair. Judging by its correspondence columns, some readers had in fact decided that already, referring to the opening celebrations in George Square – which experienced a few organisational glitches, and were hosted by the actor Robbie Coltrane – as being "in the worst possible taste and quite offensive to anyone of any intelligence or education."

> A man such as Coltrane is in no way representative of Glasgow citizens and did absolutely nothing to enhance the good name of Glasgow, particularly at the beginning of the Year of Culture.

Clearly it was going to be, in all senses, an eventful year.

Alongside the packed programme ran a series of controversies too many and too wide-ranging to summarise here. They have their place in this book, however, because they involved so many Glasgow writers, who were by now, as has been demonstrated, both articulate and well-regarded on a national and international scale. Things came to a head over the exhibition *Glasgow's Glasgow*, the saga of which merged at times with what became known as "the Elspeth King affair." James Kelman observed that the matter had occasioned the biggest postbag to the *Glasgow Herald* since Billy Graham's evangelistic tour in the 1950s.

One letter in support of King, the distinguished, energetic and popular curator of the People's Palace museum, was signed by over sixty people, including Kelman, Alasdair Gray, Tom Leonard, Edwin Morgan, Archie Hind and Alan Spence. An official reply summed them up as "dilettanti . . . well-heeled authors and critics . . . professional whingers." Another irritated letter from the depute director of festivals complained that their "pathetic, factless, anti-1990-ism . . . is an embarrassment to its city and all of its cultural workforce." It might be thought that a city's practising writers are part of its cultural workforce, but apparently that wasn't what the term meant in 1990.

Culture Year ended (with more fireworks) and receded into memory. The glossy programmes went into the archives, and the arguments of the "professional whingers" were also collected in print for the use of future researchers. The question of whether 1990 was of lasting benefit to Glasgow was impartially addressed in a wide-ranging survey of urban regeneration:

> In 1990, the citizens of Glasgow, and its visitors, undoubtedly had a good time. As for the long-term benefits to the city, continuing evaluation should provide some answers. Nevertheless, there is a danger of attaching too much importance to marketing the city. Culture, like long-term economic strength, needs to be rooted in the community.

Nearly a decade on, Culture Year can be more clearly seen as the extravaganza it was: fun, expensive, and probably quite irrelevant to Glasgow. Halfway through the year Archie Hind, in a review of the book produced to accompany *Glasgow's Glasgow*, provided a notably balanced view, finding a phrase, as well, for the shifting image of the city.

> The resonance of that possessive *s* in the title remains with me as a reminder of the human need for a place, a place not only to own but to belong to. Most of us feel neither one nor the other in regard to Glasgow. Instead we make extravagant and inflated claims that fill gaps in our relation with the reality of this place – that we are a workers' city, with a special culture and a virtuous language, or a city of culture. None of these is true. Those who know Glasgow know it with the certainty of accountancy – to the rest of us it is still a Saturday night delusion.

Meanwhile the "dilettanti" got on with their work. The tally of Glasgow fiction during the 1990s has, at the time of writing, already matched and passed the total reached in the flourishing eighties. Quality as well as quantity has been maintained and recognised: novels by Glasgow writers won the Whitbread Award in 1993 and the Booker Prize in 1994. New writers have joined the established names, and new themes and approaches have continued the demolition of any idea that "the Glasgow novel" might come from a standard mould. In a healthy development, Glasgow during the 1990s housed between thirty and forty writers' groups, often led by professional writers. Several leading names in Glasgow fiction today (though not all of them, since the writers, like their novels, resist attempts at pigeonholing) came to publication through similar writers' groups.

Alasdair Gray published a number of books during the late 1980s and early 1990s, though some were recensions of earlier work. This element, among others, was found in *Something Leather* (1990). Gray has said that the germ of *Something Leather* can be traced to a question and answer during an 1986 interview with the American writer, Kathy Acker:

[*Acker*] Have you ever worked with a woman as the main character or spokesperson?

[*Gray*] Only in some plays, but always she's been seen in relation to a man. I haven't the insight to imagine how a woman is to herself.

Unfortunately his interpretation raises as many questions as it answers, since *Something Leather* is a work of lesbian sadomasochistic fantasy (into which the "realistic" episodes, the parts imported from earlier work, irrupt with odd effect).

The novel in which Gray does give full weight to a woman's point of view is *Poor Things* (1992). As *1982, Janine* is in part a homage to Hugh MacDiarmid's *A Drunk Man Looks at the Thistle*, considering the condition of Scotland through the condition of Jock McLeish, so *Poor Things* is in part a descendant of James Hogg's *Justified Sinner*, and the question of truth, the reliability of narrative, is pivotal to the work.

The main text is an account by a Glasgow doctor, Archibald McCandless MD, of his discovery that his strange gifted colleague has "created" a woman, Bella Baxter, from the body of a suicide and the brain of the full-term foetus in her womb. It is followed by a refutation from Victoria McCandless MD, who in terms of the main narrative is that same Bella, but in her own account is nothing of the sort, being "a plain sensible woman" who will become a controversial figure active in women's issues. She tells a very different story: her theory is that her late husband Archibald made up his version out of envy and resentment, borrowing from a dozen nineteenth-century sources – a Gray whimsy, since these references (Hogg, Poe, Mary Shelley . . .) are certainly present in the work. "You, dear reader," remarks Victoria, "have now two accounts to choose between," and these accounts are flanked by a narrator's "factual" Introduction and a section of "Notes Critical and Historical, by Alasdair Gray." The dense texture of *Poor Things*, the games it plays with truth, fiction and Glasgow social history, make it ultimately a more satisfactory work than *Lanark*, and perhaps the most aware and accomplished Glasgow novel so far.

It had strong competition during the 1990s. Alan Spence's long-awaited novel *The Magic Flute* (1990) appears at first glance to be another realistic *Bildungsroman*, but it teases out the lives of four young Glasgow boys with reference to the spiritual dimension always present in Spence's work. William McIlvanney, as we have seen, coolly extends our knowledge of the unorthodox policeman Laidlaw in *Strange Loyalties* (1991). His later novel *The Kiln* (1996), possibly his masterpiece, is set for the most part in 'Graithnock', his fictionalised Kilmarnock, but McIlvanney's world is a unified one and Jack Laidlaw turns up on a holiday job in the brickwork.

Carl MacDougall, whose first novel *Stone Over Water* (1989) had moved between his fictional small town 'Invercullion' and the city streets, firmly chose Glasgow as the setting for *The Lights Below* (1993). And, as he explained in interview, not just as a setting:

> There was a real attempt, I don't know how successful, to make the city a character inside the novel. The city as much as anything affects him [the central character] and the way that he is and affects what happens to him.

Andy Paterson is just out of prison after two years (he was framed, and he has problems to work through concerning his father's death and his mother's remarriage), and is seeing with new eyes not just his own situation but also the city around him. It has changed greatly; what is almost a potted social history within the novel details the process of change as it affected the district of Possilpark (where MacDougall himself grew up, though he has emphasised that he is writing fiction, not reportage). Andy has read about, and now sees at first hand:

> . . . the new city, the emerging place. Consumerism's victory over manufacture promoted a tourism and conference centre, with no extra facilities to support the influx. Millions were coming to the city, using the same sewers, the same water, gas and electricity as served the population prior to the goldrush.

And he sees also the beggars in the prospering streets:

> Four hours a night at the Central Station and he splits the take
> with the lookout . . . "The businessmen and yuppies give you
> fuck all," he said, going down Stockwell Street towards the river.
> "And the casuals give you a kicking . . . The trouble's getting
> worse, on both sides. Sometimes when somebody stops you in
> the street to tap you, they're sizing you up for a mugging."

Andy's Granny, who takes soup, cardboard boxes and newspapers
to the down-and-outs, is perhaps the personification of the old
caring Glasgow; yet there's no sentimentality here, because she
sells the cardboard boxes for fifty pence apiece. Nor is there an
easy nostalgia. MacDougall, while celebrating the vanished
industrial city, hymns also the varied beauty of today's Glasgow.

> Commuters . . . have never smelled the George Square
> hyacinths on the corner of Albion Street at two in the morning;
> they have never seen the rabbits on the Clydeside Expressway
> or the packs of Pollokshaws foxes, kestrels in the city centre;
> they have never read a paper in the park while the band played,
> never seen the city empty at Easter, never seen a seagull raise its
> beak in the middle of Springburn, never been wakened by the
> traffic or a taxi or a shout, never seen the river change . . .

Jeff Torrington's Whitbread prize-winning first novel *Swing
Hammer Swing!* (1992) is an exceptional work in several ways. Its
setting is Gorbals, but by no means the cliché slum Gorbals familiar
from *No Mean City* onwards. The first sentence serves notice of
that:

> Something really weird was happening in the Gorbals – from
> the battered hulk of the Planet Cinema in Scobie Street, a
> deepsea diver was emerging.

He is one of the novel's recurrent minor characters, stumping the streets to advertise the film *The Yellow Submarine*. Later in the crowded weekend of the story, since a mummy film has been sent in error, he goes out again swathed in makeshift bandages and is knocked down by a bubble car:

> A pair of fat wifies . . . had stopped to do a bit of rubbernecking.
>
> "My, would you look at that, Senga!" says one to the other. "They've got'm wrapped in bandages already. By jings, that was quick, was it no?"
>
> "It's a mummy, missus," a wee boy tells her.
>
> "D'ye hear that, Lizzie?" says her pal. "It's this poor wee laddie's mammy, so it is. S'that no a shame?"

We have digressed – easy to do in discussion of this headlong, funny, yet thoughtful novel – from the situation of the narrator, Thomas Clay, who is at a point of change in his life: he and his wife (at present in the maternity hospital) are about to move from the old Gorbals to distant Castlemilk. For the novel is set in the late sixties, and Gorbals is coming down all round Clay: the surreality of the novel's opening only mirrors a greater madness.

Torrington began writing *Swing Hammer Swing!* in the sixties: he has remarked that "the demolition of the Gorbals paralleled the demolition of each tottering version of the novel." The long delay in publication was due partly to external forces (such as work, redundancy, and the onset of Parkinson's disease) but partly also to Torrington's perfectionism, his search for the right voice and structure to convey what he wants to say.

Clay's voice is gallus and lively, and his picture of sixties Glasgow not just accurate but often comic:

> A blizzard of authors was sweeping through Glasgow. To get into the boozers you'd to plod through drifts of Hemingways and Mailers. Kerouacs by the dozen could be found lipping the Lanny [Lanliq tonic wine] on Glesca Green. Myriads of Ginsbergs were to be heard howling mantras down empty night tunnels.

But there is a serious point being made too.

> The shop was crammed floor-to-ceiling with junk. Every nook
> and cranny had been utilised to accommodate the domestic
> fall-out which had resulted from that most disastrous of
> community explosions – the dinging doon of the Gorbals.
> Leaving in their wake the chattels of an outmoded way of
> living, whole tribes of Tenementers had gone off to the
> Reservations of Castlemilk and Toryglen or, like the bulk of
> those who'd remained, had ascended into Basil Spence's "Big
> Stone Wigwam in the Sky".

Torrington has spoken in interview of his anger

> . . . at how the planning authorities botched their golden
> chance to really do something positive for the community.
> After all, it was the least they could do to compensate for the
> years of atrocious living conditions endured by the
> Gorbalsonians. But they were blinkered by the "cheapest
> tender" syndrome and their misplaced affection for stressed
> concrete. (The stress was mainly on the citizens forced to live
> in such brutish habitations.)

Amidst all the humour and quickfire patter of *Swing Hammer
Swing!*, this anger is very clear. From the roof of the Planet Cinema
Clay has

> . . . a panoramic view of the Lost Barony of the Gorbals. What
> set the red nerves twitching was the utter contempt for the
> working classes which was evident no matter where the glance
> fell. Having so cursorily dismantled the community's heart,
> that sooty reciprocating engine, admittedly, an antique,
> clapped-out affair, but one that'd been nevertheless capable of
> generating amazing funds of human warmth, they'd bundled it
> off into the asylum of history . . .

Towards the end of the novel, the ever-optimistic cinema proprietor
sets out his dream of a "Gorbals House of History":

> Stairheid rammies and closemouth shirrikens could be enacted
> by out-of-work thespians, while Tobacco Lords and Snuff
> Barons, not forgetting lepers, deepsea divers and the odd
> mummy or two could be seen strolling around. Sundry items of
> sentimental value to be contemplated; a stank lid from Adelphi
> Street . . . a pub mirror from The Salty Dog Saloon . . . a pair
> of Benny Lynch's boxing gloves . . . At the Sales Points patrons
> would be able to purchase wee model slums that tinkled "I
> Belang Tae Glesca" when their roofs were raised . . .

At least one reviewer picked up the strange similarity to the real-life extravaganzas of Culture Year and we can hardly doubt that Torrington has availed himself of his novel's long gestation period to comment on Glasgow not just of the sixties but of the nineties too.

James Kelman, undistracted by the 1990 mud-slinging, published another collection of stories, *The Burn*, in 1991. Again his characters are 'ordinary' people in ordinary situations, whose thoughts and emotions Kelman lays bare to an unsettling degree, through his technique of interior monologue. The unemployed man in "By the Burn", on his way to a job interview, is taking a short cut through marshy woods; it's raining and his feet are wet, he's going to look a mess at the interview, which anyway he's dreading; but suddenly these irritations are nothing. He feels cold, "a tremor, a spasm", and he realises where he is:

> It was right across the burn from where he was standing and if
> it was winter and the leaves had fell you would see right across
> and the sandpit was there, it was right there, just on the other
> side. Aw dear, the wee fucking lassie. Aw dear man aw dear it
> was so fucking hard, so fucking awful hard, awful hard so
> fucking awful hard. Oh where was the wife. He needed his
> fucking wife. He needed her. He needed her close. He needed
> her so fucking close he felt so fucking Christ man the sandpit,
> where the wee lassie and her two wee pals had got killed.

Given the rarity of a writer who is equally accomplished in novels

and short stories, the temptation was, after *The Burn*, to claim
Kelman as, above all, a master of the short story form. That limited
view lasted only until 1994, when he published his fourth novel
How Late it Was, How Late. Kelman came to the notice of the
literary world – more precisely, that hemisphere based in London
and so far largely unaware of his work or of Scottish literature in
general – when *How Late* won the Booker Prize.

Months before the Booker ceremony, those who did know
Kelman's work had recognised *How Late* as something quite
exceptional. The central character Sammy Samuels – very central,
because of his situation and Kelman's technique – wakes in police
custody, covered in bruises, to find that he is blind. From then on
the reader is inside Sammy's head, though in a way unique to
Kelman: "consistent in voice . . . yet somehow enclosed in omnisc-
ience." More, we are inside his world, a blind man's world, which
Kelman has considered in every detail.

> He moved his right foot off the kerb, his left hand was still on
> the pole, he settled the heel of his left shoe down off the kerb
> but nudging against it, fuck sake man launch, launch, yerself
> forwards, okay, he moved his left foot forwards then his right,
> his left. There was somebody behind him. I'm just feeling
> dizzy, he said . . .
> Ye there? He cleared his throat, no, they werenay, whoever it
> was, they werenay there, unless they were saying fuck all. But in
> the name of christ man! Jesus. Wwhhh.

And we experience with particular clarity the coldness of the benefit
system, in whose Orwellian terms Sammy's condition is not
blindness but Sightloss.

> Now there are two bands of dysfunction; those with a cause
> that is available to verification, and those that remain under the
> heading pseudo-spontaneous. The former band may entitle the
> customer to Dysfunctional Benefit but those in the latter may
> not. But both bands entitle the customer to a reassessment of
> his or her physical criteria in respect of full-function job
> registration, given the dysfunction is established.

In this world we can expect no easy resolution to Sammy's problems; at the end of the novel he is still inexplicably blind. But we have come to recognise his grim humour and his resilience: "Ye've got to batter on, know what I'm saying, ye've got to batter on".

With "a few things to get sorted", he heads south to England, hailing a taxi to the station, dealing with difficulties as they occur.

> A hackney cab; unmistakeable. When the sound died away he
> fixed the shades on his nose and stepped out onto the
> pavement. It wasnay long till the next yin. He tapped forwards,
> waving his stick in the air. It was for hire, he heard it pulling in
> then the squeaky brakes. The driver had opened the door.
> Sammy slung in the bag and stepped inside, then the door
> slammed shut and that was him, out of sight.

This is the brilliant novel that was awarded the Booker prize in October 1994. It was not an unanimous decision and one of the judges, interviewed later, was particularly vocal in her objections: "I'm really unhappy. It was my least favourite book . . . What I objected to was the monotony . . . For many people it will be completely inaccessible . . . It's just a drunken Scotsman railing against bureaucracy." She wrote to the chairman of the prize committee suggesting that the voting rules should be changed; "to ensure," one commentator drily observed, "that the next time one of the panel judges a book to be inaccessible, offensive and Glaswegian she can't be outvoted."

Her outpourings seemed to express a general feeling in London literary circles that this really shouldn't be allowed. Reading through the many column inches of argument, it's hard to miss the subtext: that these are circles in which Kelman does not move. Nobody outside Scotland (it appeared) had ever heard of him; a state of affairs which the Booker controversy, if it did nothing else, did something to rectify.

Within Scotland things are different. Six months before the Booker, the literary editor of the *Scotsman* was able to summarise:

Everybody knows all about Kelman. "Kelmanesque" has already become insouciant shorthand: Glasgow mean streets, bad language by the bucket-load, a cast-list of alkies and no-hopers . . . The new novel, *How Late it Was, How Late*, will not disappoint the stereotype-spreaders . . . It is possible to argue that in no other country except Britain would such a major author be subject to such reductive labelling.

And a reader joins in with enthusiasm:

It all started with the one about the teacher [*A Disaffection*]. I was blown away. As I progressed through the others, greedily reading my way through page after page, my obsession developed . . . Great, I thought, here is a guy actually capturing what my own life resembles, I hadn't come across it much before in the stuff I was reading . . . why do I feel excluded when the literary merit of Kelman's work is under discussion by folk who can't understand the nuances and the life from whence it came?

It goes without saying that Kelman has detractors in Scotland too.

The image of Scotland presented in the majority of current novels, short stories and plays seems to be that of a nation of drunks, drug addicts and drop-outs. James Kelman is the leader of the pack with his dreary depiction of life at the bottom end of the social scale in darkest Glasgow.

Another critic offers his opinion of the one about the teacher in less than favourable terms:

Ye huv a quick look, there, and yer no sure aboot it. Hell but, gie it a chance. So ye take it hame and ye read it over the next three days and ye finish it. And ye realise its complete absolute unadulterated fuckin shite.

This review, as can be seen, is itself couched in what is generally

thought of as Kelmanesque language. The recognition of Kelman
in Scotland is confirmed, if confirmation is needed, by a quantity
of imitations, or parodies, of his style. An elder statesman of Scottish
poetry writes a sonnet in his own version of Glasgow vernacular
and titles it with laborious humour "Whippet for High Tea". A
younger wit presents "a very condensed novel" entitled "Oh No,
Another New Glaswegian Writer", reading in part:

> This writing is a pain in the butt it sure is a pain I dont know
> why I do it I dont know here comes the cleaning lady again
> here she comes,
>
> – good morning hen,
> how are you today?
> is your son better, is he feeling OK now?
> thats great, great.

Such drollery should not obscure the reality of Kelman's influence
on younger Scottish writers, which has been overwhelmingly
beneficial, in spite of the grumbles of a columnist already quoted.

> Kelman stood alone for a time as the writer who had broken
> the language barrier; he used more gutter obscenities than
> anyone else. Now, others have caught up with him and strive to
> surpass his total. Irvine Welsh is the new champion . . .
> Needless to say, some of the trendy critics have taken Welsh to
> their hearts as they did Kelman when he started, while hard on
> the heels of the Terrible Twosome comes one Duncan McLean,
> desperate to plumb even deeper depths of depravity.

The writer, in fact, makes a mistake here in his chronology of
depravity, since it was Duncan McLean who "discovered" Irvine
Welsh. As east-coast writers they may be marginal to a history of
Glasgow fiction, but McLean has made his position clear.

> Probably in common with a lot of writers my age in Scotland, I
> might not be writing at all if it wasn't for James Kelman. Or

not fiction anyway. I was still writing cabaret when I read *Not Not While the Giro* and *The Busconductor Hines* and I thought, "These are much truer to life than what I'm writing." For the first time a piece of fiction connected with my life – there was something there that I could relate to. And after I'd read it I got the notion that maybe I could write fiction too.

Equal appreciation is expressed by Janice Galloway, whose work began to be published, to immediate critical attention, in the late 1980s. Born in Ayrshire but attracted by what was going on in Glasgow, she entered a short story in a Glasgow-based competition.

It didn't win, but Jim Kelman was one of the judges, and at the award ceremony he read out a bit of it. It was as if he really understood it – it just galvanised me. I'll never forget that, it was a huge experience – someone who was called a writer, taking my work seriously.

Kelman encouraged her to seek publication and her first novel, *The Trick is to Keep Breathing*, appeared at the end of 1989. It may be possible to see his influence in her pared-down style, but she has her own slant on life. She is often categorised as a feminist writer, and certainly she writes from a woman's perspective, but a perceptive interviewer has remarked that she "doesn't write about, but through, feminism."

Similarly she doesn't write about, but through, Glasgow. Her gripping short stories often have, and need, no specific setting, focusing as they do on one moment of epiphany, of emotion, crisis or choice. Where there is a streetscape, it may well reflect not Glasgow but the bleak semi-urban hinterland where she grew up. It's near enough for those critics who choose to align her with urban realist writers like Kelman, and who manage to miss the point as thoroughly with her work as with his.

There was a very odd letter in the *Times* from the chief of police in Hong Kong . . . who said as an ex-pat Scot he was disgusted to see the stuff that Kelman and this woman

Galloway were writing representing Scotland – what do you
do? . . . The resistance you get is from the people who maybe
don't know the things you're writing about and suspect you're
making it up, it's maybe not real and this is a vogue you've
cottoned on to. That's about the kindest interpretation of it,
the other is that they know bloody well it exists but they'd
rather you didn't write about it.

Setting her apart from Kelman, however, is the element of the
surreal which recurs in her short stories, particularly in her first
collection *Blood* (1991). We have seen this earlier in the work of
Agnes Owens, but here it is eerily sustained. The little girl Janet
visits her elderly neighbour, whose black cat she admires but isn't
allowed to touch:

There was the usual tan-colour of the fire surround, the
ornamental brasses on the mantelpiece. Inside, a black-backed
roaring fire. And inside that, framed in flames, the upright vase
of the black cat, sizzling in a mound of coals. The fur was
catching slowly, jets budding along the dark outline as he
sat . . . Sheathed in golden-hearted arrows of flame, Blackie
burned. His eyes were full as green moons . . . The cat in the
fireplace, the child on the rug: their gaze met and steadied.
And Janet knew she would do nothing. She had been taught to
respect his privacy too well.   ("Breaking Through")

When the old woman follows her cat into the flames – "She
managed a half-smile as the child lifted the poker to help" – it is,
in the story's terms, both expected and acceptable. Another heir
of post-*Lanark* freedom, this is a new voice in Glasgow fiction.

The voice of AL Kennedy, who also began to write in the
late 1980s, is not only new but impossible to categorise. Her short
stories are unique in their structural power. A typical Kennedy
story opens in a wandering, casual way; hard to see what, if
anything, is ever going to relate to anything else. By the end we
know that everything has been relevant, everything connects, and
it connects with stunning force. Equally characteristic, and evident

from her first collection *Night Geometry and the Garscadden Trains* (1991), is the beautiful freedom with which her stories move between present and past. Sometimes they let us glimpse the future. After the last words of "Tea and Biscuits", for instance, or "The Moving House", what's going to happen next is all too clear.

As a bonus, they are often set in Glasgow; born in Dundee, Kennedy has settled in Glasgow, and it does seem that she is finding the city a good place to write in. It lies behind most of her work and sometimes breaks cover:

> Even where there are chip shops with metal shutters and the homes have putrefied around their tenants; even where there are beggars, really beggars, at the feet of each refurbished edifice, the light that falls here makes it beautiful. This is a city where ugly things happen under a beautiful light.
> ("The Role of Notable Silences in Scottish History",
> *Night Geometry and the Garscadden Trains*)

A similar freedom pervades her first novel, *Looking for the Possible Dance* (1993). Margaret is travelling south by train and as she travels she thinks: of her single-parent father who danced and talked with her; of her lover Colin, not always there but lastingly important; of the young people she works with and her harassing, sad, bitter boss. The book is a complex mesh of past and present held in the light framework of the journey. It's a pity perhaps that Colin, in an echo of an older Glasgow, ends up nailed to the floor. Kennedy herself has admitted some difficulty with that sequence.

> The whole of that bit of the novel is peculiar. It's actually a thing that loan sharks have done, although I wasn't aware of that until I'd written it. When I found out, I thought, "Ah, that's convenient, it looks as if I've done some research!"

But Glasgow clichés are long forgotten by the time of Kennedy's second novel *So I Am Glad* (1995). Once more we begin vaguely, deceptively, as Jennifer describes herself.

> I am not emotional. You should know that about me. You
> should be aware of my principal characteristic which I choose
> to call my calmness. Other people have called it coldness, lack
> of commitment, over-control, a fishy disposition. I say that I'm
> calm, a calm person, and usually leave it at that . . .

The truth is, of course, that her emotions are frozen, unable to operate, or at least to operate in any recognisably "normal" way. Much of the time she is calm indeed, reserved to an unnatural degree. Some of the time she is taking part in sado-masochistic sessions and beating her lover half to death.

Her job in radio calls on none of her faculties except a flexible voice which can assume any colour and tone. She lives in a bedsitter house in Partick, interacting with the other tenants to the extent demanded by good manners but no more. To the house comes a new tenant who will break the ice and set her free. So far, so hackneyed; except that the new tenant is Savinien de Cyrano de Bergerac, arrived in twentieth-century Glasgow from seventeenth-century France.

Jennifer's life is still anchored in contemporary reality – Romania, vandalism, a crumbling health service, street people – but part of it now, impossibly yet convincingly, is an articulate, friendly, haunted Frenchman who is 375 years old. Magic realism has arrived in the Glasgow novel. After some two hundred years of growth, firmly rooted in its protean, many-coloured, exciting city, Glasgow fiction seems to have further developments in view.

Notes

CHAPTER 1

An urbane silence: I am indebted for this excellent phrase to the title of Andrew Noble's article "Urbane silence: Scottish writing and the nineteenth-century city", in George Gordon, ed., *Perspectives of the Scottish City* (Aberdeen, 1985), 64-90.

two curious little shops: James A. Kilpatrick, *Literary Landmarks of Glasgow* (Glasgow, 1898), 14.

thought to be caricatured: *ibid.*, 17-18.

Scott visited Glasgow: Kilpatrick, *op.cit.*, 136-39.

make a hit: *ibid.*, 139.

Queen Victoria: *ibid.*, 139-40.

Jean Byde: see John Gilkison, *The Jean Byde Papers* (Glasgow, 1873).

biographical appreciation: J.F.George, "Bailie Nicol Jarvie: who he was and what he was. An attempt at a biographical appreciation." *The Bailie*, 15 December 1922, 79-83.

David Dale: Simon Berry and Hamish Whyte eds., *Glasgow Observed* (Edinburgh, 1987), 37.

This area, the Necropolis: Ian Spring, *Phantom village: the myth of the new Glasgow* (Edinburgh, 1990), 6.

several novelists: e.g., John Gibson Lockhart, *Peter's Letters to his Kinsfolk* (Edinburgh, 1819), and Thomas Hamilton, *The Youth and Manhood of Cyril Thornton* (Edinburgh, 1827).

population figures: Joe Fisher, *The Glasgow Encyclopedia* (Edinburgh, 1994), 295.

What tolerable Scotch fiction: J.M.Robertson, "Belles lettres in Scotland" (1888), cited David Craig, *Scottish Literature and the Scottish People* (London, 1961), 148-49, 309-10.

Though Scotland had been severely industrialised: William Power, *Literature and Oatmeal* (London, 1935), 163.

In the meantime: George Blake, *Annals of Scotland 1895-1955* (London, 1956), 10-11.

on the Kailyard School: George Blake, *Barrie and the Kailyard School* (London, 1951), 8-12.

His work: Sydney Goodsir Smith, *A short introduction to Scottish literature* (Edinburgh, 1951), 23-24.

The big, ever-expanding industrial cities: Lars Hartveit, *A study of some aspects of the Scottish regional novel* (unpublished BLitt thesis, University of Glasgow, 1956), 125-6.

Carlyle had the genius: Smith, *op.cit.*, 24.

This curious notion: William Donaldson, *Popular literature in Victorian Scotland: language, fiction and the press* (Aberdeen, 1986), 87. The following quotation is also from this work.

Clydeside Litterateurs: D. Walker Brown, *Clydeside Litterateurs: biographical sketches* (Glasgow, 1897).

strong nostalgia: S.G.Checkland, *The upas tree: Glasgow 1875-1975; . . . and after: 1975-80* (Glasgow, 2nd ed 1981), 83.

Some readers will perchance: *Scots Pictorial*, 3 (1898), 376.

CHAPTER 2

Was ye ever: *Noctes Ambrosianae* 28, *Blackwood's Edinburgh Magazine*, 20, October 1826, 625-26; excerpted in J.H.Alexander ed., *The Tavern Sages* (Aberdeen, 1992), 142.

eyewitness accounts: see Berry and Whyte eds., *op.cit.*, sections II and III, and Spring, *op.cit.*, 9-13.

Whistle-Binkie: Kilpatrick, *op.cit.*, chapter 14, 'A Literary Lounge'.

James Hedderwick: Brown, *op.cit.*, 91-98, and *The Bailie*, 21 December 1887, 1-2.

His object was: James Hedderwick, *Backward Glances* (Edinburgh, 1891), 228.

Most people have heard: "Men You Know" no. 92, *The Bailie*, 22 July 1874, 1-2.

Had he chosen the law: "Men You Know", no. 299, *The Bailie*, 10 July 1878, 1-2.

Young George's career: Hedderwick, *op.cit.*, 273-75.

Nobody that has criticised the B.B.: Letter from George Mills to George Cruickshank, 5 October 1866.

the eponymous benison: The traditional Beggar's Benison is a wish for virility and wealth, not exactly in these words. If George Mills knew of it, he chose to tone it down.

This will perhaps: Letter from GM to GC, 12 November 1866.

in the hope: Letter from GM to GC, 11 March 1869.

Mr Hawk: Letter from GM to GC, 2 May 1869.

Little known: Donaldson, *op.cit.*, 77. David Pae's work, including *The Factory Girl*, is fully treated here, 77-100.

Ellen Johnston: Ellen Johnston, *Autobiography, Poems and Songs* (Glasgow, 1867).

abusive stepfather: This suggestion is made in Elspeth King, *The Hidden History of Glasgow's Women: the Thenew factor* (Edinburgh, 1993), 75-76.

It seems probable: T.Wemyss Reid, *William Black: novelist* (London, 1902), 29-30.

contrives to get his native city: Kilpatrick, *op.cit.*, 275.

The two stood: *The Bailie*, 17 January 1877, 3.

His new novel: *ibid.*, 2 July 1879, 4.

This has accomplished: *ibid.*, 13 August 1879, 4.

In transporting: Kilpatrick, *op.cit.*, 277-79.

Henry Johnston: Brown, *op.cit.*, 99-106.

a completely forgotten: Blake (1951), *op.cit.*, 9.

As a necessary . . . result: Henrietta Keddie, *Three Generations* (London, 1911), 186.

it may be summed up: Keddie, *op.cit.*, 344.

an evangelical sentimentalising: Francis Russell Hart, *The Scottish Novel: a critical survey* (London, 1978), 111.

The impression given: "Under the Reading Lamp", *Quiz*, 15 August 1884, 230.

When Miss Keddie wrote: "Scots Worthies: Henrietta Keddie ('Sarah Tytler')", *Scots Pictorial*, 1 January 1898, 354-55.

Mrs Oliphant . . . Mrs Craik: Keddie, *op.cit.*, 289-90, 317-18.

There was Charles Gibbon: Keddie, *op.cit.*, 340.

CHAPTER 3

a city of more than Mediterranean crowding: Checkland, *op.cit.*, 18.

Paisley: *The Bailie* often calls Paisley "Seestu", which is a unique Paisley form of greeting; alternatively "The Suburb", from a speech made by Lord Brougham in Glasgow: "I visited today your enterprising suburb of Paisley . . ." *The Bailie* kept this joke going for years.

Many papers circulated: William Donaldson, *The Language of the*

People: Scots prose from the Victorian revival (Aberdeen, 1989), 4.

"A Causeyside Cork": *The Bailie,* 19 February 1873.

"Wanderin' Wull" etc: These pseudonyms recur over several issues of *The Bailie,* but see for instance 2 July 1873; 16 July 1873; 8 August 1877; 19 February 1879; 2 June 1880.

Quiz: Similarly, see for instance the issues of 24 February 1882; 9 December 1887; 21 December 1888.

utterly removed: Donaldson (1989), *op.cit.,* 10.

auction scene: *Quiz,* 4 November 1887.

I wid raither gang doon: *ibid.,* 23 September 1887.

Wee Mary: *The Bailie,* 26 June 1878.

advertisements: *ibid.,* 20 December 1876 and 31 January 1877, each running for four weeks.

Archibald Macmillan: see Brown, *op.cit.,* 139-46, from which the next quotation also comes.

the small independent burghs: Fisher, *op.cit.,* 297.

message of goodwill: *The Bailie,* 15 December 1922.

The "Jeems Kaye" sketches: "The Passing of 'Jeems Kaye'", *ibid.,* 12 August 1925.

CHAPTER 4

a dozen books: Gillian Shepherd, "The Kailyard". Douglas Gifford, ed., *The History of Scottish Literature, volume 3: Nineteenth century* (Aberdeen, 1988), 309-20. Includes a useful list of further reading.

thoroughly discussed: see for instance Ian Campbell, *Kailyard: a new assessment* (Edinburgh, 1981).

Recent studies: see for instance Eric Anderson, "The Kailyard Revisited". Ian Campbell, ed., *Nineteenth-Century Scottish Fiction: critical essays* (Manchester, 1979), 131-47, and Thomas D. Knowles, *Ideology, Art and Commerce: aspects of literary sociology in the late Victorian Scottish kailyard* (Goteborg, 1983).

re-evaluation . . . of Barrie: see for instance Andrew Birkin, *J.M.Barrie and the Lost Boys* (London, 1979) and R.D.S.Jack, *The Road to the Never Land: a reassessment of J.M.Barrie's dramatic art* (Aberdeen, 1991).

For Hardy: Anderson, *op.cit.,* 142.

"The Minister of St Bede's": "Ian Maclaren" (John Watson), *Afterwards, and other stories* (London, 1898). See Knowles, *op.cit.,* 197-204.

It so chanced: *Quiz,* 7 November 1895, 28.

To be taken out of themselves: James Drawbell, "Are there no Annie

S. Swan books nowadays?", *Scots Magazine*, vol. 89, no. 1, April 1968, 20-30.

The Sunday Post offers a market: D.C.Thomson & Co.Ltd., "The Kind of Short Story We Want" [guidelines for contributors], c. 1990.

Helen W.Pryde has conceived a Glasgow family: Blake (1951), *op.cit.*, 86-87.

Oh where is the Glasgow: Adam McNaughtan, "The Glasgow I Used to Know". Farquhar McLay ed., *Workers City* (Glasgow, 1988), 19-20.

Where is the Glasgow: Jim McLean, "Farewell to Glasgow". *ibid.*, 20-21.

a collection of Glasgow short stories: Moira Burgess and Hamish Whyte eds., *Streets of Stone* (Edinburgh, 1985).

Wee Black Sannyism: see Jack McLean, "Barrapatter and the Glasgow Myth", *Books in Scotland*, no 16, Autumn 1984, 8. "Wee black sannies", of course, are little black plimsolls, as worn (at least in memory) by wee Glasgow boys.

When we were wee: Stephen Mulrine, "Glasgow Number Seven". Spring, *op.cit.*, 152-53.

While the judges: Tom Leonard, "Dripping with Nostalgia", *Intimate Voices* Newcastle-upon-Tyne, 1984), 137.

The figures . . . are flattened out: Bill Hare, "Streetkids and stormy seas: reflections on Joan Eardley, RSA, retrospective exhibition." *Cencrastus*, no. 31, Autumn 1988, 10-15.

CHAPTER 5

Returning to Scotland: Lewis Spence, "Literary Scotland: 1910-1935; a personal retrospect." *Scots Magazine*, vol. 23, no. 2, May 1935, 92-98.

The book was published: J.J.Bell, "Introduction: the story of the book." *Wee Macgreegor*, New Library Edition (Edinburgh, 1933), 5-14.

"He's – phew – ": *Mair Macjigger* was published anonymously, but the author has been identified as Joseph W. Campbell.

I enjoyed letting myself go: Anna Buchan ("O. Douglas"), *Unforgettable, unforgotten* (London, 1945), 74.

Bell enjoyed for a space: Blake (1951), *op.cit.*, 83.

I realise its inability: C.M. Grieve, *Contemporary Scottish Studies* (London, 1926), 86.

We are as far: David Hodge, " *Wee Macgreegor* twenty-five: an appreciation of J.J.Bell." *Bookman*, vol. 73, November 1927, 106-8.

There is only one broad division: J.A.Mack, "The Changing City." *Third Statistical Account of Scotland: Glasgow*, ed. J.Cunnison and J.B.S.Gilfilllan (Glasgow, 1958), 758-71.

is a frequent contributor: "The Man You Know: no. 93a." *Glasgow Weekly Herald*, 23 December 1933.

We might see him: George Blake, "*Belles lettres* and boaters." *Glasgow Herald*, 16 November 1957, 3. The "quirk in publishing practice" presumably had to do with copyright.

My earliest memory: J.J.Bell, *I remember* (Edinburgh, 1932), 271.

kenspeckle for his height: Blake (1957), *op.cit.*

He was the gifted prose stylist: *ibid.*

Only once . . . do I remember: Bell (1932), *op.cit.*, 275.

he could be bitter: Blake (1957), *op.cit.* See also Blake's biographical introduction to Neil Munro, *The Brave Days: a chronicle from the north* (Edinburgh, 1931), 7-24.

It has been asserted: J.F.George, "Novels of Neil Munro." *The Bailie*, 9 May 1923, 14.

It was almost closing-time: "Views and Reviews", *Glasgow Evening News*, [undated cutting].

It was really written for my mother: Anna Buchan (1945), *op.cit.*, 154-55.

Perhaps if he had been conceived: C.A.Oakley, *"The Second City"*, 2nd ed. (Edinburgh, 1967), 232.

Chapter V: James Veitch, *George Douglas Brown* (London, 1952), 172-73.

The intention was: Frederick Niven, *Coloured Spectacles* (London, 1938), 26-27.

Watson the cashier: *ibid.*, 27.

Fra Newbery: *ibid.*, 29.

For the very first time: Blake (1956), *op.cit.*, 18.

His agent suggested: Letter from Mrs Niven to John Dunlop, [1954].

The further MacGill moves away: Jack Mitchell, "Early harvest: anti-capitalist novels published in 1914." H.G.Klaus, ed., *The Socialist Novel in Britain: towards the recovery of a tradition* (Brighton, 1982), 67-88.

an employee in a Glasgow factory: "Literary Notes", *Glasgow Herald*, 16 March 1907, 9. As such, "John Blair" could, of course, be a woman, though I have not pursued this possibility here.

a volume of East End sketches: *ibid.*

CHAPTER 6

The great literary need: "Literary Notes", *Glasgow Herald*, 18 July 1908. The pamphlet by James Leatham referred to is *The Style of Louis Stevenson* (Peterhead, 1908).

from time to time: David Craig, "The Radical Literary Tradition". Gordon Brown, ed., *The Red Paper on Scotland* (Edinburgh, 1975), 289-303.

The crowding of our . . . populations: Agnes Stewart, "Some Scottish Novelists." *The Northern Review*, vol. 1, no. 1, May 1924, 35-41.

Here are douce citizens: Marion C.Lochhead, "'The Glasgow School'." *Scots Magazine*, vol. 4, no. 4, January 1926, 277-81.

Where in our collection: John Cockburn, "The Scottish novel: can we uphold a renaissance that lacks the thing that matters?" *Scots Observer*, 25 February 1933, 9.

several literary histories: see for instance Klaus (1982), *op.cit.*; Jeremy Hawthorn, ed., *The British working-class novel in the twentieth century* (London, 1984); and Andy Croft, *Red Letter Days: British fiction in the 1930s* (London, 1990).

"Literature: Class or National?": see *Outlook*, vol.1, no.3, June 1936, 74-80 (Lennox Kerr); no.4, July 1936, 54-58 (Neil Gunn); no.5, August 1936, 74-80 (Edward Scouller).

I am rootedly middle-class: William Power, *Should auld acquaintance . . . an autobiography* (London, 1937), 229-30.

This great disability: "Notes of the Quarter", *Voice of Scotland*, vol.1, no.1, June-August 1938, 26-27.

I once wrote a romantic-realistic novel: Power, *op.cit.*, 218-19.

One of the "achievements": Jack Mitchell, "The struggle for the working-class novel in Scotland." *Scottish Marxist*, no.6, April 1974, 40-52; no.7, October 1974, 46-54; no.8, January 1975, 39-48. (Parts 2 and 3 are headed "The Proletarian Novel".) The full article was published in *Zeitschrift fur Anglistik und Amerikanistik*, 21(4), 1973.

CHAPTER 7

As it stands: Grieve (1926), *op.cit.*, 273

In a broadcast talk: Letter from Neil Gunn to Nan Shepherd, 26 August 1929. Neil M.Gunn, *Selected Letters*, ed. J.B.Pick (Edinburgh, 1987), 8-9.

He briskly lists: Grieve (1926), *op.cit.*, 309.

None of our young fictionists: *ibid.*, 309.

A post-industrial city of crisis: Beat Witschi, *Glasgow Urban Writing* *and Post-Modernism* (Frankfurt, 1991), 34.

returning to the same themes: *ibid.*, 51.

on her son's authority: John Carswell, "Introduction". Catherine Carswell, *Open the Door!* (London, 1986), v-xvii.

There, on Monday nights: Power, *op.cit.*, 78.

I never met her: "One of the BBC Critics", quoted in Helen B. Cruickshank, *Octobiography* (Melrose, 1976), 128.

This is a book so very rich: Review (unsigned, but by Carswell) of D.H.Lawrence, *The Rainbow. Glasgow Herald*, 4 November 1915, 4.

You have very often: Letter from D.H.Lawrence to Catherine Carswell, June 1914, quoted in Catherine Carswell, *The Savage Pilgrimage* (London, 1932), 19.

How much, when all is said and done: K[atherine] M[ansfield], "A Prize Novel", *The Athenaeum*, 25 June 1920, 831.

The principal motif: Rebecca West, [review of *Open the Door!*], *New Statesman*, vol. 15, no.373, 5 June 1920, 253-54.

nothing is any good: Letter from Catherine Carswell to F. Marian McNeill, 27 January 1926. Catherine Carswell, *Lying Awake: an unfinished autobiography* (London, 1950), 183.

The Wild Goose Chase: Letter from D.H.Lawrence to Catherine Carswell, 1916, quoted in Carswell (1932), *op.cit.*, 64.

much darker at the heart: Alison Smith, "And Woman Created Woman: Carswell, Shepherd and Muir, and the self-made woman." Christopher Whyte, ed., *Gendering the Nation: studies in modern Scottish literature* (Edinburgh, 1995), 25-47.

after a few pages: Buchan (1945), *op.cit.*, 159.

Miss Wells's special interest: Elisabeth Kyle, "Modern Women Authors, 5: Mary Cleland". *Scots Observer*, 23 July 1931, 4.

As the mise-en-scene: Frank Arneil Walker, "The Glasgow Grid". Thomas A.Markus, ed., *Order in Space and Society* (Edinburgh, 1982), 155-99.

I have only one ambition: Quoted in R. D. Macleod, ed., *Modern Scottish Literature: a popular guide-book catalogue* (Glasgow, 1933), 35.

a purely "machine-made" naturalistic "study": Grieve (1926), *op.cit.*, 310.

I am going to call it Saturday: Letter from Edwin Muir to Sydney Schiff, 7 May 1924, quoted in P.H.Butter, *Edwin Muir: man and poet* (Edinburgh, 1966), 88-89.

Though a good idea: *ibid.*, 89.

I believe [Muir] is also engaged: Grieve (1926), *op.cit.*, 116.

Most of [his novels] have reflected: Macleod (1933), *op.cit.*, 25.
simply inexplicable: Grieve (1926), *op.cit.*, 312.
Mr Blake never seems: Robert Angus, "Two Scottish Novels". *The Scottish Nation*, 6 November 1923, 8-9.
These early Blake protagonists: Hart (1978), *op.cit.*, 214-15.
She will probably develop: George Blake, "A Woman of Destiny". *Vagabond Papers* (Glasgow, 1922), 9-14.
[Blake is] likely to endure: Edwin Morgan, "Who will publish Scottish poetry?". *New Saltire*, no. 2, November 1961, 51-56.
She submitted a sonnet: Elisabeth Kyle, "Modern Women Authors, 3: Dot Allan". *Scots Observer*, 25 June 1931, 4.
I certainly have written: *ibid*.
Some of her more recent work: Grieve (1926), *op.cit.*, 311.
Her work appeared regularly: once a month in 1924, and frequently throughout the 1920s and 1930s. See *Glasgow Herald* index for the period.
angry young men: Blake (1957), *op.cit.*

CHAPTER 8
All of those [pre-war] voices: Edwin Muir, "New Paths in Fiction the Scottish novel since the war", *Glasgow Herald Book Exhinition Supplement*, 22 November 1934, I-II.
fresh air has been let into it: *ibid*.
a Scottish writer: Edwin Muir, *Scott and Scotland* (London, 1936),15
writers who in any country: Muir (1934), *op.cit.*
that Scotland never at any previous time: Lewis Grassic Gibbon and Hugh MacDiarmid, *Scottish Scene* (London, 1934).
Unfortunately: Muir (1934), *op.cit.*
asserts that there is more drama: "The Man You Know", no. 159, *Glasgow Weekly Herald*, 30 March 1935.
a serious artist's attempt: Edward Scouller, "So This Is Glasgow!" *Outlook*, vol. 1, no. 8, November 1936, 79-81.
The majority of our Scots authors: Edward Scouller, "My view of the Scots novel". *Scotland*, vol. 3, no. 4, Winter 1938, 49-52.
Glasgow life is felt: Christopher Whyte, "Imagining the City: the Glasgow novel". Joachim Schwend and Horst W. Drescher, eds., *Studies in Scottish fiction: twentieth century, 1900-50* (Frankfurt, 1990), 193-205.
In Glasgow there are: Lewis Grassic Gibbon, "Glasgow". Gibbon and MacDiarmid (1934), *op.cit.*; reprinted in Lewis Grassic Gibbon, *A Scots Hairst* (London, 1967), 82-94.

I have been told of slum courts: Edwin Muir, *Scottish Journey* (London, 1935), 116.

There are so many Glasgows: Scouller (1936), *op.cit.*

When he was writing The Staff at Simson's: Letter from Mrs Niven to John Dunlop, *op.cit.*

Mrs Barry is really splendid: Letter from R.B.Cunninghame Graham to Frederick Niven, 21 April 1933.

A noble story: Compton Mackenzie in *Daily Mail*. Quoted on jacket of Frederick Niven, *The Flying Years* (1935).

I do not like, in the last sentence: Letter from Cunninghame Graham to Niven, *op.cit.*

A lost "dear green place": see Douglas Gifford, *The Dear Green Place? the novel in the West of Scotland* (Glasgow, 1985).

It was only after his widow's death: Letter from H.S.Reid to author, 15 August 1970. "Tobias" is Reid's other posthumously published novel *Tobias the Rod* (Ilfracombe, 1968), which is not set in Glasgow.

brought up in poverty: "The Man You Know", no 159, *op.cit.*

A first novel: Edwin Muir, [review], *Scotland*, vol.2, no.6, Summer 1937, 66.

wheelchair-bound: Private information obtained in Clydebank c. 1970.

The Plottels: See Iain Cameron, *George Friel: an introduction to his life and work* (unpublished M.Litt thesis, University of Edinburgh, 1987) for valuable biographical information and criticism.

an annus mirabilis: Gordon Jarvie, "Introduction", George Friel, *A Friend of Humanity: selected short stories* (Edinburgh, 1992), [vi].

does bear some marks: Edwin Morgan, *Twentieth Century Scottish Classics* (Glasgow, 1987), 1.

to retire decorously: Blake (1956), *op.cit.*, 32.

family history: see Barke's autobiography *The Green Hills Far Away* (London, 1940).

a double parallelism: see for instance Whyte (1990), *op.cit.*, 325-26, and Manfred Malzahn, "Coming to terms with industrial Scotland: two proletarian novels of the 1930s." Schwend and Drescher (1990), *op.cit.*, 193-205.

Enough contradictions there: Malzahn (1990), *op.cit.*, 197.

"Authentic" is the adjective: [review], *Scots Magazine*, vol. 23, no. 1, April 1935, 79-80.

The Shipbuilders . . . gives us the portrait: Spence (1935), *op.cit.*, 96

excruciating sentimentality: Alan Bold, *Modern Scottish Literature* (London, 1983), 232-33.

re-reading the novel: Campbell Black, "Warscope", *New Statesman*, 31 July 1970, 127.

even when the narrative point of view: Malzahn (1990), *op.cit.*, 196.

a pseudo-proletarian writer: see Mitchell (1974-75), *op.cit.*

Blake . . . now thinks [The Shipbuilders] unworthy: Blake (1956), *op.cit.*, 32.

It may be allowed him: *ibid.*

Taken on its own terms: Whyte (1990), *op.cit.*, 326.

Glasgow of The Shipbuilders: Alison and Alistair McCleery, "Personality of place in the urban regional novel", *Scottish Geographical Magazine*, vol. 97, no. 2, September 1981, 66-76.

As a writer he had great sympathy: John R. Allan, "My Scotland", *Scotland's Magazine*, May 1958, 7.

[Barke] has entered with complete sympathy: Scouller (1936), *op.cit.*, 79.

It is too long: *ibid.*, 81.

We feel that the decisive debate: Mitchell (1974-75), *op.cit.*, Part III: "James Barke", 43.

The book is schematic: Whyte (1990), *op.cit.*, 327.

James Joyce: Croft (1990), *op.cit.*, 277.

a heroic attempt: Mitchell (1974-75), *op.cit.*, Part III: "James Barke", 42.

CHAPTER 9

Reeks with squalor: *New York Herald Tribune* (quoted on half-title page of McArthur's posthumously published *No Bad Money*, see below).

letters of outrage: see Sean Damer, "No mean writer? The curious case of Alexander McArthur". Kevin McCarra and Hamish Whyte, eds., *A Glasgow Collection: essays in honour of Joe Fisher* (Glasgow, 1990), 25-42.

novel after novel: Damer (1990), *op.cit.*

Another novel: Alexander McArthur and Peter Watts, *No Bad Money* (London, 1969). Recent research has confirmed that a third novel, *The Blackmailer*, was published in 1949, again posthumously. It was printed and distributed by a small Glasgow firm and it is not yet clear how this work attained publication.

Working-class people: Alexander McArthur, "Why I wrote *No Mean City*". *Daily Record*, 1 November 1935, 7.

among them Edwin Muir: "Glasgow slums", *Spectator*, 8 December 1935. Quoted in full Damer (1990), *op.cit.*, 30-31.

It is impossible: "A Glasgow slum", *Times Literary Supplement*, 2 November 1935. Quoted in full Damer (1990), *op.cit.*, 29.

the book may positively be harmful: *Evening Citizen*, 28 October 1935. Quoted in full Damer (1990), *op.cit.*, 31-32.

it lifted a lid: Gifford (1985), *op.cit.*, 7.

Such was the bourgeois-lumpen crap: Freddy Anderson, "Early days at Glasgow Unity Theatre". *Cencrastus*, no 46, Autumn 1993, 17-18.

crude and melodramatic: Edwin Morgan, "Glasgow speech in recent Scottish literature". *Crossing the Border: essays on Scottish literature* (Manchester, 1990), 312-29.

realist fallacy: Whyte (1990), *op.cit.*, 322-25.

several commentators: see for instance Spring, *op.cit.*, 75; also Edwin Morgan, "Tradition and experiment in the Glasgow novel". Gavin Wallace and Randall Stevenson, eds., *The Scottish novel since the seventies* (Edinburgh, 1993), 85-98.

Violent end of a hard man: *Scotsman*, 11 August 1994.

the police superintendent: see Chapter 2.

CHAPTER 10

the archetypal "dear green place": see Gifford (1985), *op.cit.*

Why? Why did men: Lewis Grassic Gibbon, "Glasgow", *op.cit.*

The greenhorn has everything to lose: Jonathan Raban, *Soft City* (London, 1974), 45-47. (Page references here and below are to the Collins Harvill edition, 1988.)

Glasgow itself becomes: Spring, *op.cit.*, 68-70.

The passage that shows best: Edwin Muir, [review of *The Albannach*], *The Modern Scot*, vol. 3, no. 2, Summer 1932, 167.

element of autobiography: see Edwin Muir, *Poor Tom* (London, 1932), and *An Autobiography* (London, 1954).

taken round Glasgow slums: see F.R.Hart and J.B.Pick, *Neil Gunn: a Highland life* (London, 1981), 168. (Page reference is to the Polygon edition, Edinburgh, 1985.)

the writing on the wall: This was Friel's original title for the whole novel (see Cameron (1987), *op.cit.*), surviving as the title of Part II.

the full treatment of Glasgow as hell: see Cairns Craig, "Going Down to Hell is Easy", Robert Crawford and Thom Nairn, eds., *The Arts of Alasdair Gray* (Edinburgh, 1991), 90-107.

there is a clear connection: Spring (1990), *op.cit.*, 97.

CHAPTER 11

well-crafted short stories: see for instance *Glasgow Herald* 1 October 1955; 10 March 1956; 21 February 1959.

George Friel was continuing to write: see Gordon Jarvie, "Introduction", Friel (1992), *op.cit.*

Jenny Stairy became: Margaret Hamilton, "Jenny Stairy's Hat". First published Maurice Lindsay and Fred Urquhart, eds., *No Scottish Twilight: new Scottish short stories* (Glasgow, 1947), 9-24; reprinted Burgess and Whyte (1985), *op.cit.,* 46-58.

See ma mammy: Margaret Hamilton, "Lament for a Lost Dinner Ticket". First published *Scottish International*, April 1972; reprinted Hamish Whyte, ed., *Mungo's Tongues: Glasgow poems 1630-1990* (Edinburgh, 1993), 216-17.

one other novel: see Dorothy Porter McMillan, "Margaret Hamilton: *The Way They Want It*". *ScotLit*, no 7, Spring 1992, 3-4.

encouraged by James Bridie: The exact circumstances are so far unclear.

The stories describe: *Glasgow Herald*, 20 June 1942.

poetic impulse: *Times Literary Supplement*, 20 June 1942.

I do not exaggerate: Wells and Muir are quoted on the jacket of Gaitens's *Dance of the Apprentices* (see below), but no original correspondence has so far been traced.

Gaitens' finely-modelled prose: Whyte (1990), *op.cit.,* 330-32.

This story is much more true: Mack (1958), *op.cit.,* 763-65.

To a reader in 1991: Edwin Morgan, "Tradition and experiment in the Glasgow novel", Wallace and Stevenson (1993), *op.cit.,* 85-98.

A compound of brilliant writing: Jack House in *Evening Citizen*, 25 December 1948.

written in 1938: see Robert Calder, "Man, poet and thinker". *Chapman* 52, Spring 1988, 21-26.

brought up in Shettleston: biographical information obtained from acquaintances of J.J.Lavin, 1994.

Novels about life in the East End: *Glasgow Herald*, 19 February 1953.

Jenkins . . . accompanied his pupils: see Isobel Murray, "Introduction", Robin Jenkins, *Guests of War*, Scottish Academic Press edition (Edinburgh, 1988), ix.

To find Mrs McShelvie's equals: Alastair R. Thompson, "Faith and love: an examination of some themes in the novels of Robin Jenkins". *New Saltire*, no 3, Spring 1962, 57-64.

CHAPTER 12

In the fiction of many rousing novelists: Neil M. Gunn, "Drains for the Kraal", *Glasgow Herald*, 4 January 1941.

ladies with a pretence: McLean (1984), *op.cit.*

This passage could have been called: Tom Leonard, "On Reclaiming the Local, or, The Theory of the Magic Thing." *Reports from the Present: selected work 1982-94* (London, 1995), 33-43.

One gusty midnight: Gunn (1941), *op.cit.*

Time must also reveal: McArthur, "Why I wrote *No Mean City*" (1935), *op.cit.*

We had a lively debate: Power (1937), *op.cit.*, 230.

McArthur was still in the working class: Damer (1990), *op.cit.*, 40.

a second novel: An extract from *For Sadie* appeared in *Scottish International*, vol.6, no.6, August 1973, 18-23. See also chapter 19.

Master Hind: see calligraphic decoration, Alasdair Gray, *Unlikely Stories, Mostly* (London, 1983), [ii-iii].

The works assume: Leonard (1995), *op.cit.*, 33.

I knew I was after a book: William McIlvanney, "A Shield against the Gorgon". *Surviving the Shipwreck* (Edinburgh, 1991), 217-38.

working-class heroism: The question is considered in Beth Dickson, "Class and being in the novels of William McIlvanney". Wallace and Stevenson eds. (1993), *op. cit.*, 54-70.

CHAPTER 13

the immense amount of stuff: J.H.Millar, *A Literary History of Scotland* (London, 1903), 680-81.

What we know as the Glasgow Novel: Allan Massie, "Seeking the real Glasgow". *Scotsman Weekend*, 15 January 1994.

Miss Caldwell and Miss McLeod: Ronald Frame, "Paris". First published *Scottish Short Stories 1985* (London, 1985), 100-10; reprinted Carl MacDougall, ed., *The Devil and the Giro: two centuries of Scottish stories* (Edinburgh, 1989), 491-98.

Wax Fruit had one of those spectacular successes: "The author who made Glasgow a best seller" [obituary, Guy McCrone], *Glasgow Herald*, 1 June 1977.

I decided that if I had any gifts: Guy McCrone, *Scottish Field*, March 1952, 36.

I found myself: *ibid.*

Clearly intended as a sketch: Mack (1958), *op.cit.*, 770.

The densely interwoven street-life: Raban (1974), *op.cit.*, 27.

One of the distinguishing marks: Muir (1935), *op.cit.*, 108.

CHAPTER 14

what . . . was happening to Glasgow: see for instance Checkland (1981), *op.cit.*, 63-80.

Oscar Marzaroli: see Oscar Marzaroli, *Shades of Grey: Glasgow 1956-1987* (Edinburgh, 1987).

The destruction of entire living areas: note by Joe Fisher in Marzaroli (1987), *op.cit.*, 209.

the secure grid: see Walker (1982), *op. cit.*

Too much of the experience: Edwin Morgan, "The Beatnik in the Kailyaird". *New Saltire* 3, Spring 1962; reprinted *Essays* (Cheadle, 1974), 166-76.

hordes of Scottish authors: Clifford Hanley, "The Writer in Scotland", *New Saltire* 5, August 1962, 5-9.

nationalism and internationalism: see Andrew Murray Scott, "Mr MacDiarmid and Mr Trocchi: where extremists meet". *Chapman* 83, [Summer 1996], 36-39.

Most critics chose: James Campbell, "Alexander Trocchi". *Dictionary of Literary Biography*, vol. 15 (Detroit, 1983), 538-41.

At a second reading: Edwin Morgan, "Alexander Trocchi: a survey". *Edinburgh Review* 70, August 1985, 48-58.

Alan Sharp, there was a big discovery!: Liz Lochhead, "Making the words and Biro ink flow to put my slant on the world". *Glasgow Herald*, 13 October 1982, 9.

achieved a fusion: Alan McGillivray, "Natural loyalties: the work of William McIlvanney". *Laverock*, [no 1, February 1995], 13-23.

revealed it in interview: see "Together to the death" [interview by Colette Douglas-Home]. *Scotsman*, 30 November 1992.

Friel had been writing . . . novels: see Cameron (1987), *op.cit.*

A fiction of working-class Glasgow: Gordon Jarvie, "Introduction", George Friel, *The Bank of Time* (Polygon edition, Edinburgh, 1994), 1-4.

Some of the critics: Raymond Gardner, "A walk on the wild side" [interview]. *Guardian*, 24 March 1972, 12.

Each novel is a carefully constructed experiment: Glenda Norquay, "Four novelists of the 1950s and 1960s". Cairns Craig ed., *The history of Scottish literature*, vol. 4 (Aberdeen, 1987); see in particular 268-70.

a very unexotic: Jarvie (1994), *op.cit.*

Percy Phinn . . . Persephone: see Cameron (1987), *op.cit.*

He sent it to Calder: *ibid.*

I wrote a story in '63: see James Gillespie, "Friel in the thirties". *Edinburgh Review* 71, November 1985, 46-55.

No account: "Pieces by Petronius", *Journal of the Law Society of Scotland*, vol. 16, October 1971, 265-66.
a structure of endless trapdoors: Norquay (1987), *op.cit.*
These final revelations: *ibid.*

CHAPTER 15

the Glasgow Group: Philip Hobsbaum, "The Glasgow Group: an experience of writing". *Edinburgh Review*, 80-81, May 1988, 58-63.
Kelman, agnamed the Cool: Gray (1983), *op.cit.*
thirty paintings and drawings: They are listed in the brochure produced for *The Continuous Glasgow Show*, an exhibition mounted in the People's Palace, 1978.
I chose characters: Margaret Thomson Davis, *The Making of a Novelist* (London, 1982), 61, 71.
I was sitting at my desk: *ibid.*, 88.
I had meant The Breadmakers: *ibid.*, 75.
a protracted journey: see Cameron (1987), *op.cit.*
a perfectly disastrous solution: *ibid.*, 89-90.
Liddell and Scott: Auberon Waugh, "Celtic twilights". *Spectator*, 29 January 1972, 156-57.
If this book is to be accepted: James Davie, [review], *Glasgow Herald*, 29 January 1972.
This is one of the greatest: Douglas Gifford, "Introduction". George Friel, *Mr Alfred MA* (Canongate Classics edition, Edinburgh, 1987), v-ix.
Wasteland Glasgow: *ibid.*, ix.
People keep judging Laidlaw: William McIlvanney, "The Courage of our Doubts". *Surviving the Shipwreck* (1991), *op.cit.*, 153-62.
The idea remained lifeless: *ibid.*, 157.
The central mystery: *ibid.*, 159.
various accusations: These points, with others, are discussed by Dickson in Wallace and Stevenson eds. (1993), *op.cit.* William McIlvanney's essays are collected in *Surviving the Shipwreck* (1991), *op.cit.*
It is necessary to point out: Allan Massie, "Sense and sensibility". *Scotsman*, 27 August 1977, from which the next two unattributed quotations also come.
My writing often has: National Book League, *Writers in Brief no 23: Alan Spence* (Glasgow, 1986).
thirteen stories: James Kelman, *An Old Pub Near the Angel, and other stories* (Orono, Maine: Puckerbush Press, 1973).

CHAPTER 16

It undoubtedly will stand: Douglas Gifford, "*Lanark* towers above all else". *Books in Scotland* 9, Winter 1981-82, 10-11.

Lanark's most remote ancestor: Bruce Charlton, "The Story So Far". Robert Crawford and Thom Nairn eds., *The Arts of Alasdair Gray* (Edinburgh, 1991), 10-21.

I didn't spend 25 years: Kathy Acker, "Alasdair Gray interviewed". *Edinburgh Review* 74, August 1986, 83-90.

The big novel continued: Charlton (1991), *op.cit.*, 13. Also see this essay, particularly the Chronology (18-21), for the novel's various submissions, rejections etc.

parts were read: Hobsbaum (1988), *op.cit.*, 62.

on grounds of length: Charlton (1991), *op.cit.*, 15.

perceptively reviewed: see P.H. Scott, "*Lanark* and the reviewers". *Literary Review*, June 1981, 16.

Times Literary Supplement: William Boyd, "The theocracies of Unthank". *Times Literary Supplement*, 27 February 1981, 219.

which had been Gray's aim: Acker (1986), *op.cit.*, 83.

adapted for the stage: the script of Alastair Cording's adaptation is in *Theatre Scotland*, vol. 4, no 14, Summer 1995, 27-44.

plans for a film version: see Allan Brown, "The Picture of Alasdair Gray". *Observer Scotland*, 19 March 1989. Alasdair Gray's storyboards for the film of *Lanark* are serialised in *Scottish Book Collector*, vol. 2, no 1, August/September 1989, and subsequent issues.

My most densely and deliberately: Alasdair Gray, *Alasdair Gray* (Saltire Self-Portraits, 4) (Edinburgh, 1988), 14.

We may accept: Isobel Murray and Bob Tait, *Ten Modern Scottish Novels* (Aberdeen, 1984), 231.

the details of the two books: Colin Manlove, *Scottish Fantasy Literature: a critical survey* (Edinburgh, 1994), 201-2.

I particularly liked: Jennie Renton, "Alasdair Gray" [interview]. *Scottish Book Collector*, no 7, 1988, 2-5.

Alasdair Gray points out: This caveat accompanies a list of the major interviews in Bruce Charlton, "Checklists and unpublished material by Alasdair Gray". Crawford and Nairn eds. (1991), *op.cit.*, 156-208.

A writer who is also an artist: Edwin Morgan, "The Walls of Gormenghast" (written 1960). *Essays* (1974), *op.cit.*, 35-42.

He was perhaps the first person: Edwin Morgan, "Nothing is not giving messages" (interview, 1988). *Nothing Not Giving Messages: reflections on work and life* (Edinburgh, 1990), 118-43.

Cowcaddens 1950: The painting is reproduced as a fold-out colour plate in Hamish Whyte ed. *Noise and Smoky Breath: an illustrated anthology of Glasgow poems 1900-1983* (Glasgow, 1983).

Unthank and Cowcaddens: Cordelia Oliver, "Alasdair Gray, visual artist". Crawford and Nairn eds. (1991), *op.cit.*, 22-36.

so little had changed: Spring (1990), *op.cit.*, 966 ff.

It is true that Lanark: Edwin Morgan, "Gray and Glasgow". Crawford and Nairn eds. (1991), *op.cit.*, 64-75.

The symbolism indicates: Douglas Gifford, "Private confession and public satire in the fiction of Alasdair Gray". *Chapman* 50-51, Summer 1987, 101-16.

If the only viable way: *ibid.*

Lanark's importance consists: Brian McCabe, "No real city". *New Edinburgh Review*, no 54, May 1981, 10-12.

Certainly of all the books: James Robertson, "Bridging styles: a conversation with Iain Banks". *Radical Scotland*, no 42, December 1989/January 1990, 26-27.

By the time of the 1970s: Witschi (1991), *op.cit.*, 58.

Surely the cause: Carol Anderson and Glenda Norquay, "Interview with Alasdair Gray". *Cencrastus*, no 13, Summer 1983, 6-10.

The reader of Gray's work: Witschi (1991), *op.cit.*, 58-59.

CHAPTER 17

What is the New Glasgow? Spring (1990), *op.cit.*, 38.

the arrival of the New Glasgow: *ibid.*, 39ff.

At Exeter Magistrates Court: *Scotsman*, 16 January 1993.

Taggart: see Spring (1990), *op.cit.*, 80-81; Joan McAlpine, "The Great Detective", *Scotsman*, 31 May 1994.

Glasgow fictional crime: see Hamish Whyte, *Glasgow crime fiction: a bibliographic guide* (1977), available in typescript at The Mitchell Library, Glasgow; new edition in preparation.

[From the thirties to the sixties]: Introduction [unsigned, probably by Douglas Gifford] to programme of Strathclyde Writers' Festival, Glasgow, May 1984.

Forced to choose: Foreword to leaflet accompanying *Book Four* (London Weekend Television), 10 April 1985.

A title to raise an eyebrow: Geddes Thomson, "The Glasgow Short Story". *Chapman* 33, vol. 7 no. 3, Autumn 1982, 5-8.

recalls with quiet amazement: Catherine Lockerbie, "Lighting Up Kelman". *Scotsman Weekend*, 19 March 1994.

The stories I wanted to write: James Kelman, "The Importance of Glasgow in My Work". *Some Recent Attacks* (Stirling, 1992), 78-84.

One of the things that goes on: Duncan McLean, "James Kelman Interviewed". *Edinburgh Review* 71, November 1985, 64-80.
You've stated that you are trying: Kirsty McNeill, "Interview with James Kelman". *Chapman* 57, Summer 1989, 1-9.
Sometimes in monologues or narratives: Francis Spufford, "Dialects". *London Review of Books*, vol. 9, no. 7, April 1987, 23. Reprinted in "James Kelman", *Contemporary Literary Criticism*, vol. 58 (Detroit, 1990), 294-306.
I remember thinking: McLean (1985), *op.cit.*, 70-71.
the funniest sexy story: Douglas Gifford, "Discovering Lost Voices". *Books in Scotland* 38, Summer 1991, 1-6.
Reviewers spoke: see *Contemporary Literary Criticism*, vol. 58 (1990), *op.cit.*, 297-302.
Let's talk about the opening sentence: McLean (1985), *op.cit.*, 77-78.
This is the closest anyone has come: Douglas Gifford, "The Authentic Glasgow Experience". *Books in Scotland* 19, Autumn 1985, 9-10.

CHAPTER 18
Owing to the influx: Introduction, William Grant, ed., *The Scottish National Dictionary*, v. 1 (1931), xxvii.
The Scots of here and now: Campbell (1981), *op.cit.*, 123
There is even a novel: Richard Cobb, quoted in Alan Taylor, "Some humour down in hell". *Observer Scotland*, 22 October 1989.
Glasgow speech: William McIlvanney, "Where Greta Garbo Wouldn't Have Been Alone". Marzaroli (1987), *op.cit.*, 13-36.
Anyone who wants: *ibid.*, 33.
I maintain: Michael Munro, *The Patter* (Glasgow, 1985), 4.
Even the famous Wee Macgreegor stories: Caroline Macafee, "Glasgow dialect in literature". *Scottish Language* 1, Autumn 1982, 45-53.
I am well aware: Bell (1933), *op.cit.*, 8.
came from Paisley: see "A Little Tale of a Grandmother", Bell (1932), *op.cit.*, 72-89.
right inuff: Leonard (1984), *op.cit.*, 120.
The seventies was a decade: Edwin Morgan, "Glasgow speech in recent Scottish literature". *Crossing the Border* (Manchester, 1990), 312-29.
if a toktaboot: Tom Leonard, "Unrelated Incidents: 3". *Three Glasgow Writers* (1976), 36; also Leonard (1984), *op.cit.*, 88.

This collection is a landmark: Alex Hamilton, *Gallus, did you say?* (Glasgow, 1982).

Auld Shug: "The Hon" appears in James Kelman, *Short Tales from the Night Shift* (Glasgow, 1978), and is reprinted with slight alterations in *The Burn* (London, 1991).

This deliberately stilted style: Macafee (1982), *op.cit.*, 50.

Like Galt: *ibid.*

CHAPTER 19

A deil o' a lassie: Alexander G. Murdoch, "Shoosie, ye jaud!" Brown (1897), *op.cit.*, 159.

There are three basic types: Carol Craig, "On men and women in McIlvanney's fiction." *Edinburgh Review* 73, May 1986, 42-49.

Here is a theme: Robin Jenkins, "My Scotland." *Scots Magazine*, vol. 62, no 3, December 1954, 218-23.

Scotland as woman: see the ongoing work of such researchers as Susanne Hagemann and Kirsten Stirling.

a few fragments: see the extract (from which the quotes here are taken) in *Scottish International*, vol. 6, no. 6, August 1973, 18-23.

Women novelists: Robert Elliot, "Women, Glasgow, and the novel." *Chapman* 33, Autumn 1982, 1-4.

accomplished novelists: see Douglas Gifford and Dorothy McMillan, eds., *A History of Scottish Women's Writing* (Edinburgh, 1997), particularly chapters 12, 24, 26, 39 and 40.

Joan Ure: see Alasdair Gray, "Portrait of a playwright." James Kelman and others, *Lean Tales* (London, 1985), 247-55.

occasionally anthologised: "Kelvingrove Park", Burgess and Whyte, eds., (1985), *op.cit.*, 175-78; "It's My Day for Leaving Home", Moira Burgess, ed., *The Other Voice* (Edinburgh, 1987), 216-19.

a taut book: Anne Simpson, "Portrait of Evelyn." *Glasgow Herald*, 8 December 1976.

They were recognised: Jude Burkhauser, "The visible woman vanishes." Jude Burkhauser ed., *"Glasgow Girls": women in art and design 1880-1920* (Edinburgh, 1990), 63.

Women painters: Jude Burkhauser, "Blinkers on our imagination." *ibid.*, 215.

As with many women: Jude Burkhauser and Susan Taylor, "De Courcy Lewthwaite Dewar." *ibid.*, 163.

CHAPTER 20

"Culture" is the motif-word: Lewis Grassic Gibbon, "Glasgow" (1934), *op.cit.*

the only culture's whit's growing: This was a popular 1990 phrase, but see Liz Lochhead's poem "Con-densation" in her *Bagpipe Musak* (London, 1991), 16-17.

The Festival city: Thomas Connolly, "The last four letter word." *Observer Scotland*, 30 July 1989.

There is widespread acceptance: Farquhar McLay ed., *Workers City* (Glasgow, 1988), 1.

with a fanfare: see *Glasgow Herald*, 2 January 1990.

A man such as Coltrane: correspondence column, *Glasgow Herald*, 3 January 1990. See also letters in agreement, *ibid.,* 6 January ff.

"the Elspeth King affair": James Kelman, "Storm in the Palace, summer 1990." Farquhar McLay ed., *The Reckoning* (Glasgow, 1990), 50-53; also Alasdair Gray, "A Friend Unfairly Treated". *ibid.,* 54-56.

One letter in support of King: see Kelman (1990), *op.cit.,* for references to this and subsequent letters and replies. See also David Kemp, *Glasgow 1990: the true story behind the hype* (Gartocharn, 1990), which comments on the various controversies. For the original correspondence, with arguments on both sides, see *Glasgow Herald*, May and June 1990.

the arguments . . . collected in print: In McLay (1990), *op.cit.* See also foreword to Kelman, *Some Recent Attacks* (1992), *op.cit.,* 1-4.

In 1990 the citizens of Glasgow: Peter Booth and Robin Boyle, "See Glasgow, see culture." Franco Bianchini and Michael Parkinson eds., *Cultural Policy and Urban Regeneration: the West European experience* (Manchester, 1993), 21-47.

The resonance of that possessive s: Archie Hind [review], *Glasgow Herald*, 23 June 1990.

The Whitbread . . . the Booker: Whitbread Book of the Year Award: Jeff Torrington, *Swing Hammer Swing!* (January 1993). Booker Prize: James Kelman, *How Late it Was, How Late* (October 1994).

writers' groups: see Janet Paisley, "Writers groups – a growth phenomenon." *West Coast Magazine*, no. 11 [1992], 31-33.

the germ of Something Leather: see Gray's Epilogue to *Something Leather*, 232 ff.

Have you ever worked with a woman: Acker (1986), *op.cit.,* 85.

There was a real attempt: Alan MacGillivray, "Interview with Carl MacDougall". *Laverock*, [no. 2], [1996], 9-17.

the demolition of the Gorbals: "Jeff Torrington in conversation with Jim Kelman." *West Coast Magazine*, no. 12, [January 1993], 18-21.

the long delay in publication: *ibid.*

at how the planning authorities: Duncan McLean, "Jeff Torrington." *Scottish Book Collector*, vol. 3, no. 10, April/May 1993, 2-3.

At least one reviewer: Joe Murray, [review]. *West Coast Magazine*, no. 11 [1992].

consistent in voice: Douglas Gifford, [review]. *Books in Scotland*, no. 50, Summer 1994, 3-4.

one of the judges: Rabbi Julia Neuberger. See interview by Gillian Harris, *Scotsman*, 13 October 1994, 15.

to ensure . . . that the next time: Ian Bell, "A joyful blow for the free word." *Observer*, 16 October 1994.

Everybody knows all about Kelman: Lockerbie, "Lighting up Kelman", *op.cit.*

It all started with the one about the teacher: Michael McCormick, "For Jimmy Kelboats." *Chapman*, no. 83, [Summer 1996], 30-34.

The image of Scotland: Maurice Fleming, "Scotland the depraved?" *Scots Magazine*, vol. 141, no. 6, December 1994, 616-18.

Ye huv a quick look: Macdonald Daly, "Your average working Kelman." *Cencrastus*, no. 46, Autumn 1993, 14-16.

An elder statesman: Maurice Lindsay, "Whippet for High Tea." *On the face of it: collected poems vol 2* (London, 1993), 53.

A younger wit: Brent Hodgson, "Oh No, Another New Glaswegian Writer." *Radical Scotland*, no. 50, April-May 1991, 20.

Kelman stood alone: Fleming (1994), *op.cit.*, 617.

Duncan McLean/Irvine Welsh: see introduction to Duncan McLean, *Ahead of its Time: a Clocktower Press anthology* (London, 1997).

Probably in common with a lot of writers: Ruth Thomas, "Duncan McLean" [interview]. *Scottish Book Collector*, vol. 3, no. 6, August/September 1992, 2-3.

It didn't win: Catherine Lockerbie, "Electrified lines" [interview with Janice Galloway]. *Scotsman Weekend*, 23 March 1991.

doesn't write about . . . feminism: Stella Coombe, "Things Galloway." *Harpies and Quines*, no. 1, May/June 1992, 26-29.

There was a very odd letter: *ibid.*, 28.

The whole of that bit of the novel: Ruth Thomas, "A. L. Kennedy" [interview]. *Scottish Book Collector*, vol. 3, no. 12, August/September 1993, 2-4.

Index